THE COLLECTED LANCER

Volume One

An Arek Lancer Collection

By Troy Osgood

DELIVERY TO ORSO

Originally Published:
Available for free from the Ossy Writes Mailing List

The ramp lowered and I saw the busy port of Buhin.

Lights, bustle, activity. And lots of it.

Bright and strobing lights, large shining signs in Tradelan and a ton of other languages. Lots of noise. Lots of languages but mostly Tradelan, the default and somewhat galaxy wide language. Buhin was one of the busiest ports, being on the edge of the Inner Worlds and Deep Space. The planet's sun would set, but the port never did.

Which was why I was landing and unloading at this horrible hour.

I should have been asleep in my bunk on board my ship, the *Nomad's Wind*. Instead I was impatiently waiting for the ship's ramp to lower so I could unload. I had the first polyplas crate on the maglift and pushed it down as soon as I heard the clang of the metal ramp hitting the metal port deck.

Time was fluid. Each planet had its own system of telling time and pilots, like me, operated on whatever one worked best for them. That was one reason why a planet's port was never closed, there were people up at all hours as they were on their own time schedule. Adjusting to a new one was always a pain in the ass. It had been just my luck that the timing of the hops to Buhin worked out to be at a period when I would normally have been sleeping.

I got a good look at the city itself when I stopped at the bottom of the ramp.

The city was built on top of a very tall cliff with the landing deck hanging out over the dark water that was so very far below. It was structurally sound. Or so I had been told. Truthfully I had no issues, had never felt the deck shake even though others swore they had. But it still made me uneasy when it was full like it was now. There was a lot of weight on it.

Ships were arranged in a half circle around mine, all with ramps facing inward. There was a limited number of spots on this dock, one of three such landing pads ringing the cliff's edge of Buhin. The entire planet was giant cliffs and mountains, and nothing but raging water below. The city was built on one of the few flat spots and in two levels. Elevators went up and down between them. I'd never been to the top level, there was nothing there that I needed.

All the good stuff was down here.

Gambling halls. Bars. Jobs.

At least for an independent hauler like me.

Buhin is on the edge of the Inner Core, the more populous and richer worlds. It's the last spot before entering the wilds of Deep Space. That makes it a busy trading stop. Where the trading collectives of the Inner Worlds walk alongside the independents like me. And we try not to kill each other.

That doesn't happen. Not very often anyways.

I leaned against the maglifter watching four beings walk my way. Three were Buhini, dressed in gray and black uniforms. Dockhands. The natives were short, about five foot six or so, but very stocky with long arms and legs. Muscular. They had to be, as they spent most of their time climbing the many mountains and cliffs of the planet. They were all dark skinned, shades of gray with almost pure white hair. Dark black tattoos were visible on their exposed skin. Two of them were pushing maglifters of their own.

The fourth being was a Kry. Light brown skin, red eyes, dark hair. Perfectly groomed and dressed. He walked slightly behind the Buhins and glanced around as if everything was beneath him. Which was true as far as the Kry were concerned. They were one of the most arrogant species in the galaxy.

Shrewd businessmen. Their entire culture revolved around it.

The Buhini stopped just in front of me, looking bored with everything, the Kry walked around them to stand closer. He looked me up and down and I could just feel the disdain. This one probably didn't like that he had to deal with someone like me. An independent from Deep Space. He probably felt dirty just associating with me. Probably cursing or whatever it was a Kry did that Buhin was an older port and didn't have the automated cargo storage and hand-off that a lot of the newer space stations and ports did.

This particular Kry was really unhappy to be here.

I just had to remember that their credits were good.

"Captain Arek Lancer," he stated.

"Yep."

He paused, expecting more. Like I was supposed to say how honored I was to be there or some such thing. I had to remember that this job was a favor for another Kry, Tesk Un Lil. One of my regular customers and maybe, kind of, probably a friend. He'd done something to get himself exiled to Deep Space. That was how the Kry saw it, exile. He was making a fortune there though, probably one of the riches Kry around. But he was still in Deep Space and been exiled, so he was still looked down upon by the rest of his people.

But everyone needs something and there's always someone that has it available. In this case, someone somewhere in the Inner Worlds needed something that Lil had to offer. And here I was, midway there in Buhin.

I could have gone to whatever Inner World it was but that would have almost doubled or tripled the transit time and this was a rush job. So well I was hopping to Buhin, this Kry was hopping here as well.

"And the other crate is," the Kry asked after waiting for me to say more and I didn't.

I pointed behind me, up the ramp.

The Kry nodded to the Buhini with a maglifter and I led him up the ramp. No one boards another ship without permission or tour guide. It's just not done. Behind us I could hear the other maglifter connecting to mine. Once the two were joined, the Buhini could easily slide the large crate onto his lift.

Once up the ramp and in the *Wind's* cargo hold I led the Buhini to the right crate. It wasn't hard, there weren't many. I could see him looking around, clearly not impressed.

Whatever.

This was a long haul with a time limit. Not like I could have taken on extra cargo. Lil's money was good, too good to pass this one up. I was hoping I'd be able to find something here needing to go to Deep Space.

The Buhini adjusted his maglifter and got the crate on it. I followed him out the *Wind* and down the ramp. The Kry had the courtesy to actually wait until I was down the ramp before sending the credits. He hit a couple buttons on his tablet and I heard a ding on my wristcomm. Looking down I saw the announcement that the sale had gone through. I'd see a transfer of credits from Lil soon enough.

"Pleasure doing business with you," I said and looked up but the Kry was already walking away.

Shrugging, I grabbed my maglifter and brought it back up into the *Wind*.

*****

I walked through the crowded streets of the city. I could have been back on the ship sleeping and out job hunting in what passed for morning at a reasonable hour, but it had been awhile since I'd been planetside on any planet and Buhin was a city that was up all night.

Even at this hour of it's night cycle it was crowded. Almost every shop was open, the taverns were packed, street vendors were out in force. Beings from all over were everywhere. All shapes, sizes, sexes. No other humans though.

Terrans, humans, earthlings. We're not well liked.

We were the newbies, only been in space outside our galaxy for about thirty years. And what did we do when we first got to other solar systems? What do humans always do?

Just look at our history. We expanded and claimed them. We had allies at least, ones that wanted us to expand.

The Thesans had come to us, had given us the tech we needed to expand beyond our own solar system, because they wanted and needed us. They needed our help to protect their own expansions. They were going up against another empire, the Tiat. They wanted our aid in the fight. The Thesans thought by giving us the means to hop systems, they could control us. They didn't do their homework on humans. But it still worked out for them, they found willing allies in their fight.

Terrans are not well liked. The Tiat are hated. By everyone.

But they're the strongest race in the galaxy.

We banded together with the Thesans to fight the Tiat. There are some complicated reasons for it all but it basically led to the Third Galactic War.

So us upstart humans helped start a Galactic War. No surprise there. That's kind of our thing.

It lasted a while. Cost a ton of lives on all three sides and beyond. We've been in a cold war with the Thesans and Tiat since. That's how I got involved in the whole mess.

I spent some time with the Earth Expeditionary Force, the 2Es. Special operations. I did the scary stuff, the wet work, the stuff no one knows about.

Out for three years now and I just needed to wander. I bought my ship, a Castellan Light Cruiser Model F497 that I named *Nomad's Wind*, and I'd been a vagabond every since. I went wherever the jobs took me. Got a cargo, went and delivered it, picked up a new one and delivered that one. So on and so on. Never in one place for longer then it took to drop off cargo and pick up cargo.

It's a good life.

I may have been out a couple of years but I still possessed enough situational awareness to know I was being followed.

Dammit.

Why couldn't this have been easy? Just deliver, grab a new cargo, leave. Nice and simple. I should have been sleeping right now.

But that's not the way things usually worked for me. Nothing but bad luck.

Casually I adjusted how my dark green jacket, left over from my EEF days, was hanging so I could get quick access to my blaster.

I couldn't spot the follower. Too crowded and well the walls of all the buildings were shiny metal, they weren't that reflective. All the polycarbonite windows were the same. Dark and unable to see anything using them.

It was all instinct.

You know when someone is staring intently at you. The hairs on the back of your neck stand up and you just get this feeling.

I had a destination, or I used to have one. There was a hauler's guild hall down the street and I hoped to find some work, but going there was out of the question. At least for now. I needed to lose my tail but I really wanted to find out who was after me and why.

Considering where I was, I had a couple guesses.

I could rule out random mugging attempt.

I'm not the biggest guy around but I'm told I look pretty intimidating. Six foot, black hair and beard starting to gray even though I was only in my low thirties, muscular. People said I had a look to me though, one that said 'don't mess with me'.

Besides, I'd seen about a dozen easier marks that I could have easily mugged.

The next choice was an old enemy from my military days. I had a few of those. I'd done things I'm not that proud of but my record was sealed. Most of that was still secret.

Next option was a trading company. As an independent hauler, I wasn't liked by the various guilds and unions. They wanted everyone operating under their charters. Guys like me mucked up the works. That was fine in Deep Space, for now, but here on the edge of the Inner Core?

Finally there was the local criminal gang.

That was my guess.

I started looking, by not looking, for places to confront my follower when I saw a group approaching towards me from down the street. I quickly turned and pretended to be looking at the assorted goods in a store window, trying to position myself so people around me were hiding my very noticeable jacket. I also started revising my guess on who was following me.

Coming down the street with six Earth Expeditionary Forces soldiers circled around him, all heavily armed, was the esteemed Terran ambassador to the Planetary Council. I knew General Frank Coulson from my military days. We ran into each other a couple of times and it never went well. I hated the bastard and he wasn't fond of me.

It had to be a coincidence.

I wasn't arrogant or paranoid enough to think he was here for me. He was here himself, so it had to be official. He was not the kind of guy to get his hands dirty with a little nobody like me. I knew some of his secrets but I still wasn't worth a personal appearance.

Had to be some official business. Buhin was a hub afterall, so he was probably on his way to Thost, the central planet where the Planetary Council met.

The Council tried to exert some control over the galaxy but they didn't have much. It was more of a symbolic organization, a way to show that we were trying for a unified galaxy when everyone knew it really wouldn't ever happen. The problem, one of them anyways, was that some species were too powerful. The Tiat controlled six systems, the Thesans had three and us Terrans had three. Lots of others had two systems they controlled. So really, the Council spent most of its time trying to stop the Tiat from gaining anymore control.

That was a full time job.

I glanced at good ol' Frank as he walked by. Looked the same as always. Hair perfectly cut to military standards, but now all gray. Clean shaven, square jaw. Blue eyes in his pale skin. Wore a dress uniform with lots of medals.

I had some of the same medals. Mine were somewhere in the *Wind*, couldn't remember exactly where.

General Coulson was ambitious and had lots of little side projects, but he was purely Terran-first. Not the best appointee to a group like the Planetary Council. A tactical genius, he was a hard ass and compromise was not something he knew how to do. He was as old school as his name.

As Coulson and his escort walked past, I took the opportunity to turn and look that way. No one could blame me for watching my species walk past. They actually were the first humans I had seen here since I arrived.

My eyes followed Coulson and his escort but I searched the surrounding crowd. Beings moved out of the way of the armed escort and I was able to spot my tail in the parting wave. Short, covered in long brown fur with bright blue eyes, long arms that hung past it's knees. A Ghini.

I knew it was my tail, too far away to see if it was male or female, because of the way it tried so hard to not be noticed. The trick to tailing someone is to be natural about it. Never stare directly at them and if they turn around, just continue walking like nothing was the matter. The Ghini had stopped and was also staring at a store window, well at the same time glancing my way quickly.

I had the urge to wave.

There didn't appear to be any other followers, just the Ghini. I didn't know much about the race. They were fast, strong and the long arms were an advantage when in close. For that reason they were usually employed as snatchers. It was kind of odd that this one was tailing me and not waiting further ahead.

Weird.

As I walked I started looking for places to duck into. The lower city of Buhin is tucked into the small shelf between cliffs. Not much space and every available inch is taken up by some kind of building that turns some kind of profit. The streets are narrow, not wide enough for hovercars. Foot traffic only. Not that many places to pull off.

So I continued walking, adjusting my pace now and then. Slowing down, speeding up.

I didn't get a chance to look behind me, but figured the change was driving the Ghini crazy. This was a trick I had learned during my special operations days. Varying the pace makes it difficult for the follower to keep the same separation. Are you stopping to look at something? Has the follower been made?

Following someone through a busy city is not easy.

I made sure that Coulson and his entourage were far enough away. I didn't want anything I might do to catch their attention. I was small potatoes for Coulson but no need to push myself back into his focus.

Walking further down I found what I wanted, a small alley off to the side, cutting between two buildings and heading towards the cliff. I shifted through the crowd, slowing as the alley approached. A dark space, barely five feet wide. It would do nicely.

Without looking behind me I quickly turned into the alley. It appeared to be a last second change in direction. Walking almost past and then turning quickly I was inside the alley. Now the Ghini would either continue walking by and try to catch me leaving the alley, which is what I would have done, or stop at the entrance and follow me down.

Which is what the Ghini did.

It stood at the entrance looking confused. The alley wasn't long, just the depth of the buildings and ending at the edge of the cliff. And it was empty. No me. The Ghini moved quickly down the alley, heading for the edge. I could understand what it was thinking. The buildings weren't tight against the cliff, so maybe I had moved behind one. Crazy but possible. It slowed as it got closer to the edge, hugging the building and holding onto it for balance. Leaning out, it looked behind both buildings.

Turns out his guess had been right.

The Ghini's head poked around the corner and got a face full of my Sig Sauer T1700. He was startled and I was able to push him back. And I could now see that it was definitely a him. Off balance the Ghini fell to the ground rolling to the side away from the cliff edge. The water far below could be heard crashing against the rocks.

Now came the tricky part. I didn't want to kill the Ghini, but I would if I had to. I was counting on him just being ordered to follow me and not kill me. Stepping away from the back of the building and into the alley I had my back to the cliff and I was standing pretty damn close to it. All the Ghini had to do was kick out or roll into me and I'd fall over the edge.

Calculated risk.

"Back up," I ordered.

The Ghini tensed, shifted a bit.

"Don't think about it," I said and made sure he heard the clicking as I shifted my blaster from stun to kill. "Back. Up."

The Ghini slid itself back, sliding along the rocky ground. It shot me a hateful glance but I didn't care. I looked it over, the parts I could see that weren't covered in the long fur and didn't see any weapons. Had to remember that Ghini were strong and those long arms gave it a reach that I had to stay out of.

I stepped forward, getting a comfortable distance from the edge.

"Why are you following me?" I asked as the Ghini hit the wall of a building. He started to get up but I motioned him back down with my weapon.

"Who sent you?"

The Ghini just looked at me, defiant. The eyes were a very bright blue, and set in a thick brow. The nose was flat, close to the face, with a mouth full of sharp looking teeth. The Ghini's long arms ended in five fingers with long claw-like fingernails. Brown fur covered the entire body, flattened in parts by the darker brown pants and shirt it wore.

"Talk to me," I said with just a hint of threat. "I don't like being followed."

He didn't look like he was going to answer me and I wondered how far I was going to have to go. How much was he told about me? He had to know that I would kill him if I had to. Just because I was out of the military didn't mean that I'd forgotten everything they taught me. Never leave a potential enemy behind if you can help it.

Killing this guy would send a message.

But make it harder for me to find out who sent him.

I admit it, I was curious.

This guy had 'hired thug' written all over him so my guess that the local criminal gang had interest in me was probably accurate. The question was why? I'd done my share of smuggling through the years and not all my jobs were completely legal, I had no moral issues there. But there were a lot of easier ways to hire me and a lot of other haulers that would be available. And probably cheaper.

I priced my services on the risk to my ship and my life. Smuggling was risky.

So this didn't seem like a job offer.

"I'm waiting," I told him, my tone getting angrier and annoyed.

His eyes darted all over, looking for a way out.

Just my luck to get the one guy that wouldn't talk. Looked like I was going to have to kill him.

Crap.

Then a thought crossed my mind. Was he stalling?

I adjusted my stance so I could keep an eye on the Ghini and the entrance to the alley.

Too late.

Two figures stepped into the alley, one slightly behind the other, but both with blasters pointed at me. The one in front was a Curdo. Skinny, could be called too skinny, with dark black skin and tufts of feathers at the wrists, ankles and around the shoulders. It's long hair was feather like with bird's eyes and a beak for a nose and mouth. It had three fingers and held a specially made weapon. The one in back was Terran like me. She was average height, blond, pretty in a harsh way, with green eyes. She held a Remington Tech5.

"Drop your weapon," she said without an ounce of warmth. The Curdo just squawked.

The good news was that they hadn't just shot me. That answered the question on if they needed me alive. Always look on the bright side of any situation.

Stepping further away from the Ghini who was pushing himself up, I kept my free hand raised and holstered my weapon. Both hands now raised I turned to the woman.

"Hi."

Three sets of eyes stared at me.

"What can I do for you?" I asked.

None of them found me amusing.

I couldn't see a way out and really wasn't looking for one. This had gotten interesting. Whoever it was had sent a three person team after me. I was a little pissed that I had fallen for the obvious tail which let his back-up get close.

That was a lot of effort to go through.

They must really like me.

Or hate me really bad.

Only one way to find out.

"Take me to your leader."

The Terran cracked a smile. The Curdo shot me.

*****

I woke up groggy. Slowly and with great effort.

Hate stun blasts. I really do.

Each weapon manufacturer has their own frequency so it's a crapshoot when using them. Each being in the galaxy is different, each weapon is different. Lots of randomness to using a stunner. You get to know what your own weapon can do and how it will affect different beings but there's still some chance involved.

I've seen stun blasts fry parts of someone's brain.

I felt decent coming out of this one. A low setting probably so I was only out an hour or two, maybe less.

As I awoke I could feel that my hands were bound behind me. I was strapped down to a metal chair. Not the first time. I'm kind of embarrassed to admit how many times this has happened to me.

I pulled at the bonds, could feel the edges of the plasticuffs digging into my wrists. Pretty secure. Great. My feet were loose, so that was a plus.

And I was clothed. Big plus.

Been a couple times I'd woken up in this position naked.

Opening my eyes fully, lifting my drooping head, I looked around.

Metal walls, metal floor, metal ceiling. Not much in the way of decorations. A single door in front of me, that I could see anyways, couldn't look behind me.

Basically a big empty room.

Good tactic. The prisoner wakes up disoriented from the stunner and can't place themselves because of the room. Keeps them off balance. Too bad it's a tactic that I had used on people in the past.

Waking up in this room, hands tied, wasn't really bothering me. I could wait this out.

I started whistling. An old Earth tune. I leaned back in the chair, as much as I could, and stretched my legs out in front of me, crossing them at the heels. I looked relaxed.

Whoever decided to kidnap me must not have known who I was, or my history. They should have known this wouldn't work on me. I'd done much worse to many people. So I settled in to wait.

It wasn't long.

The door swished open and two people walked in. First was the woman from the alley and the second was someone I knew and hoped to never see again.

Thomlin Romer

This just got bad. Really bad.

I thought I'd seen the last of his crazy ass years ago. About my height and weight but much better dressed. His hair and beard were neatly trimmed, all gray. Dark brown eyes. Handsome, there was a regal bearing to the man. Anyone that really didn't know him would think he was royalty. The outfit he was wearing, complete with a blue cape, was the height of earth fashion. The colors were picked to work with his dark skin color. He looked good, dashing.

I didn't even want to know what I looked like compared to him. Black hair always in need of a hair cut, beard barely trim. Worn out EEF military jacket. Plain shirt and pants, both picked for durability over fashion.

He had worked 2E Intelligence. Before he went freelance. Wasn't sure what he was doing now. Heard lots of rumors. Most were that he was into weapons smuggling. Looked to be successful, whatever it was.

"Thom," I said, keeping the tone casual, not wanting him to know how surprised I was by his appearance. Or how worried I was. "How's things?"

"Arek," he said stopping a couple feet from me, well out of reach of my legs. "You've seen better days."

The woman moved off behind me. I could feel her over my shoulder.

"We didn't all have your connections to fall back on," I said with just a hint of disdain. When Romer had left the EEF, under very bad circumstances, he had taken some of his contacts and connections with him. That's how he'd set up his initial freelance network.

I saw a flash of anger cross his features. Gone quickly and he was back to his salesman look. It's one I knew well. I'd seen it in operation many times.

"If you wanted to get together for a drink, there's easier ways to do it," I said, pulling at my hands.

"I didn't think you'd come if I had asked," Romer replied with a shrug.

"That's true," I said. "How was your meeting with Coulson?," I asked playing on a hunch.

Romer's face flashed surprise, gone just as quickly as the anger. Interesting. I really didn't want to know what Coulson was doing meeting with Romer. As long as they kept it far away from me that is, but it was a good way to keep Romer off balance.

"I'd forgotten how tight you two were back in the day," I continued. "Didn't know you still were. Did you know your boss was tight with the Earth ambassador to the Planetary Council," I asked looking over my left shoulder. I couldn't see the blond so that meant she was on my right. "Of course you did. That's probably why you're working for him. I can imagine the kind of jobs those connections bring." I looked back at Romer. "You look like you're doing well. Coulson must be paying you good."

Romer just smiled.

"Same old Arek Lancer," he said with a chuckle. "How long has it been?"

"Not long enough."

He moved towards the wall, further away from me, and leaned against it. Arms crossed over his chest, that damn salesman smile never left his face.

"Come now Arek, don't be like that."

I tried to shrug but it came out as some kind of weird spasm like motion, but it got the point across.

"If you let me loose, I'd be a lot more friendlier and open to whatever it is you have to sell me."

Romer studied me, still smiling. He finally shook his head.

"Not quite yet," he said.

"So why am I here?" I asked, still trying to appear casual. I was getting tired of this though. I wanted nothing to do with Romer. Too bad the blond was behind me, I could have started working on the bonds if she wasn't back there. "You obviously need me for something, what is it?"

Romer stood up straight and starting pacing across the room. It wasn't that wide, so he was turning around a lot. His boots clanged against the metal with each step. It was kind of annoying so I just looked at the door, not following him.

"First, just to be clear, I don't need you," he said and stopped, pointing at me, before continuing again. "You just happened to be here when I needed someone."

Great. More of the Lancer luck.

Also, I didn't buy it. He needed me specifically.

"I need an item delivered," he said, making it sound so simple.

There was no way it was that simple. There was a catch. With Romer, there always was.

"And," I prompted.

"And what," Romer said, still smiling. I wanted to wipe that grin off his smug face.

"Why not one of your many goons," I said and pulled at the bonds with force. I moved the chair causing Romer to jump back and the blond behind me to rush forward. I felt her hand on my shoulder pushing me down. "Why me?"

"I have connections everywhere," Romer replied, regaining his composure after being startled. "Except one place."

Now it made sense. Now I understood 'why me'.

*****

The galaxy is huge. Only about a tenth of it has been explored, if even that much. There is so much more still out there. And even in the areas that have been traveled for hundreds of years, there are remote little places that hardly anyone goes. Orso is one of those.

Not a planet but a small moon that's on the edges of explored space, in an unnamed system that's as hidden away as somewhat known systems can get. It orbits a dead world that also has no name. There's no reason to go so no reason to name.

The moon has one settlement and that's it. Just a small ball of rock.

But that ball of rock is the home base of the Yortusk, a multi-system criminal organization. You name it, they have their hands in it. It's an oddly set up group. The actual members of the Yortusk are few but they are incredibly loyal. They kind of franchise out chapters to other systems and you get all the benefits of having the Yortusk name. But you also play by their rules and if you don't, it's not pretty.

The rock, Orso, is notoriously hard to infiltrate. They only let a select few know it's actual location and even then a very few are actually allowed on the surface.

Somehow I became one of those chosen few.

It's a long story. Not necessarily a good story.

But I'm one of the few trusted by the Yortusk higher-ups.

And Romer wanted to use that trust somehow.

*****

"No," I said before Romer could continue. No way was I going to do anything to betray the Yortusk trust. I liked living thank you very much. I feared them more than anything Romer could do to me.

He just smiled. It was a smile that said I could protest all I wanted, it wouldn't matter in the end.

Smug bastard.

"Now you understand why I had to restrain you until you could hear my offer," he said.

I wanted to hit him. Badly.

"Not happening."

'You still don't know what I want," Romer said coming closer, smirking at me.

I shot him a look that was equal parts 'I don't care' and 'let me loose so I can hit you'. Maybe more of the hit one. I really wanted to hit him.

"It's a simple job," he continued, ignoring my look. "Just doing what it is you do now. Deliver. You take a couple crates and drop them off on Orso. That's it. So simple."

"What's in the crates," I asked even though I didn't want to know. 'So simple', yeah right.

"Nothing important," Romer said casually. "A legitimate order that you decided to fill this afternoon."

I was about to say something snarky but stopped, catching his words.

"What did you say?"

"I knew you needed a job when you left Buhin so I went ahead and booked you one," Romer said in his friendliest tone. I could see it in his eyes. He was enjoying this. "I found one that is going to Orso, although it wasn't advertised as such of course."

He leaned against the wall, smiling. He knew he had me.

Most of Orso's supplies came from the Yortusk themselves but every once in awhile they needed something else and put out feelers to folks like me. Independent haulers that they trust. I find that job and take it, go to Orso, get paid very well.

How did Romer learn the code they used?

And he did have me, dammit. The Yortusk would already know that I had accepted the order. I couldn't back out either. That was frowned upon because when they put out feelers like this, it meant they needed whatever it was pretty quickly. Taking the job and canceling put a wrinkle in their plans and the Yortusk hated that. Good way to find myself on their naughty list.

Doing this for Romer would find me there as well, but for different reasons.

What really sucks is that I would have taken the job anyways.

Sure the Yortusk are criminals, but I like them.

Romer waited patiently with that smug smile. I leaned back as much as I could, looking like I was thinking about it. There wasn't anything to think about, I was kind of stuck. At least for now, until I could think of a way out of it.

But I didn't want to make this easy on the bastard. The blond walked back around to the front and also leaned against the wall. One arm hung at her side and the fingers tapped against the metal. She was pretty when she wasn't holding a gun on me.

I shifted positions, pulled my legs in, tried to shrug my shoulders and settled in again.

Another couple minutes passed and I figured it was enough.

"Fine," I told Romer. "Not like I have a choice."

He stood up, clapping his hands.

"Good, good. Glad to hear it."

Romer motioned to the blond who once again walked behind me.

"You won't be going alone obviously," he said.

Of course, I figured he'd send one of his goons along. I gave him the 'I'm not an idiot' look. I really wanted to hit him.

"Valeri will be one of those going."

"Who?" I asked.

The blond smacked me across the back of the head. Ah, her. That was Valeri. Well at least the company would be good to look at.

I heard the cuffs click open. Pulling my hands around front of me, I stood up, rubbing feeling back into my wrists. I glanced behind me to see that Valeri had her hand on the handle of her holstered weapon. I smiled. She glared.

*****

It was a quick walk back to my ship.

Romer stayed behind, of course, but Valeri was joined by the Curdo. He was named Squayerit or something. She called him Yer. I didn't call him anything or say anything.

They marched me in front of them. The streets were less crowded now, the Buhin sun was rising and everyone had finally gone off to bed.

Funny how the sun rising does that, makes people go to sleep.

I'm sure there were some people working in the city but not down in this area. The buildings thinned out a bit and we turned onto the large metal deck that was hanging over the water. Ships filled the area and there was mine.

The *Nomad's Wind* was a Castellan Light Cruiser Model F497. A medium sized, when compared to other ships, metal wedge that was colored blue. A gray wing came out at the midpoint, tapered towards the back and towards the front where it extended beyond the angled front, with two large stardrive engines mounted on the wings. It was a beauty, to me anyways. Not fancy but I loved it and it was home.

Two beings stood outside of it with four crates lined up next to them on maglifters. One of them was a Kern, about six feet tall and almost a shapeless mass. It had arms and legs and a head with no neck, the shoulders and head kind of one piece. A shade of yellow, with lumpy and wrinkly skin, the arms and legs were thick as was the body. The other was another human, male, looked like early twenties.

More company that I didn't want.

The ship was designed for a crew of six but could be piloted by one. At least mine could. I'd rigged a lot of the systems. I had no other crew. Just me.

"Friends of yours?" I asked looking over my shoulder at Valeri.

She just glared at me.

She was good at that.

"What's in the crates?" I asked as we approached the ship. The human and Kern repositioned the maglifters, ready to load them.

"None of your business," Valeri replied. Apparently she was the leader. I tried to place her accent. From earth or a colony world? Hard to tell. "One of us will be in the hold at all times to keep you from snooping."

Interesting. I figured Romer had something stashed in the crates. The Yortusk wouldn't do business with him and he hadn't been able to penetrate their organization. Whatever was in the crates was probably to help him do that. Her response pretty much confirmed it.

I entered a code on the keypad mounted next to the rear ramp and it started to descend. I watched, ignoring my new "crew", and waited until it had lowered. I walked up the ramp and headed towards the far end of the hold and the rest of the ship. I heard footsteps, Valeri and not the Curdo, following me.

I paused at the door into the ship's lounge, watching the Kern and the other human pushing the maglifters into the bay. They moved over to one side where the locking plates were. The Curdo just stood by the ramp looking out into the city. I wished I had my blaster, I could take him out easily from here. They hadn't given it back to me. Valeri had it in the bag she carried over her shoulder.

That's okay, I had some other weapons hidden on the ship. Just needed to find some time to get to them.

I stepped through the door and into the ship's lounge. From there into the galley and the spiral stair in the corner that led to the upper level. A short corridor led to a longer one off of which were the quarters, three to each side and at the far end the door to engineering. The near end was the hatch into the bridge, with two storage rooms on either side. I hit the pad to open the bridge door and Valeri followed me in.

The bridge consisted of two levels with four stations facing a clear polycarbonite view window. Each station was a bunch of readouts, buttons and controls along with a chair. More readouts and controls lined the walls. Pilot was on the upper level to the right, co-pilot on the left. Navigator was on the left on the lower level and weapons on the right. The pilots station, my station, had additional controls that allowed access to the other functions.

Like I said, crew of six, but rigged for one.

Valeri sat down in the co-pilot's chair and swiveled it to face me as I took my seat. I started punching in the navorders for the hop to Orso. Flying through space is nicknamed starhopping, or just hopping. To get from A to E, you need to go to B and D and sometimes G depending on the current conditions of the various systems. Ion storms, novas, you name it. They all messed with navigation. You basically hopped from one system to another. Each hop would bring you closer to your final destination. When you went from A to B, you'd get an updated navorder in B for the trip to C or you'd get an alert that you now had to go to D.

Hops generally lasted anywhere from three to six hours, the longest single hop that I'd been on was ten hours. One reason why ships ran crews with multiple people, so there was always someone on duty in case something came up. It was a risk running with just one person, but that's the way I wanted it.

And now I had four unwanted passengers.

I mentally ran through the list of supplies. Not enough for five people.

The navcom beeped and I glanced at the readout. Five jumps, six days. Not bad. I hit a couple buttons and got it programmed in with a slight addition so it would need to be recalculated after each hop. I cleared the memory and set the navcom so that only I could access it. Just a little insurance.

"We're good to go," I said.

"How many hops?" Valeri asked.

I shrugged.

"Are your boys loaded?" I asked instead of answering, ignoring the glare she gave me. "I'll contact Buhin Dock Control and we can head out."

"Not yet," she replied and started looking around the bridge. "We're waiting on supplies. Where's the camera for the hold?"

I pointed it out to her and she switched it on. We could see the Curdo still standing at the ramp, the other two somewhere else in the hold.

"Supplies huh," I said leaning back in my chair, studying her. "Good, I didn't want to feed you lot anyways."

My initial observation had been accurate. She was good looking but had that cold and hard look to her. It made her uglier than she really was. Not that I really wanted to, but I figured I'd try to break down her walls. I had absolutely no interest in striking up conversations with the other three, so might as well with her or it'd be a long four days. I know I'm not the most charming guy around, but I do alright.

"So," I started to say but she was ignoring me.

In the camera feed I could see another figure walking up the ramp with a small crate on the maglifter. Another human, this one talked with the Curdo and both walked off screen for a couple seconds. They came back, the human pushing an empty maglifter. The supplies were loaded.

There went the idea of stopping somewhere and having an attempt to end this. Now we were all on board for the duration.

I felt a vibration through the ship and knew the ramp was raising.

"Now we're ready," Valeri said turning back to me.

Shrugging I grabbed my headset and prepared the ship for launch.

*****

The galaxy is made up of thousands, millions and maybe more, solar systems. Each system is a star in the sky. Each star is a sun with anywhere from three to a dozen planets orbiting. Out of those planets in a system, most are gas or uninhabitable. There's usually only one or two planets in a system that can sustain life. But each planet and its moons have their own gravity. Not to mention asteroids and other objects in space. This makes jumping to warpspace difficult within a system, so everyone travels to the edge of the system to jump.

Some ships, like the *Wind*, can travel in-system and larger ones have to wait at the edge and take small shuttles in deeper. Lots of heavily traveled systems have space stations at the edges where all the trading comes in. Buhin was not one of those, but we still had to travel an hour or two to the edge of the system to engage the stardrive. Thankfully it's a small system.

Once at the edge of the system, the stardrives are engaged and the ship enters warpspace, or wildspace as it's also known. This is the weird area between systems, the stuff that surrounds it. Dark matter I guess. Whatever it's called, you have to travel through that to get to the next system. The stardrives take trips that would be decades or centuries and makes them hours.

Star travel, the short version.

We got to the edge of the Buhin system and I engaged the *Wind's* stardrives.

Most ships no longer have view windows, but I love them for just this reason.

Before us was black with thousands of white dots that were the stars. As the engines started up, the dots elongated.

They stretched in continuous lines as far as the eye could see, ahead and behind. They got closer and closer together, the black disappearing, until all was white. It took on a foggy appearance, like flying through a cloud, as we entered wildspace.

I loved this view.

I caught Valeri looking out the window.

"I've never seen the transition before," she said, awe in her voice. It lost some of the harshness.

"It never gets old," I said and leaned back in my chair, arms crossed behind my head, watching the clouds of wildspace drift by.

The silence grew and there was a bit of tension to it. A 'what now' kind of thing. I was content to just wait it out. I was the kidnapped party, forced to do this, after all. No need for me to make it easy on them.

I heard the door slide open behind me and the other human walked in. About six foot, hundred and fifty, with brown hair and eyes. Clean shaven, hair cut short. Nothing remarkable about him. No idea what his name was, didn't care. He was armed with a blaster like Valeri's, in a holster hanging from a belt. Young looking, he must have been pretty inexperienced. The way he was standing, with the holster angled towards me, I could have grabbed it pretty quickly.

Lunge forward, grab and pull the gun, push him into Valeri so she can't react. Two shots and I'd have them out of the fight.

I was tempted.

Valeri must have seen me looking because she pushed the kid aside, glaring at me. I returned my attention to the console.

"Set up a rotation with Yer," she was telling the kid. "I want one of you in the hold at all times. Awake," she finished, putting emphasis on the last word.

So much for sneaking down to the hold and seeing what was in the crates.

"And one of us with him at all times," she said pointing at me as the kid walked out of the bridge. The door closed before him.

"Even when I need to use the lav?" I asked, an innocent smile on my face.

I got the glare.

It was starting to look good on her. How soon could someone get that condition where they started sympathizing with their captors?

"What about when I sleep?" I asked as I watched the *Wind's* security camera feeds through the small monitors at my station. I could see the kid walking down the stairs and into the hold where the Curdo and Kern were. They were all pretty animated in their discussion.

"Someone will be outside the door," she answered.

"You're more than welcome to be inside the door," I said and meant it as a joke, figured I'd get some kind of angry remark.

There was a pause before she answered.

"Sure," Valeri said.

I looked over to see if she was serious. No glare and she was standing up.

What the hell.

*****

If you can, I'd recommend getting kidnapped by a good looking blond that's wild in the bunk.

That made the trip much more interesting.

And fun.

I had no illusions about what was going on. It was just fun, a way to pass the time. I had no problems with that.

The other goons weren't fans, but I didn't care and apparently neither did Valeri. She was the boss. The rotation they worked out was that one person was with me at all times, one was in the hold at all times and the other two were sleeping. It went hold, sleep, me, sleep. They went on a twenty-four hour rotation. Six on, six off. There wasn't that much time to get a true pattern and routine going but I tried to establish one with my movements. Yer, the Curdo, was a mean one. He would have killed me the first time he saw me. I avoided him as much as possible and never felt comfortable when it was his turn to watch me. Those beady little eyes just bored holes into me and I could tell he wanted to not just kill but to hurt me. The Kern was named Hors Buyt. Decent enough and might have even been friends if he wasn't one of my captors. The other human was named Darm Hunir and he was an ass. Young and cocky with a touch of squirrely. He wasn't long for life. Someone would put him down soon enough.

Midway through the third day was when I decided to have some fun.

Valeri's shift at watching me was almost up and we were walking towards the galley afterwards. I wanted a beer. A good earth made beer. They were hard to come by out here and I kept a few on hand.

I walked over to the pantry, cabinets aligned against one wall, and pulled a bottle of beer out of the cooling unit. They keep telling us that replication tech is coming someday and we'll no longer need to carry food. I don't believe it. Leaning against the counter I surveyed the room.

Yer was sitting at the table, facing me, eating something from a bowl. I didn't know what it was, some special food that only the Curdo would eat. It looked gross. Valeri was digging through the supplies her team had brought aboard. They were still in a box sitting on the floor.

In the way.

Which is where I kept moving it to.

And there was my target.

Darm came into the room having just switched places with Hors down below in the hold. Probably to grab a bite before his sleep rotation.

He looked tired, irritable. Perfect.

He eyed my beer and I took a drink from it.

"Damn this is good stuff," I said to no one in particular. "Pretty rare to get a good earth beer out this far."

Grumbling something he moved to dig around in their box of crap. Valeri had taken a seat at the head of the table where she could keep an eye on me. And she was doing that without looking directly at me. I could see her wondering what I was doing. I know she had been warned by Romer that I was smart, which I was, and crafty. She had to assume that I was always up to something.

Darm found something prepackaged and took it to the table. He sat next to Yer, glancing at Valeri and noting what she was wearing. Pants and a tank top, nothing special, but it wasn't what she had on earlier. He knew what we had been up to.

I think little Darm was jealous.

"Better than that stuff," I continued pointing with the plasbottle of beer at what was on his plate. I was just speaking the truth. I didn't even know what it was supposed to be.

Setting my drink on the table, in clear view of Darm, I turned around and started pulling stuff out of the pantry. Early in the trip I had caught him in my stuff and had quickly put the locks on so only I could open the cabinets. I had to share my ship with them, not my food. It was bad enough they were all sleeping in the bunks next to mine. I'd have to pay to get their stench and germs cleaned out of my beautiful *Wind.*

What I pulled out was nothing fancy but it was much better than what Darm or the others had.

"Now this is what food should look like," I said sitting down. "So kid, you from Earth or a colony?"

"Don't call me kid," Darm grumbled.

"How'd you know I was talking to you?" I asked innocently. "I could have been talking to Yer there," I continued, pointing at the Curdo with my now almost empty beer bottle. "I have no idea how Curdo age, he could be a kid." Yer, for his part, just gave me the look that said he wanted to eat me and then kill me. "But since you responded, you must get called kid a lot."

I took another bite of my meal and another drink. I could tell he was glancing at my stuff.

"I'd offer you a beer but I don't have that many and it'll be awhile before I can get more. Besides kid, are you even old enough to drink?"

"You don't need to worry about getting more," Darm snarled.

"Is that a threat kid," I replied taking the last swig of my beer and putting the empty plasbottle down, closer to him.

"Darm," Valeri said calmly.

He ignored her, staring hatefully at me.

"Don't worry Val. I'm not worried about the kid." I could see using a familiar form of her name bothered him. He was almost twitching. This was the first time I had used that shortened form. Up until that point I hadn't even called her, or any of them but Hors, by name the whole trip.

Darm tried to calm down, I could see him taking deep breaths. Yer just stared at me, the same look. Valeri shook her head, not wanting anything to do with it, or thinking Darm was calming down. He wasn't. I could tell.

Back in my Special Operations days I'd been taught how to read people and how to push buttons. It was a great skill to have. Beings of all races were easier to deal with when they were off balance. Just a matter of finding the right screw to twist.

He finished eating and stood up, walking towards the head of the table. All eyes followed him, at least mine and Vals,

Yer continued to glare at me. I smiled at the Curdo and felt the urge to stick my tongue out.

"You didn't answer me kid," I said to Darm as he passed by Val. "You from Earth or a colony?"

I could feel Darm's eyes boring into my skull as he walked towards the sink mounted in the cabinets. I heard the dish fall into the metal bowl. He was now directly behind me.

"It's not a big deal kid," I continued and got myself ready, not showing it in my body language. "Just making conversation. I think most people your age that are in space come from colonies. Read a stat on that or something years back. Not that many kids come out of the homeworld nowadays."

Yer glanced up quickly over my shoulder so I knew that Darm was standing there looking down at me. Now to just push him over the edge.

"I don't know Val, Romer must be hard up for thugs," I said looking across at Yer. "The Curdo here, that species is tough, so that's a plus. A Kern like Hors is the same. And I understand you. But Darm here," and I motioned behind me. "That one I don't get. He's so green, a fresh faced kid. Couldn't Romer have done better? Back in the day this kid would just be a mule."

I had to give him credit, he didn't make a sound and moved pretty quick but I was expecting it.

He lunged for me, probably wanting to grab me in a headlock or push my head against the table. I darted to the side, pushing the chair back so it slammed into him. His hand just missed my right shoulder and I grabbed his reaching arm with my left. I stepped backwards and pulled him forward, his body pushing the chair against the table and into his stomach. With my right arm, while holding his left pulled out, I reached over his shoulder and cupped his chin. I pulled his head back, kept his left arm out and stepped behind him. I kicked his legs out and he fell forward but was pinned by my headlock. He struggled, trying to move his left hand and reach at me with his right but the angle was wrong and my knee in his back drove him against the chair.

Darm was coughing and sputtering.

"Dumb move kid," I said calmly.

"Let him go Lancer," Valeri said and I looked to see her and Yer standing up, both with weapons pointed at me.

I leaned forward, close to Darm's ear, well keeping my eyes on Valeri. As much as Yer might want to shoot me, he was going to follow her lead.

"They're not going to shoot me," I said to Darm. "Without me they can't land on Orso or even fly the ship. You're expendable. That's probably why you were sent along. Just a body to give them a break on watch."

"Lancer."

I released his arm and his head, pushing it down with my hand as I stood up. Darm jerked back and turned towards me, holding his chest where the chair had been against it. There was a lot of hate in that stare but I could see fear too. Kids like this, put the fear in them and they fold. I smiled.

Turning my back on him I walked towards the stairs up to the bridge. I could hear Valeri getting up to follow.

"Hey kid, clean up the dishes," I called out walking up the stairs. I didn't even bother looking back at him. Not worth my time.

I could have sworn I heard Yer chuckle. It's hard to tell with Curdo.

*****

A day later and we were on the final hop to Orso. We'd hop out at the edge of the system and it was a three hour in-system jaunt to the moon.

Time was ticking and I was going to need to make a move soon. No way was I landing on the moon with these jokers in control. And no way was I delivering Romer's cargo. I liked the Yortusk. I didn't like Romer.

Valeri got out of the bed and started rummaging around on the ground for her clothes. Aside from the first time, she never brought her blaster in. Smart. I sat up and watched her. She ignored me. Leaning forward on the bunk I grabbed my pants and briefs but didn't move to put them on.

I waited. She put on her pants and then started to pull her shirt on over her head. I stood up quickly and moved towards the refresher. There were six bunks on the *Nomad's Wind* with a private refresher and closet for each one. I moved quickly before she got the shirt all the way on.

"Be right back," I said as the refresher door slid shut behind me.

The room was small. A stand-up shower unit and toilet on one wall, sink and cabinet on the other. Functional. There was a storage room on either side of the bridge and the refresher in my bunk, the first one to the left of the bridge, backed up to the storage. Valeri and crew had searched it when they first got on, finding nothing special. It was mostly empty.

What they didn't find was the hatch between the refresher and storage.

Turning on the shower unit so the noise would hide what I was doing, I put on my briefs and pants. Slowly, quietly, I ran my hand along the wall between the shower and cabinet feeling for the catch. I found it, clicked it, and the hatch slid into the wall revealing an opening big enough to crawl through. I made my way quickly into the storage room, no light but I knew the space by feel.

The floors of the bunks and refreshers was finished in a vinyl material, warm on bare feet, but the storage was not. The metal floor was cold.

I searched in the dark and found the latch on this side, closing the hatch and shutting away the light from the refresher. Closing my eyes, letting them adjust to the dark, I opened them and looked around. Nothing had changed or been moved. A couple travel trunks and that was it. I made my way to the door, moving quietly and hit the pad that turned on the light. Yep, room was the same as I'd left it. Dust on everything except where Romer's thugs had walked in their casual review of the room.

They hadn't done a good search because I was supposed to be under watch all the time and they figured I wouldn't get into a firefight on my own ship.

They were partly right.

I moved a couple of the trunks out of the way and ran my hands along the metal wall. The walls of the *Wind's* hold and living spaces did not go all the way to the outer hull, there was a couple foot gap all around the ship. Not enough space for a person to get into but just enough space to put in some hidden compartments.

Finding the latch, I pulled a piece of paneling away from the wall and set it to the side. Revealed was a small storage compartment. Only about six inches deep, three feet wide and three feet high, the back was lined with a peg system. Hanging from the pegs were an assortment of weapons. A couple blasters and rifles.

Some of them illegal in different systems.

There were a couple boxes lined up on the side. When I had left the service, I made off with some gear. I wasn't supposed to have it, that's why it was in the hidden compartment.

I grabbed a blaster, a Remington Tech 6, the better version of what Valeri had. Not as good as my trusty Sig, but still a good weapon with a full power pack. Good to go.

Quickly replacing the panel, knowing Valeri was going to start getting anxious if I wasn't out of the refresher soon, I headed for the door. I hit the keypad, undoing the automatic opening mechanism. I didn't want the door sliding open onto an unknown situation. Listening at it, I couldn't hear anything in the corridor beyond.

Taking a deep breath I took hold of the manual handle and slowly pulled the heavy door open. The metal slid, soundlessly, and through the crack I could see the corridor outside. A nice design feature of the storage room door on this side, it was at an angle so had good sightlines down most of the corridor. I could see the three bunk doors on the other side and most of the hall's width. Couldn't see the wall and doors on this side. But there were no shadows across the metal floor to indicate someone was there.

All clear.

I pulled the door open fully and stepped into the hall. The only door I hadn't been able to see was the bridge but there shouldn't have been anyone there. I checked that first to be safe. Empty and just the way I had left it. The controls were already locked so only I could do anything so there was no worries about that.

Stopping outside my bunk door I could hear Valeri pounding on the refresher. Smiling, I entered a code into the keypad and locked the door. It wouldn't open from the inside and only I could unlock it. I closed the storage room door and did the same, just in case she managed to find the connecting hatch from the refresher. I was a little worried about her finding the weapons but I had replaced the panel and she couldn't do much damage with them locked inside the room.

I had a feeling my bunk would be destroyed when she finally got out.

Good thing nothing of importance was kept there.

I repeated the same at the other doors, locking anyone inside if they were. I had no idea where the other three were, except one should be down in the hold. The other two could have been sleeping but with my luck they were roaming the halls. The *Wind* was a small ship, wouldn't take long for us to bump into each other. Not that many places to hide.

Weapon ready, I crept down the corridor, keeping the blaster to my side. The door to engineering was closed and I leaned closer to it, listening. I couldn't hear anything on the other side but that wasn't a clear indicator. The doors and walls were solid and not easy for sound to pass through.

I hit the buttons on the keypad and the engine room door slid open. Immediately the noise level in the corridor almost doubled, maybe even tripled. The wall and door between these spaces was thick and sound proof. It had to be. I really didn't need to be in engineering, there was no reason for any of them to be there, but I wanted to make sure it was empty. I had thought about locking the door when the goon squad first arrived but it's not like they would tamper with the engines. They needed the ship to get on and off Orso. Once we were off the moon and cargo delivered, anything could happen. But that was a worry for later, for now I had set up a routine in the ship's computer to record if anyone entered the room. So far no one had but it was better to be safe than sorry.

Engineering was the largest room on the upper level. Taking up pretty much the back half. It was noisy, lots of moving parts, spinning turbines and high powered energy generators. I'd been in some rooms and they were a mess. I kept the *Wind* neat. Plenty of space to get around, easy access to the readouts and everything was as clean as they could get.

I quickly reconned the space. Walking a circuit and checking the alcove to the right of the door. This was where the out-atmo suits were kept for space walking, along with a ladder leading to the airlock and the outside hatch mounted on top of the ship.

The whole room was empty.

Time to get on with this.

I ran back, quietly, to the bridge and turned on the security cams. I felt exposed, because of the positioning of the screens I had my back to the door. There was an excuse ready if one of the others came up. Valeri was in the can. Could work long enough for me to attack but luckily it didn't happen.

After this was over, maybe adding more lockable doors to the *Wind* would be a good idea.

The screens showed Darm in the lounge with his feet up on the table. Bastard. The Curdo was the most dangerous and the cams showed me that Yer was in the hold. I couldn't see Hors. That meant he was probably in the bunk, the only places there was no camera. Safely locked away.

Back down the corridor, I checked but could no longer hear anything coming from my bunk. Wonder what Valeri was doing? At this point she knew I was up to something, she had to be. She was probably trying to understand how I had gotten out of the refresher. She'd probably find the hatch to the storage room, but was trapped in there as well.

This level was as secure as I could get it.

Now came the hard part, but the easy one first.

To the right of the bridge was a short hall that ended in the spiral stair that went down to the lower levels. It was open to the galley, which is why I had been moving as quiet as possible. All that back and forth would seem suspicious. Just to be safe I locked the door to the right side storage room. There was nothing vital or harmful there but again, safe over sorry.

Keeping the gun in my right hand, tight to my body, I walked down the metal stairs. I kept my body loose, like there wasn't a care in the world. Darm was in the lounge but he could have moved. But no, there was no one in the galley.

Across the space, the door to the lounge was closed. I crossed through the galley quickly.

At the door to the lounge I paused and took a deep breath. I forced myself to focus. This had always been the hardest part for me, the calm before the storm. My mind would fill with random thoughts, things that had no place or meaning to what I was about to do. Just distractions. But once I focused, got my mind locked down, it was like I went on automatic.

The door slid open and I walked into the lounge.

What I called the lounge really wasn't much of one. In most ships they were bigger, with lots of entertainment options and sitting areas. This one had a single couch and two chairs. Lots of empty space. It was just me, I didn't need much. The couch ran parallel with the length of the room, the two chairs on either end facing into the middle where there was a table. In front was the large vidscreen.

There was some show playing, one I didn't recognize. Not sure where Darm had found it, not one of the ones I had recorded. When a ship was in wildspace it couldn't receive any transmissions. Once you hopped out and into normal space, you'd receive a ton of stuff. Communications, anything that was set to download from the Galactic Feed.

The Feed was the communication system and organization that linked all the separate planets and races together. Using Tradelan, the common language, allowed us to communicate and the Feed allowed us to share data. The Feed transmitted through satellites placed throughout the systems and could punch through wildspace. You couldn't access it well in wildspace but once you were out everything was available again. Most people, myself included, had the Feed set up to download certain items whenever they hopped into a new system. Messages, news, entertainment. That kind of thing.

Whatever Darm was watching, it wasn't something I had programmed into the Feed. Just one more thing I was going to have to cleanse once they were gone.

Darm glanced quickly at me when I walked in and returned to his show. He didn't notice that I had one hand behind my back.

"Where's Valeri?" he asked.

"Refresher," I replied. He didn't even ask why I was shirtless. Although he did know what Valeri and I had been doing, so me being shirtless shouldn't have been that big a surprise.

He kept glancing at me, pretending not to, but my presence without someone else was making him nervous. Especially when I started walking behind him.

My old Special Operations commander, Colonel Jessups, had three rules for any mission.

First was to plan for every eventuality.

That was always the hardest because there were so many things to account for. I was treating this whole voyage like a mission. Planning and assessing my targets, Romer's four goons. Planning for every eventuality for this was in how I would approach each and where. Options had to exist for meeting the Curdo in the galley with Darm, with Hors or alone. And there had to be one for meeting Yer in the bridge or the bunk or lounge and with or without others. Lots of options. But what else did I have to do during the trip?

Second was to choose your battlefield.

This one was the hardest for me. It was my ship but there were way too many variables. The only one I could have any control over was Valeri and then only limited. What if she didn't want to fool around during one of her shifts watching me? But I knew my ship better than they did, so that gave me a bit of an advantage.

But I could control some of their reactions. Somewhat befriending Hors, so he wouldn't react as negatively to me was one way. Another was the stunt I had pulled on Darm the other day. Now he was afraid of me, wary. So his reactions would be slower and not as confident. Made him a bit more predictable.

Jessups third rule was my favorite. Be good at making it up.

All the planning in the world didn't help you once the blasting started and the chaos came, he was fond of saying, because that brings a whole new set of conditions and variables you never thought about.

I could plan with the best of them but my real strength had been in improvisation.

Pausing behind Darm, I placed my free hand on the back of the couch, making him jump a little bit.

"How are you doing Darm?" I asked.

He leaned forward, trying to ignore me. I was making him jumpy.

Good.

I turned and headed for the cargo hold door, adjusting my right hand so the blaster was blocked by my body. I figured Darm was doing his best to pretend I wasn't there, try to maintain what little dignity he had left. If you're a punk ass cocky kid, getting shown up by the older guy you're supposed to be guarding and pushing around, especially in front of the woman you have a crush on, that pokes lots of big holes in the pride.

Whatever. He could use this as a teachable moment if he survived.

I paused at the door, body blocking the weapon and could feel Darm glance at me, curious what I was doing. I looked over my shoulder and he quickly looked back at the vidscreen. Perfect. Turning around I stepped to the side so I could get a better shot around the couch and thumbed the blaster to stun. No need to accidently shoot holes in my own furniture.

Raising the weapon I took aim at Darm's chest. The angle was off and the way he was sitting didn't give me much of a target.

"Hey kid," I said.

He turned towards me, turning to face me, showing more of his body.

Thanks kid.

I pulled the trigger, a bolt of energy shot out of my gun and struck him in the chest. Darm convulsed, lines of energy sparking around his body, his head falling back and his body just sagged against the couch. He lay there awkwardly, body bent strangely, and gave little shakes. Maybe I had the stun setting too high.

Too bad.

I stepped away from the door and turned so I could cover it with the blaster. I was moving to my right, I'm right handed, so the blaster was pointing across my body to the left. Awkward but I'd be able to get a couple shots off before having to dive for cover.

Darm was no longer moving. Placing a couple fingers to his neck I could feel his pulse. Still alive. He should be out for a couple hours.

One more to deal with.

*****

I crouched down, using the couch as a kind of cover, and sighted on the door. Maybe Yer would make this easy and come in on his own.

No way I'd be that lucky.

Instead he'd be on the other side with his weapon sighted on the door and just waiting for me to enter.

If the *Wind* was bigger, there would have been space in the hull and other sneaky spots to move through. I'd been on board larger freighters where you could move between levels and rooms through the hull space. Not here.

A year or so ago I had thought about installing secondary monitors for the security cams down here in the lounge or galley area. Never got around to it. Sure would have come in handy right about now. I added it to the mental list along with more lockable doors.

I had one thing working for me. Yer couldn't kill me. Not yet anyways.

I knew next to nothing about Curdo anatomy. Had never run into them during my time in service. They lived on the far side of the known space, the far edge of the Inner Worlds. Some jungle planet called Durod. The Tiat had a small colony there but it wasn't a world they fully controlled. Which said lots about the climate and the natives. All I knew was that Curdo were tough bastards. I needed to take Yer out from a distance. No way would I win a hand to hand fight with him.

Didn't want to wait here forever either.

Keeping my blaster trained on the door, I moved that way. The keypad was on this side, which worked to my benefit. I hugged the wall, crouching low and hit the pad. The door slid open.

Blaster bolts, the green tinge of stun blasts, flew through the opening. They struck the far wall, leaving smoking scorch marks on the metal, searing off the paint. Splashes of energy moved across the wall.

Staying low I rotated around the wall and into the opening. I fired off three quick bolts, jerking my blaster so each bolt went to a corner and straight down the middle. Following behind, I rolled into the bay, came out of the roll and fired three more shots. Same pattern but lower. I could hear most of my shots hitting the metal walls and one hitting the polyplas of a crate. No grunts of pain from Yer.

Dammit.

The hold was big and empty, just the three crates that Romer's people had brought aboard. No other cover and those were down at the far end, like fifty feet away. Not good, not good at all.

I got up and ran towards the right wall. Even though they were further away and Yer was behind them, I could still make use of the crates. I fired as I ran, keeping Yer's head down. I had gotten a good look at the hold and hadn't seen him, which meant he was behind the crates. I hit the crates and some shots going wide. I didn't care if I damaged whatever was inside, I just needed to damage the Curdo more.

Yer's head poked up above a crate and he fired back at me. I managed to twist and slam into the wall. Sliding against the wall, I slide to the ground where Yer didn't have an angle to shoot me. I also didn't have one to shoot him. Crouching low I moved as quick as I could towards the crate.

I paused when I heard the squawk. It was blood curdling. Like a bird of prey dive bombing from the sky. I looked up and saw Yer crouched low on top of the crate. He was bent in a position that no human could ever get, leaning down close to the top of the crate, one hand on the crate and the other raised over his head. His three fingers were spread out, nails like talons.

There was murder in his slitted eyes. My murder.

I don't think he cared about keeping me alive anymore.

With a screech, Yer jumped off the crate.

I dove to the ground, spinning as I did. Landing on my back, I fired at where I saw the streaking form of Yer. I missed.

Yer landed with a skid, body still low, and with a shift of his weight he was turning to face me. It was one smooth motion. One quick and deadly looking smooth motion.

"Romer's plan won't work with me dead," I said as Yer took a quick step towards me. It was more a slide, his body low and flowing. I could hear the talons on his hands clicking against the metal floor. It echoed through the empty hold.

I was only going to get one shot at this. I needed to guess right. Fifty/fifty chance.

My back was to the crate and I used it to hold myself steady. I raised my blaster and aimed at Yer's head. He reacted how I knew he would. The Curdo darted to the side, moving incredibly fast.

But not fast enough.

My shot took him in the lowered shoulder, sending the Curdo sprawling and sliding across the deck. He squawked in pain.

I had guessed right. Sometimes the Lancer luck works in my favor.

Can't believe I guessed right.

Standing up I walked over to the struggling Yer. He was watching me, hate still in his eyes along with pain and was trying to push himself up.

I pointed my blaster at him and clicked it off of stun. That little noise was infinitely loud in the hold.

The noise of the blaster bolt was even louder.

*****

Romer was right.

I had to take the job once he put my name on it. The Yortusk would not have been happy to be stiffed and pissing them off was not conductive to my continued career or health. So I had to go. He had hoped his goons would keep me in line and deliver his cargo.

That didn't work.

And well I never told them how long it would take to get to Orso, or exactly how many jumps, I had purposely gone out of the way.

In reality Orso's system is only two quick jumps away from Buhin. I went out wide and started to come back in. I never headed directly for it either.

I didn't think he had, but Romer could have put a tracker in the cargo.

Tracking a ship through hops is extremely difficult, at least if you're trying to follow the path. Turning one on, keeping it on while the ship hops in and out of wildspace, is a good way to screw up the data and reception. Like the Galactic Feed, signals get blocked and interrupted by wildspace. A tracking signal can get scrambled. It goes into wildspace in one system, the ship comes out in another and the signal shows it in yet another system. Then there's ion storms, novas, and all that.

Wrecks havoc with a continuous signal.

So most tracking is done from point to point. Leave a fixed point and the ship hops out at the final destination and the tracker is turned on, connects to the Feed satellites and you have your location. You can turn the tracker on at each hop but it takes time for the device to connect, and most midhops aren't that long. And you don't need to know the path, just the end point.

I made sure none of the stops between hops were long enough for Valeri or one of the others to connect a tracker. The next part was where I was making some assumptions and hoping I was right. I was counting on Romer overthinking it and trying to compensate for my involvement.

If one of his people were carrying the tracker, they could switch it on as soon as we hopped into the system. But I was counting on him thinking that I'd have a jammer on board, which I do, or that the Yortusk would block outgoing signals from within the system. Maybe they do, I don't know.

So the most accurate and surest way to get a tracker signal from Orso was on the moon itself and the safest way to get it there was as part of the cargo. Once on planet, activate the tracker and walk away.

That's what I would have done anyways.

But this is where I think Romer got cute. Orso and the Yortusk operations are a huge unknown and that bothered Romer. He wanted to know more so instead of just finding out where Orso is, he wanted to bug it. That was my guess anyways. Knowing where the moon was wouldn't do Romer any good. It's not like he would forcibly take it. He could have tried to get a spy but there were easier ways to do that.

No, some kind of bug made the most sense.

Which was why I was tearing apart the three cargo containers.

Yer was dead a couple feet away from me. Darm was tied up and thrown in one of the bunks. Hors and Valeri were still locked in theirs and I'd locked in the last hop coordinates.

Just a couple hours from the system. Plenty of time to find the bug.

There was nothing special about the crates. Standard polyplas. Four foot by four foot by four foot. And the bug wouldn't be in them as they'd get reused or trashed. So whatever it was, would be inside one of the crates attached to the cargo. Right?

Was I starting to overthink this?

I took a couple steps back from the crates. I needed to think like Romer. Which was hard. The guy had decades of experience as a spook and I grudgingly had to admit he was one of the best. It was in his blood and every fiber of his being. He was smarter at it then I was, no question there.

This was giving me a headache.

Going to the storage closet in the hold I pulled out the crowbar. The crates were locked and closed but not keycoded. Placing the bar at the lip I pushed and started popping the top off one. Inside were stacked boxes of foodstuffs. Nothing sinister. The others contained more foodstuffs, clothing and other miscellaneous innocent items. I really didn't want to go through each item but I would if I had to.

But before I did that, it was time to examine the crates again.

There was one other thing that Colonel Jessups liked saying about any mission planning. Keep it simple. Don't overthink it.

Romer had been involved in a lot of those missions.

Think. What was Romer's goal here?

Ultimately he probably wanted to overthrow or replace the Yortusk.

There was something here, had to be, otherwise why keep someone in the hold with the crates at all times? They didn't want me looking at these things.

Running my fingers along the edge of the crate I found it on the second one.

A slim piece of circuitry. About an inch long and very thin, almost invisible under the lip of the crate.

I pulled it off. Just a circuit board with a push button switch. Some kind of transmitter. They would turn it on when we arrived and probably remove it from the crates once they were unloaded. Long enough to get a tracking connection.

Could it even be one of those new burst transmitters that I had heard about before I left the service? Devices that could send a signal to any wireless or satlinked network. Depending on the strength of it, they could bypass firewalls and send or receive data. Not a lot. Could Romer use this to install some kind of virus in the Yortusk system?

How would Romer have gotten such a device?

Coulson?

This just got a lot more interesting.

Using my finger nail I disconnected the switch so the device wouldn't turn on.

To be safe I looked over the rest of this crate and the next. Nothing.

I walked back to the bridge and could hear pounding coming from my bunk. Valeri was slamming something against the door. I'd probably have to redo my entire room when this was done, what was left of it anyways. She was shouting something but couldn't make out the words. Nothing from Hors side of the hall.

Only a couple more hours and I'd be done with this.

*****

The white clouds of wildspace disappeared. Bright one second and then the black with white dots of space that was the field of stars. I could see the distant bright point that was the system's sun and a couple of larger bodies that were the closest planet and its moons.

Taking manual control, I reorientated the *Nomad's Wind* and pointed it at a spot beyond the planet. I engaged the insystem thrusters and settled in for the next part of the flight.

Insystem travel was a lot slower than starhopping, outersystem warping, but it was quick enough considering the distances traveled. Most of the larger ships couldn't do insystem for various reasons, mostly because they were too big to land on planet and not equipped for space transfer, but the *Wind* was just small enough. Just one of the reasons why the busier systems built space stations near where ships hopped in. Planets didn't like a lot of traffic in and out, so the stations helped regulate it.

Orso was not like that. Only the moon got any traffic and that was already tightly controlled.

It took an hour to get where I could see Orso. A small moon, the planet it orbited was barren. As I got closer I could see lines of red crisscrossing the planet's surface. Not a hint of green or blue, just dark black and gray with the hints of red. Not a vacation spot.

The moon didn't look much better. Circle of gray rock floating in space.

I hit some commands on the comm station, sending a coded signal, as the *Wind* adjusted and shook entering the moon's gravity field. I had approached with the moon at the top of the viewwindow and now the surface swung around so it was at the bottom of the viewwindow as the *Wind's* compensators orientated with the surface of the moon. The *Wind* was now flying over the surface of Orso, still a couple hundred feet up. The ship followed the curve of the moon and soon lights could be seen in the distance.

The lights turned into structures built onto the surface.

A large ring was cut into the surface of the moon, the edges covered in metal and built up. Lights flashed along the surface and a red glow around the inside circumference, the lights of the magbarrier. A structure was just off to the side, lights flashing along the metallic surface. Well it was one large building, there were different levels and structures.

Some round, some with angled sides. I knew from experience that most of it was unused. The real buildings were under the moon's surface.

The base had started out as a research facility that was abandoned. No idea who the previous owners were but the Yortusk found it and took it over for their needs.

I took the *Wind* over the opening ringed in metal and adjusted the thrusters. Slowly I lowered the ship down. There was a shaking and bright flash across the canopy as I passed through the barrier and into the artificial atmosphere of the base.

Looking out the view window I saw cut rock mixed with metal panels. Blinking lights of various colors and polycarbonite windows cut into the surface. I could see people moving in the rooms and halls beyond the windows, all of them carrying weapons. I knew there were blaster cannons hidden in the walls behind some of the metal plating.

Watching the readouts I adjusted the thrusters and set the *Wind* down nice and easy. There was a slight shaking as the ship settled on the landing skids. I hit the switches and powered the engines down.

I had kept the bridge door open so I could hear any noises from my prisoners. Valeri had stopped shouting once she realized the ship was done jumping. I think she realized at that point that they really had never been in control of me or the ship.

Walking by I had expected her to start yelling again, but there was just silence.

She knew where we were and what it probably meant for her.

*****

I stood at the end of the cargo hold watching the ramp lower. As it descended I could see the stars and void of space through the magbarrier, tinged in red, then the rock walls and metal plating and finally the Yortusk that came out to meet me.

They were all Dyer, three men and a woman. Green skinned humanoids, all different shades, with blue or purple shades of hair and purple eyes. All were dressed in various styles of clothing, all in good condition, and looked like they could fit in almost anywhere in the galaxy. Four of them here but I knew there were more near. All armed with weapons held loose but ready.

Leadership of the Yortusk, which meant everyone on this rock, was all Dyer. They were a race from the Manis system, one of the few with three livable planets. The Dyer had colonized all three without much expansion beyond that system. They were a strict society, very rigid in their codes. Which made the criminal gang very odd indeed. I'd always suspected that the Yortusk was tied tightly to the Dyer government.

The ramp settled against the metal floor of the Orso hangar with a slight bang. I started down the ramp, hands held far off to the side, away from my holstered blaster.

"Captain Lancer," the Dyer in front said, nodding his head.

"Shirrit Yurn," I said, returning the nod.

A smile came across his face and he laughed, the others lowering their weapons. I reached out a hand and Yurn took it, pulling me in for a hug. Most Dyer are more reserved. Yurn is an oddity. Probably why he was in charge of the Yortusk.

"It's good to see you again my friend," he said stepping back. "I was glad to see that it was you that had taken our order."

"Yeah," I started and paused, glancing up into the ship. "About that."

*****

Yurn had sent for more Dyer, people to take away the Curdo's body. They had also scanned the contents of the crates and were scanning the rest of the ship to be safe. I had no problem with that. Darm had still been out when they took him away. Yurn didn't say what his fate would be and I didn't ask but I could assume.

Didn't really care.

The kid was fated for a short life so why not now?

With Yurn, I led a group of six up to the bunk corridor. We were not quiet, I wanted the occupants to know there were multiple people out here.

We stopped in front of the room that Hors was in. I banged my fist loudly on the metal and hit the button that activated the intercom into the room.

"Hors," I started. "I'm out here with six armed men. We're going to open the door and you're going to come peacefully right?"

There was a grunted acknowledgement from the other side.

I hit the command to unlock the door and stepped back. It slid open to show Hors standing on the other side, hands out to his side. He was slumped and looked tired. The Dyer had weapons raised and pointed at him.

"Are you going to give us trouble?" Yurn asked.

Hors just shook his head. He didn't bother to look at me as two of the Dyer led him off the ship. He moved quick enough, surprisingly for one going to an unknown fate.

"He seems decent enough," I said to Yurn leaning in and speaking quietly so Hors wouldn't catch it. "Might be able to turn him."

Yurn watched the Kern disappear around the corridor, listening to his heavy steps on the metal circular stair.

"I've always liked Kern," he said as quietly. "Dependable people." He turned and pointed at my bunk and the last prisoner. "What about that one?"

I thought about it for a bit. Would Valeri turn on Romer? If she didn't, there was no illusions about her fate. The Yortusk would try to get as much information out of her as they could and then they would just end her. Even if she didn't stay loyal to Romer, I couldn't see her talking to the Yortusk out of stubborness. They'd have to torture her.

"No," I finally said, knowing I had sealed her fate.

I'm not a nice guy. I have no problem with killing. I just don't like when it's a waste like this.

"Valeri," I said into the intercom. "I have armed guards with me. I'm going to open the door now. Come quietly."

There was no answer.

I looked at Yurn who positioned his men to cover the door and I unlocked it on his nod. It slid open and there was Valeri inside sitting on my bunk. Surprisingly there was no damage. Nothing broken, nothing turned over. Just as I had left. She had shut off the shower though.

She looked up at me as I followed two Dyer in. Their weapons were pointed at her, two plasma rifles, but she didn't give them the time of day. Just studied me. There was some respect there.

"We were never in control were we," she asked.

"No, not really."

"Romer underestimated you," she said standing up.

"He always did," I replied.

One Dyer stayed in the room, weapon following Valeri as she followed us out. I stepped aside, hanging back with Yurn as another Dyer proceeded her and the rest followed. It was a quiet procession as we went down the spiral stairs and into the galley. From there, into the lounge and into the hold.

Valeri stared ahead, the only time she paused and looked was at the scorch mark on the floor of the cargo hold. Dark black, sooty, against the shining metal. She glanced back at me with a question.

"Yer," I replied and she nodded.

She didn't even glance at the crates or the scattered contents. The Yortusk had been a little rough in searching them. Understandably but it had made a mess. They didn't even end up keeping any of the contents, not trusting them now. Which was a bonus for me, I could turn around and sell what I could for a nice extra profit. Not like I was going to get paid for delivering them.

We walked down the ramp and Valeri looked around at the entrance to the base. The walls of rock and metal got a cursory glance but it was the stars that got the most attention. They led her towards the nearest door into the structure built inside the moon's rock and she paused a last time looking up into the stars. She closed her eyes.

I stopped, wondering what she was doing. Yurn looked annoyed. The guards never took their weapons off her. She didn't move, just stood there with eyes closed. She knew she was dead, just a matter of time, so was she making peace with it?

I realized what she planned and reacted too late.

Valeri lunged to the side, pushing aside the nearest Dyer. She grabbed at his weapon as the man fell, pulling it free. Crouching down she fired off one shot, hitting another Dyer, before the rest unloaded on her.

Multiple bolts struck her. Chest, shoulder, leg. Smoke rose from the wounds, the weapon falling from lifeless hands as she fell backwards and lay unmoving on the ground.

Dammit.

"Hopefully the Kern has some answers," Yurn said motioning to the guards.

Two bent down and picked up her body, started to drag it away. The other went to help the one that she had shot, now starting to stand up, smoke rising from his shoulder. They all disappeared into the Yortusk base just leaving me and Yurn outside.

I looked down at the small scorch marks where Valeri's body had been. Plasma bolts at this range would burn through a body. Painfully. I had to give her some respect, she had chosen how she was to die. The Yortusk would have gotten what they wanted from her but this way she didn't break and give up any secrets and went out fighting.

"Here," I said and took the transmitter from my pocket, handing it to Yurn. "This was what they were going to activate."

He studied it and put it in his pocket.

"What are you going to do now?" he asked.

It wouldn't take long for Romer to find out his little enterprise had failed and once I popped back up in any system, he'd probably come looking for answers. Just one more thing to add to the list.

I looked away from the scorch marks and up at my ship. Not the prettiest but it was home.

"Got any cargo you need delivered?" I asked Yurn.

KINN'S PIRATES

Originally Published:
Available for free from the
New England Speculative Writers
mailing list

"Pirates," I cursed looking out the *Nomad Wind's* view window. Alarms blared throughout the ship's small bridge even though I was the only person on board to hear them. "Out here?"

The sensor screen showed a large ship, larger than the *Wind* anyways, approaching from the right, which was planetside, coming around the dark side of that moon where it had been blocked from my scans. Standing up at the pilot's station and leaning, I could just see the bulk of the approaching ship in the corner of the window. It looked like a massive barrel. Round, with two wings coming off the side with engines attached, the front was rounded like a dull cone. I didn't recognize the make and model but it definitely had seen better days. Battered was a good word to describe the ship.

Piracy wasn't that rare out here in the fringes but it wasn't that common either.

The way space travel worked, hopping from system to system, made it difficult to track specific ships. There were some traveled routes, but each ship had different speeds and differences in travel paths from one place to another were common. A ship didn't go directly from one system to another. No, it hopped from that first system into the next closest and so on until getting to the destination. Jumping into wildspace, that somewhat unknown space between systems, and back out again.

Which meant that most pirates had to sit and wait for prey to come to them. Long waits in the depths of space, just hopping a trader would wander by and not the other side of the system.

I'd never heard of pirates operating out in this area. They normally worked closer to the Inner Worlds, where there was more trade and travel. Out here in Deep Space, on the fringes of the known galaxy, there wasn't enough travel to make sitting and waiting profitable.

Lucky me to run into the one ship of pirates out here.

I looked over the scanners, studying the approaching ship. I could see multiple gun ports on the hull. It was slow but heavily armed. I could try to out run it, there's no way I could outshoot it and just a couple shots would destroy the *Wind's* shielding. The *Nomad's Wind*, a Castellan Light Cruiser Model F-497, was a hauler not a fighter. I had limited weaponry.

This was not good.

It was odd that they were bothering with the *Wind*. A small freighter like this didn't have enough cargo to really warrant an attack by a ship that size. So were they after me directly? I didn't believe in coincidence so I had to assume they were.

Now what part of my cargo were they after?

I watched through the scanners as the barrel ship rotated around my smaller one. It was about one and a half times the size of the *Wind*, but the shape made the difference seem greater. It created the impression of dwarfing the *Wind*, looming over it.

Or maybe that was just my imagination as I could almost feel the presence of the pirate ship.

I shut off critical systems, leaving life support and just enough power to keep the *Wind* hovering in place, thrusters adjusting to keep it relatively motionless. I sure as hell didn't want them firing on me but I also wasn't going to make it easy on them. I keyed in a distress signal but knew it was useless. The planet of Rewe, my destination, was still an hour away and it would take at least that long for help to arrive. This would be over in minutes.

Stepping out of the bridge and into the bunk corridor, the door slid shut behind me and I code locked it to keep anyone that wasn't me off the bridge and away from the controls. It wouldn't keep a good codebreaker out for long but it would be a block in their way. The corridor stretched out, the door to engineering at the far end and three doors on each side leading to the ship's bunks. The *Wind*, all Castellan Light Cruisers of this make, could carry a crew of six and be operated by as many as two or three. I had rigged up the systems so my ship could be crewed by one. Just me.

I had no need for additional crew.

Didn't want any. I'd spent enough time in the Earth Expeditionary Forces to get my full of working with others. I'd been out four years or so now and been on my own that whole time. Just the way I liked it. No one to bark orders, no commands to follow. Just me doing what I wanted when I wanted. I could take any cargo I wanted for anywhere at anytime. I wandered, one system to another. The *Wind* was my home.

Which is how I found myself here.

I'd taken a quick job in the Touy system. Deliver two systems over, from Touy to Rewe and the planet of the same name. Simple enough. One hop, the system in between, and only four hours in wildspace between each hop. Good pay day for not much work.

The perfect job.

Or it would have been except for the pirates.

To my left was a small corridor that ended in a spiral staircase. I ran down that, my boots clanging on the metal. This emptied out into the galley. A pantry was along one wall, shelves along the other with a table and chairs in the middle. A door on the far side wall led to the next room and on the near wall was another door. I paused at this one, thinking.

The thought didn't last long. No way was I taking the escape pod and leaving my ship behind.

From the galley and into the lounge, which sounded better than it was. A couch, a couple chairs and a vidscreen mounted to the wall. Through the lounge and into the cargo hold. Polyplas crates lined the walls, not that many and not filling up the space, only half a dozen or so. The *Wind's* hold was never as full as it could be. The latest cargo, the one that I thought got me into this mess, was on the left side.

Four small and gray polyplas containers maglocked to the floor.

The ship shook as the pirate's engaged their transfer tube. I crouched behind a crate and drew my trusty Sig Sauer T1700, an earth made plasma blaster. I'd been using this model since my old soldiering days. I switched it to lethal. There was more shaking as the *Wind* rocked under the weight of the other ship's intersecting gravity field.

Transfer tubes were segmented pieces of polycarbonite or some other material that would extend out from a ship's airlock and magconnect to another ship. Inside the tube, the pirate's airlock would open and they would make their way to my ship. There would be gravity inside the tube. They had to link up with the *Wind* and bring both ships into the same rotation so the two gravity fields would interact. Once that was done, they could walk through the tube easily.

The Tubes had controls that would interface with the connected ship so that air pressure and breathable air could be synced up between the two vessels. Both doors on either side could even by interlocked so only one could open at a time and the air between be cycled out.

Not all ships came equipped with tubes, but the majority of them had the necessary connectors on their hulls. Even the *Wind*. Though mine was codelocked.

I heard thumps against the metal hull. Small and localized. The pirates coder accessing the *Wind's* tube connector controls. It may have been coded, but it wasn't that deep of one. Wouldn't take long for their coder to get access.

It took less than a minute.

The *Wind's* hold has a ramp that folds down and in that ramp is a smaller sliding door. I watched as that door slid open and two figures darted through.

First was a Guykik. Large, reptilian and scaly. It looked like a bulky giant humanoid lizard, shades of green with a brown chest visible around the clothes it wore. The thing was twice as wide as me and I'm not small. I stand 6'-0", 200 pounds, broad shouldered and muscled after years in the military. The Guykik made me look puny. It had three clawed fingers on hands that were big enough to squeeze my head. A long ridged tail swung in the air, the ridges continuing up it's back. The face was wide, the snout was short and filled with sharp teeth. The eyes were bright yellow with black slits that scanned the hold. It held a bulky weapon in one hand.

The second was a Yurig. About my height, but green skinned with large round and yellow eyes. No hair, the head was oblong with a lot of forehead, slits for a nose and a small mouth. The fingers were long and held a blaster pistol.

I didn't want for them to get far before firing two shots from my weapon. The first hit the Yurig, dropping him to the ground, smoke rising from his chest. The second hit the Guykik in the middle of it's barrel chest and did nothing, the energy fizzled around the alien's body and faded. The thing made a noise that was probably a laugh.

I'd heard that a Guykik's leathery hide was resistant to plasma blasts, now I had proof of it. I could have done without ever learning that first hand. I didn't waste time with surprise, instead I fired two more shots at its head. One hit the cheek and the other an eye. The Guykik dropped, falling on top of the Yurig.

Bolts came out of the opened door and I had to duck. This allowed more of the pirates to enter the hold. Four of them. Two humans and two Yurigs. All four kept firing, all aiming at the crate I hid behind. Polyplas was strong stuff, but nothing could hold up to this barrage for long. Already pieces of the crate were melting and breaking off. It wouldn't be cover for much longer and once it was gone, I was done.

But really, I was done no matter what.

They weren't going to kill me unless I gave them more cause to. Pirates didn't waste anything. They'd take the ship and sell it or use it. They'd take the cargo and sell it or use it. And they'd take me and sell me.

Slavery was illegal in most systems but there were a few that took slaves and asteroid miners were always looking for new meat for the mines. Those weren't technically slaves but the mine owners would buy your ransom from the pirates and you'd have to work off the debt, in the mines or the areas that supported them, at very low wages. Which meant you never worked it off.

It was time to get control of the situation.

"Enough," I yelled out and threw my blaster into the hold away from me.

The firing stopped and I stepped out from behind the crate, hands behind my head. The humans moved behind me, the Yurigs stayed in front. I was in the middle of four weapons.

Laughter came from the transfer tube, a weird kind of squawking laugh. Out stepped a creature almost the size of the Guykik, but instead of muscle and bulk it was fat. It was covered in tan feathers, some lighter and some darker. It's face was angular, a large beak with two large eyes. Behind the eyes were two horns of bone, short and close to the skull. Growing from between the eyes was another horn, this one a lighter color and coming from a ridge. Where the other two lay flat, this one was raised a bit. It held no weapon in it's two fingers and thumb. Dressed in blues and oranges, a weird mix. The whole creature was odd but the little thing perched on its shoulder was odder. It looked like an earth monkey, only about nine inches tall with dull brown fur. Long arms and legs with a tail that was as long as it's body. The face was very humanoid, almost like a person. It held onto one of the bones for support.

The being was a Curon. I'd never encountered one before, it was rare to see one off their homeplanet of Cur. The planet was home to a Tiat colony, the largest empire in the galaxy and even they had not completely conquered the place. Beside the Curon, it was home to another bird-like species, the Curdo. Neither species belonged to the races that had their own startravel, this meant they had no development of their own ships. Each had to rely on others to get them offplanet. Both were said to be scary fighters so I knew not to let this Curon's bulk fool me.

It glanced down at the two dead pirates and laughed again. Just such a weird sound. The creature on it's shoulder copied it, making its own weird laughter.

"Where is the rest of the crew," it asked in heavily accent Galactic, words punctuated with squawks and chirps. It walked towards me and stopped between the two Yurigs. As tall as the Guykik, the Curon had to outweigh me by a hundred pounds.

"There isn't any, just me."

The Curon tilted it's head, studying me. The thing on it's shoulder hopped up and down.

"Lies," the weird monkey thing said.

"Squeeg thinks you're lying," the Curon added.

I shrugged.

"Just me."

Looking past the Curon, I saw another figure step out of the tube. Small, only about four feet tall, the newcomer was a Xertin. Basically a small human but purple with black hair and darker purple eyes. This Xertin, she held a tablet in hand and seemed a little skittish. Another human and Yurig followed.

"Captain Kinn," the Xertin said in a high pitched voice. "I can't override the ship's systems. I need to be on the bridge."

The Curon, Kinn, nodded.

"You two," Kinn said pointing at the two humans behind me. "Take him to the brig. You'll make a good miner," he said poking at me with one of his thick gloved fingers. "The rest of you search the ship. Let's see where our booty is." His large eyes started looking around the cargo hold, focusing on the crates picked up on Touy.

"Booty," the monkey thing yelled.

One of the humans pushed me and I stumbled. Kinn laughed and followed the rest of the pirates into my ship. The Xertin trailed behind, eyes looking everywhere, clutching the tablet tight. She must be the pirate's coder.

The way Kinn had said 'our booty', confirmed what I had guessed. He knew what I was carrying. Someone in the Touy system must have given him the heads up.

A short hop from Touy to Rewe, that wouldn't take a lot of guesswork on when the hop would have come into the system. Star hopping is about going from point to point, so in each system there needs to be a somewhat fixed point for navcomputers to set coordinates to. This was usually the last planetary object in that system. A planet, a moon, a large asteroid belt. Something that maintained it's relative location as the entire system rotated around the sun. Depending on where the fixed point was in the rotation, the hop time would change.

All Kinn had to do was set up somewhere between the hop point and the planet and wait. This short of hop, the wait wouldn't have been long. Even accounting for transmission lag from system to system, he would have had plenty of time to wait for me to arrive.

Wonder why he wanted my cargo so bad. I had no idea what was in it. I'd learned long ago to not ask. It was none of my business. I was hired to pick up and drop off, not question.

At the prodding of the pirate, I picked up my pace and stepped into the transfer tube. Made of shining metal segments, black seal between the pieces, the tube was just that. A segmented metal grated walkway was held up from the bottom of the tube, a flat place to walk. Ahead I could see the entrance to the pirate's ship.

"What's the name of the ship," I asked and motioned towards the approaching hull.

The two humans, one in front and one in back, glanced at each other. They were surprised I was as calm as I was. I should have been panicking. I was their prisoner, losing my ship and would soon be an unwilling miner or worse. This is not how I should have been reacting.

I never did what I should. Even when I was a soldier in the Earth Expeditionary Forces Special Operations where you had to follow orders. I never really did and somehow I had gotten the rank of Captain. I could never figure out how that happened.

"The *Uinh Geriyu*," the one behind me said. "In Terran it means.."

"Iron Raptor," I finished for him, recognizing the language. Tiat.

*****

The galaxy is huge and there's only like a tenth of it explored and in that tenth there are hundreds of solar systems and each system has one or two inhabited planets and most of those systems have discovered some form of space travel. And all those traveling races wanted to explore the galaxy.

We know what explore really means though. It means to take. So there's a whole galaxy full of people that want to take the other planets. Some were successful and some not. Us earthlings, or Terrans as we are called by the other races, were one of the newest starfaring races. Forty years. That's it. And we're only here thanks to another race, the Thesa.

Humans being humans, when we reached for the stars, we decided we wanted to take a couple of them. So we did. The rest of the galaxy aren't big fans of us. That's probably because along with our Thesan allies, we started the Third Galactic War against the Tiat.

That lasted about ten years. I came in on the tail end when I joined the service and well the war officially ended, the fighting did not. I kept busy in the ten years I was in EEF

Special Operations. I'd only gotten out a couple years ago. Had enough of the crap. The orders, the missions. It was time I was on my own.

We all make choices in our lives that lead us to certain points in our journeys. It's not always the big decisions that decide our course. Sometimes it's the little choices we make. One of those little choices had led me here.

*****

The door to Kinn's ship slid open and the lead pirate stepped through. I followed and stepped into a hallway. The hall ran left and right, probably around the perimeter of the ship with the functions inside and not along the hull. Left went to the bridge, right to engineering. Directly ahead was a large sliding door, probably going to the hold. This style ship had an elevator that lowered out of the bottom to load and unload cargo. I glanced behind me and saw the outline of a larger sliding door. At the edge of that door's size, in the corridor in both directions, I could see blast doors that could close when needed to form an airlock.

A ship of this side needed a crew of about twelve and there would be another twelve or so pirates on board.

So say a minimum of twelve and a maximum of twenty-four.

I killed two, there was six on board the *Wind* including the captain, these two with me. So that left a possible two to fourteen pirates onboard the ship.

Hopefully no more Guykik. Those things are a pain to kill.

The pirate nudged me to the right and I went down the corridor. It wasn't wide enough for two to walk next to each other but it wasn't cramped. The Guykik, and even Kinn himself, could have brushed the sides. Too tight to do anything.

Large access was through the doors we had just entered or through the bottom so the engine room would connect to the hold. This corridor, and one on the other side of the ship and on the next level, would give access around the perimeter, ending at the engine room and probably up front at the bridge. That's where most of the activity would be.

Fine with me, I didn't need those areas for what I had planned anyways.

We stopped in front of a door on the left side of the corridor. The pirate in front hit a button on the keypad and the door slid open to reveal a dimly lit hall with doors lining both sides. The brig. The room and spacing of the doors indicated small cells, five by five and probably that deep. Nice and cramped. Three to a side. A quick look at the keypads outside each showed that none were in use, none of the pads showed locked.

I paused just inside the door, in range of the sensors so it wouldn't close. The lead pirate continued, not paying attention, towards one of the doors. The one behind me stopped before bumping into me and nudged me with his weapon.

"Move," he said.

I didn't.

Now the one in front started paying attention. He turned and walked the couple steps back towards us.

"Move," he said.

I still didn't move and the one behind nudged me again. I stumbled forward, exaggerating the move. I fell towards the ground, tucking into a roll and came back up directly in front of the surprised pirate. He tried to move back but couldn't. I planted a foot solidly, placed my second foot between his, grabbed his weapon, and twisted.

Surprised and off balance, tripping around my foot, the pirate fell into the motion of my pull. I threw him behind me, ducking down at the same time. I ripped the weapon out of his hand and felt the heat of the other pirate's blaster bolt over where I had been. The first pirate hit the wall and I turned and dropped, now facing towards the door.

I fired and got lucky, my quick and unaimed blaster bolt striking the pirate in the chest. He fell, flying back against the far wall of the corridor. The bolt had been green, a stun blast, and I switched the weapon to lethal.

Standing up I shot the pirate still on the floor and then the one in the corridor. With one hand, I pulled that pirate into the room and searched them both quickly. Not much of value, no keycards or anything else but one of them did have a small vibroknife that I stuck into my pocket. Luckily both rifles had straps, so I hung one off my shoulder and stepped out into the hallway.

Left to engineering, right to the bridge and access to my ship.

I went left.

*****

Moving as quickly as I could, but keeping quiet, weapon ready, I made my way down the corridor. I encountered no one and it was a short distance to the door that led to engineering. Security was pretty lax, the door wasn't locked. But then pirates weren't known for their discipline and they had no cause to think anything was wrong.

The door slid open and I was assaulted by the noise.

All engine rooms are loud. The turbines, generators and other assorted equipment puts off a lot of noise and a lot of heat. The *Nomad's Wind* room was quiet compared to this one. The *Wind* runs smooth, everything purring along. For the most part. But this engine room? There was stuttering to some of the generators, whines where there shouldn't have been any, leaks from overhead piping.

I was surprised the ship was even running.

A large room taken up by lots of equipment, there was barely an order to the chaos. Enough space to move around and I could see the larger doors that led to the hold, the way that new pieces of machinery and computers got brought into the space. On the *Wind*, the engine room had its own hatch that opened up in the rear of the ship. This one, the *Uinh Geriyu,* handled everything through the lift in the middle of the ship.

I walked through the room looking for a specific terminal. The layout was different, not a build I knew, but things were usually kept pretty generic to make it easy to perform maintenance. Ship's travelled all over the galaxy, you wanted to be able to get it worked on no matter where you were. There were plenty of truly unique ships in the galaxy, but for the most part things tried to be the same.

The terminal I wanted was on the other side and I had to make my way about the generators and drive motors. It consisted of two monitors, lots of dials and readouts and an input station. I started typing, bringing up the maintenance log and hoping it wasn't codelocked.

It wasn't but I also got distracted in the menus.

"Who are you," a voice asked and I turned to see a Yurig standing about ten feet behind me. He was dressed in maintenance coveralls, a magwrench in hand. He didn't look wary or cautious, just surprised. "What are you doing?"

"The ship is a little wobbly in the connection," I said, making something up. "The Captain wanted me to come check to make sure we didn't disconnect from that other ship."

The Yurig stepped closer, tilting his oblong head in confusion.

"The coupler was checked last week when we made port," he said and stopped. Now I saw surprise on his face, more confusion. "Who are you."

I shot him. The blast took him by surprise, sending the Yurig falling against the motor. The wrench clanged against metal as it hit the motor and then the floor. A small trail of smoke drifted up from the wound.

Did I feel bad killing the Yurig? Nope. Not at all. He was a pirate, he chose this life and the consequences that came from that. These were people that were willingly going to sell me into slave labor on some asteroid somewhere. How many other people had they sold into slavery, hard labor or other even worse things? How many lives had they ruined?

With the rifle I rapidly scanned the engine room but didn't see anyone. There were a lot of places to hide though. Had to make this quick.

I rapidly scrolled through the menu options and found what I wanted. I turned off all the overrides and safeties and cranked up the generators. I could hear the whine beginning. Satisfied I ran to the large doors looking for the keypad.

No time to be fancy, I just shot it. Sparks and pieces of the pad flew through the air, the pad completely useless. They wouldn't be getting through that any time soon but now I had to move.

Back out in the hallway I shot the outer keypad as the door slid shut. I could hear running feet now, a variety of sounds against the metal deck. I ran and made it back to the brig door, ducking inside and closing it before the noises ran past.

Leaning against the wall I popped the power pack from the second rifle and dropped the rifle to the ground. It landed where I wanted it to, on the body of one of the pirates. Helped muffle the sound of the metal weapon hitting metal deck. Taking the small vibroknife that I'd taken from the dead guy at my feet, I pried open the power pack. A little rewiring and it was good to go.

Opening the door, I looked both ways and the hallway was clear. Whoever had run by, had sounded like two or three different sets of beings, must be trying to open the door to the engine room. Stepping out, I turned left, back towards the engine room.

When walking that way I had noticed indentations in the wall. Indications of a blast door. Or so I thought. Only one way to find out.

I connected the last two wires together and could feel the power pack heating up in my hand. I tossed it beyond the indentation in the wall and turned, running the opposite direction.

It didn't take long. The pack overheated and exploded. It was loud, the blast confined by the close walls of the hall. I could feel the shock wave, heat and force, against my back and then it stopped. The echo of a blast door slamming into place echoed down the hall.

It wouldn't have been a big explosion, but being in the cramped space would help. I didn't need it to be. Just needed to shut the blast doors and lock some people in the other side. Killing or hurting them was a bonus.

*****

I slowed as I neared where I had entered. The wider door was now open, on both sides, indicating that the pirates had been loading cargo from my ship to theirs. I could hear people talking excitedly, moving from the tube to ship's hold. They were anxious, curious and worried. Wondering what the noises were. They had heard the sound of an explosion.

An alarm started to blare throughout the ship.

There was shouting now, sounding like Captain Kinn, and the noise of beings disappearing deeper into the hold. Which made sense. The sound of an explosion had come from the corridor, so the safer entry would be through the hold.

Some of the talking became screams and grunts, beings and objects slamming into the walls as the large ship tilted. It canted to the side, artificial gravity keeping people aligned with the floors. Loud noises; bangs, whistles and the grinding of metal; came from the engine room. The whines continued through the hull, the metal plates straining.

I had been expecting it to happen and I still slipped and slammed into the corridor's side. Because I knew what was happening I was able to recover quickly, bracing myself with one foot on the floor and one on the wall.

New noises came from the transfer tube, metal straining. The *Wind*, because of its own thrusters and programming would stay where it was. The pirate's ship, and attached tube, was starting to rotate at a different pace. Soon enough the tube would either pull the *Wind* with it or break apart.

I didn't want either.

It was time to get off this ship.

It was an awkward walk, one foot on the floor and one on the wall, as I made my way to the tube. I couldn't see anyone, all the noise indicating they were inside the hold. I almost fell as the ship righted itself, the pilot adjusting for the tilting. Normally a ship's antigrav generator compensates for a ship spinning through space and approaching a planet upside down or on it's side, keeping the occupants in what is considered upright and perpendicular to the floor. But it has a hard time doing that when someone sets it to overload so the generator wouldn't compensate for the movements of the ship. Setting the thrusters to fire randomly wouldn't help either.

Ships naturally rotate well in the vacuum of space. The *Uinh Geriyu* was doing just that. The strain I heard from the transfer tube was the larger *Geriyu* spinning at a different rotation with the *Wind*. It's all pretty complicated and I'm not an Aeronautical Engineer, I just knew the basics, and what I knew was that the pilot wouldn't be able to compensate for long and the tube would break or the larger ship would pull the *Wind* and destroy it's thrusters.

I had to be on the *Wind* before that happened.

Stopping at the open doors I looked into the hold. I could see Kinn, that weird monkey thing hanging off his shoulder, yelling and screaming. Others moved around the door, some standing and watching. Humans, Yurigs and another Guykik. Kinn didn't branch out much for his crew. The hold was a mess, crates where everywhere. Most were locked in place but others had not been. A couple had broken against the far wall and some of the crew were nursing obvious injuries. They all had their attention on trying to get into engineering and seemed to have forgotten the possibility of their prisoner having escaped.

Really lax. That should have been the first thing they checked.

I ran into the tube, wanting to get across before the pilot lost control.

The door to the *Wind* was open and I couldn't see anyone in my ship's hold but I kept the gun ready.

I leaned against the cold blue metal of my ship, feeling the familiar vibrations. Turning around the opening I looked in to see an empty hold. The pirates had taken the three crates I had picked up in Touy as well as the others that had been in the hold. Bastards. But that was okay, there hadn't been anything of real value in them. At least they had been nice enough to take the dead bodies.

There had to be some pirates still on board. They were going to take my beautiful, to me at least, ship to salvage. But they weren't in the hold. So just enough to pilot the ship? I didn't like the idea of having to take back control of my own ship.

That would be relatively easy though. The hardest part was coming.

The tube locked onto the *Wind* from outside the ship. The controls on this side. With the tube disengaging, the *Wind's* rear door would shut to keep the hold's atmosphere intact. There wouldn't be much time for me to get onboard.

That left one option and it was going to damage my ship. Someone was going to pay for that.

Stepping into the familiar hold of the *Wind* felt like coming home. The familiar creaks and vibrations.

Quickly I moved to a storage lock along the wall and took out a breathing mask and magline. I attached the magline to a connector plate to the left of the door, next to a grab bar mounted to the hull, and the other end to a plate on my belt. Turning my body to look both ways, towards the access to the *Wind*'s hold and down the tube, I pulled the power pack off the pirate's weapon I had. Some quick fiddling and connecting of wires and I could feel it heating up in my palm.

A quick toss and it landed on the tube's walkway.

I moved out of the way and held onto the grab bar, pulling the breathing mask on.

I hated this.

*****

The explosion wasn't that loud or that big, not confined like it had been in the pirate's ship. I could feel heat and wind as the blast wave extended into the *Wind*'s hold. Immediately I heard the alarms from the ship as a grinding noise came from outside the door. The tube was ripped off, straining and groaning.

It started small but as more of the tube fell away, the atmosphere was ripped out of the *Wind*. The vacuum of space pulled everything from the hold. The pirates had done me a favor emptying it. The noise was the rush of wind, which was odd that there was noise at all. Space had no sound but all that force rushing past the closing doors made the oddest whooshing noise.

I could feel myself being pulled towards the closing doors, tightening my grip on the bar.

The galley door opened, a pirate stepping out in surprise. It closed behind him, a couple small plates and forks sucking into the vacuum along with the pirate who didn't have time to catch himself. He hurtled through the hold, screaming and thrashing, watching the void of space approaching.

The *Wind*'s door closed with a slam, the rush of escaping atmosphere stopping. The pirate dropped to the ground hard, his momentum carrying him further. He slid across the floor and slammed into the hull. Before he could recover, a swift kick from me and he was knocked out.

I grabbed his weapon. Didn't recognize the manufacturer. Some non-earth brand built for five fingered humanoids. Nowhere near as good as my Sig. I'm leery of those weapons designed for multiple species use, there's always something wrong with them. But for now, it would do.

It even had a stun setting.

Which I used on the guy laying on the deck next to me.

No one else came running to see what the problem was, so that meant there was a good chance no one else was aboard. With the door closed and the tube ruined, I couldn't see what was happening on board Kinn's ship but at least it wasn't connected to mine anymore.

I ran through the hold, my footsteps loud on the deck. I winced with each bang on the metal. But there was no time for quiet. I was on the clock. Through the door as quick as I could, ducking low, expecting blaster bolts but there was none.

The lounge was empty and a bit of a mess. The pirates had begun tossing it, emptying cabinets and looking for anything of value. Luckily they hadn't had much time. There would have been plenty when they took the *Wind* to salvage but my sabotage had ruined those plans.

I could see into the galley, the door open. It was in a little better shape, they had just barely started going through the cabinets there. It was also empty. I moved quickly through the room checking the escape pod to be safe. Still there, no one hiding.

Quietly I went up the spiral stairs, pausing just as my head cleared the floor. I couldn't see anyone down the short hallway and the door to the bridge was open. Someone there was whistling and tapping away on my keyboard. Probably screwing everything up too. I had the *Wind* perfectly where I wanted the controls set and now someone was messing with it. Would take me forever to get it right again.

Slowly, keeping an eye on the hall, I stepped up onto the level and made my way down to the intersection. I looked down the bunk corridor, all the doors still closed and showing red lights which mean the locks were still in place. Same with the door at the far end into engineering. Good. The pirates hadn't gotten there yet. Probably saving it for the trip to where ever the salvage yard was.

That left just the bridge.

With my back to the wall, I edged my wall to the open door. I peeked around the corner and could see stars and distant planets outside the view window. Three of the four stations were empty and someone was sitting in my chair.

Or more accurately they were standing in it.

The Xertin had to stand and lean to reach the controls. It didn't seem to bother her, probably use to it, as her small hands darted across my control board. She was calm as she corrected the tilt of the *Wind*. I couldn't tell what tune she was whistling. Really, it didn't matter.

I stepped into the bridge and pointed my borrowed blaster at her.

"Hi," I said.

She jumped, almost falling out of the chair. Sitting down hard, she looked over at me, staring at the end of the blaster. To her credit, as scared as she was, she didn't say anything.

I stepped into the bridge, behind the co-pilot's chair, the end of my blaster always pointing at her. I used it to motion her into the corridor. Hopping off my chair she headed out of the bridge.

"Left."

Turning she paused at the door into the small storage room off the corridor. This one was smart, she hadn't even bothered trying to go down stairs. Stepping closer, I held the gun awkwardly pointed at her. She was two feet shorter. I'd fought a Xertin hand to hand before and it was a pain in the ass. The size difference was to their advantage but this one was too scared to do anything.

Unlocking the door and opening it, I motioned her inside. She went in quietly and gave a small squeal and jump when the door closed and locked behind her.

Back at my pilot's station I was surprised that the Xertin really hadn't messed with much. I got the *Wind* stabilized and started moving away from the pirate's vessel. Scanners showed that it was no longer tilting but they picked up some damage. Nothing from the pirate's ship indicated that it was getting ready to pursue. In fact, it was moving away from the *Wind*.

Kinn was cutting his losses. He got what he came for, my cargo, and had lost too many men and had a damaged ship. I'm sure he wanted to destroy my ship and torture me, but there were more important things to consider. He had to know I had sent a distress signal so forces from Rewe would be showing up soon. Revenge would have to wait.

Worked for me.

I accelerated the *Wind* as fast as I could, not wanting to take chances. The sooner I was out of weapons range the better.

It didn't take long for the two ships to get far enough apart and I could breath a little easier. I was safe enough.

Twenty minutes later the two patrol ships from Rewe hailed me.

Better late than never.

One ship remained in the area, searching for Kinn's ship on the chance that it had been unable to hop out. The other escorted me to the planet.

Rewe was a very green world. Small with one little moon. Fourth from it's sun, the planet looked like a green sphere, lots of different shades with a bits of blue mixed in. I broke atmosphere and flew down over fields of endless grass. No mountains or large hills visible, the world was very flat. Lots and lots of grass.

The patrol ship veered off, returning to space, well I cruised over the surface. I could see metal shining in the distance and came upon the only piece of civilization on the planet. Rewe is a frontier world. It's at the edge of known space and is held by Terrans, or earthlings as we like to be called. From here there are numerous excursions into the unknown regions. It's not exactly lawless though, Territory Protectorate maintains a large presence with an Earth Expeditionary Forces base on the surface as well.

Clusters of metal buildings, most one story but some three, started to dot the grassy plains. Small, a few homes and businesses for colonists, they were spread out showing some growth across the planet. There was a lot of construction ongoing. The largest concentration of buildings, in size and completeness, was the space port. Three story square and blocky buildings in a u-shape around a cleared space. No grass grew there, just expanses of metal decking with painted stripes and lights.

The vast space was filled with ships, all earth designs. Port Control directed me to a bay near the center. It wasn't a busy port as it was really just a staging area. The large exploration ships couldn't land on the planet so only supply ships ever got down here.

Settling the *Wind* down where directed I shut the ship down.

As I headed for the staircase I paused at the storage room door.

"It's almost over," I said through the door, not sure if the Xertin could hear me.

She was a pirate but I felt kind of bad for her. She was out of her element, that much was obvious. I kind of doubted she enjoyed working for Kinn. Maybe she didn't have a choice? Soon enough she wouldn't be my problem or concern.

Calmly I walked through the ship, only drawing the blaster as I got into the hold and stopped to examine the stunned pirate. Still out for a couple hours. I gave him a kick to the head for good measure.

Stepping out of the ship I was surprised that the open plains weren't brighter. There were clouds in the sky, but not many. Clear and blue, if this had been earth the sun would have been very bright. It was pleasant here. Warm, but not hot, a nice little breeze. I could see people moving about the ships, mostly human techs but a couple of native Rewens.

There were forests on the planet, but spaced far apart and not large. Which was odd since the natives of the planet resembled trees. Tall and skinny, the smallest at seven foot, they had skin in various shades of brown and it was rough and cracked like tree bark. They had long arms that hung past their knees, long legs and narrow heads. Eyes and mouth deep set in the bark like features. The Rewens walked with a stiff gait. They were strong, even if they didn't look it.

The six figures approaching the *Wind* had my attention. Four were uniformed members of the Territorial Protectorate, the Prots but jokingly called the TeePees, the police forces on terran controlled worlds. Where the EEF was the military arm, with jurisdiction in space and warzones, the TeePees had jurisdiction over any problems planetside. Black boots, blue pants and shirts. These four wore riot gear. Armored vests, helmets and carrying blaster rifles.

They were accompanied by two plain clothes officers. One was male, older and my height. His hair and beard were gray with streaks of silver. Pants, a vest and tie; he wore his badge attached to his belt along with a holstered blaster. He walked a couple steps behind the other officer.

She was short, eyes even with my shoulder, with long black hair pulled back in a ponytail. A couple strands fell down on either side of her face. Very striking, she had dark eyes and tannish skin. Even though she was short, she carried herself in a way that warned people not to mess with her.

I knew from personal experience that she was tough.

Black pants and boots, holstered blaster, dark blue shirt and black jacket. Her badge hung from a chain around her neck.

Back on Earth, he would have been classified as Arabic and she would have been Latina, but up here in space they were just human. Every race on every planet had different ethnicities but out in the wilds we all ended up belonging to just the one race.

It was an old earth concept. Even though I was in my early thirties, I had been born on earth itself. The first time I'd seen space was when deployed on my first tour with the 2Es. There were a lot of humans that had never stepped foot on Earth itself.

"Lieutenant Higareda," I said, smiling at the woman.

She smiled back but it was one that warned me not to give her any crap. Behind her, the older man just shook his head. Lieutenant Waleed Abboud knew how this was going to go.

"Captain Lancer," Lieutenant Kristin Higareda answered, stopping in front of me. "Arek," she added less formally. She looked past me at the ship and the large burn and scratch marks on the hull. "Any problems?"

"Not really," I said with a shrug. "It went how we figured it would. Did you find your snitch?"

"We did," Higareda said with a genuine smile. I'd known her for a couple of years and the only time I saw her truly happy was when some criminal got busted.

About a week ago, I had been approached by Higareda. It seemed that a pirate had been making life hard for the colonists on Rewe. Most of their shipments got hit coming into the system. It was discovered through her investigation that it was the ones coming out of Touy. So they organized a sting but decided to go out of the Protectorate for help. She had guessed, rightly, that there was a mole leaking shipping schedules.

The operation wasn't well received by the higher-ups. But Higareda only cared about results, not kissing ass or making anyone happy. One of the reasons I liked her.

"He's under surveillance," Abboud added. "He'll lead us to this pirate's home base."

"Kinn," I told him. "Captain Kinn. A Curon. Crew is mostly human with some Yurigs and Guykiks. A ship called the *Uinh Geriyu*."

"Excellent," Abboud said, making notes on his wristcomm.

"And," Higareda prompted. She knew me well.

"His ship will need repairs, a gravity generator and transfer tube," I said. Those were specialized systems and should be somewhat easily trackable where repairs would be made. "He's also down a couple crewmembers."

"I'm surprised you didn't gift wrap Kinn for us," She said.

I shrugged.

"There are a couple presents on board," I added pointing behind me.

Abboud signaled to the four uniformed Protectorate officers. They ran off past me towards the *Wind*.

"The *Wind* looks a little damaged," Higareda mentioned, pointing at the large scorch mark and scratches along the hull.

I looked over my shoulder at the damage. It wasn't that bad and wouldn't prevent operation of the ship. The *Wind* itself never looked in that great of shape, this just added to it's charm. But Rewe seemed a nice planet and I had nothing pressing going on.

There was no cargo to deliver right now. Kinn and his pirates had it all. Of course it was all fake cargo planted by Higareda and her people.

"Since the Protectorate will be paying for the repairs, I suppose I'll be here for a couple of days," I said turning to Higareda. She was smiling. Abboud was rolling his eyes. "So when are you off duty?"

THE EUROPAN SWITCH

Originally Published:
Never before published

"What is that," Hert said looking up from the hologame board between us. "Never seen a species like that."

I ignored him and the kind of insensitive comment. But that was Hert, I was used to such things from him. An Engyn, they were a very blunt species with no filter. They didn't try to offend, they just didn't think before speaking. To an Engyn, that was a waste of time. They resembled humanoids carved from stone. Blacks and grays, same height and size as humans, Engyn's bodies were faceted, like stones. Hard lines and angles, similar to a diamond but dull like stone.

Of course, when dealing with so many different beings and cultures, everyone learned to not take offense right away. Most just accepted the Engyn's bluntness as part of their culture, which it was.

I concentrated on the hologame. I was losing and it was pissing me off.

Savik was a Thesan game, a cross between checkers and chess but with some other rules thrown in. I was usually good at it and could beat Hert nine times out of ten, but today he was crushing me. I was down three games to one and was losing the fifth. That didn't make me happy.

Hert was an independent freight hauler like me, the competition really, but that hadn't stopped us from forming a friendship over the last couple years. I'd first met him during my soldiering days and it was Hert that helped set me up as a hauler when I left the Earth Expeditionary Forces. Didn't run into each other that often, so when we did it was time for a game or twenty and a drink or thirty.

Ten or fifteen years older than me, maybe even twenty. It was hard to tell an Engyn's age. He'd seen and done almost all of it. The good and the bad. Legal and illegal.

So to hear there was a species he hadn't seen, that was a surprise.

I was curious but dammit, I wanted to win this game.

There had to be a way to salvage this and win. If I could just win this one game I could get a streak going. Ending the day tied in win/loss would be good enough. No way did I want to leave with a losing record. Hert wouldn't let me forget it. Ever.

"*Grak*, whatever that thing is, he's fresh," Hert continued, looking past me at something over my shoulder.

Interesting, some unknown species that was new to port. Still not enough to take me from the game. When he was annoyed, Hert switched back and forth from Tradelan to his native language. He was also always annoyed to some degree.

"*Grakking* Pierd. I hate those *hireks*."

Pierd were notorious swindlers. Great businessmen, almost as good as the Kry, but they always looked to get the best part of any deal especially if it meant taking advantage of the other party. Newbies to port were a Pierd's favorite target.

I finally turned, there was no way I was winning this game, and immediately could see what had caught Hert's attention.

This area of Corric Station was busy. Just off the connecting corridor to the docking bays, it was lined with bars and shops. And beings. Lots of beings of all kinds. But it was easy to see the one that stood out and had caught Hert's attention. Directly across from the bar's open to the corridor seating were a couple of shop stalls, both run by Pierds. The shopkeeper was loudly berating a specific customer. Pointing, shouting. The poor customer didn't know what to do. It was drawing a large crowd.

I knew what species it was, one of the rarest in the wider galaxy.

Easily seven feet tall, it was twice as big as the Pierd but was cowering before the smaller being. It was covered in a dusky gray, of various shades, long fur. The body was shapeless, with no neck, just a head at the end of the body that bent forward and was blunt and rounded. Long arms and small legs ended in webbed digits, with a thick and small tail that dragged along the ground. Tiny black eyes on either side of the head, whiskers around a small nose and a wide mouth with sharp teeth.

It wore crisscrossing bandoliers and pouches, no other clothing except a biosuit. Tubes ran up it's arms, crisscrossing down it's front and back, along the legs and connected to a tank it wore on it's back. The suit was to keep the being cool.

Biosuits were somewhat unique, each created to fit the individual beings requirements. Most times, you had no idea what specifics a biosuit was for. Some carried breathable air for the species, others had gases that kept the species wet or dry or oily. Lots of different species, lots of different uses for biosuits.

I only knew what this one did because I recognized the being. It was amphibious species from an ice moon in the Sol system. My home system.

It was a Europan.

*****

The galaxy is huge. Billions of stars, each of those stars housing a system of planets, moons, asteroids and all sorts of things. Rarely the conditions in that solar system are perfect so that life evolves. Even with as many types of life and beings in the galaxy it's still rare because there are more empty and lifeless systems then those with natural life, that which evolved in the system. Colonists don't count. Out of the billions of star systems, maybe only a couple thousand or hundred thousand have natural life. That's rare. Even more rare are those systems that have multiple planets or moons capable of creating and sustaining life. Even more rare are those systems that have multiple species within. Not multiple species on one planet, that's everywhere that creates life. I mean multiple species on different planets within the same solar system.

My home system, Sol, is one of those.

Us humans, or Terrans as we are called in the greater galaxy as we come from the planet officially called Terra, are expansionist. We're never satisfied with just what we have so we try to get more. This led to us wanting to explore our own solar system, and eventually the galaxy. We first had to come up with a way to travel the great distances within the solar system. That happened and we established the colony on Mars.

Because of that we came to the attention of the Thesa who were looking for allies in their expansion battles with another race, the Tiat. The Thesa helped us develop the hopdrive, which allowed us to finally leave our system and explore other systems, to expand beyond Sol.

That turned us into a starfaring race, or hoppers.

Even though we got help, we would have done it eventually. And this way the Thesans insured that when the aggressive human, Terran, species expanded beyond their system they did it allied with the Thesan. It was a good call on their part.

There are two kinds of developed life on a planet. Starfaring, or hoppers, and planetlocked, or grounders if you're being polite. Hoppers are those that have developed star travel, the ability to leave their own system. They create and build their own ships, developing the level of technology necessary for that. Grounders do not. They may leave their planet, but only because others allow them to. They hitch rides on the ships of others. Which is where the not nice term for them, stowaways, comes from. Or just stows for short. To some, that's a major insult.

Europans are grounders. Europa is the largest moon around Jupiter and the only other planetoid in the Sol system that could create life and that life lived in the cold waters and in caves within the layers of thick ice that surrounded the moon. We had encountered them early on, after the Mars colony and before the Titan colony. Primitive by our standards, they very rarely leave their planet. As a species, they're not well adapted for living outside their homes on Europa.

Some could be found sometimes at the Sol Station, the large space station at the edge of the system, but up until now I had never seen one outside of the system itself.

*****

The Europan looked scared. Terrified. It's eyes darted everywhere, trying to avoid looking at the Pierd. A crowd had started to form, beings of all kinds stopping to watch the entertainment. Some were pointing at the Europan, wondering what it was. It knew it was the center of attention and was shrinking as much as a seven foot pile of fur could.

On one hand, it's somewhat amazing that after all that these beings had seen, as wide and varied as the small part of the known galaxy was, there were still things that surprised everyone. But I was starting to feel bad for the Europan. They were a gentle and non-violent species. The sights and sounds of a busy and crowded place like Corric Station were always overwhelming even to a jaded flyer like me. I couldn't imagine how worse it could be to someone like a Europan experiencing it for the first time.

The Pierd was more than half the Europans size, but it wasn't backing down. If anything, the timidness of the Europan as well as the gathering crowd was pushing the Pierd to yell louder and make a bigger scene. Only four feet tall, two feet wide, covered in a light brown fur and a head like a block, the Pierd was definitely playing to the audience. It was gesturing wildly, fingers pointing at the taller Europan. One finger poked into the Europans chest and it took a step back.

From here I couldn't make out what was being said.

I turned back to the game. Whatever was going on, none of my concern.

"I give up," I told Hert pointing at the board. "You win."

"Of course," he said, his gravelly voice chuckling. "So you know what the *grak* that thing is?" He hit a button on the side of the table and the game board flickered. All the pieces disappeared and came back but in their original locations.

"A Europan," I replied studying the board and planning my moves. Savik was a game of strategy and thinking multiple moves ahead while anticipating your opponents gambits. I'd lost the last round so I started this round. "From Sol."

"Ain't that your home system," Hert asked watching as I moved my first piece. He studied the board, hand on one piece before changing his mind and moving another.

Inwardly I smiled, that was precisely what I wanted him to do. He was playing into my hand. Or was I playing into his by what I was going to do next, reacting to his move in a predictable way? It was very easy to lose Savik by overthinking it. Thesans reacted on instinct and the game was based on that. It was meant to be played instinctively, making moves quickly but in a strategic manner.

"Yep," I replied. "Europa's a moon, one of our colonies."

I moved another piece and Hert quickly moved one of his. No thinking. Dammit.

He lifted his head up higher, looking past me. There was still a commotion going on at the shop.

"Poor thing," Hert said shaking his head. "I don't know what he did but no one deserves the beating the Pierd is giving him."

I fought the urge to look. I knew I'd get involved if I looked. I didn't want to get involved. I tried to concentrate on the game board.

Dammit.

I stood up, turned around and headed for the shop.

I can't stand bullies.

*****

"Is there a problem," I asked pushing my way through the gathering crowd.

They stepped aside, not that they wanted to. I made them. Not the biggest guy around, six foot and two hundred pounds, but I have a presence. Or so I've been told. Apparently I'm just naturally intimidating. It comes in handy. More often than I would like.

The crowd was a mix of everything. There were a couple of Dyer, a Thesan or two, another couple Pierd, a Kern, a group of Kry and even a couple more humans. They all watched me step into the clear circle that had formed around the Europan and the Pierd. It wasn't every day that you got to see something like this.

The stall was a general goods shop. A mix of different things; food; clothing and trinkets that appealed to a wide variety of beings. Three walls and an open front. A small space, shelves and displays close, I could immediately see what the problem was. On the floor near the front opening was something broken. Lots of little pieces, looked like some kind of metal, scattered across the floor of the shop.

All this over some broken piece of crap?

The Europan looked at me and it looked like it's eyes lit up. Probably happy to see a friendly face. Us humans have a good relationship with the Europans. Surprisingly, considering our history and how we treat the natives in our colonies. A friend of mine, a xenobiologist, said this was in part due to the Europans looking like giant otters. It created a kind of familiarity for us. Same as Thesans and looking like humanoid cats.

I'm not an xenobiologist. I don't know if I bought into that theory or not. I just knew the Europans were innocents. Not jaded by life in the galaxy.

The Pierd ignored me. Just continued to angrily berate the Europan in the Pierd's native language. It was a series of squeaks and chirps. They can't speak Tradelan, the common language and their language is hard for almost any other species to speak but somehow they are among the galaxy's best business people. Not sure how that one worked.

"I asked if there was a problem."

The Pierd finally turned to look at me, probably because I stepped directly in front of him. He paused for a second, looked me up and down and continued but in a somewhat gentler but still angry tone.

"Slow down," I told him.

It was pretty obvious what happened. The Europan accidently hit the shelf, the item fell down and broke. Pretty simple and should have been handled as such. Was this a language barrier issue?

The squeaks and chirps did slow down and the Pierd started controlling it's gesturing. He pointed at the Europan, who I could feel looming over my shoulder, and then at the broken whatever on the floor.

"He hit the thing and broke it?" I asked pointing at the Europan and then at the pieces. I was speaking Tradelan which the Pierd understood even if couldn't speak it.

The Pierd nodded and held up the palm of his hand. He pointed at it empathically.

He wanted to get paid.

Understandable.

I turned to the Europan, having to look up. It was awkward because the big guy was so close to me and the way his head bent down I really needed to take a step back but the Pierd was in the way. Why do I always involve myself in crap like this?

Most Europans understand english, which the Pierd most likely did not, so I switched to that. It's the main language of Earth, my first language, but I spent so much time speaking Tradelan that it felt odd to be speaking english.

"Was it an accident?"

The Europan nodded, it's fur shifting and rustling with the motion. It made a moaning sound, different pitches and undulations. I didn't speak Europan. I knew people back on earth and the Sol Station that understood it, but like the Pierd's language it wasn't speakable by other species.

"Can you pay for it?"

A pause, long and drawn out, and a shake of it's head. Dammit.

He hung his head even lower.

I studied the Europan. I was no expert on the race but I knew enough. This one was young. Had decided to go out and explore the wild galaxy. Now in way over his head. Not an uncommon story. Sadly. Not just Europans either. So many of the races, spacefaring and grounders, would go out to explore and wind up in the same spot. Or worse.

It was pure luck that any of us managed to survive, let alone thrive, out here.

I turned back to the Pierd, looking past and down at the broken piece of whatever. The material wasn't exactly metal. It looked like it, but it was shiny and had a glow that refracted the light hitting it. Some alien material that I didn't know. Didn't matter. It was probably expensive.

As an independent freighter I wasn't rolling in credits. Most times I had just enough to keep my ship, the *Nomad's Wind*, flying and buy the important things. Like ale.

"How much," I asked the Pierd with a sigh. I saw his eyes light up. "The real price," I said putting some threat into my voice.

The Pierd made a motion with it's blocky body, some kind of shrug, and went back into the shop. He didn't go far, keeping an eye on me and the Europan the whole time. Coming back out he handed me a tablet. I glanced at the screen and cursed.

Yep, it was expensive.

Taking out a credit chip I inserted it into the tablet. The Pierd hit a key and I was a whole lot poorer. Smiling, at least

I think it was a smile, the Pierd walked back into the shop as if nothing had ever happened. Seeing that there was no more excitement the crowd began to fade away. The Europan just stood there looking at me.

"Follow me," I told it and walked back towards the bar where Hert was watching and laughing.

He walked away from the table, meeting me halfway, still laughing. An Engyn's laugh is not a nice sound. It's like two rocks grinding against each other.

"Arek Lancer, the hard ass," Hert chuckled. "You're just a big softie."

"Shut up."

That just made Hert laugh harder.

Hert walked around the Europan, studying it. As he was same height as me, the Europan's bent head was still higher than Hert was.

"What are you going to do with him now?"

Good question.

"What's your story," I asked the Europan.

It was meant to be rhetorical, neither Hert or I could understand him, but he started talking anyways. The hoots, moans and undulations went on for awhile. His whole life story and I didn't understand a word of it. He spoke with his hands as well, moving them up and down, around. One hand reached into his fur across his body and scratched before rejoining the other in the odd movements that accompanied the hooting.

The Europan spoke for almost a minute before stopping.

"I have no idea what you're saying," I told him with a sigh, glad the story was finished.

"His name is Eretut," a voice said from off to the side.

I turned and saw two women walking towards us, about ten feet away. Human, pretty. Both had auburn hair, one was long and the other was cut short. They looked alike, sisters. The one with short hair was the older and taller. Probably about my age, low thirties. I pegged the other in her mid twenties. And the prettier of the two. Both wore form fitting pants, shirts and jackets. They looked good.

Both were armed, weapons strapped to their legs. Each had the same weapon, some kind of blaster in a low slung holster. I couldn't make out the make and model of their weapons.

I was also armed. My trusty Sig Sauer T1700 in my low slung holster strapped to my right leg. Hert was armed as well. And pretty much everyone else on the Station. The only one that wasn't armed was the Europan.

"Came in on a shuttle earlier," the one with short hair said. Not the one that spoke first. "Credits for the flight here and back with a little left over but sounds like he got cheated at a shop and lost all of the extra."

"He's on some kind of rite of passage," the one with long hair continued. "Not something I'd heard Europans were doing."

"Me either," I said glancing at Eretut. He was nodding that wide head as the women talked. Smiling, his mouth revealing some sharp looking teeth.

He spoke some more and I glanced at the women who were now right next to me. They were prettier than I had first thought. Striking green eyes on both of them. The older looked more jaded, a little harder. She was an inch or two shorter than I was and the younger was another inch or so shorter than that.

"Says thank you," the older one translated.

"You're welcome," I told Eretut with a nod of my head. He returned the nod. "Arek Lancer," I said turning to the two sisters.

"Jada Welker," the older replied.

"Tani Welker," the younger added.

"Hert," he interjected but wasn't smiling. He was studying the two women, not the same way I was. They were almost completely ignoring him. Which was a bit odd.

"From Titan?" I asked the sisters.

One of Earth's colonies, neighbor to Europa.

"Yes," Jada replied. She didn't seem as happy as Tani did.

"What did you say your name was," Hert asked.

Jada shot him an annoyed look but Tani answered.

"Welker," she replied and turned her attention to me. "We saw you intervene and thought we could help."

"I appreciate it." I gave her my best smile, which she returned.

"So big guy," I said turning to look up at Eretut. "When is the shuttle heading back to Sol Station?"

He moaned some and we both looked to the sisters.

"An hour or so," Tani replied. She paused as Eretut spoke some more. "Europans don't travel much outside the system but it's starting to become a thing for the young to leave Sol. A way of showing they are more adventurous than their elders. They normally only go a hop or two beyond. He says he's gotten further than anyone else from his tribe."

Eretut stood straighter, puffing himself up, proud.

"Your rite of passage cost me a lot of creds."

He instantly deflated and sagged. I felt bad for the kid. I could understand what he was trying to prove but this was still not a good place for him.

"Don't worry about it," I told him and he nodded, moaning something quietly.

"He says that he owes you a debt now," Tani translated taking a step closer to me. "Debts of honor are important to Europans," she added.

Eretut nodded. Very enthusiastically.

"He can pay that debt by getting on that shuttle and going home."

He deflated again. Did he really expect me to bring him along until he repaid this debt? Not that I needed it repaid but I know how some of these cultures could be about things like debts of honor. I had no desire to have anyone following me around. My ship was a Castellan F497 Light Freighter and was designed for a crew of six but as small as three. I'd rigged mine to be flown by a crew of one. Me. No one else.

"Look," I started taking a step back so I could see Eretut's eyes that were on either side of the flat head. "You're not ready to travel in space. Spend some time on Sol Station. Learn how to interact and communicate with other species. It takes awhile to get it." I pointed at Hert and chuckled. "Hell, some like him never get it."

"*Hirek*," Hert replied with that stone on stone grating chuckle.

Eretut started to speak but I held up a hand to stop him.

"Don't bother. If you really want to repay this debt, you'll head home. The galaxy is not a nice place."

He looked like he was going to say something else but stopped, sagging. Without another word, Eretut turned and walked away. His shoulders drooped, his head hung lower.

Dammit. I felt like a jerk.

But the kid needed it. He was out of his element in so many ways. My advice was good. Hang out on Sol Station for awhile. It was no Corric Station but there was a good mix of species there. And it was close to Europa, with some others of his kind on the station. A good place to get his feet wet before venturing into the wider galaxy.

Watching the kid walk off, even though I was right, I still felt like crap.

"Eretut," I called out. He stopped and turned. "Just remember, you got further than anyone else."

That seemed to perk him up. The shoulders didn't droop, head was lifted, and he walked away with some pride to his step.

We watched him go long enough to make sure he was going to the right place, down the connecting corridor to the docking bay. He received lots of stares but that was it. I was half afraid I'd need to go through the whole thing again before he got to the shuttle.

"Come on Arek," Hert said heading back to the bar. "We have a game to finish and more drinks that need drinking."

He was right. Maybe I'd manage to win a hand or two before having to leave.

"Ladies," I prompted. "Would you care to join us."

I liked Hert, but having two good looking woman around would make losing more bearable. I was starting to think that Tani might be interested in me as well.

"Sorry but we have things we need to do before we leave the Station," Jada answered.

Tani looked disappointed.

"It was nice meeting you Arek," she said, lagging a little behind as her sister walked towards the connecting corridor. "Maybe we'll see you around."

I nodded as they disappeared into the crowd. Turning I went back to the bar and Hert.

"The old Lancer charm failed I see," he said as I took my seat and looked down at the gameboard. He'd cleared it and started a new game.

As I studied the board to make my first move Hert looked towards where the sisters had walked away. He tapped at his chin, making a small thunking noise. He only did that when he was thinking. Which wasn't often for Hert.

"What did they say their names were?"

"Jada and Tani Welker," I answered as the server put a new plasbottle of ale down in front of me. It wasn't exactly ale, not like on Earth, but it was close enough. And it was good. That was the important part.

"Yeah, it sounded like something I'd heard before," he said. "But not sure."

I finally made my first move and leaned back, waiting for Hert to make his. But he wasn't paying attention to the game board. He had leaned back in his seat, fingers tapping on the table, eyes staring at the metal ceiling and lights above.

"Not the name," he said. "But who they are. Two Terran sisters."

"What are you talking about," I asked.

"A couple months ago, on Dynuit Station, I was talking to a Curdo who mentioned something about two Terran sisters and to avoid them."

He paused, leaning forward, eyes closed in thought.

"What was it he said?"

The tapping on the table increased as he thought back.

The eyes opened, gained focus as Hert looked up and stared at me. He'd remembered and it wasn't good.

"Slavers?"

*****

The galaxy is a huge place and with all the trillions of people alive, why would there be a need for slavery? There's no lack of beings and they all need work of some kind.

But it exists. Illegal in most systems but there are a couple where it's still allowed and some of the smaller and deeper mining asteroids have slaves masquerading as 'paid' employees.

Cheap labor is always desired. Any merchant that tells you otherwise is lying. But there are some that take it to far. Slaves are as cheap as they come. Just barely feed and house them. Because of that, there would always be a market.

Slavers are the worst. The only thing equal is ship thieves. Pretty much everyone hates slavers but everyone loathes ship thieves.

But everyone also has a good fear of slavers.

Space stations like this are their shopping centers. The naive, the weak. Those are their targets.

A being like Eretut would be irresistible.

*****

I was afraid I'd be too late.

Most space stations follow the same general layout. There's the central tower core that has the shops, restaurants and other services. As well as housing for the people that live on the station. Then there are the connector tunnels that lead to the docking ring or rings.

The sisters and Eretut had headed towards the nearest connector. No elevators needed, the tunnel wasn't that far from where we had been.

But it was far enough.

I ran as fast as I could, Hert not that far behind. The level wasn't that crowded, but there was enough that I had to push some and slalom around others. Which slowed me down. They didn't have that much of a headstart but it was enough.

The problem was that as soon as they got into the docking ring I could lose them. I had no idea where there ship was, in which direction I'd have to run. The ring was huge and it would take a long time to get all the way around it and there were a hell of a lot of dock doors. More doors than actual ships.

The galaxy was huge and there were a lot of shipbuilders out there. So lots of different designs and lots of different sizes. And space stations had to deal with them all. Most stations just put in extra dock doors and airlocks so they could take different size ships. Sometimes coming up to a station and it's docking ring, it was like a jigsaw puzzle with all these different ships maglocked to it. Made it fun to try to fit your own ship into that mix.

I hit the connecting tunnel and pushed my way into it. I kept scanning the crowds, looking for Eretut's tall form. The tunnel was large and round, the floor at the halfway point of the circumference. The lower half, that we couldn't get to, was used for transferring cargo and goods. The top half was for people. Multiple conveying belts lined the metal floor, half coming towards the station and half moving towards the docking ring. The curved walls were made of a shiny metal with large windows evenly spaced that looked out onto the blackness of space.

Luckily the tunnel wasn't that full. I could see almost the entire length. No large and furry Europan towering over everyone else.

I ran past people, jumping from conveying belt to conveying belt to avoid and move around the various beings. Lots of different races, lots of different sizes. I bumped more than a few. Which could be dangerous. Some species took great offense to being bumped into, even accidently. More than a few fights had started that way.

But I lucked out and ran onto the docking ring a couple quick minutes later. I could hear Hert further back, shouting for me or grumbling as people got in his way. He was trying hard not to run into any being. Engyn's were heavy and could easily hurt someone in a collusion.

Pausing, catching my breath, I looked both ways. I really wasn't out of breath. Nowhere near the shape I was a couple years ago when I was still a soldier, but I kept in shape. I needed to pause, to relax a bit in case I needed to sprint.

The ring was lined with doors spaced along both walls. Different sizes and shapes, fit into any space available. The ones across from me led to airlocks that connected to more doors on the outer ring. The ones behind me led to storage bays, each assigned to a docking position. Move the cargo into the storage bay and then it could be collected and moved by the recipient later. Some even had lifts to below to connect to the lower level of the connector tunnel. It was a pretty efficient system. Freight haulers like myself could drop off the cargo and never even see the buyers.

But it was really for the buyers, so they never had to associate with folks like me.

To my right I couldn't see anything. No one pushing through the crowds. No one moving quickly and nothing standing out like Eretut would.

I turned to my left and saw him. About fifty feet down the ring. Just standing there looking lost and confused. He towered above everyone else, standing against the outer wall to try to get out of the flow of beings. Oddly enough, he was almost directly next to the door that connected to my ship the *Nomad's Wind*. No sign of the two sisters.

Quickly I made my way to where he was standing. My eyes scanned everywhere and I tensed as I passed each door, expecting an ambush from one of the sisters. I didn't think they'd try anything here, too public, but better to be safe. That was probably what happened with Eretut. They tried to get him on their ship and something must have spooked them.

"Eretut," I said holding up my hand to catch his attention. At the sound of my voice he turned and I could see him standing up straighter, more confident. The confused look somewhat disappeared. He was glad to see a familiar face.

He took a couple steps towards me, gesturing with his arms and not paying attention to the beings he almost hit. I could hear the moaning and grunts as I got closer but still couldn't understand a word he said.

"Whoa big guy," I told him stopping in front of him. "I don't know what you're saying. Where are the sisters?"

His head tilted like he wasn't sure what the word was but then the eyes brightened as he figured it out. Eretut gestured behind him with more moans, grunts and a couple hoots. I got the general idea. They'd fled that way. So it meant time to get Eretut out of here.

"Follow me," I told him and headed a couple dock doors down. I glanced behind me but couldn't see Hert through the crowd. He must have gone the other way around. No big deal, he knew where the *Wind* was docked.

It had been a couple years since I'd been out of the 2Es, the Earth Expeditionary Forces; and while I wasn't in the same operational shape as I had been, my instincts were still pretty sharp. I didn't feel like anyone was watching us or approaching but I still glanced in both directions before entering the code into the large sliding door.

The door parted in the middle, sliding apart smoothly to reveal a large and square room. Across from us was a blue and gray metal ship's hull, blue above and gray below. I knew what to look for so I could see the larger outline of the ramp that could be lowered in the gray lower half of the ship and the smaller one that was the sliding door in that ramp. The walls of the room where they hit the ship were ringed in a black material, the gasketing that surrounded the maglocks connecting the *Wind* to the airlock we were in.

Eretut looked at all of it with wonder. He examined the segmented floor plating beneath our feet, the walls and jumped when the door slid shut behind us. Had he never seen an airlock before? Even with the passenger ships, everyone exited through an airlock that looked basically the same.

Something about his behavior was a little off. It was like he was playing the part of the bewildered species out of his element. Overplaying it really.

The thought hit me as I touched the final key on the pad mounted to the *Wind's* hull. The smaller hatch slid open to reveal the nearly empty cargo hold of my ship as some other stuff fell into place.

When I had just found Eretut, it was too calm. If the sisters had been run off there should have been some sign in the crowd. Some excitement, some indication. The incident with the Pierd had drawn a bunch of onlookers. Shouldn't there have been some in the docking ring?

The sisters were also pretty quick to show up once I had brought Eretut away from the Pierd.

I felt like an idiot.

I'd fallen for one of the oldest cons in the book.

I rolled to the side just as Eretut's heavy hand swung towards me. Instead of my head, he caught my shoulder but it was still enough force to slam me into the side of the *Wind*.

I turned to see him standing over me. He was roaring now, angry. No more innocence or bewilderment. He knew exactly what he was doing.

Which was trying to kill me.

He thought he had me pinned to the side of the ship, unable to move out of the way. Most people it would be true, but I doubted he knew the extent of my training.

Instead of trying to duck away from the swing, I kicked out. His arms were longer than mine so he was further away than I would have liked, but I still connected with his knee. Or what I hoped was his knee. Such small legs it was hard to tell.

He took a step back, that was it. It still kept me in range of the arms.

I knew the blow was coming and took it on the shoulder and let the momentum carry me to the ground. I crawled away from him, heading back towards the airlock door. I could feel the next blow coming and rolled away from it, laying on my back and coming up against the wall. Eretut was bent over, arm hovering above the metal decking and body twisted towards me, the flat head and eyes staring at me.

No way to grab my blaster in a small space where Eretut had the advantage. I had to change the situation before he managed to grab me. At that point, it would be all over.

There was a mad glint in the black eyes as Eretut slowly raised his hand. He extended the fingers and with an audible slicing sound two long claws slid out of sheaths on his wrists over his fingers. Long, sharp and with a serrated edge. Europans lived in caves and cliffs of ice, of course they would have claws designed for cutting into the ice.

Or flesh.

I shifted so I was somewhat sitting up, my legs under me and ready to push. Eretut took a step back, sliding the claws out on his other hand. My hand hovered, inches away from my holster. I shifted to the right, towards the docking ring airlock doors and the pad that was mounted to it on my side. Eretut moved a tiny bit that way.

Leaning like I was going to dive for the door I jerked that direction and Eretut took the bait. He lunged for where he thought I would be, claws out, but I quickly shifted and bent my body awkwardly the other way. I landed hard on the decking but was up and running for the open hatch to the *Wind*.

I needed space and the *Wind's* near empty hold had lots of it.

The big Europan was quick to recover. I scrambled through the door just as he twisted and lunged after me. I had a couple steps on him now though as he had to come into the hold fully. He was so tall that he had to crouch to get in. The way his body was made, one long shape with the head at the end that bent forward, his eyes were even lower when he stepped through.

For a second he wasn't looking directly at me.

Which was all I needed.

I'd pulled my blaster as I dove through the door. Landing on the deck of the *Wind*, I used the slick surface and my momentum to turn and keep sliding away from the door. On my back I aimed towards the door well I kept sliding. Not the best firing position but it would do.

Pulling the trigger I moved it diagonally up, strafing the door with multiple shots. I knew most would miss, hitting the metal and damaging my ship.

As I came to a stop I heard the soft sound of plasma blasts washing over metal followed by the grunt and moan of Eretut. Not as loud as I had hoped but at least one blast had hit.

Smoke rose up from scorch marks on the gray metal of the *Wind* as well as from the fur of Eretut. He stood in the doorway, both feet inside, arms held out with claws extended. I caught the scent of burnt fur and saw the wound on his upper left shoulder and another lower down on the right and his stomach. Neither wound, fur smoking and burned away and the wound blackened flesh, seemed to bother him as he took another step into the ship.

I hated aliens that were immune or resistant to blasters.

But now I had time to aim and I'm a pretty good shot.

My first shot caught him in the other shoulder, staggering him back. My second grazed his arm but did what I wanted it to. The cooling tubes of his biosuit started leaking. My third shot took him in the neck, where his head bent forward.

That one made him howl.

He took a step forward, glaring at me with hate, smoke rising from the blaster scorch marks across his body and stopped as he felt liquid dripping down his leg. Already a good amount was pooling on the floor of the *Wind*. From here I couldn't tell what it was. Some kind of coolant.

Eretut shook that arm, drops and spray flying everywhere. He was aggravated and turned back towards me, growling now.

I shot him between the eyes.

It took his body a bit to register that it was dead. He stood there, the eyes still dark, a new blaster mark in that small forehead region he had just above the noise. The body toppled forward, hitting the deck. Coolant continued to leak out of the biosuit tube.

Standing up I walked around the body, kicking it a couple times to make sure he was dead.

This is what being a good samaritan gets me, becoming the target for ship thieves. They probably thought they had found an easy mark, not a trained spec ops soldier. Ex-soldier but still, not what they were expecting.

Surprise and strength go a long way and even with my training I had come close to getting hit by Eretut.

I got lucky.

*****

I stepped around the growing puddle of coolant. Not sure what kind it was, no way I wanted to touch it. Some of that stuff could be pretty nasty. And volatile. The tube was only an inch diameter and there really wasn't that much of it, not for Eretut's size. Europa was a very cold world so whatever he had going through the biosuit tubes had to be pretty strong.

So what was the next step for the thiefs? Eretut plays the part of the lost lamb, the naive traveler out of their element, and then ambushes the mark. What were the sisters doing during this? How was he to contact them?

They had appeared pretty quick after I had first encountered Eretut. At the perfect moment. Right on cue. Had they been summoned? Would make sense. I bet if I did some digging I could find a lot of encounters where this had worked for them. They probably had the timing down.

How did he contact them? Nothing visible. No wristcomm, headset or anything.

He would have needed to activate some kind of transmitter so they knew when to show up or had some kind of listening device on him. Being careful not to touch any of the leaking coolant, I searched him pretty thoroughly. I ran my hands through his fur, feeling for anything that would be attached. Nothing on his back so I rolled him over.

As soon as I had him on his back, looking down at the body with his head flopped back, I remembered an odd movement he had made. It had been before the Welkers showed up. He'd been telling his story, his arms waving around, but had stopped to scratch himself. The only time he had done that.

Sure enough, in that area, I found the transmitter. A small box with a single button tied into his fur next to the skin.

Thankfully it wasn't a listening device, just a signal. The sisters didn't know I'd taken him out. They were probably somewhere nearby waiting for him to transmit the all-clear.

No reason to keep them waiting.

I hit the button.

*****

There could have been some kind of prearranged pattern or something that Eretut was supposed to send them. I didn't know and didn't care.

I only hit the button that one time.

Either it would be the all-clear signal or it wouldn't and they would know something was up.

Plan for the worse. That's what my old commander always said and what I tried to do.

I was planning for them to show up knowing it was a trap.

Starting a fight that you could avoid because you were embarrassed wasn't a smart play. I was angry at myself for falling for the obvious con. Even with Eretut dead, their operation could still continue. There were a lot of ways that two good looking women could get onto a ship. That really wasn't my concern. If someone else fell for it, that was on them. I just wanted to teach them a lesson for messing with me.

Really it was me taking my anger at myself out on them.

*****

I left the door between the airlock and the docking ring unlocked. A clear invitation.

When it opened I couldn't see but I could hear. The *Wind* was silent and the doors sliding apart in their tracks were quiet. It was the noise from outside that alerted me. Even half crowded docks like this one created a ton of noise. Conversations, hovercars, doors. Just so much to make a loud background noise.

That noise disappeared as the doors slid closed and I waited.

I could imagine what they were thinking. The unlocked doors, the empty airlock with visible blast marks, and the open hatch into the *Wind*. There was a chance it wasn't a trap, that Eretut had done his job and been wounded. They would play it safe and cautious. They would move through the airlock, approaching the open hatch slowly.

But once there they would see it.

Eretut's body.

It had fallen right at the hatch so I had pulled him further into the *Wind's* hold. I didn't want them to see it right away.

Now that they could see him, what would they do?

"You can come in," I yelled out from where I stood at the far end of the hold, out of their sight. "I won't shoot."

I still couldn't see them, they were smartly staying just outside of view. It limited their look into the hold but limited my view of them. Which was fine. I didn't need to see them clearly but I did need them to get fully into the hold.

Most likely they were talking with each other, maybe had even stepped further away. Run or confront? I figured the older sister, Jada, was preaching caution and the younger, Tani, thought they could still get their prize. It was two against one afterall. Which would be the most convincing.

It was Tani.

She stepped into the *Wind* first. Her weapon was drawn and she kept her profile tight to the hull as she scanned the open space. Not many crates, there never was and just the one door at the far end that led deeper into the ship. No sign of me. Tani moved to the side and Jada stepped in. She did the same, weapon out and scanned.

I waited until both were committed fully. They had taken a couple steps away from the hatch, moving away from the other and eyes still looking everywhere. Neither had really glanced at the dead body of their partner. Both had targeted in on the most likely location for me. The only place where crates were stacked two high.

"That's far enough, I said and stepped around those crates, my weapon drawn and pointed towards them.

They turned towards me, pointed their weapons at me but didn't shoot. Why would they? As far as they were concerned I was outnumbered and well I could shoot at one of them, there was no way I could stop the other from shooting me. It was a stand off of a sort and they felt like they had the upper hand.

Also they were curious.

Who was I? How had I taken out Eretut?

Risky? Sure. But they were ship thieves. Everything they did was risky.

"How's it going," I asked smiling at Tani. "We could have been having some fun right now instead of pointing weapons at each other."

She smiled back and shrugged.

"It would have been lots of fun," she replied with a smirk. "But my sister and I will still end up having a good time."

"We'll get a good amount of credits for your ship," Jada added. "Even if it's not in the best shape."

"Ouch. Insulting a man's ship," I said with a shake of my head. "That's not very nice."

Silence fell and I let it linger a bit. The sisters glanced at each other, waiting for one of them to give the go-ahead and make a move. I wasn't going to do anything but wait on them. I could be patient. Missions with the 2E special forces had taught me that.

Jada took a couple steps forward, Tani a little slower but following.

"Far enough."

"I don't think so," Jada said. "We're going to take your ship."

As they moved forward the sisters put more space between them, walking close to the sides of the hull. It was a smart move.

"You're not taking my ship," I told them pointing my blaster at Tani and looking at Jada. "Or any others."

Both of them paused. There was a lot of confidence in my statement. More than there should have been. When someone is trying to sound tough, make a threat, they need confidence in their tone to make it work and sometimes the person on the other end can see right through it. See that it's a bluff. But then there's the time when the person isn't sure. The speaker has such confidence, sounds so sure, that you have to start to wonder. That's what was happening to the sisters.

"I could kill you both," I told them, no doubt in my tone of voice. "Or you could end up killing me but I doubt that happens."

"How do you figure that," Tani asked with a chuckle.

"You ladies really need to vet your targets," I told her, watching as they got closer.

Most criminals in space don't have any specific or special training. It's something they just fell into. Could be there was no choice, forced by family, or a myriad of reasons. Doesn't matter. They became criminals and use amateur tactics and fighting styles. Usually just brute force. They succeed with a lot of shock and awe attacks. It's amateur to someone like me that has seen real shock and awe.

The Welker sisters were doing exactly what I wanted. My blaster was in my right hand, pointed at Tani. Both sisters were creeping along next to the ship's hull but Tani was not directly across from Jada, she was lagging behind a couple steps. Because I had the weapon pointed at her.

Predictable. She was doing what I wanted.

"Yeah, Eretut almost got me," I admitted but pointed down at his body with my left hand. "We all see how that still turned out."

"So," Jada barked. "What are you, some kind of super human?"

"No, just former Earth Expeditionary Forces Spec Ops."

That made them both stop. Which I wanted them to. Still doing what I predicted. Even though I could guess what their reactions would be, there was a lot that could and would go wrong. A plan is only good until the first blaster fire, my old commander used to say. So far the plan had gone perfectly.

Their next action, which I hadn't predicted, made it even better.

They glanced at each other.

It was only a split second but it was enough.

I followed with my original plan of attack. Their slip-up just made it easier on me.

My weapon was pointed at Tani, the natural target, but I moved it and shot at Jada. I pulled off two quick shots and dove to the ground, also in that direction.

Tani was quick and her plasma bolt slammed into the hull, only a couple feet away from where I had been. My shots, green blasts, came close to Jada. One on either side. It caused her to stop and pull in on herself, trying to make herself smaller. My dive put me beyond the plascrate and a clear shot at Jada.

Laying on the ground, I held my blaster steady against my other arm, aimed and pulled the trigger.

The green blast slammed into Jada's chest and sparks of energy wrapped around her body. She fell backwards, collapsing against the hull.

"Jada," Tani yelled and just started firing wildly.

Idiot.

Keeping low I moved from crate to crate until I got to a good firing lane. Standing up I took aim and pulled the trigger. Tani fell just like her sister.

And it was over.

Neither sister was dead. I'd hit them with stun blasts. I could have killed them easily, but why bother? I'd done my share of killing when I was a soldier and I was tired of it. I'd still do it when necessary, but that wasn't now.

If the sisters ever crossed my path in the future then it would be necessary.

*****

The airlock door slid open to reveal a near panicked Hert. His stony face, which rarely showed expression, was definitely worried.

"What the *youki*," he said as he stepped into the room. The door slid shut behind him and he looked around. There were the scorch marks on the floor but nothing else besides me and the large plascrate on the maglifter that I was towing.

I had been about to leave when he appeared.

"Are you okay?"

"Yeah," I answered. "Especially now that you're here to help with this thing.," I said and pointed at the crate.

"What," he asked, still surprised and not sure what was happening.

I lifted the top of the crate and he looked inside. Eretut's body was on the bottom with the two sisters piled on top, both still stunned and would be for a couple hours. They were also tied together with flexline. I wished he had shown up earlier. It had been a pain to get all three inside the crate, especially Eretut. The Europan was heavy.

Hert took a step back and shook his head.

"I knew I shouldn't have been worried about you," he said with a chuckle. "What happened?"

So I told him and explained what I was planning on doing.

*****

Finding an empty storage bay on the station's docking ring was pretty easy. Hacking the lock to get in, just a little more difficult. Lugging the large plascrate through the docking ring and opening the door without attracting attention? The easiest of all.

Pretty much everyone flying in space holds to the idea of minding their own business.

If I had followed it, I wouldn't have been dumping a crate with a dead Europan and two stunned Terrans into a storage bay. But here I was.

The sisters would be out for another couple hours and would have a hard time getting out of the crate. A very tight space with no room to move. They'd be stuck together for awhile. Sometime soon they'd be found. Bays didn't remain empty for long. Most likely the station's law enforcers would be informed when someone found them.

Once they were in the law's hands, it wouldn't be long before their history came out. They'd probably be arrested and sent off somewhere.

Not my concern.

I figured it would be best to be off station when all that happened so I never got to finish the game with Hert or have another drink. We said our goodbyes and I launched the *Wind* into space.

Before I hopped into wildspace I sent some feelers out to a couple contacts.

To fly from solar system A to solar system D you basically hope from A to B to C and end up in D. Well hopping you enter the space between solar systems, what we call wildspace. Well in wildspace you can't send or receive transmissions. So it would be awhile before my contacts were able to get back to me.

So it was a couple days and hops later that Lieutenant Kristin Higareda of Earth's Territorial Protectorate got back to me. Where the Expeditionary Forces were the military arm that went around fighting Earth's wars in space, the Territorial Protectorate were the law enforcement on the various colonies and worlds that Earth controlled and settled.

I'd known Kristin for a number of years, both professionally and personally. Good friend.

She confirmed some suspicions.

Turned out that part of Eretut's routine was real. He had been on some kind of Europan pilgrimage but had run into the sisters before anyone else. It hadn't taken them long to get their hooks into him and convince him to join up with them. The Welker sisters had been on the Protectorate's most wanted list for awhile. They'd been busy the last couple years and got busier when they hooked up with Eretut about six months ago.

Then they had the bad luck to run into me.

They wouldn't be busy much longer.

Kristin was happy to learn they were still guests at Corric Station. She was personally on her way there to pick them up. No word on what had happened with Eretut's body.

I felt bad for the Europan. He'd still be alive if the sisters hadn't gotten a hold of him.

But like I had told him, the galaxy is not a nice place.

THE LAST CHILD

Originally Published:
May 26, 2018, eBook on Amazon

CHAPTER ONE

"That's it?"

The Pierd in front of me just mumbled something in it's language, which I didn't speak. It sounded like rocks grinding against other rocks, long sentences made with lots of short words. It, I can never tell the Pierd sexes apart, stood four feet high and two feet wide. Short and stocky. All covered in brown fur with a head like a block. Flat nose, beady eyes.

They were shrewd traders and this one was trying to cheat me.

It held out a credchip good for one thousand creds. Not close to what I was owed for this job.

The cargo itself wasn't a big deal. Relatively small. It was the delivery location. CU145792 was a large asteroid in the Callic Cluster. This was Deep Space. The outskirts. As far out as you could get and still be in the known galaxy.

My territory.

The place didn't even have a real name. Part of an asteroid belt that orbited a dead planet called Untun, CU145792 had been hollowed out and mined by the Culkin Union. Not a friendly or welcoming place but it still needed goods to survive. The problem being that it was so far out of the way that the larger shipping concerns didn't want to waste the fuel needed to get there. That's where freighters like mine came into the picture.

Trips like this were barely profitable for me. As long as I got paid.

"Give me the full amount or you don't get your cargo," I growled at the Pierd.

It's name was Yunil and it ran one of the local general goods stores. The asteroid was home to miners, miners and more miners. Along with the services and people that supported them. The Culkin Union was a Pierd group, so beings like Yunil were in charge of everything on the rock.

Yunil yelled at me some more. I'm sure it translated to "cheater", "scammer" and so on. It ended with what was likely "I already have the cargo" and the Pierd gave me what I assumed was a smirk, thinking he had the upper hand.

I leaned in close, giving it the look.

I'm six foot, two hundred. Black hair and beard, with streaks of gray. Brown eyes. Ruggedly handsome, so I've been told. Not the most intimidating at first glance, there are many bigger, but I've worked hard on 'the look' and it gets results.

The Pierd took a step back, even though it weighed as much as I did, things still get intimidated by those bigger leaning over them. Yunil glanced around the lobby to its shop, especially at the transaction window and the office behind the blastproof polycarbonite window. Yunil had wanted to stay back there to conduct our business, the circuitry of the window would have translated it's words to Tradelan, Terran or some other language I could understand. But it would have been behind the protection of the carbonite. I made it come out here.

I'm not stupid.

"I'll take back the cargo, sell to your competitor and break some stuff on my way out."

Most of that was a bluff. I knew it, Yunil knew it. First there was no competition on the rock. Yunil's shop was it. I could take the cargo back to more populated areas of space, but that would cost me fuel and the job would be a major loss. Second, if I was to break stuff, the Culkin Union would have me arrested or fined. Neither of which was good for me. Yunil looked up at me, studying and thinking. How much was a bluff and how far was I willing to go?

The Pierd made a noise that I assumed was a sigh because it handed over another credchip. Good for another thousand credits and paying me what I was owed. Yunil had figured it wasn't worth the hassle of calling my bluff.

Which I knew he would have.

Yunil isn't a bad sort. We'd done business before but times were getting rough on the asteroid and he was trying to save every cred he could. Can't blame it. Times were tough everywhere.

"Thanks," I said biting back a sarcastic remark.

Which was hard for me. Sarcasm came naturally.

But no need to annoy one of my regulars.

I needed the work Yunil offered.

With a last huff, Yunil turned its blocky body around and headed for the door. The Pierd's people had unloaded the cargo from my ship when I had first arrived and it was probably already lost within all the supplies the shop carried. The door slid open into the metal wall and Yunil disappeared.

I turned, pocketing the credchips, and walked out the shop's lobby. The asteroid was a backwater, no automatic scanning of cargo and deposits like at some of the bigger stations. Still did transfers the old fashioned way. I tended to like that more. Personal. Got to look the being in the face and eyes. If they had eyes.

Like most Pierd establishments, there was an empty lobby with a display board that would list the shop's wares. You'd order from the board, under the watchful eye of the shop owner behind the window, and one of the employees would bring your order to you. Larger orders would be picked up out back. Efficient with minimal interaction.

Just as the Pierd liked it.

The shop's door slid quietly shut behind me and I was out on the street.

Being an asteroid, everything was carved out of the interior. So the gray stone surrounded everything. Only about twenty feet high, the cavern was carved like a ring through the stone with shops on both sides. About three miles long in total, it was very busy. The workers and homes were in side caverns, the entrances scattered around the oval. The hanger was another tunnel, midway around the north side of the ring.

The city, for lack of a better word, was called The Oval. Not very imaginative but it did the job.

It was dark and crowded. What little light there was came from the shops and glow lamps hanging from the ceiling. The smell of dozens of aliens of all species mixed in the refreshed air from the circulators mounted in the cavern roof. Beings moved in both directions, pushing against each other, not caring. Most were dirty, miners off their shift. No one looked wealthy. There was an air of resignation everywhere, people given up on life.

Not a fun place.

Not that I blamed them. If I was stuck inside an asteroid that didn't even rate a true name, I'd be pretty depressed too. I couldn't wait to get off this rock.

Just needed to find a job first.

*****

The life of a freighter is not glamorous. Not by any means. Don't let the books and vids fool you. They like to make it seem better than it is. The daring swashbuckler off on another adventure.

Tired of your mundane life stuck on your backwater world? Become a freighter and see the universe. Visit exotic locations. See all that the galaxy has to offer.

Sounds like the same pitch used to get people to sign up for the Expeditionary Forces.

Sadly, it works. For both.

Sure, some haulers get the good runs. Get to see the inner core worlds. Visit the good places. But those are the ones that sign up with the big interplanetary outfits. The others, the independents, like myself, we get stuck with running small hauls out to worlds and asteroids like this rock.

Nothing glamorous about CU145792.

The void of warpspace gives a solo pilot plenty of time to spend on contemplation. So I have lots of opportunities to reflect on my life and the choices that got me here. It's not just the time in warpspace either. Sitting in dingy and rathole bars while waiting for a job offer gives that same kind of time.

Dingy and rathole bars like this one.

It didn't even have a name, just a sign over the door written in Tradelan that said 'bar'.

The room was large and square. No windows, just the door. The bar counter was along the back wall, lots of stools that could adjust in height to accommodate various sized beings, and built out of solid rock. Nothing fancy, got the job done. Tables filled the rest of the space. No organization, just as many tables as would fit. Some were broken with cracks and even missing pieces. There wasn't enough chairs for every table, so some beings had to stand along the edges.

I'd taken a chair at a small table in the corner where I could watch the door as well as the vidscreen mounted to the wall. It was behind a sheet of somewhat clear blastproof polycarbonite which made the picture a little fuzzy but still watchable.

Wonder who has the contract for bringing polycarbonite here? They use a lot of it.

The vidscreen was showing some news from the inner core but it was on a station controlled by the Culkin Union so it was filtered but still broadcast in Tradelan, the common language of the galaxy. Filtered a lot. So is every station, everywhere. There are so many Unions, planetary governments, the Planetary Council and others controlling the news that you never get an unbiased report. But if you know how to read between the lines you can get a pretty good idea of the truth.

See all the galaxy has to offer.

Sighing, I took another swig of my ale. Technically it was not ale, not by the earth definition. But it was close to it, one of the closest I'd found. Some drink called gaurt from a planet called Uduy.

I kept one eye on the vid and one on the door, and I waited.

As an independent freighter, I take a job to one place and when I leave that place it means I usually need to leave with a job. That sends me to my next destination. That's life. One planet, moon or asteroid, hop to another.

The problem with a rock like this one is finding a job when I leave.

The asteroid needs a lot of stuff but not a lot of stuff leaves. Ore, sure, lots of that. But the Union controls that. A guy like me needs to find something else.

CU145792 is so out of the way that it doesn't even have a jobs board like the Inner Core worlds do. A centralized location where people looking to ship have a place to post what they need and people looking to do the shipping can find them. In some Inner Core worlds, the shipper never even meets the shippee and it's handled through a third party.

The bartender, who doubled as the server in this place, a big lump of a Kern, had just dropped off my second glass when I saw my contact enter. He looked around the place with an air of disdain. Quickly finding me, he started making his way through the crowd. Tesk Un Lil was a Kry from the planet Kryot in the star system of the same name. One of the Inner Core systems. He'd done something to anger his superiors so had been banished here to the dredges of the galaxy. He represented the Kry on other worlds and rocks in the local area of Deep Space. We ran into each other a lot.

Lil had light brown skin, bright red eyes and perfectly combed and cut black hair. He wore expensive looking clothes. He worked hard to present an image, that of an Inner World businessman. Someone important.

He really wasn't. He knew it. I knew it. Everyone here knew it.

Stopping at my table he looked down at the empty chair with a sigh. It was a dirty chair and Lil was in his full snob mode. He sat down, back straight and hands held above the table as if he didn't want to touch it. He was laying it on pretty thick.

"Arek Lancer," he said in near perfect Tradelan, not a hint of a Kryan accent. I mean the guy spoke it better than I did and it was my primary language. It was rare that I spoke english nowadays. "How are you?"

"Doing good," I replied and pointed at my mug, offering him one. He shook his head and I held up one finger for the Kern to see. "You?"

"Business is looking up," he replied finally settling his hands on the table. He pulled out a cloth first and wiped off a section, looking down at the surface with disgust. He held the cloth away from himself and shook it before disdainfully putting it back in his pocket.

He was lying. Business was not looking up.

Tesk Un Lil wanted back into the Inner Core. Badly. He constantly worked to get there, going after bigger and bigger deals to try to convince his people that he deserved to be in the Core. He was still stuck here, which meant business was just the same as it always was.

That was the big problem with Deep Space. Once you were stuck here, it was very hard to get out.

"You called me so I assume that means you are looking for work?" Lil asked. More of a statement than a question.

"That's right. Just dropped off a shipment for Yunil. Need a shipment to head back out with."

Lil leaned back but without actually touching the chair. He tapped his long fingers on the table. The Kern bartender brought my drink and dropped it on the table, spilling some of it. Without a word he took the empty, not even bothering to clean up the spill or apologize. I leaned back, actually touching the chair, and waited for Lil.

The Kry had excellent memories. Their minds were almost like computers. They could process a lot of information quickly and were very good at multitasking. They rarely had to write anything down or input it in a computer. This meant they rarely forgot anything.

Another reason Lil was having such a hard time getting back to the Core.

Right now he was going through all the various deals he had in place, what needed to go where and when. He was also factoring in which ones didn't accept cargo from Terrans.

Yeah, fancy that, we're not that well liked out here or anywhere in the galaxy for that matter.

I took a drink and watched the vidscreen well waiting on Lil.

"I have a couple crates that need to go to Dynuit," he said finally. "No rush."

Picturing the trip from here to there in my head I worked out the fuel calculations and the time factor.

"How much," I asked knowing what the minimum would need to be.

"2,500 cred."

"That'll work," I said holding out my hand. Minimum and a little bit extra.

I wanted to laugh as Lil awkwardly reached out and clasped mine. His face was priceless. Kry don't like to touch or be touched, and Lil was worse than most of them. I made him shake my hand on every job we did. I thought it was funny. I doubt he did.

It's the little things that make life fun.

*****

By the time I left the bar it was well past dark. Or would have been if the sun was visible inside this rock. Instead I knew it was late by the type of people that were out. Every planet is the same. Night comes and a different class of being comes with it.

CU145792 was no different. It's surprising, but even on a rock this small with a tightly controlled workforce, there were still criminal gangs. Maybe not that surprising really.

As I made my way through the street and around the clusters of people, I kept a hand on my gun. I wore a low hanging holster on my right leg. It was strapped to the leg and my belt, a holdover from my old army days. As was the blaster itself. Hand on gun and the general "don't mess with me" vibe I gave off kept people away from me.

I wouldn't be able to leave the rock for a couple hours or even load Lil's cargo until morning, or what counted as morning, so I had some time to kill. Time was relative. Each planet or system had its own day and night cycle. Could play havoc on a traveler as they always had to adapt to local time. Or they did what most of us pilots did, kept their own cycle. In other words, they kept odd hours.

There's wasn't much to do on the asteroid but I knew I could find a card game or something along those lines if I wanted to.

But I didn't.

What I really wanted was to sleep.

Well I really did want to play cards, but money was tight and I didn't have any to risk.

So sleep it was.

I was near the tunnel that led to the hangers when I heard the commotion behind me.

Turning, hand around the grip of my blaster, a military issued Sig Sauer T1700, I saw people being pushed aside. Something or someone running through them. I could see two tall figures near the back, coming closer, the ones pushing people out of the way by force or just their presence. I couldn't see anything they could be chasing.

And then I felt something slam into me.

Something small, a foot or more shorter than me and much thinner, hit me. I almost fell but was able to keep my balance. It hadn't hit hard but had momentum behind it. So short I had missed it when looking at the crowd.

I looked down at what hit me.

"What the hell," I said.

It was a she.

A young girl.

A Thesan and she looked scared.

CHAPTER TWO

I looked down at her and she up at me with big eyes that were on the verge of tears.

She wasn't just scared, she was terrified, reaching out and holding onto my jacket. She looked over her shoulder at the two tall forms that were continuing to push their way through the gathering crowd, coming closer. People were coming out of shops and buildings to see what the commotion was.

I didn't need this. I had stuff to do and places to be. It wasn't my business.

"Dammit," I said aloud as the girl looked up at me.

Thesan, they're allies of us earth folks. Terrans is what the other races call us. From Terra, which is what they call earth. Thesans are one of the few allies we truly have out here.

And the girl was alone.

And young.

She was typical for her race and age. I placed her at mid teens, maybe on the low end. She was about five feet tall with gray and black fur. Thesans are covered with a light fur from head to toe, tufts at the wrists and ankles, and hair that goes down their back and connected to their bodies. Their ears are small and pointed and their eyes are bright yellow with green irises. She wore a nondescript set of worker's coveralls that were too big. Probably meant to hide her form. Thesans tended to stand out. It was the long tail.

They looked like humanoid cats.

This one had a pleading look to her eyes. Like I was her only hope.

From the noise I knew whoever was chasing her had come to a stop in front of me. The crowd was murmuring and all footsteps had stopped around us. I looked up.

And cursed.

A Tiat.

Two of them. The one in front of me and another behind looking at the crowd which was quickly moving away. Staring them down.

I studied the one in front of me.

Tall, light blue skinned, cold purple eyes and white hair. Dressed in a perfectly fitting uniform, no creases, no stains, no blemishes. Rigid. About a foot taller than my six feet and thin. But not spindly. Still looked balanced and tough.

That's the thing about Tiat. They may not look like much but don't let it fool you. They're tough bastards. Bones like steel, muscles and tendons like wire. They don't look it, but they're strong. I'm not a xenobiologist, don't know why, just know that they are.

Tiat were the galaxy's bullys. I tried to avoid the bastards as much as possible.

They were militaristic, their matriarchal empire spreading out and taking what they wanted. We had fought a war with them that in some places and ways was still ongoing. It'd been five years since I left the Earth Expeditionary Forces and it'd been that long since I'd been face to face with a Tiat.

Punching one is like hitting a wall. Getting punched by one is like getting hit by a hammer.

Been there, done that.

Not something I wanted to do today or any other day. Something I never wanted to do again in this lifetime.

But it appeared there would be no avoiding it.

The girl still clung to me but I managed to push her behind me, using my body as a shield.

I looked up at the Tiat standing five feet in front of me and tried to keep the second in sight. That one had shifted to my left so he could look around his friend. It helped me keep an eye on him but also helped keep me in his view.

Why were two Tiat chasing a Thesan? I thought there was a non-aggression pact between the two races? Just like the one between Terrans and Tiat. Which is violated on a regular basis. I'm sure the same was true of the Thesan and Tiat one. But how could that involved a young girl?

"Can I help you?" I asked, keeping my voice calm.

"Move human," the Tiat said. A command, no room for anything but doing what the big guy said. His voice was firm, deep.

It occured to me that I didn't know the score here. I could be stepping into the middle of something big and bad. The Tiat could have a legitimate reason to be chasing this Thesan. They could and I could also be the richest guy in the galaxy, which I'm not. Not even close.

I hate Tiat. I hate bullies.

I could feel the girl trembling against me.

There really was no choice.

I was probably going to regret this.

"Sorry, what did you say," I said to the Tiat, watching his eyes.

Always watch the eyes. You can tell when they're going to move by the eyes.

Sure enough, his eyes twitched and he took a couple steps towards me, reaching out with his arm. Giving the Thesan girl a light push backwards, I stepped forward and into the reach of the Tiat. He was bigger than me, longer reach than me, outweighed me because of his bone density and stronger than I was so he had lots of advantages.

But I had leverage.

I grabbed his reaching arm with mine, hooking mine around his. I pulled him down and twisted my body so my free shoulder was slammed into his chest. It hurt, like hitting a wall, but my shove had put the Tiat off balance. I leaned down, taking the weight of the Tiat on my shoulder. He fell forward, off his feet, and when I had the full weight and it was a lot of weight, I pushed forward. The Tiat fell to the ground. Hard. And I released its arm.

When I had moved the other Tiat had moved. The bastards were quick.

I glanced at him and ran to the girl. Poor thing was frozen in fright, watching it all. Granted it had only been a couple seconds but still. She grabbed for me and I took her hand. I had the urge to grab my blaster but there was no way I was opening up a firefight in the middle of The Oval.

We ran down the lighted hall towards the hanger. The walls were smooth, metal and curved to the ceiling. No exposed rock here. Bands of lights ran along the top, making the hallway the brightest thing in the asteroid. It was wide too, the only way to get cargo from the hanger and into the center of the rock.

People, aliens of all sorts, moved through the hall in both directions. They stopped to watch us run by. I could already hear the Tiat behind us. They moved fast.

I wished the hall was more crowded. We needed to lose them before we could make it to my ship. I didn't want them getting a look at it or the registration codes painted on the hull.

Not long, the hall emptied out into the large hanger. A wide open space carved out of the rock with metal lining the walls and floor and rough rock ceiling. It was a couple hundred feet long and deep. I could see the far end open to the void of space. Just a magbarrier between us and the vacuum. Black background, white stars and other asteroids floating by.

The hanger was filled with ships of all shapes and sizes. CU145792 was limited in how many ships it could hold. The asteroid was only so big and most of it was used for the mines. The center of the docking bay was open, lines painted on the metal with running lights that would direct ships from the berths into the center where they could pass through the magbarrier and out into space. Because of its size, the traffic was tightly controlled.

Even if we made it to my ship unseen, we weren't leaving until the scheduled time and that was a couple hours away still. We needed some place to hide now so the Tiat couldn't follow us to my ship.

I wouldn't have come this way in the first place but I'd already been heading this way when the girl bumped into me. There are plenty of places to hide back in the Oval, but not in the hanger. I knew the Tiat were right behind us but I took a couple seconds to look around and try to come up with something.

Ships lined the perimeter, the back wall where we were and the sides. Crates and other equipment between the ships. Maybe thirty ships total. Lots of crates. No good places to hide.

Think Arek, think.

I was already regretting doing this until I looked down at the Thesan. She looked up at me with those eyes and they spoke volumes. They said she believed in me. She gripped my hand tighter, but not from fear but reassurance.

Dammit.

I looked around the space, thinking harder.

There. I hoped.

I pulled the Thesan to the right, heading for a group of aliens two ships down. About four of them stood together, watching another two pushing a couple maglifters up a ship's boarding ramp. Crates were stacked near them, two on each maglift. We were running towards them and it had caught their attention. I could see a couple lowering hands to blasters strapped to their sides.

Different shades of green skin and blue hair, purple eyes and humanoid. The same size as Terrans, they wore neatly tailored and matching uniforms. One of the many trading consortiums. I didn't know which one, I only knew their species.

Dyers.

I didn't know much about them as a species or their world, the few that I knew were independents and not that connected to their people. Dyers had a very strict society.

Very regimented and controlled. There were reasons for it, or so I had been told. Almost every aspect of their lives was controlled by the ruling government. Independents, like the ones I knew, were rare and considered an anomaly. What I did know is that no Dyer was a friend of the Tiat. The two races hated each other. It was only because the Dyer weren't as strong as the Tiats that prevented them from going to war. The Tiat knew this and teased the Dyer with that knowledge.

I slowed, holding up my free hand, glancing behind me, trying to convey that I meant them no harm. The Thesan girl looked behind us, fear in her eyes. I knew it was genuine and the Dyers were picking up on it. They glanced at me and the girl, a couple looking behind us. I changed my angle so I would go past them and quickly turned to be behind them. One followed us with his eyes but the others were focused on the entrance to the hanger and the two Tiat that had now entered.

Looking both ways, the Tiat split up.

The Dyer that had been watching us looked to one of the others who was staring at the Tiat. Without looking towards us, he nodded. Another Dyer motioned to me and started walking to their ship. I followed, pulling the Thesan tighter to me. The Dyer adjusted his pace so he was between me and the approaching Tiat. One of the crewers pushing the maglifter stopped and moved so it was now blocking us. He kept the maglifter even with us as we walked up the ramp into the ship.

The hold of the Dyer's ship was long, the full length of the vessel. It was an underneath hauler, meaning the hold was the bottom half with the rest of the ship's functions above. This design allowed for a lot of cargo. Inside I saw lots of crates of various sizes organized throughout. The Dyer were mostly known for their efficiency and it showed. Their regimented lifestyles carried over to all aspects of their lives. The ship was clean, well maintained. The maglifter continued on and our Dyer escort led us to a storage closet against the wall.

Still without a word he hit a button and opened the closet door. He motioned us to enter.

It wasn't that large, barely enough room for me and the girl. It was dark and I wasn't sure about letting someone else control the door but I was already throwing a lot of faith into this, trusting in the Dyer's hatred of the Tiat.

The Thesan looked up at me and I smiled at her, trying to be reassuring. Hoping I faked it because I sure didn't feel it. Taking a breath, I nudged her into the closet. I pulled her closer, arms wrapped around her and felt hers tighten around me as the Dyer closed the door and we were lost in the darkness.

*****

The girl wouldn't stop shaking and I couldn't blame her. I lost track of the time and the air was getting stuffy in the small space. There were no vents to let new air in. We got some from the ship's ventilation system, but it still wasn't comfortable. I patted her shoulder, trying to comfort her.

I had no idea what I was doing. I didn't have kids, barely knew anyone that did. I had been a soldier, a frontliner, Special Operations, never had time for that kind of thing. My sister, who I had not seen in a long time had a couple. I forgot how many.

Some uncle I was.

What was I doing? I still had no idea what was going on. I didn't even know the girl's name. I was running on instinct.

Which had never really run me wrong before.

So we waited in the dark.

We heard footsteps, boots on metal decking, coming our way and I tensed. The girl felt it and she grabbed me tighter. I wanted to loosen up but I needed to be ready for anything.

There was no space in the closet to draw my blaster. The footsteps stopped and I heard the sound of buttons being depressed.

The door opened with a soft release of pressure and I breathed deep of the cooler air in the ship's hold. I looked out, ready to see almost anything and was relieved that it was just the Dyer that had led us here.

"This way," he said, turning and leading us to the ramp.

I followed cautiously.

I could see the hanger through the still open ramp. No maglifters were moving up, the hold was now filled with the crates I had seen outside. I couldn't see anyone or anything in the hanger from this angle. Another of the Dyer was standing at the top of the ramp looking out into the open space of the docking bay. He was dressed in the same uniform as the others, but there were some additional bars on his collar. He turned as we approached.

An older Dyer, streaks of darker blue in his hair, he had a scar along his right cheek from jaw to scalp. Old and puckered, a battle wound most likely. He stood military straight, his hands clasped behind his back. He studied me, looking up and down. I still walk like a military man and he could tell. He studied the Thesan girl, who held my left hand with both of her smaller ones.

The moment creeped on. I let it. This was the Dyer's play. He had helped us.

"I don't think I want to know what this is about," he finally said.

"I wish I did," I answered and the Dyer gave me a weird look.

"The Tiat left the hanger," he said and I took that as my cue.

"Thank you," I told him and held out my hand. "Arek Lancer."

The Dyer shook and smiled.

"Garrin Delt," he said. "Earth Expeditionary Forces?"

"Captain," I replied. The Dyer nodded, satisfied. "I owe you one."

"It was my pleasure. Anything to annoy the Tiat."

I laughed and led the Thesan down the ramp. Even though the Dyer had said the Tiat were gone, I still looked both ways and kept my head on a swivel as we walked to my ship.

CHAPTER THREE

Making our way from the Dyer ship to mine, only six ships down, was painful.

We moved slow, trying not to look out of place. I gave the girl, who still had not talked, my dark green military jacket to help hide her shape. She pulled the collar up to hide her features and hunched a little. I was very aware of the security cameras mounted on the walls.

This was a Pierd owned asteroid and there was no reason to suspect that they'd work with the Tiat, letting them review the security footage, but better to be careful. The Tiat had gotten a good look at me in The Oval and I really did not want them to figure out which ship was mine. My face was attached to my ship's identifiers, which would now be in the asteroids system. So I kept my head turned away from the cameras.

I had the urge to run but that would draw attention from the Pierd security forces, who were probably already combing the Oval for me and the girl. They might not have responded to the fight yet. Fights were very common in places like this asteroid so security rarely reacted unless there was a death.

But this was the Tiat I was dealing with and they wanted this girl for some reason. They could put a lot of pressure on the Culkin Union if they really wanted to.

It's funny how quickly old instincts and training come back.

I can't remember how long it had been since I'd run an infiltration mission but this was starting to feel like that. Keep moving, don't draw notice and pay attention to everything. My eyes darted all over the place, checking everyone and everything. I watched all the different beings in the hanger, their movements, which ones looked towards us. I noted when one started walking towards us, studying its hands and movements. I let out a breath I didn't know I was holding when the alien, a species I didn't recognize, continued past us.

I really wanted to question the girl but this was not the time or place. That could wait.

The last ship before mine was a giant cruiser that blocked our view. Not good. I lightly touched the girl and slowed her down. If the Tiat had already figured out who I was, they'd be there waiting.

Or I was being overly paranoid.

Deciding to be cautious but not paranoid, I stepped around the cruiser and looked on my home.

Compared to the cruiser behind us, the *Nomad's Wind* was nothing, not even half the size of the Dyer's ship. A Castellan Light Cruiser Model F497, built back on Earth, it wasn't much to look at. I'd heavily modified it but the lines were unmistakable. The Castellan's were not the most original ship designers, all their stuff had the same basic style.

Essentially two levels, cargo and some living on the bottom and the rest of the living plus engineering on the top, the mid part of the ship on all sides but the back had a gray metal "wing" that came off the blue metallic sides and went around to the front. It extended beyond the front of the ship and angled in. The wing ran to the back of the ship but didn't extend beyond, also angling in towards the hull. Mounted on top of the wing at the back were two large engines. The rear of the ship was straight making the ship look boxy from that view, the cargo doors and ramp on the lower half. The front was different, the top and bottom halves were angled, sloping away from the wing.

Basically a blue wedge with a gray triangle attached to it.

Not the prettiest but it got the job done.

Designed to crew six but could be run by two or three, I'd modified mine so it only needed one crewer. Me.

There were three decent sized crates stacked outside the *Wind's* closed ramp.

"Crap," I said and the girl looked up at me, worried. I gave her shoulder a squeeze to let her know it was nothing to worry about.

I'd forgotten that I'd agreed to deliver some cargo for Tesk Un Lil.

This complicated things.

I led the girl to the side of the ship and keyed my code into the plate. The door slid up into the hull and I gave her a slight nudge to enter. There wasn't much reluctance, for some reason the girl seemed to trust me.

First time for anything I guess.

I paused as I stepped up into the opening, giving the hanger one last look. Nothing caught my attention. No one paid any attention to us and I couldn't feel any eyes on us.

Time to get some answers, I thought as the door closed behind me.

*****

The girl was starving. I led her to the galley which was on the lower level and handed her some food. She tore into it.

"Stay here," I said and she nodded.

I had to do something about Lil's cargo. If I took it onboard, I'd have to deliver it. A hauler that didn't deliver wasn't one that got jobs again. But if I left it out there and canceled my contract with Lil, I'd have the same issue. Chances of finding work, especially with the Kry, would be difficult. My options were already limited, I couldn't afford to limit them more.

Moving into my ship's small cargo hold, I grabbed the maglifter from where it was stowed against the wall and took it to the back. Hitting the controls the ramp lowered. I tensed, watching as more of the hanger was revealed, expecting to see Tiat or Pierd Security Forces standing there just waiting for me. But there was no one there.

Anyone watching would just see a hauler loading cargo but it was an act. I was wired, tense. It had been years since I had been in a situation like this. My life wasn't much, but it was my life and it was relatively peaceful. I had left war behind and thought I had left this kind of thing as well.

Pushing the maglifter down the ramp, my eyes searched the hanger. Nothing had changed. It had only been a couple minutes but that could be a lifetime to a trained professional.

I paused once the crate was on the maglifter.

What was I doing?

I hadn't stopped once the girl had bumped into me. Just running on instinct. The Tiat were chasing her, she was a young girl. Was that really all I needed to know?

No. I needed the story.

But would that change anything?

Without thinking I had agreed to help this girl. Why? There was no way I was leaving her alone now. I was taking a huge risk. This could put me on the Tiat's list and I had worked long and hard to stay off that.

My record from my time in the Earth Expeditionary Forces was under lock and key. If the Tiat knew about some of my black ops missions, I would have been on their radar no matter what. That was part of the reason why I mostly operated out in Deep Space and not the Core where the Tiat's influence was greater.

I didn't regret anything I had done. It was war. Was it right? Not all of it.

Look through the history books, us humans really aren't that much better than the Tiat. Even our recent history, the last thirty to forty years since we got out to space, has not been that good. Humans get space travel and find a galaxy filled with inhabited worlds. What do you think happened?

But I'm human and between us and the Tiat? I'll take us.

It still didn't explain why I had instantly chosen to help the girl. I had friends that were Thesan. They had been our first allies when we got into space. I'd fought alongside them. But that wasn't enough.

What was I doing?

Sighing, knowing there probably wasn't an answer, I pushed the maglifter up the ramp. The *Wind's* hold was empty, so just stored the crate against the wall and maglocked it down. Didn't take long to finish loading the other two.

The *Wind* was longer than it was wide, so the hold was shaped that way. Seeing the three crates lined up on one side and the rest of the space with nothing, that just made it seem emptier if that was possible.

I needed more jobs, bigger and better. I was just getting by. Thankfully I didn't have a crew that I had to worry about paying.

One last look out the hanger and I closed the ramp, setting the security locks. Checking my chrono, I still had an hour before my scheduled launch time.

Hopefully the girl was full because it was question and answer time.

*****

She was right where I had left her, kind of.

She was no longer eating, the plates and stuff still on the table, but she was in the galley. The girl was curled up on the one chair in the room.

The galley was a long room on one side of the front half of the lower level, a spiral stair in the corner. Going up the stairs you came to a small hall that led to the bridge and turning down the bunk corridor that ended in engineering. On this level, the hold took up most of the space with the galley and next to it the lounge. Simple and straightforward design. Like I said, the Castellans are not the most original shipbuilders out there. What they are known for is efficiently operating ships that rarely break down and are tough as rock.

I'd had the *Nomad's Wind* for almost five years and she had never let me down.

Cabinets and shelves lined one wall of the galley, with the door to the lounge in the middle, the appliances and more shelves on the other. A long table took up the middle of the space with one cushioned chair in the corner, opposite the stair, bolted to the floor. The chairs for the table were attached to sliders on the floor, so they could move but were essentially locked in. There wasn't too much loose furniture anywhere on the ship. Things tended to slide while the ship was moving.

The Thesan was looking at me, legs pulled up to her chest with arms around them. She was still frightened, but more than that she looked tired. I pulled out one of the chairs at the table, hitting the button under the seat that would unlock the slider. I hit another button and swiveled the chair around. Taking the seat I studied her as she studied me.

"Hi," I said. It sounded dumb but I didn't know where else to start.

I never really liked kids. Never had much to do with them. I had been too busy being a soldier to think about kids and once I got out, this life was no place for a kid.

She didn't reply back, just kept looking at me with those bright eyes.

"My name is Arek. What's yours?"

Nothing.

It wasn't a blank stare. She could understand me. She just didn't want to talk. Or maybe she couldn't?

I leaned forward in the chair.

"Look, you ran into me and needed help, so I helped. But now I need to know more," I tried to keep my voice even, calm and soothing. This is something that I had no training for. "I can't help you unless you talk to me."

She lowered her legs and held her hands out in front. Her fingers started dancing, moving quickly in patterns and shapes. It wasn't random. She was forming specific shapes. She was trying to speak.

Sign language. Great.

"Hold on," I said leaning back. "I don't know what all that means."

So she couldn't talk. That would make this much more difficult.

"We'll start simple okay?"

The girl nodded.

"We can get into why the Tiat want you later, but for now you want to avoid them?"

A nod.

"Did they take you from your family?"

A nod and a sadness crept into her eyes. She was trying to be strong, to keep it out but it wasn't happening, it was too painful. I gave her a minute to compose herself.

"Is your family here on the asteroid?"

A shake of the head. No. I had a follow up, asking about the fate of her family, but figured that one could wait.

"Is there anyone here that you could go to? Friends? Other Thesans?"

Another shake.

What to do with her? I sure as hell couldn't leave her here. Not with the Tiat. Even without the Tiat, I couldn't leave a young girl alone on a rock like this.

The chrono on my wristcomm beeped. Time to start the preflight as my designated departure was almost here.

I guess I was stuck with her for now.

"You can come with me," I said. "For now. I have to go to Dynuit to drop off cargo and we'll figure out what to do with you there. Okay?"

The girl moved quick. She was out of the chair and had her arms wrapped around me pretty damn fast. Quicker then I had thought she would move. I had to remember, she was a young girl, but she was still a Thesan with everything that meant.

I pushed her away and stood up. She was smiling as she sat back down.

"I need to go get the ship ready for the flight. It's a long trip so we'll have plenty of time to talk then."

Her eyes followed me as I moved to the stair. Metal steps, grated, with a tight radius. I looked at the girl looking at me as I walked up then, trying to give her a reassuring smile. She quickly disappeared from view as my head passed the room's ceiling. I stepped out onto the upper level corridor wondering how I'd manage to communicate with her.

I needed answers.

CHAPTER FOUR

"Acknowledged control," I said into the communications headset I now wore. "Have a good one."

I clicked off the connection to CU145792 Dock Control and concentrated on flying the *Wind*. I lifted off the dock floor, using the thrusters mounted underneath. The ship shook a little and I heard the Thesan girl walk into the bridge. I had left the door open so if she came up from the galley she could find me easily. She took a seat in the co-pilots station and looked out the view window at the magbarrier and stars beyond.

I loved looking at the field of stars. Bright white dots on a black background. Each one with so much possibility and mystery. Some I had been to and some that no one had ever been to in the entire history of the galaxy. It's crazy to think of. The galaxy is huge and it's just one of an infinite number of galaxies. Only like a tenth of this one had been explored so far. So many inhabited and uninhabited worlds. So much to discover.

So much to be afraid of.

I adjusted the controls and flew the ship into the middle of the hanger, following the lights and lines painted on the metal floor. There really wasn't much I needed to do, just some fine tuning, as the asteroids guidance system kept the ship on the right path. There was a time when landing in docks like this was all manual, but nowadays every place was automated; even backwater rocks like this one. It was rare to find a dock that wasn't. Unless you were a fighter jock, flying a starship wasn't that difficult.

The *Wind* turned so that we were facing the magbarrier and large opening of the hanger directly. The guidance system pushed the ship forward and the opening grew larger and larger until all we could see was the starfield outside. There was another shudder of the ship as we crossed the barrier, everything getting tinted in blue, and we were floating outside the bay with the thrusters pushing us away from the asteroid.

I hit the controls and the engines that had been in standby came to life. The ship picked up speed as it switched from thrusters to the drive engines. I fought against the limited gravity of the asteroid and took the ship in a loop away from it.

I turned the ship so that the girl could get a good look at the asteroid belt that contained CU145792. Lights dotted the rock as well as the large opening of the hanger. Lights could be seen on other asteroids in the belts, more mines owned by the Culkin Union, but only CU145792 was inhabited. It had probably been stripped of all it's ore awhile ago and now just served as the living quarters.

Turning the ship again I headed towards the edge of this system on a course that would avoid other asteroids and junk floating in space. I could leave the system on any trajectory and still get to my destination but that might mean more jumps.

Hopping system to system was like plotting a course on a map. You went from point A to point B to get to point C. You could try jumping from A to C, but that could lead you into uncharted ion storms, nebulas or any of the other thousand dangers of the wild space between systems. All jumps started and ended at the edges of the different systems. That led to hours of in-system travel at normal drive speed and not jumpspeed. Slow. But in-system hops were dangerous. Safer to go the long way.

Inner core worlds built large docking stations at the edges of their systems to help cut down on the amount of in-system traffic. A freighter the size of the *Wind* could go in-system and even planetside, but larger ones had to stop at the stations.

I keyed in the navorders for the hop to Dynuit and once the computer had finished calculating I hit the activation button.

Technically it's called Outersystem Warping into warpspace using stardrives but everyone calls it starhopping, or just hopping, into wildspace.

The stars that were points of light elongated and disappeared as the *Nomad's Wind* shot into the wild space between systems. The view outside the window became nothing but a foggy white with streaks of black. The fog looked like it drifted around the ship as we flew at speeds that blew the mind when you tried to think about them. No one knew what this space between systems was really made of, dark matter was the prevailing theory, but I didn't care. Looking at this always filled me with peace.

Ships didn't really need view windows and a lot of the newer models didn't have them. I'd never own a ship that didn't. The views well flying were spectacular.

The Thesan girl leaned forward at the station for a better look. She was smiling, eyes wide with wonder. She'd probably never seen this view before. Not many people took the time to really see what space had to offer.

Where the girl was sitting gave me an idea.

The *Wind's* control room, cockpit, bridge and whatever other words it was called, had four stations. The pilot's on the right, co-pilots on the left and down a couple steps were the navigation and weapons stations or what amounted to weapons on this ship. A couple plasma cannons for defense but that station also controlled the shields. The pilot's station had secondary controls for all those functions. The walls were covered in dials, buttons, displays and read-outs. Lots of flashing lights. Each station was a desk with the controls and a chair. Each desk had a couple monitors and an input keyboard.

Dynuit was three jumps from the asteroid. Each jump was about six hours long. That seemed like a long time but when you measured distance in light years, it was crazy to think of the distance covered in just six hours.

It gave us plenty of time.

I stood up and the girl looked at me. I walked over to her station and pointed at the input keyboard.

"You understand spoken Tradelan but can you write it?" I asked.

The girl looked at the keyboard in thought, finally looking up at me and smiling. She looked down at the keyboard and with her long fingers that ended in short nails, she started typing.

On the screen I saw the word YES.

Now we were getting somewhere.

I shifted so I could look at her and the screen.

"Let's start easy," I told her. "What's your name?"

KAYLIA

"Nice to meet you Kaylia," I said, speaking it slowly and looking at her to see if I got the pronunciation right.

She smiled. Nailed it the first time.

"How old are you?"

THIRTEEN SEASONS

"Where are you from?"

TURESA

That was one of the Thesan's colony worlds. Not in their home system, but a neighboring one. Turns out most systems are like Earth's, only one or two habitable planets and a bunch of uninhabitable ones. Because of this, some of the more empire-leaning beings had expanded out into other systems. Thesa had four colony worlds in different systems. Us earthlings had three and counting. The Tiats had seven or eight. I did a quick mental calculation of how many jumps it would be from Dynuit to Turesa. Seven possibly? Nine most likely. It was on the edge of the Inner Core but on the opposite side of the spiral.

"Kaylia," I said gently and she looked up at me. "It's time for the hard questions, okay?"

She took a deep breath and nodded.

"Did the Tiat take you from your home?"

YES

"Why?"

She didn't type, just shrugged. Didn't know.

"Did they hurt you? Is that why you can't talk?"

NO. BORN MUTE

"Did they hurt you at all?"

She shook her head no.

GRABBED HARD BUT THAT WAS IT

"How did you get away from the Tiat on the asteroid?"

She typed for a while, the words coming fast.

THEY TOOK ME ON SHIP TO THE ASTEROID AND LED ME THROUGH THE STREET TO A BUILDING. WHILE GETTING INTO THE BUILDING I BIT ONE AND MANAGED TO GET AWAY.

So she had only been on the asteroid for a couple of hours at most. Interesting.

"Are your parents on Turesa?"

She lowered her head, hiding her eyes. I hated asking that question because I was afraid I knew the answer. But I needed to be sure.

After a minute or two Kaylia lifted her head enough to look at the keyboard. She started typing, slower than before.

TIAT KILLED THEM

She sagged back in the chair, looking out the view window at the fog of wildspace. I took a step back, leaning against the pilot station.

Why would the Tiat attack a Thesan family on a Thesan colony world and kidnap a young girl? Thesa and Tiat used to be at war. Twenty years ago. It was what had allied us, the Terrans, with the Thesans. We took their side in the conflict. That war had ended with a stalemate and non-aggression pact between the three. There were minor conflicts and each side, the Thesans and Terrans versus the Tiat, would try to sabotage the others operations. Real cold war kind of stuff. Walk up to the line but don't do enough to step over or at least not get caught. No one in the galaxy wanted another war.

This though, the killing and kidnapping of citizens, could be what finally crossed the line.

So why? There had to be more to the story.

The girl didn't look like she wanted to answer anymore questions and I didn't want to ask anymore. I doubted she'd have the answers I wanted. Like the 'why'. But there was one more I did need.

"Kaylia," I said gently leaning forward. She looked over at me, wet lines marking the light fur on her face. She had been silently crying. "Last question." She nodded. "Is there anyone on Turesa that I can take you to?"

She lifted her head, looking up at the ceiling, thinking. She finally started typing, pausing as she tried to think of the right words. That was the problem with Tradelan. It did great for the basic things but there were concepts that were unique to one race that didn't translate into something others could understand. This led to lots of misunderstandings as you tried to put the concept into Tradelan and it got misinterpreted by the other side.

Kaylia had stopped typing and I looked at the screen.

MOTHERS LITTERMATE

Litter? Thesans gave birth to litters? That was interesting. I wonder if it was in numbers similar to earth cats or if it just meant twins. Hard to tell and not really relevant.

"What's her name?"

YOTERRA

"Will you be okay if I leave you with her?"

Kaylia nodded. Not enthusiastic but it would have to do. Enough questions for now.

I stepped back and waved at the door.

"It's a long trip to Dynuit. We have three six hour jumps. Let me show you to a room where you can sleep."

Kaylia stood up, stretching. I wished I had some clothes she could change into and get out of the coveralls. A one-piece suit with a zipper, the Tiat had most likely put her in them. The clothes held her tail down and that had to be getting uncomfortable. I wondered if I had anything that would fit her small frame. Probably not. She was shorter than I was and a lot smaller body wise.

And it wasn't like I had a wide variety of clothing.

I wore my dark green military issue jacket all the time. Long sleeved shirt underneath, blue in color today, and dark pants with boots. Didn't have a need for much else.

We walked out of the cockpit and into the hallway. Doors led off, four to each side. Six led to sleeping compartments and the other two to storage rooms that were on either side of the control room.

"This is my room," I said pointing to the second door on the right side, the first of the bunks.

There wasn't any markings on the doors. Nothing to indicate that one specifically as mine.

"The rest are empty, you can take your pick."

Almost immediately, without any thought, she pointed to the one directly across from mine.

I nodded and showed her how to use the keypad, teaching her the code to open it. The door slid open into the metal wall and we entered the room, the lights turning on automatically to show a decent sized room. Along one wall was a bed attached to the wall and a desk. The other wall had two doors, the closet and the private refresher. A comfortable looking couch was against the far wall that faced a viewscreen mounted to the side of the door.

It was identical to the other five rooms.

There was no decoration and the room had a disused look. No one had been in it for five years. The ship's air rotation units kept it clean of dust but there was still a musty feel to the room.

"It's not much," I said as Kaylia walked in and looked around.

She turned around and ran to me, giving me a hug, holding tight.

"Hey, it's okay," I said, putting my arms around her awkwardly. "You're going to be okay."

She stepped back and raised her hands, moving the fingers in a pattern.

"Does that mean 'thank you'?" I asked and she nodded, smiling.

The pattern repeated, slower with more emphasis on the finger movements.

I duplicated them. My motions were jerky which probably gave my sign language an accent but Kaylia smiled. I did it a couple more times, getting the movements down.

"How do you say 'You're welcome'?"

She showed me. It took a couple times but I got it.

Smiling, she walked over to the bed.

I walked out of the room, closing the door behind me.

*****

I waited until I was sure Kaylia was asleep before I started searching the news.

The galaxy is a big place and there is always a lot of news floating around out there. I didn't keep up as much as I should have. Part of it was by choice. I'd made the decision to isolate myself when I got out of the military, to be a vagabond and just go from place to place. No home, just me and the ship. Being out of the loop meant I didn't catch anything from earth. The other part was about the galaxy being so big.

Each planet had its own news. Each cluster had its own news. Each system had its own news. And then there was the galaxy wide news. I didn't know many people that kept up with it all.

Luckily there was the Galactic Feed. This was a galaxy wide application that took all the different news feeds from all over and condensed it into more easily digestible segments.

You could modify the Feed to give the news you specifically wanted. The Feed was also a connection to galaxy wide entertainment, shows and music.

The problem was still that it was a lot of information and what I specifically would be looking for wouldn't be available.

That was because of the other problem with the Galactic Feed and any cross-galaxy communications.

It didn't exist while in wildspace. Each ship was isolated. There was no way to get a signal through, into or from wildspace.

There were millions of relay satellites all over the galaxy, hundreds in each system, that would give a boost in power to the signal so that it could go from system to system, but it was as a signal that couldn't be deciphered well in wildspace. So a ship would enter a system and get an infodump of everything.

All of it at least hours, if not days, out of date.

I had the *Wind's* systems programmed to get me a dump whenever I was insystem for a couple hours. No point doing it if just insystem to do the next jump.

If the Tiat had taken Kaylia from Turesa to CU145792 that would have been at least 42 hours and up to 54 or more hours ago. She'd only been on the rock for a couple of hours so that helped narrow it down. Like an idiot I hadn't asked when she had been taken. But in my defense, I was new at this rescuing kidnapped people thing.

I was on that rock long enough to get an infodump so I might get lucky.

Turning on the vidscreen, I entered my password for the Feed and started my search.

Back in my Special Ops days, I worked with a lot of intel operatives. I was the muscle, the direct action gunner, but I was involved in enough behind the scenes planning that I had picked up a couple of things in how to analyze intelligence.

First you started with what you knew to be true.

In this case it wasn't much. And while I was running through the small amount of facts in my head, it occured to me that Kaylia could be making it all up. She could be lying about her name and everything else.

I paused, leaning back in my chair and thought about it. I didn't think so. My instincts told me that she was telling the truth. She was a lost and scared girl that for some reason had chosen me to save her.

I almost laughed at that. If my old unit could see me now. I was not a nice person. I didn't go out of my way to help others. I looked out for me and me alone.

Leaning forward I started typing search commands into the Feed.

What I knew: a young Thesan girl was kidnapped by the Tiat and her parents killed.

Yep, that's a lot.

I started with the news from Turesa going as far back as a week ago. I started scanning headlines, using the Feed to narrow it down with some keywords. I started with "missing girl" and variations of that.

Nothing.

The Tiat would have wanted to keep this quiet, that's why they went out of their way to hide on CU145792. But would the Thesans? I changed my search tactics and looked up the missing persons news feeds.

Nothing.

The Thesans hadn't reported her missing? That was very odd.

Why would both sides be keeping it quiet? Who was she?

Changing the tactics again I started looking for family deaths and for good measure I threw in the name Kaylia had given me. Yoterra.

That found something.

A family had died in a small farming settlement outside the major city on Turesa. Father, mother, two sons and their only daughter. Yoterra wasn't listed as the mother's littermate, still wasn't sure what that meant. Instead she was listed as the regional governor of the planet.

That was a surprise. She was a pretty high ranking Thesan.

The news had a video of her speaking, talking about the tragedy. She was pretty enough for a Thesan. Tall, couple inches shorter than me, couple years older. Coal black fur with gray highlights, wearing what I assumed was the height of Thesan fashion. She looked every bit the part of the regional governor speaking at a tragedy of people she knew personally.

But there was something else about her that caught my attention. The way she stood, her bearing.

Yoterra was military.

Why would the Tiat kill a farming family and kidnap the daughter? Along with faking her death? And why was the only other person I knew involved the regional governor? Who was or had been Thesan military?

I was starting to worry that I had stepped into something very big and very bad.

CHAPTER FIVE

I searched the Feed for a while longer, not finding anything else. I even looked for more information on Yoterra but all I could find was standard stuff for a regional governor on a colony world. Nothing about military. Nothing about why she might be of interest to the Tiat. I had gotten to thinking that they had taken Kaylia to use as leverage against Yoterra.

The idea had merit but it just didn't feel right. Not completely. There might be something there but there was also something else.

Not even midway through the first jump and I had run out of ideas. I didn't think I was going to find out anything else from the Feed. And I didn't think Kaylia could or would tell me more. She probably didn't even know. Wouldn't be the first time an innocent and unknowing kid had been involved in something adults should have left them out of.

I had one more avenue to explore. I composed a quick message and programmed it to send once we got to the first hop point.

Checking the chrono on my wristcomm I saw it was approaching what would normally be dinner time for most species. I kept an odd schedule so never ate on a regular pattern. Most ships carried two pilots, working alternating shifts, so one would always be up when hit a hop point. Normally those were safe, no problems, but there was always a chance and so a pilot was on duty. It was just me so I couldn't always do that. I needed to sleep.

The *Wind's* navcomputer would automatically recalculate the next hop, accounting for the normal variables of ion storms and orbits, and take us into wildspace. There was nothing for me to do, not really. But I normally was awake and in the cockpit when hitting the hop point.

That was a ways out and I was getting tired. It had been a weird and stressful day. Probably could use some food.

I left the cockpit and entered the hall. I lightly tapped on Kaylia's door.

"You up? I was going to make some food."

No response but I thought I heard some rustling and banging.

Concerned I hit the controls and opened the doors. It was dark, nothing but shadows. I could hear flailing from the bed, a banging as she tossed and turned and hit the metal wall. The lights were turned off by the bedside controls so I hit the manual override. Kaylia was on the bed, the sheets and blanket thrown on the floor and she was thrashing wildly.

It was like she was trapped in a nightmare but worse. She was flailing her arms, like she was attacking something. Tossing back and forth, banging her arms and legs against the wall. I was surprised I hadn't heard it in the cockpit.

"Kaylia," I said, quietly at first but repeated it louder.

No response.

I took the couple steps to the bed and stopped. Her fingernails had elongated. They were now claws and they looked sharp. Her face was a mask of rage and pain. Tears flowed down her cheeks, her eyes tightly closed.

This was no normal nightmare and I wasn't sure what was happening to her but I had to stop it. She looked to be in so much pain.

"Kaylia," I yelled reaching for her hands.

I managed to grab one and was surprised at how strong she was. For such a small thing, there was strength there. I could barely hold on. The other arm came close and I managed to grab it as well before the claws could connect.

I held her steady and slowly the fit, or whatever it was, stopped but she still shook. Through it all she had made no noise. The shaking stopped.

Her eyes were now open, looking up at me in shock, and more tears fell. She was silently crying.

I sat down on the bed, noticing that her fingernails had shrunken back down to normal size. I gently pulled her up and wrapped the crying girl in a hug. I wasn't sure what else to do so I let her cry into my shoulder for as long as she needed.

*****

Kaylia calmed down eventually and we went into the galley to make some food. She sat at the table and watched as I attempted to make a well balanced meal.

I'm a single guy. Well balanced was not normally on the menu. I had plenty of ale, true Earth variety, and junk food but not that much for a growing girl. I'd have to stock up when we got to Dynuit. We'd make do until then.

She was now wearing one of my older jackets. Faded and worn, it was big on her but in a way it fit. She seemed to like it.

"Sorry I don't have anything that fits you," I said. "When we get to Dynuit, we can see about getting you some real clothes, okay?"

Kaylia nodded and smiled, no trace of the sadness and misery from before.

The whole episode was weird. It wasn't just crying from the loss of her parents. I'd seen that kind of grief before. This was something else. Grief and rage, a madness to lash out. It kind of scared me to be honest.

And the fingernails turning into claws?

Thesan nails were strong and normally longer than other species. They could be sharpened to a point and used as a weapon. It was a remnant from an earlier time in the Thesan's evolution, when they were more wild and animalistic. Their nails could not grow into claws. Not like I had seen with Kaylia's.

I was tempted to ask about that but she was so peaceful at the moment.

We finished eating and I cleared the dishes, putting them into the washer. Grabbing a bottle of ale from the cooler, I turned around. Kaylia was looking at me.

"There's a vidscreen in the lounge," I said and pointed that way. "Not many vids to watch though and can't get anything else well we're in wildspace. I have cards but don't know any games that a kid should play."

She gave me an annoyed look and her fingers started flying. I could guess what she was getting at. Took offense to the kid comment.

"Slow down," I said. "I don't speak that," I added and moved my fingers randomly.

Kaylia laughed. It was silent, but her whole face lit up. Her body and face performed the action of the laugh, eyes sparkling, even with no sound.

It made me smile.

"So here's a thought," I said when she finally stopped laughing and looked at me again. "Why don't you teach me that sign language?"

She nodded. Enthusiastically.

I was probably going to regret this. I'm not a good student.

*****

The time passed quickly. Turns out, I was pretty good at her sign language, parts of it anyways. It was a combination of Tradelan with some Thesan concepts thrown in. I already knew her language, or enough to get by, so that made learning the sign that much easier. There were still some of the Thesan words I missed but I could get the basics of what she was trying to say.

When we weren't doing that, I taught her the basics of ship control. She learned how to program the navcomputer, work the weapons and the basics of piloting. Kaylia was a quick study, even though she didn't get a chance to put it to practical use.

This part took longer as she had to ask questions in sign and I had to first interpret what she was getting at then describe it to her. It took a bit to get into a pattern but we got there.

And the hours passed.

Kaylia was smart. Very smart. She picked up on things quickly, grasping concepts that took me months to understand. I was impressed. The kid was also funny and sarcastic.

Surprisingly I was enjoying having her around.

She was in the co-pilots station, watching the controls and watching what I did as we hopped out of wildspace and into the outer edges of the Dynuit system. I had disconnected the co-pilot's board so she could hit the buttons and move the controls and not do anything to the ship. She followed my movements as I changed over to the sublight drives for in-system movement, reorientated the ship and started us towards the Dynuit Station.

The Nuit were part of the Planetary Council; like the Terrans, Thesans, Tiat, Dyers and most of the other spacefaring species in the galaxy; but they rarely involved themselves in politics. They like staying neutral and keeping to themselves, relatively. They had two planets out of the seven in the system, only their home being habitable and they had never expanded out of this system. I didn't know the names of the planets and they didn't allow much non-Nuit traffic onto the planets themselves. Not Deep Space and not Inner Core. They had copied the Inner Core though and built a station at the edge of their system.

"Kaylia," I said pointing out the view window at the shadowed object that was in front of the nearest planet. It looked small at this distance. "Do you see that?"

She leaned forward in her seat and looked where I pointed. Turning to me excitedly, she signed.

Is that the station?

"Yep," I answered.

The station grew as we got closer. At sublight speed it took about thirty minutes and Kaylia was staring at it the whole time. I got the feeling she hadn't done much space traveling and the Tiat had most likely kept her locked up.

It went from a dark shadow to hundreds of bright spots of light that started to define the shape. Dynuit Station was a long cylinder with a much wider disc shape at the top. The length had four giant solar panels attached to it and widened as it connected to the disc. That was two thicker rings with a thinner connecting ring and some structures built on top. Lots of lights could be seen in the rings. An arm came out of the thinner ring with a relatively smaller structure attached. Ships of different shapes and sizes could be seen coming in and out of that structure, the docking pad. The Nuit Military were housed in the cylinder as well as the buildings on top of the disc. All station operations, housing and shops were in the three rings. The whole station rotated around and orbited the gas planet beneath it.

I put on my headset and keyed the comms.

"Dynuit station this is *Nomad's Wind*, Terran registration SE6890, requesting permission to dock."

I glanced at Kaylia and saw her slump a little in the chair, eyes downcast. She was no longer as excited. I wondered what happened, it was a sudden shift, and was about to ask when station controls came back.

"*Nomad's Wind*, you are free to dock at bay 29."

"Acknowledged control," I replied and disconnected.

I took the headset off and realized why Kaylia was now sad. There had to be some communication between ship and docking. She was realizing that she could not do that part. It could prevent her from actually flying the *Wind*, or any ship.

"After we leave Dynuit, remind me to teach you how to automate the ship's comms to send docking messages," I said as I brought the ship in closer to the ring.

I didn't look over but I could see Kaylia smiling again.

I hit a couple of keys and a series of dots and lines appeared on the viewing window. The *Wind* had connected with the stations docking system and was being guided in towards the berth we had been assigned. I followed the directions on my screen, turning the ship. I kept it at an angle so Kaylia could see all the other ships already docked. There were large freighters, small cruisers, a couple in-system cruisers and even a couple of yachts.

"This is the hard part," I told her drawing her attention.

The docking bay was an exterior connection, no hanger to fly into and no magbarrier. It was airlock only, meaning the ship had to connect directly to the exterior wall. Once there, the stations own gravity held it in place, but it took a bit of maneuvering to get the connection right.

Bay 29 showed up, between a yacht, of a make and model I didn't recognize, and a Yourikal Vessels Heavy Freighter. Using the thrusters I slowed the *Wind* and turned it around so it was facing away from the station. Kaylia stood up, trying to look out the view window to see the station.

"Watch your screen," I directed and turned on the vidcam at the rear of the ship.

Her monitor at the co-pilots station now showed a view of the *Wind's* rear and the rounded exterior of the station's docking ring, black gasketing around the perimeter. She watched as a door slid open showing a square room and another door beyond. Out of the room a metal rectangle, the same size and shape of the space, extended out with a black rubber gasket around the edge. Magnetic couplers could be seen at the four corners. The circular ring extended as well, a second layer of connection in case the rectangular connecting tube couldn't get a good seal.

The tricky part was aligning the rear of the ship with the extended gangway, getting the couplers in the right spots so my rear hatch could still open and making sure the gasket fit tightly.

Slowly, with controlled use of the thrusters, I backed the *Wind* up against the gangway. There was a loud bang and four sharp taps as the couplers engaged with the hull of my ship. Lights flashed green on my control panel and I knew we were lined up correctly.

I turned off most of the power to the *Wind* and started to get out of the seat.

"Let's get the cargo unloaded, get paid and do some shopping."

Kaylia was down the hallway towards the stairs that led to the cargo hold before I was even fully out of the chair.

*****

We stood in the *Wind's* cargo hold looking at the metal doors waiting on the signal from Dynuit Docking Control. Kaylia was impatient, she wanted to go and explore the station. She still wore my oversized coat and I'd given her a hat to hide her hair and ears. With the coat and hat, tail still hidden by the coveralls, she really didn't look Thesan.

Which was good.

"The Dynuit are a tribal society," I explained as we waited. "An old custom from their pre-space days was the exchange of gifts. One tribe visiting another would bring a gift and get a gift in return. They still do that today."

A green light flashed on the display and I hit the button. The doors slid to the side and revealed the gray colored interior of the gangway and two aliens, Nuits. They stood my height with a slight stooped posture. Their legs were short with a long body and very long arms. One was gray, the other more black. Both were bald and wore matching uniforms. Their eyes were dark pits of black, almost hidden in their flat faces. No noses, just two angled slits below the eyes.

The one in back held a rifle of a manufacture I didn't recognize. His eyes searched the hold of the ship behind me. The other held a datapad and looked more official, some chips of something on it's uniform probably signifying rank.

"Welcome to Dynuit Station," the one in front said in heavily accented Tradelan looking at the datapad. "Your cargo has been cleared," it said and looked up into my hold with a little bit of surprise.

The three crates stood out as the only things in the hold.

"Slow day," I said.

The Nuit made a gesture that I assumed was a shrug. It was a movement of the shoulders anyways. He could have been giving me their equivalent of the finger for all I knew.

"Your cargo can be unloaded into the secure storage just outside the doors, Bay 29," he said pointing behind him towards the rest of the docking bay. "We have dockhands available for a small fee."

"I'm good thanks."

The Nuit made the same gesture. The one with the weapon studied Kaylia and me. I didn't like the attention he paid Kaylia but had to admit she looked a little suspicious in the oversized jacket and hat. He looked from her to me. I gave him a look that I hoped was just enough 'back off, mind your own business' but not aggressive and threatening enough to cause an issue.

"As you wish," the lead Nuit said and looked right at me. "Welcome to Dynuit Station."

"Thank you," I replied, reaching into my pocket and pulling out a couple credchips that I placed into the Nuit's open and waiting hand.

He glanced at the chips, nodded, and turned. The other followed with one last glance at Kaylia and me.

"Enjoy your stay."

The airlock door swished shut behind them.

I turned to go get the maglifter when Kaylia tugged at my sleeve. I looked down at her hands and she moved them through a series of gestures.

You bribed him?

I laughed as I led her to where the maglifter was stored.

"Remember how I said one tribe gave gifts to the other?"

She nodded.

"That was our gift."

Kaylia thought about it for a minute and then signed something in reply.

What about their gift to us?

"They let us land at their station."

She thought about it some more. Just another example of how sheltered I was finding her upbringing to be. I didn't think Kaylia had learned much about the way the world really worked while living on Turesa.

That is not how it should work.

"No kiddo, it's not," I agreed. "Now come on. I'll teach you to use the maglifter."

*****

The gangway doors opened to a large space. Pushing the maglifter Kaylia stepped out and stopped, her head turning every which way. I smiled as I stepped up next to her. It was a common sight for me, but could see how it would be amazing for her.

Bright metal with track lighting built in stretched in both directions for a good distance. The docking ring was so big that you could barely make out the curving at the far ends. Doors like the ones we had passed were spaced along the outer edge, each with large writing above them in a variety of languages from Tradelan and Nuit to more obscure but common ones. Different sizes. Some for cargo, sized like ours and bigger for larger freighters, and small personal doors. I saw Pierd, Tiat and even Dyer. The walls curved up, the top half of the ring, the bottom curve hidden by the floor we were on. Lines of light along the metal floor formed and controlled traffic patterns, directing people where to go.

The ring itself was not that wide, about forty feet to the doors to the wall. Across from us was writing that matched that above our door. Our designated storage. Doors faced doors as the airlocks opened onto the travel ring and across from the corresponding storage rooms that took up most of the space inside the docking bay.

There was so much incoming and outgoing shipping happening at this station, and similar, across the galaxy and between so many varied beings with different languages, monetary needs and morals that systems had been developed to handle it. You offloaded into a designated locker and got a code. Once payment had been made, you gave the code to the buyer and both parties inputted acknowledgment to the stations Dock Control. The shipper could no longer access the storage, only the person taking possession of the cargo. For outgoing it worked the same way just in reverse.

It helped protect both parties and insured one got paid and the other got their product.

There were ways to cheat the system of course and there were still a lot of illegal and back alley deals, but the system helped a lot.

It also sped up the process as the system could be set up to do automatic payments once all the cargo was scanned and put into the storage unit. Since each crate was scantagged, it worked pretty well and the cargo's recipient didn't ever need to physically meet with the freight hauler.

A lot different then dealing with asteroids like CU145792 out in Deep Space.

Once all three crates were in storage, I was technically free to leave the station. Normally I would have gone looking for another delivery but this time was different.

I ended up taking the maglifter from Kaylia, she was spending too much time looking around.

Couldn't blame her.

The ring was crowded.

Beings of all shapes and sizes roamed the hall. It was an orderly chaos. Maglifters moved crates and other containers. Hovercrafts moved people from one end to the other. I stopped to let one pass and had to grab Kaylia by the collar and pull her along.

Unloading the three crates with one maglifter and by myself, well keeping an eye on a young Thesan that was interested in everything, took a bit of time. Really the thing that took the longest was moving the crates across the ring through the crowds, having to stop for hovercrafts and larger maglifts. I should have hired one of the Nuit's dockhands with their larger maglifts and could have had this done in one trip. I could have found a way to charge Lil.

The last crate was put in the hold and the door was closed and locked. My wristcomm beeped almost immediately to let me know that I had received my pay. There was also a note with another job offer from Tesk Un Lil. I quickly scanned it. Would have been a good little job but it was the opposite direction from where I was going. I hit a couple buttons and declined the offer. I told him I was already booked, that way he would still use me in the future.

"Come on kid," I said tapping Kaylia on the shoulder. Her eyes had been following a family of Tusgars. "Let's do some shopping."

CHAPTER SIX

I led her down the ring towards the arm that connected it to the main station. Her eyes still looked everywhere. She was definitely sheltered. Probably here and the Oval on CU145792 were the only other places she had been, and on the asteroid she had been running and scared with no time to sightsee. I didn't think Turesa was that big and probably didn't get much traffic but it did get some. Some of these assorted beings shouldn't have been new to her.

But Kaylia was acting like everything was new.

How sheltered had she been?

We walked with the flow of people heading in towards the station. The path was lined with lights and painted, helping keep the traffic moving. Middle was reserved for small cargo with the edges made for walking. Right moved towards the station, left moved towards the docking bays from the station. Beneath us were the larger tunnels used for transporting bigger cargo. Efficient and easy to understand regardless of what planet you were from or what language you spoke. You walked in on one side and out the other.

Space stations were all built relatively the same. It was an easy to duplicate design, could be retrofitted for most any type of species. And keeping it similar helped the people that went from station to station. Like me. There were differences obviously, like the armed Nuit standing at guard periodically, but they were close enough that someone visiting a new station could easily find their way.

We turned with the traffic into the connecting arm and almost got run over as Kaylia stopped dead in her tracks.

"Sorry," I muttered to the beings behind us as I pulled her over to the side. Got lots of annoyed glances, I gave some back.

Kaylia was looking up. I smiled, realizing what new wonder had got her attention. This one was worth pausing for. It was a beautiful and cool sight.

The arm was about thirty feet in diameter, the floor was a moving walkway in two directions, but it was the walls that caught her attention. They were clear, made of polycarbonite, and you could see the stars. The station itself loomed over everything but it just added to the breathtaking sight. The large cylinder, millions of lights and windows, with the black of space and the bright spots of the stars behind it. The gas giant to the bottom, asteroids further out and ships moving around.

A sight I'd seen so many times but standing there with Kaylia I was reminded of how amazing it really was.

"Come on kid," I said and nudged her onto the walkway.

She stood at the edge and looked out at the vastness of space beyond. The walkway moved us along and she just watched space. I smiled. There was a naivete about Kaylia, complete innocence. I knew there was more to her story, but that could wait. For now, she could just enjoy the stars.

We got to the other end quickly and reluctantly Kaylia followed me to the bank of lifts, one last look at the stars. There were over a dozen large ones, all speeding up to the various levels that made up the station. If I remembered right, the Dynuit station had ten levels in total, five above the docking arm and five below. Some of the ones above were living quarters for the stations inhabitants. The rest were mercantile and entertainment.

Many people lived on the stations, some were born and died there; never setting foot on a planet. Weird.

We entered one of the lifts along with over a dozen other beings, the door closing behind us, and I went to hit the button for the seventh floor. That was where the gambling hall and my favorite bars were. I caught myself in time and switched to the fifth floor. The shops.

Had almost forgotten the kid was with me and we weren't here for fun. We were here to get some clothes for her, some supplies and then leave.

A couple seconds later and we stepped onto a floor I had never been on. I was just as overwhelmed as the kid had been. Shops lined the walls as well as the middle of the floor. Some back to back forming walkways between them So many stores. It was like a miniature city.

There were a ton of beings too. Lots of young ones, kids. The signs were all bright, there was some kind of music playing and it was loud. So very loud. And annoying.

I was already getting a headache.

*****

The next level we went to was more my speed. It wasn't as loud, but it was still packed. At least it had ale.

Level six was the restaurant level. After shopping for some clothes, we came to get some food. Kaylia was still wearing my oversized jacket and the hat. She liked it for some reason and refused to take it off. Which I was fine with. Probably still smart to hide her identity as much as possible. The overalls were gone and she had bought a decent outfit. Pants and boots, brown and black, with a short sleeve shirt. I'd had her buy a couple different outfits. It was a couple days journey to Turesa.

Her tail was swishing back and forth, happy to be free probably.

The food was good and I was able to relax for a bit.

I hadn't realized how much adrenaline I'd been running on. Even the downtime from the asteroid to here had been pretty hectic. I really hadn't relaxed since I had met Kaylia. Once we got back on the *Wind* and heading for Turesa, I'd be amped up again.

I watched the kid eat for a bit wondering when she had gone from being the Thesan girl to being the kid. Taking a drink of the ale I looked around the crowd. I had chosen a restaurant that had an open wall that overlooked the main walking area and a decent view of the lifts. Having Kaylia wasn't affecting that habit of mine, I always wanted a view of the exits and where I could get the lay of the land.

There was nothing out of the ordinary. Just beings of all kinds going about their business. No one seemed to be paying us any attention. Which was good.

I kept my eye out for Thesans, but didn't see any.

The thought was to hand Kaylia off with them. She'd probably be better off with her own kind, right? But doing that just didn't feel right. It felt like passing the buck, ditching the responsibility. She had chosen me, by accident sure, but she was now under my care. It might have started as an accident, but all my actions since was me choosing her.

Finishing up her food, her hands flashed at me.

Can we look around at the other levels?

"Sorry kiddo, we need to head out," I said standing up and looking around again. Always take another sweep before moving out. When you started to make a move, that's when the calm around you started to shift as others reacted. Look to see who reacts to your movements. That was a holdover from my old Special Operations days. I'd never lost that habit because some of the jobs I took on were dangerous and I had my share of enemies.

Kaylia stood and nodded, obviously disappointed. Probably realizing that once she was home on Turesa the chances of seeing a place like this again were slim.

We stepped out of the restaurant and into the crowd. I kept one hand on her shoulder to help push her along, she was still wanting to look at everything, and the other laying lightly on my holstered blaster. We moved slowly towards the elevator, my eyes searching everyone in front of us.

I should have been looking behind as well.

We were maybe twenty feet away from the doors when I saw an alien step next to Kaylia and grab her arm. Before I could do anything I felt the tip of a blaster hard against my back. It had happened quickly and smoothly. Professionally.

"Don't do anything stupid," a rough and deep voice said quietly. "Follow them," it added with a nudge of the gun.

The being holding onto Kaylia looked over her shoulder at me. A female Garand, a little shorter than I was. Long silvery white hair, very pretty face with dark purple eyes and blue gray skin with horns a shade different coming from the sides of her head behind her large pointed ears. The horns curled back and down to her neck with the tips turning out. Four tendrils, two on each side, grew from below the horns and hung over her shoulders, the ends capped in a soft gray metal. She wore nondescript brown shirt and pants, her thick tail hanging down to her knees, banded in the same gray metal. I looked down at her legs, bent backwards at the knee and ending in what looked like a hoof. I looked back up into the pretty face with eyes that were cold, hard and unfriendly. Kaylia looked back at me, scared, and I just nodded trying to project reassurance even though I didn't feel it.

This was not a good situation.

Chances were good that I could disarm the guy behind me and get out of this. But not with the second person and Kaylia being involved. The crowd didn't help any either. The being with the blaster in my back might not open fire in the middle of the crowd but could still do some damage.

Best bet was to let this play out for a bit.

"Right," the one behind me said and nudged me that direction.

The Garand guiding Kaylia pushed her that way. We were heading towards a door, pushing our way through the light crowd. No one paid us much attention, beyond the angry glances at being forced to move. With so many different people and cultures, no one wants to ever get involved.

The unmarked door was set in the wall between the first shops and the lifts, a keypad next to it. Probably to the maintenance corridors and employee areas. The Garand reached out and hit numbers on the keypad, the door sliding silently into the wall. The room beyond was dark and she pulled Kaylia into it.

I paused and looked around quickly. I didn't like going into a dark room and that they knew the code meant they had most likely been in the room already. They knew the layout, I did not.

"Move," the Garand behind me said and jammed the blaster hard into the small of my back. I was assuming he was a Garand because they usually operated in mated pairs so it was a safe assumption.

I couldn't wait to shove that gun down it's mouth. Male Garands were big bastards, but that wouldn't stop me.

I stepped into the room a couple of feet and heard the door shut behind me. There were no lights, it was dark and I could barely make out the darker shadows that were the female Garand and Kaylia. The one behind me pushed me forward hard and I stumbled a bit.

The lights came on and I saw we were in a square room, a couple storage closets along the wall, a hanging rack that was currently empty and what looked like lockers on another wall. A door was directly across. The female Garand had turned Kaylia around so she was facing me. The Garand had her arm hanging on Kaylia's shoulder and under her chin. A clear sign to not do anything.

Kaylia was putting on a brave face. I knew she would be close to breaking. Kidnapped and now being held prisoner like this? She had to be wondering why this was happening to her.

I was getting angry. If they hurt her in any way they were dead.

Turning I saw the male Garand and he was a big one. About six inches taller than I was, but almost twice as wide. Garands are broad shouldered and built. Big and strong. He had the backwards bending knee and hooves like the female, along with the dark purple eyes and bluish gray skin.

HIs face was blocky with horns that curled to the side growing from his forehead. Hanging from his chin were four long tendrils with another two hanging down his back coming from behind his pointed ears. I could see the end of his tail behind him, just hanging there. Unlike many other species with tails, for some reason the Garands wasn't used. It was just there.

He still had the blaster pointed at me. A Duig Model XC. Decent gun. Good range, accurate and had a stun feature.

"Who are you," I asked. I moved and shifted so I could see the male Garand, and his mate with her arm around Kaylia's neck as well as the two doors. I took a couple steps back to get some more distance.

"I was going to ask you the same question," the male Garand replied. "But it doesn't matter. We're just interested in her." He pointed at Kaylia with his free hand, the point of the blaster never wavering from me. "Let us leave with her and you won't get hurt."

"Why do you want her," I asked.

The Garand's eyes never left mine, neither of them. The female held Kaylia tight but wasn't watching her.

"There's a big bounty out on a Thesan girl matching her description. Traveling alone or with a non-Thesan companion."

Great. Bounty hunters. But they didn't have my full description. That was good. I was surprised that the Tiat would go to bounty hunters but it really was the only way to spread the net across the galaxy. They probably limited it to a select few hunters. No way this was broadcast to everyone. I'd known a few hunters through the years and while they were all out for the money, some of them had a moral code or just hated the Tiat.

"This isn't her," I tried. "You got the wrong girl."

"Maybe we do, maybe we don't," the male said with a shrug of his shoulders. "Only one way to find out."

Of course these would be the moral less kind of hunters.

"Might as well drop that blaster," the Garand said looking down at my weapon. "Slowly or the girl gets hurt," he added.

Keeping my hands out, left one up where they could see it, I lowered my right to grab my weapon. I had to find a way out of this. These two would take Kaylia and turn her over to the Tiat. I couldn't let that happen. I used a couple fingers to grab the blaster and lift it out by the grip. I was looking at the male Garand, his gun pointed at me and concentrating on my hand and gun, when there was a sudden movement from the female and Kaylia.

The female Garand yelled in pain, sharp and loud.

I looked that way quickly, fingers turning into a firm grasp on my blaster's grip. Kaylia's fingernails had grown again, long and sharp like claws. One hand was buried in the Garand's side and the other in the arm across Kaylia's neck.

There was an angry hiss and growl that I realized was coming from Kaylia. With her claws buried in the Garand, Kaylia pulled the arm free. Her other hand ripped out of the Garand's side, prompting another scream of pain. Kaylia turned and somehow her small body had the strength to push the bleeding Garand to the ground. Blue blood dripped from the Garand's wounds and from Kaylia's claws.

The male Garand was stunned and so was I. Neither of us moved. I was frozen in the act of drawing my weapon. The Garand frozen half-turned with his weapon turning to point at Kaylia.

She crouched down, fury in her eyes, blood dripping from her claws. She hissed and growled at the Garand and took a step forward.

I pulled my weapon out of the holster and aimed at the Garand but he had recovered faster. His weapon was pointed right at Kaylia now and he pulled the trigger. A bolt of blue-white energy shot out and struck her in the stomach, streaks of energy cascading around her. She fell backwards a couple of feet, falling limply to the ground, hitting hard.

"NO," I yelled. A sound of pure rage.

I hoped the Garand's blaster was set to stun. Mine was not.

I pulled my trigger, a greenish bolt of energy shooting from my weapon hitting the Garand in the chest, just below his head and between the tendrils. The alien fell to the ground, smoke rising from the wound.

Keeping my weapon pointed at the female Garand, who was trying to stop the bleeding from her wounds and trying to pull herself across the floor to her dead mate, I ran to Kaylia. She lay in a heap on the ground, her fingernails back to normal but stains of blue blood on the tips.

I saw her chest rising slowly. Stunned.

Breathing a sigh of relief, weapon still pointed towards the Garand, I bent down to pick up Kaylia. Her body was so light, she was so small. How had she managed to throw the much heavier Garand? Where had that rage come from?

She was awkward but there was no way I was using two hands to carry her. The male Garand was dead and while she was wounded, the female might still be dangerous. She didn't look it, bleeding out of multiple wounds and cradling the head of her mate. I regretted killing the bounty hunter but he had shot Kaylia.

Stun blasts were supposed to be non-lethal, but they could still damage a body. With the wide variety of beings in the galaxy, there was no way to create a stun frequency that treated all the same. It was just impossible. Each manufacturer had their own frequency which complicated things even further. Most humanoids were generally the same size, which was what most stunners were set for, there were still occurrences of permanent damage from being stunned.

I needed to get Kaylia back to the *Wind* where I could run some tests on her, make sure she was okay.

Opening the door against the far wall, I stepped into a long corridor that ringed the outer shops of this level. I looked back into the room and met the eyes of the female Garand.

There was hatred there, pure hatred. The door closed behind me. I leaned Kaylia's body against the wall and aimed for the control pad. The blast was loud in the silent hall, the metal cover falling apart and sparks erupting from the crackling wires.

Holstering my blaster, I picked up Kaylia and ran down the corridor looking for a way out.

CHAPTER SEVEN

Why me?

Kahlia signed at me from where she lay on the bed in her room.

"I don't know kiddo," I said pulling the blanket up around her. "But I promise you that we'll find out when we get you home."

What is happening to me?

She held up one of her hands and looked at the remnants of the blue blood that was around her nails. Once we had gotten back to the ship, and that had taken a while, I had cleaned her up the best I could. She had woken from the stun blast midway to the ship, which was a surprise. That blast should have had her out for hours. So far everything seemed fine, no lasting effects from the blast.

"I don't know but we're figure it out," I replied and it felt weak, inadequate. I brushed a loose strand of hair from her check. "Get some rest. Next stop is Turesa."

I stood up as she turned on her side and closed her eyes. She'd be asleep in no time. The stress from the short fight and flight as well as still shaking off the effects of the stun blast, would have her out. But it wouldn't be a restful sleep.

As I walked out of her room, I turned the light off, and headed for the bridge.

We were already in wildspace, our first hop would take three hours. I had laid her in the lounge well I got us out of Dynuit Station. I had carried her through the back corridors and out a door midway around the station. I'd managed to get to the lifts without drawing attention but it was a nerve racking walk. Couldn't move too fast, had to carry Kaylia in a way that wouldn't draw the eye, and had to keep my eyes out for the other Garand and any other hunters that might be around. Finally had managed to get to the lift and down to the docking ring. She'd woken up as we were in the lift.

Groggy, she hadn't been scared at waking in the changed surroundings so I had been able to explain what happened.

Once on the ship I had to get Dock Control to give me an immediate departure slot. That took a bit of doing and convincing. Half an hour later, the first hop calculated and we were out of that system. That's when I finally managed to put Kaylia to bed.

I wanted to go back to the galley and grab an ale but as we flew out of the system I had noticed a message had come in on the Feed well we were on the station and avoiding bounty hunters. Now that Kaylia was resting, I could view it.

Putting the headset on, so the noise wouldn't carry out of the bridge, I hit the play button.

The vidscreen filled with the head of a man, human. Much older than me, hair all gray with brown eyes. The hair was close cut, a military style, and he wore the uniform of an Earth Expeditionary Forces officer. There were wrinkles around the eyes and he had a face and look that had seen a lot and barely survived it. Colonel Terrence Jessups.

My former commanding officer and one of the few people in the galaxy that I trusted.

"Captain," the message began and that voice brought back a flood of memories.

Even though I was no longer in the military, Jessups still called me by my rank. Just hearing the voice made me want to snap to attention. Some habits were never lost.

"I looked into that name you sent me. I couldn't find much and most of what I found was classified far beyond my paygrade. What I did find was that a Thesan named Yoterra was part of their War Applications Division. You know the stories associated with them. That was all I could find. Sorry Captain." He paused and the look changed, the military commander fading and a man that was like a father to me replaced it. "I don't know what you got yourself involved with, but the coding on the files I found was pretty high up. That along with what the Thesan War Applicators were up to, you're getting into some deep waters that you may not be able to swim in. Watch your six."

The message terminated and I took off the headset, leaning back in my chair.

I really needed that ale now.

*****

Forty years ago the Earth developed the tech to explore our solar system. We settled on Mars and one of the moons of Jupiter, Europa. We couldn't escape our solar system yet but our advancements had caught the attention of the Thesans. Thirty years ago they had helped develop our warpthrusters and once we had those, we expanded out into the larger galaxy and the Earth Expeditionary Forces, nicknamed the 2Es, were created. We're human, so our first impulse was to expand and the Thesans were happy to do that with us.

Turned out that the Thesans were looking for allies to help them expand and protect their territory. Another species, the Tiat, were aggressively taking over more and more systems. The Thesans wanted to strengthen their own forces and expand their influence, while using us as a buffer against the Tiat. They thought they could dominate us, as we were the newbies to space. That was quickly proven wrong.

The alliance didn't necessarily start out on the right foot, Terrans and Thesans have been strong allies since that day. It's kind of a mutual aid thing. No one else really likes us. Or the Tiat. But the Tiat are strong enough to stand on their own.

One of the first places beyond our neighboring systems that humans expanded into was a system that the Tiat had designs over as well.

And the Third Galactic War happened. The Tiat versus the Thesan/Terran Alliance. It went on for years and spilled out into other systems. Billions died on all three sides, as well as countless members of other races caught in the crossfire. The Tiat outnumbered our Alliance and the Thesans were starting to get desperate.

That's where the War Applications Division entered the picture. They were the idea factory. Anything that could help end the war in the Thesans favor. Some of the stuff never saw the light of day, thankfully, but the stuff that did was pretty bad. Not the brightest spot in Thesan history.

I'd run into some remnants of War Applications stuff during my time in service, and that was years after the war ended with the non-aggression treaty signed between the three parties. What I had seen was enough. I couldn't imagine what they had been up to during the height of the war.

What did a former member of the Division have to do with Kaylia?

Had a feeling that I wasn't going to like the answer.

*****

The next stop wasn't Turesa. We had to stop half way there at a station in the Hui System to refuel. Kaylia stayed in the ship well I was dealing with Hui Station Control to get what we needed. The first day of the trip after Dynuit, she had spent in her room recovering and dealing with the realization that something was happening to her. It was hard as she had no idea what was happening, the changes to her body as well as people hunting her. I tried to comfort her as best I could, but this was beyond my limited abilities.

I did some research and it definetely wasn't normal Thesan development. At her age, Terran kids started going through puberty. I had hoped this was a Thesan equivalent. Nope. On top of the wildness and other changes associated with it, she also had the Thesan version to still look forward to.

Poor kid.

We spent most of the early time after leaving Dynuit either on the bridge or in the lounge working on my sign language.

I did wonder at a couple points why I was bothering with this. I'd be dropping her off soon and then back to my life. It wasn't a great life, constantly moving and by myself, but it was my life.

I read a lot, it's a good way to pass the time while flying through wildspace, and Kaylia dug into my collection. I had a couple tablets connected to the ship's library and she took one as her own, downloaded a couple of books onto it and would disappear for hours into the novel. When we had stopped at Hui Station, I showed her how to get more books from the Feed and she grabbed a couple that fit her interests. From Hui Station on, we were either in the bridge or lounge and there was usually a book being read.

We didn't talk much and it was fine, a companionable silence.

The trip was only a couple of days and we settled into a routine that surprisingly I found I enjoyed. I was used to being by myself and now I had this kid along. I was okay with that.

But it was only for another couple days then back to normal.

I didn't question her anymore, there was no need. Everything would be answered soon enough. Kaylia asked me a couple questions about myself; where I came from and so on. I told her. I didn't hold anything back. I didn't go out of my way to give all the details but if she asked, I answered truthfully.

She had given herself to my protection and she deserved to know who I was, what kind of person I was.

Why the..

Kaylia started to sign and paused, unable to figure out the right way to say what she wanted. She waved her hands to indicate the ship, reaching over and patting the back wall of the bridge.

"Why is she called *Nomad's Wind*?"

She nodded.

I leaned back in my chair, looking around at the control stations with pride.

"Nomad means wanderer. And a nomad's wind is what pushes the nomad around so they don't stay in one place for long."

She thought about it for a bit and nodded, satisfied with the answer. A couple seconds later she was back buried in the book.

I looked around the bridge, thinking back to the day that I had bought the ship. There had been no name picked, I wasn't even sure what I was looking for. Just a vague idea of what I wanted to do. I'd been in the military for so long and I was ready to just roam. I saw the ship and the name just came to me, fitting what my life was going to be. A nomad, going where the wind took me.

*****

Turesa came into view.

A small blue green planet, mostly green with some blue, that had a single small moon orbiting it. The system had four planets revolving around the sun and Turesa was the third and only inhabited one. They had no space station, all traffic going to the planet. Out of the way and colonized by the Thesan, there was no native race to the planet, the traffic was relatively light. And since the war, the Thesan heavily patrolled the system.

Our hop put us at the end of the system, just past the fourth planet.

Kaylia was looking out the view window at the planet before us.

Is that Turesa?

"No, I don't know what it's called," I replied to her signing. She hadn't actually said the planets name but I knew what she meant. She had signed 'home'. "No one lives on it. See that larger bright spot just beyond?"

I stood up so I could point. She came around and leaned against me so she could use my arm to help find the spot. Her fur tickled the bare skin of my arm.

"That's Turesa."

She stayed standing as we flew that way. The fourth planet grew larger as we passed it, filling up most of the view window and then disappearing behind us. I saw the moving points of light before she did. Her eyes widened as she caught the movement and turned towards me.

Shooting stars?

"No, other ships."

I had known they were coming, they had shown up on the scanners a couple minutes ago.

The streaks, two of them, came closer and details could now be seen. They became gray pyramid like shapes, the point facing us with the lower half of the pyramid larger than the top half. A wing separated the two. Lights dotted the ship, some blinking and some constant. The barrels of two weapons could be seen mounted to the ends of the wings.

They each came along the side of the *Wind*, taking up position behind me. Kaylia looked both ways as they passed. She recognized the shapes.

Those are Thesan.

"Yeah, patrol ships, should be hailing us," I started to say when they did.

"Freighter, identify yourself," the voice said over the comms.

I had turned the speakers on so Kaylia could hear.

"*Nomad's Wind*, Terran registry bound for Choni City."

During the hops to the system I had asked Kaylia where she was from, which was a small settlement outside the capitol city. I then needed to figure out the best way to get onto the planet. I had no official cargo documentation, no cargo flying in and no order to pick some up, so we needed a reason to be allowed to land.

"Please transmit documentation to land."

"I have none but I am seeking an audience with Governor Yoterra."

This was the hard part. They could just choose to ignore me, in which case I wouldn't be landing. If that happened, we'd leave the system and I'd have to track down a cargo or try to contact the Governor from off system.

Why didn't I do that in the first place? Too many eyes and ears that way. Bringing a cargo would have taken time and all incoming ships could be watched by the Tiat or whoever else was involved. If I had been them, I would have set up a trap using cargo knowing I would need a way to get on planet. No one would really expect me to just go straight to the top There would be a lot of ears that could and would hear this request but now it'd only be hours compared to days.

And with bounty hunters looking for Kaylia, the quicker she got to the safety provided by Yoterra, the better she'd be.

"Reason for the audience," the pilots voice came back and the tone was one of annoyance. Could tell the pilot would have rather given me the brush off but someone on the other end had told him to humor me. The oddity of the request would have made someone interested.

And here came the risky part.

"Tell the Governor that I have something she is missing."

I was making a lot of assumptions. It started with assuming that Yoterra knew Kaylia had survived, that the Tiat had faked her death. That led to there being a cover-up of some kind to keep the news quiet. The Tiat were keeping it quiet and there had been no broadcast by the Thesans, so that was a safe assumption to make. If the Tiat had bounty hunters out looking, another safe assumption was that the Thesans would also.

That all led to me assuming that if I told Yoterra that I had what she was missing then she'd see me.

The minutes dragged as I waited for a response. We were still heading towards the planet and the patrol ships had yet to warn me off, so that was a good sign. Kaylia had sat back down at the co-pilots station and was looking worried. I flashed her a thumbs up and what I hoped was my most reassuring smile.

"*Nomad's Wind*, you are cleared to proceed to Choni City," the pilot finally said and I breathed a sigh of relief. "Proceed to docking pad 13."

"Acknowledged," I said. "Pad 13."

Kaylia smiled, not looking as worried. I kept the reassuring smile on my face. I didn't want her to know that was probably the easiest part.

The more I thought about, the more the whole situation stunk. My gut told me that Yoterra could be trusted with Kaylia, but I wasn't ready to relax just yet. Something about all of this still bothered me.

Scanners showed one of the patrol ships veer off, back on it's route. The other stayed right behind the *Wind*, where I couldn't get at him but he could get at me. Nothing I could do about that one, so no need to worry about it.

The course set in, I leaned back in the chair and tried to relax. At these speeds, Turesa was about an hour away. Kaylia watched the planet get bigger and I tried to run through scenarios of what to expect once we got planetside.

I wondered what Kaylia was thinking. She sat in the co-pilot's chair, legs pulled up tight, and looked out the viewwindow not showing any emotion. This was where her parents had died, so she would need to confront that. But she was also going home after being kidnapped, so she had to be happy about that. She was probably also wondering how safe she really would be. No family and not knowing why the Tiat had taken her. Would they try to do it again?

Turesa loomed larger; the blue, green and white of the clouds filling the viewwindow. Less and less of the black of space was shown, replaced with a full view of the planet. The *Wind* shook a little as it entered the atmosphere.

I glanced down at a screen on my console and saw coordinates and navguidance. I didn't let them have control of the *Wind* but I followed the route they outlined. The patrol ship was still behind us and as we broke atmosphere and came in under the clouds, the ship veered off. It flew across our front, letting us get one last look and a last warning that they'd still be around, before returning to its patrol.

We came in over an ocean dotted with small islands with a larger landmass ahead. I could see buildings appearing, a seaside city. Details sharpened into focus. The city was made up of short structures, only ten stories at the most and that was very few of them. Most of the buildings were only five stories with many down to two. Built of brown colored metal with curving architecture. There were a lot of windows, with rounded shapes and decorations. Visible beams were at the edges, extending up past the curved roofs and out past the walls. Small ships could be seen flying around the city in what looked to be orderly chaos. None got that high, never over the tops of the tallest buildings. There were even ships on the water, just floating along.

The route had us turn so we lost our view. Choni City had looked interesting. Not overly large, maybe only a hundred thousand citizens. The water below us was crystal clear, a bright blue. Waves crashed against the shore and the cliffs.

Sunlight glinted off what appeared to be buildings off to the side along the top of the cliffs. We were directed towards them and saw rows of long hanger buildings. The ground was a dark gray with lights embedded in it forming traffic patterns. Even the hangers were curved, half circles. That made them larger than they needed to be but made for interesting shapes. Like the buildings, there were visible beams that extended out past the edges.

The one we were directed to was near the front edge. I could see many ships of different shapes and sizes but most were of Thesan construction, civilian and military. Where their buildings were rounded, their ships were all sharp angles like the patrol ships. I saw none of those there, so they must have been docked somewhere else. I half expected to see some hovering over the hangers but nothing was visible.

I figured there were some space defense cannons somewhere tracking the *Wind*. I had that itch between my shoulderblades that I used to get when someone pointed a gun at me. Not a comfortable feeling.

Slowing the *Wind*, I brought it to a hover over the designated landing spot, a ring of lights in front of a hanger. The doors were closed, a clear indication that I was not to park inside the building. Yeah, they definitely had some weapons pointed my way. The thrusters mounted to the underside of the ship held us up and I slowly lowered it, turning in a circle so the nose was pointed the way we had come.

The nice thing about a starship in atmosphere was that it didn't need a specific direction to fly in order to get off the planet. Get into the air and point it anywhere. But this direction I was facing towards the city and put the *Wind's* aft towards the other ships. That was where the strongest shields were.

With a little bumping the *Wind* settled down on the ground. I shifted the engines to standby and unbuckled from the seat. Kaylia stood up, setting the tablet down on the console.

"Come on kiddo."

She tried to smile but it faded. She was nervous. I put an arm around her shoulder and pulled her into me, squeezing. We walked out of the bridge and she ran her hand along the smooth metal wall of the bunk hall. I took the spiral stairs first, walking down into the galley. Kaylia was slow, somewhat reluctant.

The hold was empty, it seemed giant and our footsteps on the metal seemed to echo through the space. We got to the aft mounted door and I stopped and turned, pointing Kaylia to the side where she was out of sightline from the door.

"Wait here."

She looked up at me questioningly. I shrugged. There was no real reason why she couldn't come out with me. I was probably being paranoid. Or maybe I wasn't ready to hand her over yet?

Either way she was staying right there for now.

"Wait here and I'll call for you," I said and added. "Don't come out for anyone else okay?"

Kaylia nodded. She was a smart kid, I think she got it.

I checked to make sure my blaster was on stun. A good rule of thumb when dealing with different cultures is to not kill. There have been plenty of misunderstandings that usually can be talked around if you only stun someone. Killing tends to end negotiations and encounters.

Keying in the code, the door slid open and I stepped out onto Turesa.

The air was thick, humid. I hadn't realized that it was a jungle world. The sun was bright in the sky and I reached a hand up to shield my eyes.

In a small group in front of me were half a dozen Thesans. Two looking official, one of them I recognized as Yoterra and a male that was probably her assistant. The other four were military, dressed in uniforms I recognized from my time in service, and all armed. None looked on alert so that was a good sign.

I took a couple steps forward, hands hanging loosely at my side.

"You are Arek Lancer, Captain of the *Nomad's Wind* and former Captain in the Earth Expeditionary Forces," Yoterra said, a statement. She looked exactly like she had in the news article but the film had not captured her commanding presence. She stood straight, hands clasped behind her back. If she was nervous or excited or anything at all, she didn't show it.

Attractive but stark. There was no softness to her.

"That's me," I said.

"You said you have something that I'm missing," she prompted. This was not a woman that had a lot of patience. From the tone of voice, I could tell she knew what my message had meant.

I glanced at the others around her.

"You can trust them."

Nodding I studied her. She was a Planetary Governor, she had power and she had to be somewhat ruthless to get to that position. She had been in the Thesan War Applications Division, which told me another thing about her. Willing to do what needed to be done for her people. I searched harder and there it was. In her eyes. She held her body rigid, controlled, but the eyes. There was hope there. Worry and caring.

"Kaylia," I called and watched Yoterra's eyes.

I could hear Kaylia behind me, stepping down out of the *Wind*. Yoterra's facade cracked. She smiled, her eyes lighting up. I glanced behind me and saw a similar smile on Kaylia's face. Kaylia was about level with me when I saw a motion out of the corner of my eye. One of the guards.

"Down," I yelled and dove at Kaylia.

I grabbed her, twisting so we fell onto my back and heard the sizzle of an energy blast hit the side of the ship. The sparks flew, falling around us, as the bolt dissipated into a fury of energy.

"For A New Thesa," a voice rang out.

Standing up, pushing Kaylia behind me, I drew my blaster and switched it from stun to kill.

I pointed it at a shocked looking Yoterra. She was looking at me or Kaylia but at one of the guards, who was now surrounded by the others. His weapon was on the ground and he was being forced to his knees. The other official looking Thesan looked like he wanted to run away and hide.

"What the hell was that," I said angrily weapon pointed at Yoterra.

The guards now saw my weapon and pointed theirs at me.

A stand-off.

I could feel Kaylia behind me. Her body was shaking against mine. The girl was crying silently.

Someone was going to hurt for this.

CHAPTER EIGHT

I kept my blaster pointed at Yoterra while two others were pointed at me. The guard that had shot at us was down on his knees, the last guard's blaster at his head.

Yoterra took a couple steps forward, putting herself between me and her guards. She turned from one to the other, hands up.

"Lower your weapons," she ordered her guards. They hesitated and finally did at a commanding look from her. She turned to me, hands still raised. "Please Captain Lancer, lower your weapon."

I didn't.

The guards moved away from Yoterra, so now I was back in their sightlines and she wasn't. They didn't raise their weapons but they held them ready. I pushed Kaylia tighter behind me and moved us towards the still open hatch to the *Wind*.

"Give me one reason why I shouldn't just board my ship and leave," I said the point of my weapon never wavering.

There was a long pause, Yoterra studying me as I inched us closer to the hatch. She turned and nodded at the guard with the weapon pointed at the prisoner.

The shot of a blaster was the only sound. Followed by the thud of a body hitting the ground.

Smoke drifted out of the hole in the dead guard's head, the one that had shot at us was now laying on the ground.

I didn't lower my weapon but stopped moving us.

"Please," Yoterra said, almost pleading.

"Who was he," I asked motioning at the dead body.

With the prisoner dead, the last guard was now able to point his weapon at me. I hated having blasters pointed at me and now there were three of them.

"A fanatic," Yoterra replied staring down at the body. "I do not know how he got into my personal guard."

"What kind of fanatic?" I didn't care how he had gotten into her guard, just that he was there. Was he the only one?

"The kind that believes in a pure Thesan culture," Yoterra explained. "He and his kind want to erase the sins of our past, not learn and grow from them. They do not like that we expanded beyond our own solar system and they do not like what we did during the war to protect those expansions."

We had folks like that on Earth. They hated the Earth Expeditionary Force and our 'expansionist' ways. They wanted to keep us on earth and not out into the stars, or if we did go out to not take territory. They saw the Third Galactic War as our fault and we should atone for all those lives lost. On one hand they were right, we shouldn't take territory from others and that was what started the war. But on the other hand, if the 2Es hadn't fought the war then we'd all be speaking Tiat right now.

I know which side of that argument I fell on.

"That's great. What does it have to do with Kaylia?"

Her head poked out around my body. I could see streaks of tears down her cheeks. She looked at the dead body and quickly buried her head in my side. She was clutching me tightly. The wind blew the last of the smoke from the wound away.

Yoterra was facing me, but not looking at me, she was looking at Kaylia. Lots of emotions flew across the Governors face. Regret being a big one.

"The Third Galactic War was a terrible one," she began. "You were in the Terran forces, and while it was before your time, I'm sure you've heard the stories. The Tiat were winning and so we started looking into alternative weapons. They outnumbered us and we needed something to even the odds. I oversaw many of those projects."

She paused, shaking her head and looked off towards the city. Her gaze drifted back to me.

"Tell me Captain, have you ever heard of the Thesan Wilders?"

I thought back through all the war stories I had heard or been told. I'd met lots of vets from those days as well as what was told during my classes in basic training. I was a kid for the later part of it, so there was even some stories I had heard when a kid. There had been some stuff on the Thesans and their tactics. What they had done that was different from how we fought a war.

And there was something about a group called the Wilders.

The way I had heard it from an old sergeant was that there were some Thesan special forces. Scary and lethal. If they got dropped into a fight, it was going to be bloody and the Thesans would win.

"A little," I told her. "Thesan special forces. Really black ops, wetworks kind of stuff."

"Yes but not just any special forces." She paused again, taking a deep breath. The words were being forced out of her, like it was something she had not talked or thought about for a long time. "Like you Terrans, we have evolved through the ages. Early Thesans were more primal, animalistic and savage. We had claws, senses that were sharper. Stronger and faster. We were the apex predators and supreme hunters of the jungles."

Claws? Early Thesans had claws? I thought about Kaylia's fingernails and how they seemed to grow into claws. I was afraid of where this was going.

"What if we could somehow get back that savagery but with the intelligence our species had now," Yoterra continued. "It took years but we made it happen. We were able to genetically alter some members of our species. They retained all the knowledge and abilities they had but gained the traits of our ancestors."

I glanced down at Kaylia, she was focused on Yoterra, listening to every word.

"We unleashed them on the Tiat," Yoterra said and there was a touch of pride in her voice. "The Wilders inflicted substantial damage to the Tiat war machine, killing many high ranking officers and government officials. After the war they were retired to live out the rest of their days in peace or so we thought and hoped."

"The Tiat started killing them off," I reasoned.

It wasn't a hard assumption to make. The Tiat were unforgiving and even though the war was over, there had been rumors of hit squads roaming the galaxy. A couple of old Terran generals had been killed and these hit squads were rumored to have done it. There was no proof and so no one could do anything. Legally in the galactic sense, the Planetary Council washed their hands of it. But that was okay, we had our own hit squads that got our revenge.

Or so I heard. Wasn't like I was on one of those squads.

I could see the Tiat doing the same to the Thesans.

"We put the last surviving Wilders into hiding," Yoterra said continuing the story. She was looking at the dead body now. "Not just from the Tiat but some of our own people. They were ashamed of what we had done, what had needed to be done."

"Kaylia's parents?"

I felt the kid stiffen as I asked. Her hands grabbed hold of me tighter. I could feel her trying not to shake.

"They were the last," Yoterra said and her eyes returned to Kaylia. "Except for their children."

*****

I had lowered my blaster but kept it in hand, out of the holster. The guards lowered theirs but kept them ready. I concentrated on Yoterra but glanced at the others to make sure there were no sudden moves.

"And Kaylia has the genetic code of these wilders?" I asked though I already knew the answer.

Kaylia let go of me long enough to look at her hand and fingernails. I put my free arm around her shoulder, giving her a reassuring squeeze.

Yoterra saw the two gestures and raised her eyebrows, questioning me. I ignored it.

"We believe so," came the reply but it was Yoterra's assistant who answered. "There has been no evidence of it." He pause and added quietly well looking at Kaylia, "that we know of."

Silence grew as Yoterra let the information sink in. I glanced down at Kaylia, she looked scared. Very scared. She'd just learned that her parents had been genetically engineered and that changed DNA had been passed down to her. That explained a lot. She was at that age, like Terrans, when the body went through changes. Her's would be even more severe with this cocktail of crazy DNA inside her.

I sighed. Time for the big question. I squeezed Kaylia tighter.

"Why didn't the Tiat kill her?"

Again it was the assistant that answered. He was the same height as Yoterra, younger, with brown fur and darker patches. He wore a tailored suit and carried a tablet. He had looked frightened when the shooting had happened but was now composed again.

"We believe they think they can reverse engineer her," he said in a matter-of-fact tone, like he wasn't talking about dissecting a kid. I didn't like him. "So they can find out how the DNA was altered and possibly use that knowledge on themselves."

The thought of mutant Tiat was pretty damn scary. Terrifying really.

"That's not going to happen," I said and held Kaylia tighter. The idea of someone experimenting on her; Thesan, Tiat or Terran; made me very angry.

"No it will not," Yoterra said, steel in her voice.

Was she concerned with Kaylia or concerned with someone experimenting on Thesans?

I looked down at the body of the Thesan fanatic and then up at Yoterra. She understood what I was getting at.

"I kept her and her family safe and hidden for almost twenty years," Yoterra began, the steel breaking. "I failed them. I will not fail again."

I could tell she took it personally. Kaylia's family had essentially been under Yoterra's protection and had died. I'd take it personally as well.

"Captain Lancer," Yoterra said looking directly at me. "Please."

I holstered my blaster and looked down at Kaylia. She had loosened her grip on me, still holding on with one hand, and had taken a couple steps out from behind me. She was studying Yoterra.

"What's your history with her," I asked. "Kaylia said you were her mother's littermate?"

Yoterra smiled and chuckled. The sound reminded me of a Terran cat's purr.

"Uhunia was not my littermate in truth," Yoterra said but looked at Kaylia like family, like an aunt would. "I was responsible for their safety and we became friends over the years, close enough to be littermates. I've known Kaylia since she was born."

I felt Kaylia grab me tighter at the mention of her mother's name.

"What do you think," I asked Kaylia looking down at her.

She looked from me to Yoterra and back, slowly nodding. Her hand released me and she took a couple steps forward and then some more. I watched her go and went through a lot of different emotions. This was why I had come to Turesa, to hand her off. But part of me wasn't sure that I wanted her to go. I'd grown attached to the kid and liked having her onboard the *Wind*. But this was better. She belonged here and not flying around the galaxy.

Kaylia reached Yoterra and the older woman enveloped her in a hug. That cemented the deal. That was a hug of love. Yoterra really did care for the girl.

With reluctance Yoterra pulled Kaylia out of the hug. She held the girl by the shoulders and smiled.

"It's good to have you home," Yoterra said. She turned to the assistant and the guards. "Please take Kaylia inside and summon a medic to check her over." The Governor was all business again. The assistant walked away, holding an arm around Kaylia to lead her but not touching. One of the guards turned to go with them.

They had gone maybe ten feet when Kaylia turned and ran back. She slammed into me and wrapped her arms around me tightly. I hugged her just as tight. She stepped back and brushed at some tear streaks down her cheeks. I held her shoulders and leaned down to kiss her on the forehead.

"Take care of yourself kiddo."

You too.

She turned and ran back to join the assistant and guard. They continued walking towards a building further down.

"Thank you," Yoterra said, turning back to me.

I stared beyond her, watching Kaylia and the other Thesans turn a corner and go behind a hanger. Why were they going that way? The building Yoterra had indicated was further down and completely in my line of sight?

"Please tell me where you found her? We know approximately when the Tiat kidnappers arrived here but have not been able to figure out how they got on planet."

"She ran into me on CU145792, an asteroid in the Callic Cluster," I said and paused, taking a step forward. Something was wrong.

"What was..," Yoterra began and turned to look behind her, hearing the same thing I was now.

Blasters.

CHAPTER NINE

I ran. Fast. I reacted quickly, quicker than the Thesan guards. I was past Yoterra before she finished her question. I drew my blaster as I went.

One of the guards finally reacted and kept pace alongside me.

We pounded across the metal surface of the ground, booted feet clanging and thumping. I didn't hear any more blasters which wasn't good.

The guard got a couple steps on me. He was in shape. I was not. I don't do much running nowadays. I thought I had managed to give it up since my military days. The hangar building drew closer. There were other Thesans, along with some assorted other beings, stepping out of the hangar and looking confused. They had heard the blasters. They gave us strange looks as we passed. I could see others running towards us, more guards and officials.

Slowing as he rounded the corner, the Thesan held his weapon ready. He disappeared around the corner of the building, between two hangars where I had seen Kaylia go with Yoterra's assistant and guard. Blaster in hand I turned the corner and stopped.

There was a body on the ground, dark in the shadows of the walls. I thought the worse but forced myself to calm and examine the scene, my spec ops instincts taking over. The body was too long for Kaylia and as I walked closer I could make out the uniform of the guard. The other guard was already down at the far end of the hangar, looking at another body. That one was out in the sun and I could tell instantly that it was not Kaylia.

I stopped at the first body long enough to examine it. The Thesan had a large blaster burn on it's back, smoke still rising from the wound and sparks in the clothing. Shot in the back.

At the end of the alley, the other body belonged to a technician. Some tools were scattered on the ground and this one had been shot in the front, laying on his back, the wound still smoking.

Must have surprised the assistant.

I knew it was a leap, but the assistant's body was not here and the guard had been shot in the back. So much for Yoterra being able to trust her people.

Stepping out into the sun I shielded my eyes with my free hand, the light reflecting brightly off the clear water. The guard was a couple steps off in the direction of the city, studying the ground. He turned when heard my footsteps, weapon raised.

"Relax," I said and he lowered his weapon. "What do you have?"

He stood up and pointed.

"That way."

"Lead on," and I motioned him to go, impatient. I knew he'd be the better tracker and I couldn't hear any footsteps or noises. The big drawback of Kaylia being mute was she couldn't scream.

I followed the guard at a jog, making our way through the ankle high green grass. The wind blew in off the sea, making the plains wave. The sun hit the back of the hangars, not reflecting as bad as I thought it would. Some kind of non-reflective paint or material. The assistant had dragged Kaylia and she had been struggling. I could start to see patterns in the grass, wide spots that would have been Kaylia fighting against him.

The Thesan hadn't looked that big or strong, I wondered how he was managing to pull Kaylia after him. I was also wondering why she wasn't fighting harder. When the Garand had held her, Kaylia had reacted and turned into that savage Wilder form. Why wasn't she now?

Then it hit me. The assistant knew about her heritage and what it could mean. He had probably drugged her.

Bastard. When I caught him, I wasn't going to kill him. Not at first. He was going to get hurt but still be able to answer some questions. He wouldn't be alive long after that.

We passed by two hangars. They couldn't be that far ahead of us. There was no way the assistant was moving faster than we were. Yeah, he'd had a bit of a head start but we should be catching up. That's when I heard the whine of thrusters.

Dammit.

The third hangar had a rear door open and we picked up our pace but it wasn't fast enough.

A small hovercar flew out of the opening, turning towards the city. It was a couple feet off the ground, pushing the grasses aside. Fairly standard model, open top with a windshield on the front, thrusters on the bottom and a larger engine mounted to the back. I couldn't see Kaylia but could make out the head of the assistant. He looked panicked.

He should be.

There were two others in the car. Taller, thinner and hooded head to toe. One was driving and the other turned to us. Holding a blaster.

I dove to the side, rolling on the ground, as the bolts hit where I had been standing. The Thesan guard , brave but dumb, knelt down and raised his weapon to his shoulder. He fired off a few quick shots, aiming for the cars rear engine. Without that, it would just hover. It was a good idea, but he missed as the car swerved. The attacker fired a couple more shots and the Thesan grunted as a bolt took him in the shoulder. He toppled over.

I watched as the car sped away, cursing. The wind took the attackers hood off and I caught a glimpse of a pale blue face.

Tiat.

*****

"You okay," I asked as I held a hand out to help the Thesan guard up.

He grunted, cursing which came out as a hiss. Grimacing in pain, he clasped my hand and I pulled him up. His left shoulder hung limp, a blaster scar along the edge. He'd been grazed, which was how he was able to stand, but it still hurt.

We heard running, the sounds of people across the grass. More guards fanned out around us, some looking at me and especially the blaster I still had out, but moving on. I heard the sound of hovercars from the other side of the hangars. Sirens, alarms.

"What happened?"

It was Yoterra. She came running up, more guards surrounding her. These ones wore more armored and had bigger and stronger weapons. I could see another hovercar further back behind her, this one with a mounted weapon. The Thesans were out in force.

Too late.

"Your damned assistant," I said, holstering my blaster. I turned and looked the way the hovercar had gone. "He took her and met up with some Tiat."

"Tiat here?" she asked, shocked. "Are you sure?"

"I know what those bastards look like. I caught a look at one."

"Find them," she yelled at a guard next to her. I could hear him speaking into some comms system. "Follow me," she ordered and turned, stalking away.

I followed. I don't know if she had meant me to or not but there was no way I was sitting this one out.

The Thesans were running all over the place, in and out of the hangars. All armed, all in groups. I saw some storming ships, searching. People were gathered outside on the metal between hangars, looking worried, confused and everything else. I followed behind Yoterra as we headed for a building at the far end.

Where the hangars all had the industrial look, even with the Thesan aesthetic, this building looked more like the rest of the city. Square walls, two stories with the second story not as large as the first, with curved supports at the front. There were smaller curves over some of the windows and the entrance door. It lacked some of the beauty I had glimpsed in the city itself, but there was a charm to it. The door slid open to reveal a hallway. The floor was metal, the walls as well but with wood panels spaced evenly. Dark wood, light wood, some designs.

My mind wasn't really on the building and the decorations.

I stayed a couple steps behind Yoterra, flanked by a couple guards. I kept expecting them to ask for my weapon but they didn't. Not like I was going to give it to them. I wasn't trusting anyone in this place, not anymore.

Down the hallway and to another door. I could see through a long window what looked to be a control room. Monitors, stations and lots of people and activity. Yoterra walked in, a couple of the guards stopping and taking up positions on either side. I moved to follow and one of them stepped in my way.

"Move," I said. No threat, just a command.

The guard didn't move. I could feel others behind me. None took a step but they were waiting.

"Out of my way," I told him calmly.

I tensed, shifting slightly.

"Let him in," Yoterra's voice came from the control room.

The guard moved out of the way. I walked in. The door closed behind me.

Not large, the room was crowded and dominated by one large monitor on the wall. I watched an overhead shot of two figures running towards a hangar and then a hovercar flying out and turning. I saw some scattered blaster fire, one of the figures diving and another getting shot. I really didn't need to see that part, I had lived it.

The hovercar sped past the spaceport, heading towards the city. It turned as it neared the outskirts, following the edge of the buildings and moving across the plain. The screen flickered and now the hovercar was around the other edge of the city, cutting into the buildings. It was now a live feed we were watching, coming from some satellite in orbit. It was an area of single story large buildings, warehouses. There was generous amounts of space between them, all with the Thesan architecture. The hovercar moved in and out of view as it flew deeper into the buildings. It finally disappeared inside a building in the middle of the cluster.

"Keep surveillance on that building," one of the Thesans said. He was standing at the rear of the room, in a white uniform. Gray and brown fur. "We'll lock down flight patterns over that part of the city," he told Yoterra turning to face her.

"Very good," she said and nodded to one of the guards. "Captain Hunil, you have your target."

The Thesan, one of the heavier armored guards saluted and motioned to two of the others.

"I'm coming with you," I told him. It wasn't a request.

"You do not need to Captain Lancer," Yoterra replied.

I just looked at her. Different from my 'don't mess with me look', but along the same lines. This one said 'don't bother' mixed with 'I'm going no matter what'.

"Very well," she said with a nod. She studied me for a minute, an odd look, before turning back to the screen.

I followed Hunil out the door where two more guards joined us. We ran down the corridor at a jog, outside and towards a nearby hangar. Running inside I saw a tactical hovercar. I'd seen the style before during some battles alongside the Thesans. It was heavily armored, walls and roof with a weapon mounted to the top. It was a tank. Our small group climbed inside and one of the guards took the controls.

"You will follow my commands," Hunil told me pointing at a seat. He spoke in heavily accented Tradelan.

"Right," I lied.

We entered the labyrinth of warehouses from the other side, our hovertank stopping a couple buildings back. I didn't have the layout of buildings memorized, but I had seen enough to have a general idea of where we needed to go. We filed out of the tank and Hunil put me in the middle of the group.

I noticed that he didn't offer me any armor or other weaponry.

Whatever, I hated wearing blastarmor anyways. Heavy and bulky.

Moving silently we made our way to the target building, crouching against the wall of one warehouse and looking across the open space at the target. It looked like all the others. Nothing noticeable. I wondered how the Tiat planned to get out of here. I think whatever original plan they had was spoiled by the actions of the assistant but they had to have a ship somewhere but no idea where that could be.

"Where's the nearest spaceport," I asked Hunil in a whisper.

He looked over his shoulder at me, annoyed, but then registered what I had asked. He hissed, the equivalent of a Thesan curse, and spoke quickly into his comm unit.

"Some of these warehouses have private docks," he said angrily. Probably upset he hadn't thought of that himself.

We both knew the skies above were locked down but we both also knew that really didn't amount to much. Sometimes you could prevent a ship from taking off but if the person was really adamant about leaving, they would leave. Once a ship was in the air, there was no way of stopping it short of shooting it down.

I didn't think Yoterra would risk killing Kaylia and the Thesans would want to question the Tiat to discover how they had learned of the kid's parents and gotten onplanet in the first place.

So they would want to capture the Tiat alive.

Which meant we had to prevent them from launching.

Which meant we had to move now.

If I was the Tiat, I would assume we had tracked the hovercar and were quickly moving in. They'd have their ship prepping to launch and scanning the skies for the patrol ships. It would be risky but they'd want to establish a pattern in the patrols and find the best moment to launch. They'd only get one shot. It would take some time to open the bay doors on the buildings roof and longer to get the ship out and into position to fire the thrusters and get off planet.

It gave us some time, but not much.

"Tighten up the patrol paths," I told Hunil. "Don't give them a window."

He gave me that annoyed look again but relayed my plan. I recognized enough of the whispered Thesan to know that he also took credit for it.

Whatever. I didn't care. Let him take the credit. He'd take the blame if this went wrong.

Or he'd transfer it to me, the offworlder who had forced himself onto the operation.

If this went wrong, I'd be blaming myself also.

"There is low level jamming," Hunil said after speaking to the command center. "We can't scan inside the building."

So no idea how many there were. And just the six of us. I assumed more Thesans were moving into backup positions but for now we were it.

"What's the plan," I asked. Hunil gave me a surprised look. He must have thought I'd butt in with some brilliant idea. Any idea I had would be brilliant but this was his home. "It's your city," I told him.

Nodding, Hunil gathered the six of us close and told us the plan.

Simple. I liked it.

*****

Only six, we split into three teams of two. I was with Hunil.

Glancing up, I could see the shadows and dark shapes of the Thesan patrol crafts moving through the clouds. They were as close to the buildings, and each other, as they dared to go. I would have liked the pattern tighter, even from here I could see gaps that I could fly the *Nomad's Wind* through, but it wasn't my call.

Hunil led us around the side of the warehouse, keeping to the shadows before we'd make the run across the open space. This reminded me of my time in the military. I'd run a lot of ops like this but mostly those were kill missions not rescue. I hadn't run many rescue missions and usually the enemy didn't know we were coming.

The Tiat in the warehouse were expecting us. Maybe not right this minute, but they knew the Thesan forces were close. We didn't have the element of surprise.

Holding a hand up Hunil called a halt. I leaned out a bit to get a look beyond him and didn't see much. Lots of open ground between us and the target. No windows facing us though, that was a plus. I could hear chatter through Hunil's comms. Coordination between the teams. He looked back at me, checking to make sure I was ready.

"Waiting on you," I whispered.

I got that annoyed look again.

A couple seconds later and we were running across about a hundred feet of open space. We both kept low, eyes looking towards the target building. Hunil concentrated on that but I kept my eyes moving as well, trying to see off to the sides. If it had been me, I would have put people outside. All I saw was another one of the Thesan teams, the last on the opposite side of the building. Maybe that meant the Tiat didn't have people to spare? Wishful thinking.

We pulled up tight to the building and I could feel the cool metal against my hands. Colored brown, it was smooth with no markings. I kept watch as Hunil turned around and faced the wall. He ran his hands over it and took out a device. Holding it in one hand, I heard a faint hum as he ran the device across the wall. He traced an oval about a foot off the ground and six feet high, only a couple wide.

Hunil slid the device into the middle of his oval and hit a button. He stepped back, the device stuck to the wall. Pulling a small controller, he motioned me away from the wall. I didn't need the encouragement, I'd seen what a breacher could do. I probably didn't want to mention to him that I had one aboard the *Wind*. On most planets it was illegal for a civilian to own a breacher, that included Thesan and Terran controlled space.

About ten feet away, directly facing the device and wall, I got down on one knee and raised my blaster at the oval.

As Hunil hit the button on the controller I saw lines of energy spark out from under the device. It crept along the wall, following the path Hunil had traced. The oval was lined by the blue sparking energy. It crackled and snapped. Another push of the button and the lines of energy flared.

Smoke rose from the brown metal as the energy started cutting through the wall. It was bright and I wanted to turn away but I needed to hold steady. It only took seconds before the energy disappeared and the sound of metal hitting ground echoed through the buildings.

The smoke cleared and I could see inside the building. White metal walls, furniture. An office of some kind. Empty.

"Go," I said.

Hunil, keeping to the side and out of my firing lane, ran to the edge of the building. He leaned against the wall next to the opening and pivoted around it. He stepped over and through the hole and was in the office. When he moved into my line of fire, I lowered my weapon and quickly moved up to the new opening.

It was an office. It was empty and looked unused.

Already at the door, Hunil impatiently gestured at me to enter. One last look around the yard, at the alleys in between the buildings, and I stepped through the hole.

I could hear activity beyond the door. Blasters firing and shouting. The other Thesan teams had breached. There was noise through Hunil's comms. Just loud enough for me to hear it, not loud enough to understand any of it. Rapid fire Thesan, too low for me to get any words.

And of course Hunil was not sharing with me.

He was making no move to open the door. No signal for me to cover it. Nothing. I was getting impatient. At some point the Tiat would cut their losses and kill Kaylia.

I hit the door release on the keypad and let it slide open. Hunil shot me an angry glance. So much for following orders. I ignored him and stepped out of the office. We needed to move quickly.

CHAPTER TEN

The door opened onto a large space, the main warehouse. The walls were curved, metal beams supporting it that were thin at the top and got thicker as they went down to the ground. They were spaced close together on the ends, leaving an open spot in the middle. Smaller beams spanned between them. No windows, but lights hanging up high. Large doors could be seen along the far wall. A couple more small offices were to our right.

The warehouse was mostly empty, some polyplas crates scattered around, except for a light cruiser in the middle. Fast and mobile, it was a Devret UT15. Common ships, they were found everywhere. Not too flashy, they were usually used by merchants and other business people as they were reliable and parts were cheap and easy to get. This one looked old and well used. If I had to fly under the radar, it's exactly what I would have picked.

A side benefit, the Devret couldn't carry that many passengers so that limited the number of Tiat we had to deal with.

I could see blaster flashes on the far side. Hear bolts hitting the walls and the ship. Sparks were erupting everywhere.

Cursing I crept out into the warehouse. What were the Thesans thinking?

Holding up behind a crate I took in the scene. The ship's ramp was lowered and two Tiat were crouched on it firing at the far end of the warehouse. I could see two more behind crates. They had heavy blasters, the weapons loud in the confined space. The return bolts from the Thesans seemed weak in comparison.

Hunil came alongside, crouching behind another crate. I pointed at the two on the boarding ramp. He nodded and took aim. Lifting my blaster, I held it steady with two hands and stood up. I took careful aim and pulled the trigger.

My bolt sailed across the short distance and hit my target, the lower of the two Tiat. He fell and the other one above him had just a second to look down in surprise before he also fell dead.

We ran forward and I crossed in front of Hunil. He ran towards where the other Tiat were, firing from behind cover. I made for the boarding ramp. Smoke rose from the blaster wounds on the dead bodies. I kicked their weapons off the ramp, not taking any chances. I also fired at one of the remaining Tiat, but I was moving fast and missed.

There were only two left. Hunil and his team could handle them, I had more important business.

I paused at the top of the ramp. The hatch opened onto a hall moving left and right and a body was slumped against the wall. It had slid down showing a blaster scorch mark against the metal. A matching one was on the bodies chest, no longer smoking.

The Thesan assistant.

I was kind of upset that I didn't get to kill him.

Turning right I headed towards the bridge. I had no idea where Kaylia could be but I could at least disable the ship. I'd been inside a couple Devret UT15s before so knew the general layout. The entrance corridor ran left towards engineering and right towards the crew compartments, lounge areas and bridge. The only other entrance was the loading hatch underneath for cargo. I had to hope that the Thesans could cover that. Anyone lowering it would be visible from their positions.

Moving slowly, cautiously, I crept up the corridor. The paneling was old, faded and scratched, even missing in some places. The hall curved, following the line of the hull. It ended just ahead, turning left to go into the compartments and right to the bridge. I strained to hear, anything, something. But it was silent, no idea where Kaylia could be.

Holding myself tight against the outer wall, I turned and tried to see down the intersecting hall that led to the compartments. I could see doors, all closed, but nothing else. I pivoted around the corner and faced the bridge. Set up much like the *Wind's*, four stations on two levels, and it was empty.

Keeping one eye on the hall, I stepped over to the pilot's station and looked it over. Controls on most ships were the same, some small variations, but pretty standard. Some were fancier, others basic, but all in relatively the same locations. Made changing ships easier. So I knew where the power cut off for the Devret was.

I hesitated before flipping the switch. Anyone still on board would know I was here if I did that. There were only two places that the entire power could be turned off, the bridge or engineering. No help for it.

The click was loud in the silence of the ship. The lights shut off, everything going black, and then the emergency lights came on. Strips of small lights along the top and bottom of the halls, just enough light to see and walk by. The ship was now effectively grounded. Power could be restored, but it would take awhile, fifteen or twenty minutes, before there was enough to take off.

I stepped back out to the hall, weapon raised, and looked down it's length. The strip lights made it dark, increasing the shadows. Six doors, three to a side and the hall ending in a large room.

Clearing all six would take time that I didn't have and leave me open to someone from other rooms or the lounge at the end. This was why we never did something like this without back-up in my 2E days. One cleared the room, the other covered.

It didn't take me long to figure out my best move.

I played the odds.

Quickly I moved down the corridor, ignoring the doors, and stepped into the lounge. I moved to the side, so my back wasn't to the corridor. Better safe than sorry.

The lounge wasn't large, chairs and tables with a vidscreen against the far wall. Serviceable, nothing fancy. But in front of the vidscreen was a Tiat.

With Kaylia.

*****

"Let her go."

The strip lights gave some detail but not much.

Tall, light blue skin and dark colored hair. Not in a standard Tiat uniform, which made sense considering. She was average height for the species, putting her taller than me. Hard face, could be attractive but this one was cold and hard. The commander of this team. To be given this assignment she had to be good. I knew what it took to be a special operations soldier and what it took to get these kinds of assignments.

Tiat were matriarchal. Ruled by the Empress, the officers were always female.

This one had one arm around Kaylia's neck, the other holding a blaster to her head. I pointed mine at the Tiat's head, visible over the shorter Kaylia. For me, an easy shot, but the Tiat could still get off a shot and kill Kaylia. I forced myself to wait.

For her part Kaylia was remaining calm. She stood still, straight, with no tears. There was relief in her eyes as she looked at me. Confidence and hope.

"This is none of your concern Terran," the Tiat said. Her voice had the steely calm, lack of emotion that was common to the race.

"Let. Her. Go."

"I should have killed her," The Tiat said. I'd never known one to be talkative, but then I'd never encountered one in this position. She knew her time was up. "The mission was to bring her back alive for study." I almost pulled the trigger at the way the Tiat said that. No emotion, as if Kaylia was just an object. "But better dead than free."

Keep her talking I thought as I looked for a way out of this stalemate. I could shoot her, but she'd pull her trigger and shoot Kaylia. She knew it. I knew it. She had nothing to lose, she was dead no matter what.

"Why didn't you," I asked. Holding my weapon steady I tried to line up a shot, but the Tiat was moving just enough. Side to side, just a step, bringing Kaylia with her, forcing me to keep adjusting.

"I wanted to see how this played out," the Tiat replied, still with that matter-of-fact tone, as if nothing mattered anymore, which was true. "But mostly I wanted to see who was causing us all this trouble. She should have been kept on that asteroid. That team failed. Mine was sent here after you took her from us."

That was a bit of a shock. That meant they had stayed relatively close to Turesa. It was only a couple days ago that I had rescued Kaylia from the asteroid.

"I was surprised to be told that a Terran was involved," the Tiat continued and I wondered if she was stalling for time. Additional back-up?

Then it dawned on me. She was stalling. But not for her back-up. She was waiting for more Thesans. She intended to die and take Kaylia and as many with her as she could.

Dammit.

That changed everything.

I released my two handed grip on the blaster, holding it with my right hand and pointing it away from the Tiat. In the near darkness I couldn't see her eyes but figured she was wondering what I was doing. She knew I had to try something. It was my move.

"I was just in the wrong place at the wrong time," I said, keeping my tone casual. With my left hand, I started moving my fingers. I moved them slowly, carefully. I know I didn't make the gestures right but hoped it was enough. "Wasn't my intention to get involved. I just don't like bullies."

The Tiat laughed, a cold chuckle.

"The Thesans will pay for what they did to my people," she said and for the first time there was emotion in her. "This brat will pay the same as did her family."

That was the wrong thing to say.

I had expected Kaylia to react, I had told her to with my clumsy sign language, but not react like she did. I had thought she'd do the same to the Tiat as she had the Garand. This was different and it came from somewhere deep inside the girl. Some deep and primal instinct.

The fingers grew to claws, a red rage came to her eyes and she growled. It was a mean growl, full of pure hatred. The claws of one hand stabbed down into the Tiat's chest, cutting deep wounds as they dug. The other hand went up to the Tiat's face. The angle wasn't right, the arm swing awkward, which was the only thing that saved the woman's life.

She screamed as the claws cut lines down her face. Three deep gashes, down the left side of her face, through her eye. The arms slackened around Kaylia, who slipped out of the grasp. The Tiat tried to bring her weapon down, her arm had instinctively shot up pulling it away from Kaylia's head. Even in her rage she tried to take aim but my shot took her in the shoulder. She dropped the weapon and fell against the wall.

Hissing and growling, Kaylia jumped on the Tiat. Holding the woman down with one hand, a strength born of rage, the other was raised up to kill.

I leaped across the room and grabbed Kaylia by the wrist, stopping the blow. She looked back at me, hissing, her eyes red. I wanted to step back, the girl I knew wasn't visible in those eyes, but I couldn't. She fought in my grasp and I had to avoid a swing of the other arm with those claws dripping purple blood.

"Kaylia," I said calmly, letting her hear my voice. "It's me. It's okay."

Her normal color returned to her eyes, the red fading. The claws retracted, blood dripping from the ends and Kaylia collapsed against me. She fell into my hug, face deep in my shoulder, and cried.

The Tiat didn't move, didn't appear to be conscious. I couldn't tell if she was alive and really I didn't care. I heard footsteps and the Thesans ran into the room. I didn't care.

I just held Kaylia tight.

CHAPTER ELEVEN

It went quickly after that.

They came for the Tiat. The commander was still alive. Barely. They had questions for her. Mostly about how many traitors there were, how they had gotten to the assistant, how they had gotten to the planet. That kind of stuff. It didn't concern me.

They came for Kaylia. She refused to let me go and I refused to let them take her from me.

We sat on a couch next to each other, she was curled up tight against me and had finally stopped shaking. Kaylia kept looking at her hands, holding them in front of her. They were clean, no traces of blood. But she remembered the blood dripping from her fingers, both times.

I remembered this last time.

It was my fault.

I felt horrible that I had made her go through that. But there had been no other way.

The Thesans had found a detonator on the Tiat, connected to the ship's engines. It would have caused an overload and ignited the reactor. The ship would have gone up and who knows how far the explosion would have gone.

Yoterra's assistant had screwed things up. He'd panicked and went to the Tiat instead of them getting another shot at kidnapping Kaylia. Knowing pursuit was on the way, and chances of escape were slim, the commander had decided on suicide. She just wanted to take as many Thesans with her as she could, so she had waited.

I didn't know what the Thesans were doing with the Tiat commander and I really did not care. She could burn. Torture her. Whatever. Besides the Thesan traitors, she was apparently high ranking enough to be valuable. The Tiat were tough but eventually she'd break. I'd be long gone when that happened.

But what was going to happen to Kaylia?

We were left in a lounge in the main building at the hangar. Thesans medics had looked Kaylia over, no injuries, and left us alone. I sat on the couch, the kid next to me and I looked out the window. I had a view over the landing field and could see the *Nomad's Wind* at the far end. Just sitting there waiting for me to board and go somewhere. Anywhere.

No destination. Just me and the stars.

I looked down at Kaylia, staring off at nothing, and brushed a loose strand of hair out of her face. She was a good kid. Didn't deserve this.

Hearing footsteps I looked up to see Yoterra approaching. She had a tablet in hand and sat down in a chair across from us. She looked tired.

"We think he was working alone," she said leaning forward, resting her arms on her knees and head in her hands. She gave a loud sigh and sat up straighter. "I hold myself responsible."

She was but didn't need to hear it from me. I didn't say anything.

"But we don't know," she continued. "Where there is one traitor, there could be others." She looked down at Kaylia and smiled, a small and sad smile. "And add in the faction that the guard belonged to, the ones that want to forcible erase our..," she paused, thinking about how to phrase it and just shrugged. "We didn't always do the right thing but erasing it is not right either."

The silence stretched before I spoke.

"How will you protect Kaylia," I asked, feeling the kid shift. Some of her own people wanted her dead. And for what? Something her parents had done, Yoterra and others had done? The kid was innocent and she was paying for the mistakes of others.

Yoterra stood up and walked over to the window. She stared out over the field, watching the ships and people moving around. Kaylia sat up and watched the older woman. Yoterra turned around, looking sad and tired and defeated.

She walked over, stopping in front of us. Reaching down she ran her fingers through Kaylia's hair. Yoterra took the seat opposite us again and studied me intently.

"When I left the War Applications Division I destroyed all records of the procedure that made the Wilders," she said, locking eyes with me. "I wanted them to live the rest of their lives in peace. After what they had done for their people, they deserved it." She looked down at Kaylia and smiled, a sad smile. "As much as I will try to stop it, it will come out that she is alive. People like my assistant will want to destroy her and others in the Thesan government will want to use her to recreate the experiments."

She reached out a hand and took Kaylia's smaller in hers, smiling at the girl.

"I can no longer keep her safe."

With a sigh Yoterra turned to me.

"Will you?"

I had begun to expect that question was coming and I already knew how I would respond.

There was only one answer.

ARMAGEDDON THEFT

Originally Published:
September 3, 2018; eBook on Amazon

CHAPTER ONE

It was a great dream.

Me, a beautiful redhead, a sunset on the resort planet of Tortugan.

And it was spoiled by a pounding on my bunk door.

Loud and obnoxious.

I pushed back the sheet and sat up in bed.

"What?" I growled. "I'm up," I added a little nicer.

There's only one person that would be pounding on my door and it wasn't right of me to snap at her. She'd only do it if it was important.

First good nights sleep I'd had in awhile though.

The last couple months had been a whirlwind and I was being overly paranoid which added to the stress level. At lots of reasons for that. I'd managed to probably piss off the Tiat, the galaxy's largest empire and biggest bullies. I'd also probably managed to piss off a faction of the Thesans, the Terrans closest allies. There were probably still some bounty hunters out there looking for me as I doubt the Tiat removed it.

All because of the person pounding on my door right now.

The metal door slid into the wall and she ran into the room. Not a big room, two doors along one wall, a bed and chair on the other, couch against the far wall. Didn't take her long to get from the door to the bed. I wasn't even fully out before she was grabbing my arm.

"Slow down kiddo," I said letting her pull me up.

Thankfully I didn't sleep naked.

The kid that was excitedly pulling at me was a young teenage Thesan. I'd literally run into Kaylia on a mining asteroid where she had escaped the people that had kidnapped her. The Tiat. Long story short, Kaylia was the last surviving member of a Thesan military special unit called the Wilders. More accurately her parents had been. Poor kid was just the unlucky recipient of the Wilders altered DNA.

Wilders, during the Third Galactic War, had killed some pretty high ranking Tiat. It was the kind of thing the Tiat didn't forget or forgive. They spent years hunting down the Wilders until only Kaylia was left. They'd taken her to experiment on her. That's when I had found her and saved her.

Tried to return her home to Turesa, a Thesan colony world, only to find out that some of her own people wanted her dead or gone.

Safest place for her ended up being with me.

How scary is that?

Arek Lancer, former Earth Expeditionary Forces Special Operations soldier, current vagabond independent freight hauler and guardian to a thirteen year old Thesan girl.

Life is weird sometimes.

Kaylia kept pulling at me, urging me out of the room. I grabbed at my t-shirt over the chair as I stumbled past. It's hard to walk when a teenager is dragging you by the arm. There was something frantic and urgent to her pulling.

"Kid," I said trying to calm her down. "What is it."

She didn't say anything. She couldn't. The kid was mute. She didn't bother trying to sign anything to me, instead pointing to the ship's bridge a short distance away. The bunk hall, three to a side, is on the top level of my ship, with the door to the bridge at one end and the entrance to engineering at the other. My bunk is the closest to the bridge so as soon as I stepped into the corridor I could hear what had Kaylia so excited.

I had been sleeping and she had been on duty, which meant she wasn't ready for bed yet and sat in the bridge's co-pilot's station watching the stars out the view window. We'd just hopped into this system on the way to delivering the latest cargo, one we needed as credits were getting low, and I'd been in bed for only an hour or so. Should have only been in the system for fifteen minutes before the navcom automatically hopped us back into wildspace.

That's why Kaylia had been so urgent in waking me up. There was a limited time to respond.

I could hear the signal playing on a pre recorded loop. Same message, short, repeating.

Sitting down in the pilot's station, Kaylia hovering over me, I hit the commands that delayed the hop and concentrated on the message.

It was in Tradelan, the somewhat common language of the galaxy, and was being broadcast on all channels. Even the emergency ones which is how Kaylia was able to receive it.

"All ships that receive this, we are requesting your aid in evacuation of Storw."

I shut off the reception of the message.

Kaylia tapped me on the shoulder and I looked down at her hands, her fingers moving in intricate patterns rapidly.

Evacuation?

I nodded and pulled up the star charts. We were a quick four hour hop from the Wils star system on the edge of the Inner Worlds, where the planet Storw was.

"Remember that news item from last week," I said as I started programming in the new set of coordinates. I'd have to remember to send a message to the client telling them why their cargo was going to be late. How late? Good question. "About the asteroid threatening a planet?"

She nodded, moving over to the co-pilots station.

"That was Storw."

Not a big planet or even a popular one, Storw had been in the Galactic Feed news a lot lately. A rogue asteroid had entered the system, on a straight line for the planet. Nothing could be done so evacuations had started. The natives, a race called the Storwos, had no colony worlds and had to scramble to find places to take the refugees.

It was huge news. There hadn't been a planet destroyed in the galaxy in a hundred years. Which was longer than us earthlings, or Terrans as we were called, had been roaming the stars.

Receiving news is interesting out in the wilds of space. Travel is done by hopping from star system to star system, crossing the incredible distances in wildspace. When in that strange area between systems you can't receive anything from out of wildspace. So you can go hours or days with no updates. You get the news in spurts. Which is why travelers hop from system to system, cutting down on the amount of time spent in wildspace.

It had been a couple of days since had heard anything about Storw beyond evacuations were continuing. I figured the planet would have been destroyed by now and the last of the people on their way to their new homes.

I wonder what went wrong.

Something had to if they were sending out an all-ships request.

I heard the tap on the console. The sound of Kaylia getting my attention.

We're going to help?

"Of course we are," I replied and hit the buttons that locked in the navcourse for Storw.

*****

I'd like to think that I would have gone to help even if Kaylia wasn't on board the *Wind*. But would I have?

*****

We hopped out of wildspace, the cloudy white replaced by the black of space with the millions of white dots that were the stars. My ship had a view window, one of the few nowadays that did, but there wasn't much to see. Coming in at the edge of the system, this far out there weren't even any planets visible.

I didn't know much about the Wils system, only what I could get from the information stored in the *Wind's* Feed directory, but I knew that it was a rare system in that all the planets were gathered in close to the sun with a lot of empty space beyond. We were still a couple hours out from Storw. I adjusted the scanners, sacrificing fine tuning for range, and picked up multiple ships in the area. Too far away to see, both entering and leaving the system.

The scanners indicated lots of different sizes. Only one of them was a large passenger liner, a ship designed to carry a lot of people. Some were freighters larger than mine. The *Nomad's Wind* was a light freighter, I wouldn't be able to hold many but every little bit helped.

The door to the hall slid open and Kaylia walked into the bridge. The room wasn't that big, four stations on two levels. Pilots and co-pilots on the upper with navigation and weapons on the lower level, only a couple steps down. Until the kid had come on board, I was the only crew and while the ship was designed for six and could be flown by three, I had rigged things so it could be flown by one.

She yawned and stretched, looking out the view window, her tail swishing in the air. Standing about five foot three, Kaylia was basically a humanoid cat. Gray and black fur in a kind of spotted and striped pattern, long tail, short and pointed ears. Large yellow eyes with thin green irises. There were tufts of fur at her ankles and wrists and her hair fell down her back, parts of it connected to her body like a mane. When I had first found her, the kid had been stuck in worker's coveralls. Since then we'd managed to get her some clothes of her own but she preferred wearing one of my old Earth Expeditionary Forces military jackets most of the time.

It was way too big for her slender form but if she was happy, that's what mattered.

You were supposed to wake me when we arrived.

Her sign language was quick, containing a mixture of Tradelan and Thesan. It had taken me awhile to get used to the mix but I was pretty fluent in Kaylia now. There were times when she signed too quickly for me to catch and I had to tell her to slow down.

"We're still a couple hours from the planet," I told her turning my attention back to controls. "Figured you could sleep longer."

Too excited.

"Understandable," I replied. "Not everyday something like this happens."

There are evacuations all the time.

The kid had been born at the tail end of the Third Galactic War to parents that had lived it. She had to have heard stories from them and in school history lessons about the battles. Settlements had been evacuated for various reasons during the War, mostly to get innocents out of the way of battles or because there was no sustaining the colony anymore because of battle damage.

I had participated in a couple during my time as a soldier.

"True but not for this," I told her. "Not for the destruction of a planet."

I could hear her fiddling with some controls, fingers tapping on the keys. One of her duties as co-pilot of the ship was to update the Galactic Feed when we hopped into a system. There was an automatic pre-programmed download that happened at each hop, but sometimes we wanted to add to it. That was her job and she was looking for updates on Storw so we'd know what we were getting into.

Communication from system to system is spotty and not quick. There are satellites in most systems that bounce the signal around, punching it through wildspace to the next receiver, but because of the nature of wildspace none of those signals can be picked up well there. The Feed is the galaxy wide communications system, everything from messages and news to entertainment videos or books. But because of wildspace and the lag across systems, when you hop into a system you're behind on the current happenings.

Usually only a couple of hours but those hours can be important.

There was one time on a mission for the 2Es, we'd gotten a signal from a forward base hidden in an asteroid belt that all was clear and the mission was a go. We hopped into the system in the middle of an ambush from the Tiat.

Most of us didn't make it out of there. Those of us that did, we were lucky.

"Any updates," I asked the co-pilot.

I looked at Kaylia and she pointed back at one of my monitors. A face appeared, human, male, neatly dressed. Some kind of newscaster. I switched the volume on and hit play.

"The evacuation of Storw was interrupted when the rogue asteroid itself encountered the rings surrounding one of the Wils system gas giants. It was hoped that the ring collision would send the asteroid off course but instead it sent parts of the gas giant's rings hurtling into the center of the system. These meteors struck Storw's largest moon as well as the planet itself. Due to the damage to the planet and the moon it was deemed too dangerous to continue with the evacuations. The hope is that things will settle down and evacuations can continue. As of now only three quarters of the planet has made it off."

I shut off the newscast and cleared it from my monitor. Adjusting the scanners I looked to see where we were in relation to the gas giant. Thankfully we were coming in from the side, not in the path of the asteroid or the gas giant that would be going crazy with it's ring destroyed.

Kaylia tapped on the console. She had been watching the vid over my shoulder.

How many people on the planet?

"Twenty million," I replied after consulting the Feed archive. "About the same as Turesa." That was the Thesan colony world she was from.

It doesn't seem like much in comparison to some of the Inner Worlds or even Terra, or Earth as we natives like to call it. When I left Earth, there were five billion on the planet itself. Our Mars colony had twenty million. Europa was one million, Titan was five hundred thousand and the Sol Station had fifty thousand. Earth's fleet of government ships numbered in the hundreds with the largest having a crew of five hundred and capable of carrying a thousand soldiers. The largest passenger liner that I knew of had a crew of a hundred and could carry six hundred.

If three quarters of the population had made it off planet, that still left five million Storwos that needed to be evacuated. No wonder they had sent out the all-ships request. No single race, even the empires, had a fleet capable of taking that many people at once. The evacuation was in chunks, a hundred here, a hundred there. If they were requesting ships like the *Wind*, they were desperate.

When your planet is going to be destroyed and you're trying to save as many of your people as you can, nothing is too desperate.

*****

The planet Storw came into view.

A small planet, blue and green with white cloud cover. Nothing special about it.

Except for the broken moon in orbit.

The gray rock globe was missing a large piece of it, smaller pieces floating in space around the wound. Cracks streaked across the surface, more chunks of rock breaking off and drifting into the void. A trail of rock debris led from the moon towards the planet, pieces drifting at different speeds.

Dozens of ships were orbiting the planet, large ones that couldn't enter the atmosphere, smaller shuttles swarming around them. Others, maybe another dozen, could be seen entering and leaving, breaking through the cloud cover and dragging puffs of white behind them.

And there in the distance the streaks across the starfield that marked the meteors ahead of the planet killing asteroid.

Storw didn't have much time left.

CHAPTER TWO

"*Nomad's Wind* to Storw Control," I spoke into the comms system. There was some static in the system and I made some adjustments.

"Storw Control, we copy you *Nomad's Wind*." The voice that answered, still a bit staticky, was melodious and a lot calmer than I would have been. "And we thank you for your assistance."

"Where do you need me?"

"Make of ship," the controller asked. No small talk, which was understandable. Probably had a checklist of things to ask to figure out the best use of the vessel.

"Earth registration and manufacture. Castellan Light Freighter Model F497. Crew of two."

There was a couple minutes of silence as the controller processed the information, probably bringing up whatever specs they had available on the ship. I had a data packet I was ready to transmit if need be. It didn't list any of my special modifications of course.

"How empty is the cargo hold," the controller finally said.

"Quarter full," I replied and could imagine the controller's expression. A freighter of any kind with an empty hold like that wasn't normally a very good freighter. The benefit of a crew of two was they didn't need as much to keep afloat.

"Thank the *Gursn*," the controller said. Probably the Storwo deity. Definitely not part of the script. First time anyone, including me, had been happy with a near empty cargo hold. "*Nomad's Wind*, we are transmitting you coordinates now to a small farming settlement called Touryon. Population of five hundred. Ground control will give further guidance once you land."

"Roger that," I said and studied my board. "Coordinates received," I added a couple seconds later.

I adjusted the *Wind's* course to bring us to the far side of the planet before we entered atmo. I wondered how many people they were hoping to cram into the ship.

The planet curved below us and I pulled the navguide up on the view window, superimposing it over the polycarbonite. A small green dot appeared on the horizon, an indication of where our destination was. We could see other ships passing us, different colored dots on the screen and even one visible to the eye, some rising from the surface and some landing. I'd never seen this much ship activity, not even at busy ports. In the corner of the view window the distance counted down. This was a feature I had rarely used before Kaylia started traveling with me. When it was just me, I could see all this on the screens at my station. Normally it was stuff shown at the navigation station and I had tasked to mine.

Seeing it on the big screen was much more interesting.

The cloud cover was thick in this part of the planet, not as white, more gray. We could see streaks of lightning cutting through the cover. A storm and it looked pretty planetwide.

I adjusted the thrusters and guided the *Wind* down through the cloud bank. The window filled with the clouds, similar to hopping through wildspace except for the blue flashes of lightning. Rain started pelting the window, drips splattering against the polycarbonite. The ship shook, nothing bad, but enough that I had to hold the controls steady.

From the corner of my eye I saw Kaylia grip the console tightly.

"Turbulence," I told Kaylia. "Just a storm."

It really wouldn't be just a storm. I had wondered what effects the damaged moon were having and I think we were about to find out.

We passed through the clouds and into the raging storm. Winds buffeted the ship, the thrusters compensating. Rain pelted off the metal, now audible with the force. Lightning strikes slammed into the planet, some so strong they caused small explosions. Fires could be seen dotting the land masses. Flying down closer to the surface, we could see massive waves across the oceans. The edges of the landmasses were getting swamped with the waves.

It was rockier here, less green.

And less ships. I hadn't seen another one on the scanner in a couple of minutes.

The distance flew by, the storm lessening. The land dropped away, becoming smaller islands in the raging seas. We could see structures on some of the islands, the remains of docks along the shoreline. Waves crashing onto the land and flooding the streets. They looked abandoned.

Hoped they were abandoned because the inhabitants had already been evacuated. But somehow I doubted it. Some of the waves were completely covering the smaller islands.

"There it is," I said as the green dot on the view window grew larger.

We passed over a wider stretch of ocean, no other land masses, except the one directly ahead. Larger than many of the others, the structures were visible from further away. It set higher up, cliffs surrounding the land and no visible beaches. With these waves, it was the safest bit of land around.

Two and three story buildings filled the near side of the island, trees further away and some fields beyond those. Gray and square, windows filled with a dark material. There wasn't much appealing about the architecture or the island itself. I wondered what it had looked like back in the planet's prime.

I slowed the *Wind* and raised it well above the buildings. No need to add the force of the ship's passing to the strong winds that were already buffeting the city. We could see people, small from this height, running through the city. All seemed to be converging at a single point. No details could be seen, most were covered to protect from the rain and wind.

Between the buildings and the trees was a cleared spot. A smaller area recently cleared much larger. The ground was hard packed dirt, no metal landing field. There was a single small square of metal nearer the buildings, the island's original ship pad, but it had been expanded rapidly. The old pad wouldn't have handled a ship the size of the *Wind* and it was not a huge ship and the pad barely held the military style boxy transport that was on it now. It appeared that only passenger shuttles ever really came out to this remote island. Farming island? They must not have exported much.

The cleared trees could be seen piled against the still living ones, branches and leaves still on them, the ends ragged from quick cutting. Stumps and mounds of dirt ringed the field.

As did a large contingent of armed guards and barriers, a crowd of people surging against it.

There weren't five hundred people, but there was way more than the *Wind* could take.

I brought the *Wind* into a hover over the field, the view out the window changing so we no longer had to look at the crowd. I glanced at Kaylia, wondering what she was thinking. She had her legs pulled up tight, arms wrapped around them and was staring at the storm. The ship shook, winds pushing at it, as I lowered it to the ground.

*****

I didn't open the *Wind's* cargo hatch, not yet, instead exiting by the sliding personal door mounted in the larger ramp. I didn't like the looks of that crowd. They could surge at any moment, nothing is scarier than a frightened crowd, and I wanted to limit access to the ship. I made Kaylia stay up in the bridge. She was able to monitor everything through the security cams but at least she was safer up there.

She hadn't protested.

Smart kid. She knew what could happen.

I'd never forgive the Tiat for taking away her innocence.

I stepped out on the ground of Storw, hand on my holstered blaster. I wanted the crowd to know I was armed. I noticed a couple of things right away as I used my free hand to shield my eyes from the dirt and small stones kicked up by the wind.

First there was a crowd of about fifty people off to the side alongside a dozen or so crates, adults and children. One of them was walking my way, bent against the storm.

Next was that the Storwo were short. They could only be five feet at the highest. Thin and a weird aqua coloring. Humanoid, with different shades of pastel colored hair and eyes.

As I looked out at the crowd behind the barriers, about a hundred and fifty of them, the last thing I noticed was that they weren't rioting. At all. They were standing there calmly, as if the arrival of the *Wind* wasn't their salvation but just a rare occurrence. In the crowd I saw looks of resignation and acceptance. But no anger.

Not what I expected.

The Storwo coming towards me looked official. Older, his bright hair a little less bright, dressed in somewhat cleanish and well tailored clothing. He carried a tablet of some kind that he held close to his chest out of the driving rain. He looked tired. Focused but tired, as if he was barely keeping it together.

"Captain Arek Lancer?" he asked, shouting to be heard over the storm.

"Yeah," I replied pointing towards the open hatch of the ship. "Come in out of the rain."

He followed me into the *Wind*, having a harder time stepping up and over the threshold then I did. Inside he used a hand to wipe the dripping water out of his eyes, looking over the empty hold.

"You did not empty your cargo hold on our accord," he asked.

"Caught us at the right time," I replied and winced. Not the best choice of words.

He gave a small smile, understanding.

"My name is Inhito, I am the local administrator in charge of the evacuation," he looked down at his tablet, running a finger along the surface. He spoke excellent Tradelan, barely a trace of an accent. "We have you slated for fifty passengers and cargo to go to the refugee camp on Hoin."

I nodded, doing the calculations in my head. Hoin was an independent system. Large planet, not a large population. A good place for refugees. I had wondered where all the Storwo were being scattered. Hoin was seven or so hops from here, eight or nine hours in between. Fifty-five to sixty-five hours total. I did a quick estimation of fuel and it would require a stop.

A long trip and a crowded hold. That was a lot of people to squeeze into that space.

"The cargo is foodstuffs as well as a limited number of documents on datachips and important cultural relics," Inhito continued running down a checklist on his tablet. "Each passenger is allowed two bags for clothing and personal effects they are responsible for."

I was working through the logistics, how much of the hold would be filled up with cargo versus people when Inhito continued by solving the problem before I could.

"Dock Control sent us the specs on your ship," he said still running off the checklist. "We utilized the space as best we could. Your hold will be filled as will the adjacent Galley and Lounge. With your permission, of course, we would like to place three families in your spare quarters."

The crowd still stood there calmly. The rain crashed down, the wind blew through the buildings. The soldiers, guns across their bodies, were there just for show. It took a second or two before what Inhito said to register.

"What? My spare quarters?"

"If you do not want them in there it is understandable," he replied finally looking up from his tablet.

"No," I said shaking my head. "It's fine. But you said three?"

"You have a crew of two," he said glancing back at the tablet to make sure he had the data right.

He should, I gave that information to Dock Control.

"Yes, but you said three families?"

"One of the cabins is set aside for a," Inhito paused, trying to think of the right word. I could tell that he wasn't happy having to do this.

"Nope," I said before he got the chance. "The cabins are for families."

"Very well Captain," he said, suddenly a little happier.

I looked at the gathered group that would be my passengers, small clusters of them huddled together. A couple kids held by their parents. The crowds contained kids, not that many but still a couple. Their parents also held them close. Too many kids.

"How long does the planet have," I asked looking up into the sky as if I could see the rogue asteroid already.

"Three days," Inhito replied, tired and resignation in his voice.

"When is the next ship?"

"Next ship?"

"Yeah," I said pointing up into the sky and then motioning at the *Wind*. "The next ship to get these people out of here?"

He glanced up at me quickly, a long look out the still open door at the crowd of people and back to the tablet, back to focusing on the task.

"We do not know."

I knew that would be the answer. Whatever ships had responded, like we had, that was it. The last group. I focused on a young Storwo at the front of the crowd, his mother's arms wrapped tight around him to protect him from the wind and rain and to provide comfort.

Would Kaylia mind? Of course she wouldn't. She'd be pissed if she found out I didn't offer.

"Find a fifth family," I said pointing at the crowd.

Inhito looked up again with a genuine smile. The first break in his routine.

"I will," he replied, almost bobbing with happiness. Just the thought of saving another family, saving more of his people, was enough. "They, we, will be most grateful."

I nodded, wishing I could do more.

CHAPTER THREE

Kaylia found it amusing that there were a whole race of people shorter than she was.

When she stepped out of the *Wind's* hold, following the lowering of the cargo ramp, she smiled and laughed as the Storwo used maglifters to bring the first crates onboard. That didn't last long as she came to truly understand the gravity of the situation when she caught sight of the crowd standing there in the wind and rain and watching, knowing that it was not them that got to escape a dying planet.

She was all business after that. I had her direct the families to the bunks on the upper level well I helped load and stack the crates. There wasn't much for me to do really. Inhito had already done up a quick layout on his tablet, using the crates to form barriers and make little areas so people had some privacy.

How many times had he done this the last few months?

The last of the families assigned to the bunks, those with the youngest and most children, boarded the ship, a lone mother with four children. She kept glancing over the heads of the crowd and into the city. The kids were all crying, hugging each other, as she led them deeper into the hold. Kaylia ran over and the kids were all attentive. They had never seen a Thesan before. She let them brush her fur, pull at her tail, all while laughing her silent laugh.

Nomad's Wind was filling up quickly. All the designated cargo was on board and almost all of the designated Storwo. I wanted to give them some time to get situated, to see if there was any way we could fit more of their people onboard.

Three Storwo guards, armored and carrying weapons, stood at the bottom of the ramp. One of them, rank insignia on his shoulder, checked everyone's identification before they boarded the ship. I wondered how people were selected.

The crowd still did not react, just stood there. I stood at the top of the ramp watching them, they watching me.

It was a steady stream of people now. Some kids, but only one or two with their parents, mostly middle aged adults. No elderly, which in a sad way made sense.

"Thank you Captain," one of the women said, stopping in front of me and holding out her hand, which I took. She was average height for a Storwo, bright purple hair cut short and eyes that matched. Not pretty but not ugly, somewhat plain. Friendly smile.

I nodded and she continued into the hold and I watched the rest of the people file in. They carried oddly shaped bags, filled with clothes and family heirlooms, important documents and all sorts of other things. In the past I'd seen some of the strangest things stuffed into a refugees bag. It was funny what some people found important. I didn't understand it. I owned very little and most of it was packed away. If it was lost, I doubt I'd miss it.

"They hope there will be more ships," a voice said next to me, her Tradelan accented.

A small Storwo woman had come up alongside me. A couple inches shorter than their average, which put her over a foot below my six foot height, she had bright purple hair and flashing green eyes in the light blue skin. A little older than me, but not much, she was a pretty woman. She wore green pants and boots, with a gray poncho.

"I hope so too," I replied. "I have to be honest. I was expecting the crowd to riot."

She was silent for a minute before replying, her tone sad.

"At first there was rioting. There was much destruction and death. Much looting. I hear the cities are still that bad but out here there was quickly acceptance."

Her eyes constantly searched the crowd as well as back into the ship's hold, like she was looking for something. Or someone.

"I am Dresla," she said abruptly, turning back to look up at me. I revised my opinion, she was very pretty.

"Arek Lancer."

"Thank you Captain," Dresla said, turning and walking back into the ship.

I watched her go, a commotion at the bottom of the ramp catching my attention. The guards had shifted, loosening the grips on their weapons. The officer held his hand up, stopping a Storwo man. It looked like he had pushed ahead of the line, huffing like he was out of breath. He was fumbling around in his pockets, looking more tired and torn than the others, a wide brimmed hat hiding most of his face. Oddly, he only carried a single bag and a small one at that.

The man was frantically searching, looking for something in his pockets. He wasn't finding what he wanted. Glancing down he realized he was carrying a bag and quickly searched it, pulling out a small and slim card. He presented that to the officer who stepped back, nodding to the guards. Quickly the man ran up the ramp, ignoring me, clutching the bag tight.

*****

"Captain, excuse me Captain."

The line of Storwo continued up the *Wind's* ramp. They moved quick enough, getting checked in at the bottom of the ramp and then up into the hold. Kaylia along with Inhito and it looked like Dresla were helping herd, for lack of a better word, the passengers and getting them organized. There was a lot of people, not much space left.

I looked behind me to see an elegantly dressed Storwo picking his way through the crowd. He moved through the line, not excusing himself. Inhito looked up, saw who it was, and looked away quickly. Not a good sign.

He was dressed in a suit. It didn't look like a Terran suit, but it was definitely a suit. The Storwo equivalent. I hated wearing suits and I didn't tend to like those that wore them on a regular basis, especially in a time like this. Water was dripping off the cuffs and pants but it was still neatly pressed, no wrinkles. I was kind of amazed that he had managed to keep it so clean and neat in this storm.

Not a single one of his bright green hairs was out of place.

"Captain Lancer," he said coming to a stop in front of me.

"Yes," I replied, curious what this guy could want. It was going to give me a headache, no matter what, that I knew. "What can I do for you?"

"I was supposed to get one of your ship's cabins," the Storwo said, his tone of voice indicating that he was shocked that it hadn't happened. "I was told that you gave it to someone else?"

I really should have guessed. Everything about this Storwo screamed of his self-importance.

"No."

He nodded, satisfied.

"Very well, I will inform them that they must vacate."

He turned and started walking away. I let him get a couple steps before stopping him.

"No," I said again. "I gave it to a family."

"But," he turned around, shocked and now a little angry. "That cabin was to be mine."

"And you are?"

"I am City Administrator Cortl," he replied actually puffing himself up.

"Well Administrator Cortl," I started taking a couple steps towards him. I'm not the biggest guy around. Six foot, two hundred. Black hair and beard with some gray. But I've been told that I can be very intimidating when I wanted to be. Right now I really wanted to be. Stopping only a step or two away, I smiled down at him. "It's my ship and I gave that cabin to one of the families."

"But," he stammered looking up at me, a little fear in his eyes. He tried to stand there looking important, he could feel all the other eyes on him, but he wasn't doing a good job of it. Cortl seemed like the kind of guy that used his position to bully others. I didn't like bullies.

"No buts. You find a spot in the hold here or you find a spot out there," I said pointing behind me. "Your choice."

Cortl tried to glare at me but couldn't manage to do it. He seemed to shrink as I stood over him. Turning he scurried back into the hold.

I caught Dresla and Inhito both hiding smiles.

*****

"That is the last one," the officer told me.

The rain pelted off the bottom of the open ramp, a tingy sound against the metal. The wind continued to push it sideways, the whole ramp wet, some getting inside the hold.

"Let me see what it looks like," I told him as we both looked out at the crowd of desperate faces. There was longing and hope. They knew the last of the designated passengers was on board and they hoped there would be room. I wanted to make some. "I might be able to fit a couple more."

The officer nodded, hopeful.

"Commander, Captain."

We both turned to see Inhito leading a woman through the crowded hold, weaving around people and bags of belongings. The small woman was crying and I thought I recognized her. The mother with the four children. Inhito had his arm around her, both of them searching the faces that were all now turning to watch them. Kaylia was behind them, worried.

"It seems we are missing someone," Inhito told us, checking his tablet. "Madam Certy's husband is not on board."

"I checked everyone's cards," the officer replied double checking the list he held. "Everyone was accounted for."

"Did you check everywhere," I asked Kaylia. "The storage rooms and airlock?"

I checked engineering as well.

"You're sure he's not here," I asked looking down at the woman. She was crying harder now, looking out at the crowd, looking for the familiar face.

"Positive," Inhito said and the woman nodded.

"But he's checked off," the commander said again, showing Inhito his own tablet.

Looking down at it, I could see the list of names. Sure enough, they were all cleared.

"Do you remember who checked in under that name," I asked.

The Storwo shook his head. I didn't blame him. I watched most of them enter and couldn't tell who was who, let alone single one person out.

I glanced at Inhito. He was rapidly scrolling through the tablet, searching. The poor woman just stared out into the distance, looking into the buildings beyond the crowd.

Madam Certy mumbled something quietly in Storwoi, the native language. I didn't understand a word.

"He went back to get some personal effects," Inhito translated. "He should have been back already."

I didn't think it really registered with any of them what all this meant. Someone was on board using the husband's card.

A rumble of thunder shook the *Wind*, causing everyone to shift and catch their balance. A young child started crying from somewhere in the ship.

I looked out past the buildings and could see a storm building. A big one. Lightning slammed into the water, sending up massive geysers. A wall of almost solid rain was coming our way. What we had now was nothing like that storm coming. It was still a good distance out, which was good because we had a more immediate problem.

We had a stowaway.

CHAPTER FOUR

From a distance the city of Touryon had seemed bleak. Not just from the circumstances. It was all gray stone, blocky and drab. Up close as I ran through the city streets, it was still gray and all stone but there was nothing drab about it. There were designs carved into almost every surface. No straight lines to them, whorls and swirls, circles. Some formed pictures, others just random imagery.

The Storwo themselves were bright, skin and hair both, so they saw no need to decorate their city with colors. But they still decorated it.

I wanted to stop and study some of the art. It would soon be lost forever but we were out in the city for a reason.

The commander of the guard, Hunio, ran ahead of me. He knew his way around the city. I did not. It was an awkward run for me as I had to move slower to not outpace the shorter Storwo. My instinct was to go full tilt, as fast as I could. But I couldn't. Hunio was going as fast as he could.

Luckily the city was nearly empty, most of the remaining citizens were either on the *Wind* or in the crowd that was now dispersing, going back to their homes to wait out the oncoming storm.

Two and three story buildings, close together, blocked my view of the ocean beyond so I couldn't track the storm but I knew it was going to be a bad one. We could feel the thunder as it shook everything around us. The flashes of lightning were visible through the gaps. Lots of flashes.

The *Wind* needed to be in the sky now. The atmosphere was already going to be rough because of the storm front and the closer it got the worse it would be. Even though a spaceship like the *Wind* could travel to a planet's surface, it was still ungainly and heavy. No real maneuverability. It was no starfighter.

But instead of leaving I was running through the city looking for a lost husband.

We heard a crack and a crash, the sound of glass breaking.

It had come from a building down a side street to our left. Hunio paused, looking down that way. I stopped next to him.

"Come on," I said, motioning at him to continue. I needed him to guide me through the city.

I could tell that he was torn. He knew we needed to find the husband but he wanted to find out what was happening. Turned out that Hunio was not military, he was law enforcement.

This was not what we needed right now.

Not sure why I was out here hunting down the husband but I was. Any potential looting was not my concern.

Dammit.

I took off running down the street, heading for the noise. I could hear Hunio behind me, pushing to catch up. This street ran straight, nearly identical buildings and homes on either side. About a hundred feet down we found the source of the noise.

Glass, real glass and not polycarbonite like most windows, littered the ground. Small pieces, big pieces. All came from a shattered window, large, that looked into a nearly empty shop. Standing in the street, the heavier rain starting to come down, we could see shelves and display cases. Along with two Storwo.

They stared at us in shock, frozen in the act of pulling some clothing or something out of a recently locked case. Their eyes looked down at my holstered blaster and at the rifle Hunio carried. There was no way these two were older than sixteen. The clothes they wore were soaked and ripped, old and frayed. They had been pulling newer clothes out.

I looked down at Hunio and shook my head. He nodded.

"Go home," I said to the two Storwo. They just looked at me blankly, not understanding.

Hunio repeated it in Storwoi.

They didn't move so we did. We could hear them grabbing the clothes and running away.

*****

The building was like any of the others. Two stories, gray with elaborate carvings. An exterior staircase led to the second level, windows looked out onto the street. The neighboring buildings were so close there was no alley between them.

Nothing special, nothing to mark it as the one. But Hunio said it was. The door was closed, the glass windows intact. There was nothing suspicious about the building at all.

That was what made it suspicious.

It looked like no one had been there in days.

Your family is on one of the last ships, if not the last ship, off your dying planet and you're not there? Yeah, no way was he missing the ship on purpose.

I was afraid of what we would find.

The storm was closer, the raindrops heavier, the wind stronger. Thunderclaps were closer together, the lighting flashes near constant. From here I could look down the street straight to the ocean and it was scary. Dark clouds, the lightning and the waves were high. The drops were thick, almost hurting as they hit.

We ran across the street and under the exterior stairs. They provided some cover, but the wind was blowing the rain sideways against us.

Hunio knocked, loudly to be heard over the storm.

Pausing he waited. Nothing. Knocked again.

He tried the door. Locked. He knocked again.

We didn't have time for this.

I pushed Hunio out of the way and took a couple steps backwards. Raising a booted foot I slammed it against the door. The wood cracked around the handle and I kicked it again. The door flew open to reveal an empty house.

No lights and what I could see was a mess.

Hunio pushed past, weapon raised and I followed. My blaster was still in the holster. I didn't think we were in any danger.

The room was dark, no lights and the windows closed and shaded. Furniture, smaller scale for the smaller Storwo, was scattered everywhere. Drawers were pulled open, various pieces of art and other objects thrown and tossed aside. Only the important stuff was taken and the room looked as if someone had tossed it looking for the important stuff. Every room would look like that.

Hunio was heading for the stairs against the far wall when we heard a thumping. Random, hard, like something hitting the ground. It was coming from a back room. Hunio moved slowly in that direction but I just walked past him.

He gave me a dirty look that I ignored.

We didn't have time for this.

I opened the door onto what looked like a kitchen and dining room, Storwo style. Dark gray cabinets made out of that wood like material, a small table, everything a little smaller. Thankfully their ceilings weren't that much lower.

Inside the room, on the floor, was exactly what I thought we'd find.

A male Storwo was tied up. Polyline bound his feet together at the ankles, more holding his wrists together behind his back. A piece of clothing was stuffed in his mouth. His eyes were huge as he saw me walk in, scared.

Madam Certy's missing husband.

I held my hands out to the side, showing I meant no harm.

"It's okay," I told him, not sure if he understood Tradelan.

Moving aside I let Hunio in behind me and the bound man seemed to breath a sigh of relief.

This room wasn't as messed up as the others. It was the eating space. No need to bring food and nothing else of major importance would have been in here. In the back corner of the building with no windows or doors, there wouldn't be much chance of any sounds getting outside. You'd only hear someone if you were inside like we were.

A good place to hide someone.

Hunio pulled the cloth out of the man's mouth and he started speaking in non-stop Storwoi. I didn't catch a word of it but I could guess.

"He says he came back to get a picture that he had forgotten," Hunio translated as he went to work on the man's bindings. "Someone hit him from behind and he woke up here."

Yep, just what I figured happened.

"Did he get a look at the person that hit him?"

Hunio asked him in Storwoi and the man replied. It went back and forth a couple times.

"No," Hunio replied with a hint of disappointment.

Probably hoping for one last arrest.

A crack of lightning followed by thunder that shook the house signaled that it was time to go. At this point, it didn't matter who had hit the man. We had to get him to his family and get off this planet before we were grounded by the storm.

We stepped outside into a wall of rain. Thick drops blown sideways from the wind. Worse than before. These were hitting with force and in a steady sheet. I couldn't see more than a couple feet in front of me.

Hunio helped support Mister Certy and we started pushing our way back to the ship. Luckily the wind was behind us, helping drive us, but we were soaked instantly.

*****

My back felt battered and bruised. I kept the two smaller Storwo in front of me, trying to protect them. The wind driven rain, thick and heavy drops, felt like being hit by rocks. There was no one else out and about, the sane people riding out the storm under shelter.

The *Wind* should have been in space by now.

I stumbled as a strong gust came in from the side, rain splashing us. It dripped from my hair, into my eyes, down my face. There wasn't a single part of me that wasn't wet.

The rain was a wall in front of us, clouds moving in to make it all dark. No lights were on in the city, adding to the darkness. I hoped that Hunio was able to tell where we were going. The sound of thunder and cracks of lightning were getting louder, getting closer.

My mind went back years. The rain and wind, darkness and strength of the storm, reminded me of a mission during my Earth Expeditionary Forces Special Operations days. I couldn't even remember the planet or the details, they blurred together after a while, but the details of that storm stuck with me. Rain dripping off my rifle, off my helmet, struggling to see the objective. So much like it was now.

I shook my head, sending wet strands of hair flying, as I brought myself back to the present.

Hunio turned us down a street and ahead I saw a light in the dark. Small, but getting closer as we struggled with the wind and rain hitting us in the side. Buildings started to block the storm and we could see the light turning into the open loading ramp of the *Nomad's Wind*.

Four shadowed figures stood on the ramp, two further down and two at the top. Three were about the same height and one was taller with a tail. Details got clearer. Kaylia and Inhito lower on the ramp. Madam Clerty and the one called Dresla at the top. Dresla had her arm around Clerty, pointing towards us.

One of the two Storwo in front of me ran forward, racing as fast as they could. The husband dashed past Kaylia and

into the arms of his wife. Hunio and I walked up the ramp, a
steady stream of water falling from us to join the river that
ran down the ramp.

You're a mess.

Kaylia smiled at me, stepping back as I flicked water from
my arm at her.

The three of us walked to the top of the ramp, watching
the Clertys move deeper into the hold. The wife was crying,
not caring that her husband's arm around her was soaking
wet. They huddled close together, stepping over others who
pulled their things out of the way to not get wet from the
stream coming from Mister Clerty.

"Thank you," Inhito said.

I nodded scanning the interior of the cargo hold, looking
at all the faces I could see. I wondered which one was the
stowaway, the one that had knocked out Clerty and stolen
his ID. I wanted to find the bastard and throw his ass out.

But we didn't have time.

"Prep the engines," I told Kaylia. "Get us ready to go."

She nodded, running through the hold, lightly moving
around the people. She was almost dancing. Show off.

I heard receding footsteps, turned and saw Inhito and
Hunio walking away.

"Aren't you coming," I asked.

Hunio continued but Inhito stopped.

"We must prepare for the next ship," he told me looking
over his shoulder.

I wanted to say something, anything, but wasn't sure what
to say. We both knew the chances of there being another
ship were slim to none.

He continued walking down the ramp. I stepped up to the
edge, watching him join Hunio at the bottom. The wind and
rain had picked up again, their forms nothing but dark
shapes as they ran to the nearest building. I watched for a
bit before hitting the button and closing the hatch.

I walked through the cargo hold, moving around the refugees. Nowhere near as nimble as Kaylia had been. I left puddles of water behind me.

CHAPTER FIVE

The *Wind* shook as it broke through the atmosphere. The storm was stronger here, winds pushing the ship around. My ship had wings, great gray ones coming off the wedged shaped blue metal body, with the engines mounted on those wings. It was what allowed the ship to go on planet. No wings, like some ships had and especially the larger ones, and they couldn't enter atmo. The wings also created nice big areas for the storm to hit.

Wind, rain and lightning.

The bridge door was open. I'd left it open so I could hear the activity throughout the ship. There wasn't much, everyone was trying to hold onto something. I could hear people grunting and mumbling as the ship was buffeted every which way.

Next to me, strapped into her chair, Kaylia had a death grip on the console.

I had a death grip on the controls.

A spaceship's inertial dampeners helped with dissipating the g-forces of space travel, but it did nothing for the turbulence in a planet's atmosphere. Just a little bit more and we'd break through the storm.

"This is fun," I said and glanced at Kaylia. She rolled her eyes.

I laughed.

The ship could take it. The storm was nothing really, not to the *Wind*. It just made for a bumpy ride. As long as we didn't take a direct hit of lightning.

Rain splattered against the view window, sheets of it, making it impossible to look out. We could hear the drops breaking as they struck. Everything was gray, rivers of water running down the window blocking all sight.

The sound stopped, the sheets falling away and we could see the black and white dots of the stars ahead of us. We'd broken through the storm. The ship settled and I released my grip.

"Smooth sailing," I said. "Can you do a quick run through the ship and make sure the passengers are okay," I asked Kaylia.

She unbuckled herself from the harness and left the bridge.

"Excuse me," I heard a voice say and looked over my shoulder.

Dresla stood in the doorway, turned around and watched Kaylia make her way through the ship. She turned and looked out the view window, mouth dropping open.

"Never been to space," I asked.

"No," she replied and stepped onto the bridge.

Didn't ask permission of the ship's captain, which would be me, but if she had never seen space from this angle then she'd never been on a ship before and considering the circumstances, I could cut her some slack.

I angled the ship, turning the window so it was looking out at the larger ships beyond. They were pretty distant but visible, not much detail but I saw Dresla take another step. She was in awe, amazed.

"Never get tired of the view," I said.

And it was true. I never did.

"It's amazing," she said. "I've seen stars from the ground of course but this," she paused and waved her hand vaguely at the window.

I adjusted the Wind, turning away from the ships in orbit and into deeper space. We broke atmo away from the rogue asteroid but could see the moon and some other asteroids further off.

"Got about an hour before we can hop," I said keying in the navorders.

"May I," she asked pointing at the co-pilot's chair.

I nodded. Kaylia wouldn't mind.

Dresla sat down, having to kind of jump to get into the chair. She looked like a full grown adult, and a good looking one at that, but was the size of a child. I'd never realized how much of the *Wind* was sized for average human adults.

"I know the basics of space travel," she started rotating the chair so she could examine all the instruments and controls. She just looked, not touched. "But I have never been out in the stars before."

"What do you know?"

"A ship moves from space into the...," she paused looking for the right word.

"Wildspace," I supplied. "And it's called hopping."

She nodded and started over.

"A ship hops into wildspace and then comes out in another system."

"That's about all there is to it," I said and leaned back in my chair. I put my feet up on the corner of my console, hands behind my head. The ship was basically on autopilot until the hop point. "It really doesn't get more complicated. I mean the theory behind it all is complicated. The math is extremely hard to follow. I tried looking at the calculations once but it gave me a headache."

Dresla laughed. Like all of Storwoi, it had a melody to it.

"But don't need to understand the math to know it works," I finished.

We watched the stars through the view window. Noises carried up from other parts, people talking. I glanced down at the internal systems readout. I wasn't concerned with the weight of all the people. The *Nomad's Wind* was a freight hauler, it was made to transport weight. But it wasn't made to handle this many bodies. The air handlers, refreshers and other systems were only built for a maximum of six. There was a lot more than that now.

They'd overload long before we got to Hoin.

I leaned forward and adjusted some of the settings, dialing back the climate control and the water settings. We'd be stinky and uncomfortable by the time we got to Hoin but it was better than anything breaking from overuse. Ships were fine tuned instruments. Problems in one area inevitably led to problems everywhere else.

Wouldn't take long for these many people to use up the oxygen reserves if life support went out.

"How long have you had the ship," Dresla asked, looking over to study me.

"Five years," I replied. I knew I was considered ruggedly handsome. Six foot, solid build, two hundred pounds, black hair and beard. But I was starting to wonder what her interest was. "Before that I was a soldier."

"I knew it," she exclaimed with a smile. "I thought it was that. Solider or law enforcement."

"That obvious?"

"If you know what to look for," she replied. And she was right. Us vets did have a swagger that if you knew what to look for it was there. A way we walked and carried ourselves.

"Your Tradelan is nearly flawless," I told her with a chuckle. "Better than mine. Where did you learn?"

"I was a coordinator at the Storw landing port," she explained and looked out the window, quickly turning away from me. Hiding something maybe? Not the full truth, that was for sure.

There was a tap on the door frame and we both turned to see a frazzled looking Kaylia. Her hands moved rapidly, too fast for me to follow. I was getting pretty good at her sign language, but times like this when she moved them this quickly, I got lost.

"Slow down kiddo," I said and she did.

Help. I can't understand them.

"Looks like there's a language barrier issue," I translated for Dresla. "Can you help?"

She stood up and headed towards Kaylia who was smiling, glad for the help.

"Take your tablet so you can communicate with her," I told the kid. It would have been interesting seeing Dresla try to translate for Kaylia when she didn't know the sign language.

I watched them walk down the hall, stopping at the door on the right. Kaylia went in as it opened. That was my cabin, Kaylia's normal one was across the hall but we'd given it to a family so she was crashing in mine. She came out with her tablet in hand and led Dresla towards the stairs down to the lower half of the ship: the galley, lounge and hold.

Dresla had said it was obvious that I had been a soldier or law enforcement.

I wondered if she realized how obvious she made it as well.

Which was she? Soldier or law? I was leaning towards law.

*****

The black background punctured by white dots of stars turned to the cloudy white of wildspace as the stars stretched into lines. The *Wind* hopped into that weird space between systems. Dark matter, wildspace. No one really knew what it was. No transmissions penetrated it, so a ship was flying blind. There were stories of some ghost ships being lost in this void and some beings freaked out while here but I found the fogginess of wildspace to be calming.

I hadn't seen Kaylia in awhile. She must have been wandering the ship getting Storwo's situated. I should have done that as well, get an idea of just how many people there were. Between loading, chasing down that errant husband and the stormy take off, there hadn't been a chance for me to really assess what the situation on board the *Wind* was. It wasn't a large ship by any means. It was going to be tight.

That thought only reminded me that there was someone on board that shouldn't be here, that had knocked out a legitimate passenger and stolen that spot. I wondered how much trouble that would cost. I mean, the reason why was obvious. They wanted off a dying planet. There would be no reason to cause trouble unless someone went looking for them. So was it better to just leave it alone?

Probably.

Easier for me to just let go and keep the drama to a minimum. It was already going to be a rough trip. Did I really need to go adding to it?

Nope.

Leaning back in my chair I started to relax, watching the swirling clouds thinking I'd go grab an ale from the stores.

The peace and calm didn't last long.

I could hear the argument before I heard the actual words. They were in Storwoi and one was raised voice, the other quieter and weaker. It came from the hallway outside the bridge, where the bunks were.

Getting up I stood in the doorway. I could see a Storwo about midway down on the left side. He was standing in an open door, not going into the room, almost yelling at someone inside. I recognized him as Corti, the City Administrator.

I knew what this was about.

Was it too late to throw his ass off the ship?

"What's going on," I asked stepping into the hallway.

He jumped, startled, and fell back a step. At least he looked guilty.

"Shouldn't you be down in the hold?"

I looked into the doorway and saw a family. Two kids sat on the bed, young. They looked scared, a boy and girl. Two other kids, both somewhat older boys, stood against the opposite wall. The mother was against the back wall. The father was a couple steps in. He looked relieved to see me.

"Again, what is going on," I asked Corti turning to him, putting on the full weight of my size advantage.

He was an older Storwoi. Up close I could see the wrinkles in his pastel colored skin. His bright green hair had a few small streaks of duller color, the Storwo version of the gray in Terrans. Did Storwoi dye their hair? I would have bet that he did. He worked hard to maintain his appearance. I wondered how quickly it would fall apart on this trip, especially living down in the hold.

Corti started to say something but it was in his language. I held up a hand to stop him.

"Tradelan," I told him.

Standing up a little straighter, taking a deep breath, and smoothing his suit coat Corti composed himself. This one was pure politician and I hated politicians. They had been nothing but trouble during my time in the 2E Special Operations. Lots of friends had been killed because of a politician's stupidity.

"I was merely trying to negotiate with this family to gain possession of the room back."

I rolled my eyes. He looked annoyed.

"One," I started and pointed a finger at him. "It was never in your possession. I don't care if someone said you could have it back on planet. The second you stepped onto my ship you lost whatever rights were given you. My ship, my rules. I decide who gets what."

He started to speak but I didn't give him a chance, pointing at him with two fingers now.

"Two. That didn't look like negotiation. That looked like intimidation."

Taking another step back, I saw a smirk crawl onto his face. He thought he had me now.

"Intimidation," he said now looking directly at me. Had I mentioned how much I hated politicians? "Similar to what you are doing to me now?"

I laughed. That caught him off guard.

"My ship, my rules." I jabbed my finger at him with each word, aiming for the forehead, but not quite touching. It was rewarding to see him squirm back as it came close each time.

Inside the room the mother had come closer and was standing next to her husband. The kids were quiet on the bed, the older ones almost laughing. The parents watched with interest and a little amusement.

"But tell you what," I continued taking a step back from Corti, lowering my arm, appearing at ease. "There is a room that you can have if you'd like."

He looked at me in surprise and a little concerned, not quite sure how to take it. Curiosity and his self-importance won over and he stood up straighter again, back to politician mode.

"Why thank you Captain. That would be perfect."

"It's the airlock."

This time I smirked at him.

His self-satisfied expression dropped and he looked at me angrily, upset at looking foolish.

"Back down stairs with you," I said and pointed towards the stairs going down.

Trying to muster as much dignity as he could, Corti walked down the hall. He didn't bother looking in the room, or at me. I turned to watch him go. Dresla stood at the end, a smile on her face. Corti did his best to ignore her as he stalked by. She walked down the hall and looked into the room.

She said some words in Storwoi, the father inside the room saying something in return. He looked up at me and nodded, thankful. I nodded back. Thanks and your welcome. Men can speak volumes with just a nod.

They closed the door leaving me and Dresla alone in the hall.

"He thanked you for the help," she said. I knew that was what he said, didn't really need a translation. It had been in the nod. "Even on Touryon, Corti used his power to intimidate others."

"What exactly is a City Administrator?"

"Just what it sounds like," she replied. "He was in charge of the city. Touryon may not have looked like much, but it was a vital city. The only island in that part of the world with the ability to dock large cargo ships and spaceships. Being the Administrator of the city gave Corti a lot of power."

I'd seen the spaceship landing pad and it wasn't that big. What size ships were they used to on that planet?

"What about Inhito? Isn't he an Administrator as well?"

She shook her head.

"No. Inhito was not from Touryon. He was sent by the planetary government when the evacuations started, along with Hunio and the rest of his guard. It was Inhito's job to organize the evacuees," she paused at the word and grew silent. I let it linger, understanding where it was coming from. "It was his job to prepare us," she finally said. "To decide who would leave first and who would wait."

"Tough job."

"There were riots at first," she said continuing as we walked the short distance back to the bridge. "But those calmed soon and order was restored. The government instituted a lottery system to be fair and it worked well at first but then the moon cracked and..."

She drifted off, lost in thought again. I could imagine what happened. The evacuation ships slowed as the storms started, tides rose and all sorts of other natural disasters that resulted from the moon cracking. At that point, people just gave up and accepted their fates. They'd get off or they wouldn't.

Same attitude that I'd seen in people in the middle of a war zone. Either they'd get bombed or they wouldn't. Life goes on and you live it as long as you can and in the back of your mind you hope for the better result.

I sat back down in my pilot's chair. Dresla stood in the open door looking out at the cloudy emptiness, lost in thought.

After a time Dresla wandered off.

There wasn't much to do now. We were in wildspace, our course set. We couldn't receive transmissions from the Galactic Feed, we couldn't communicate with anyone not on the ship. Nothing ever really happened in wildspace because you never encountered another ship. If you were traveling with a fleet, which happened sometimes, you had to sync your coordinates for each to appear the same distance apart in the other system when you arrived. There were stories of ships hopping on top of each other.

Can imagine how that ended.

But during the trip, it was as safe as space travel could be. If something went wrong with the ship, we'd hop back into normal space. It would be jarring and a little scary, but we'd survive. As long as it was nothing catastrophic. There were stories of ships being lost in wildspace, breaking down and not being able to leave, just drifting aimlessly forever.

I tried not to think about that aspect and just enjoyed the flight.

Footsteps, light and nimble, told me that Kaylia had returned. I looked over my shoulder as she stepped onto the bridge, yawning.

"They all settled in?"

Yes

"No problems?"

Not yet

Only thirteen, she was a very smart kid. Had seen a lot in her short life. A lot of the bad things in the galaxy and even in her own people. During her first week with me, I'd caught her checking the Feed for all she could find on the Thesan Wilders, her parents and where her DNA came from. There wasn't much but what she found was pretty bad. She knew what was lurking in her genes and she didn't like it.

But a strong kid, Kaylia didn't let that bring her down. I was proud of her. In the few short months we'd been together, the kid continued to impress me.

So she knew what having all these people on a small ship like the *Wind* could mean. We'd just have to hope nothing bad happened. There wasn't much we could do about it.

*****

I left Kaylia on the bridge. I'd make her go get some sleep soon.

We'd decided, or more accurately I had, that one of us would try to be up at all times. There would come a time in the trip that it wasn't possible, but we'd try. I was thinking of teaching Dresla how to operate the various systems and check the controls. It would be nice to have a third set of eyes so we could rest and I had a feeling I could trust her.

I'm a decent judge of character.

For the most part.

We'd see how the first couple nights went.

I kept the *Wind* on a standard Earth cycle. Twenty-four hours, a 'day' of twelve and a 'night' of twelve. Didn't mean I slept on that cycle, but it helped maintain some sense of time. Every planet, space station, moon and inhabited asteroid kept it's own local time. It made landing confusing as sometimes it was the middle of the local night or it was what you thought of as the middle of the night but a bright day on planet. Glancing at my wristcomm I saw that it was only early evening on the *Wind's* day.

It would mess up Kaylia's sleep cycle. I didn't keep normal hours but I tried to get her to maintain some. But it couldn't be helped.

Stepping out of the bridge I turned left and took the side corridor that ended in the spiral staircase leading down. On the hop to Storw, Kaylia and I had taken all the important stuff and locked it in the two storage rooms on either side of the bridge, behind a code lock. Someone could always try to hack it, but I wasn't worried. Well it wasn't a strong code, it would still take some time and on a small ship like this time alone was not something anyone would have a lot of.

My weapons stash was hidden at all times. I'd only kept my trusty Sig blaster and that was now locked in the safe in my bunk. So for the most part, there wasn't much of anything valuable or important that was out where anyone could get at it.

The stairs were a tight spiral, the deck between floors only a couple feet. I could hear noise in the galley, the stairs opening right into that space. Cabinets along one wall, more cabinets and the cooking appliances along the other, a table and chairs in the middle, door to the lounge on the opposite wall. Nothing fancy but functional.

Only made to sit eight, the table was covered in containers of various sizes and shapes. There were maybe a half dozen Storwo moving about the galley preparing food. Some were organizing containers along the table, setting up a buffet line well the others were cooking. I only recognized Dresla and she smiled at me as I passed through the room.

The lounge was full. The viewscreen mounted on the far wall was off, the door to the side that led to the airlock and the escape pod was closed. Kids were scattered around the room, a couple Storwo adults standing against the wall watching them. The kids played with some games or other toys they had brought.

I weaved my way around the kids, nodded to the adults and stepped through the open door into the hold.

And didn't even recognize it.

The Storwo had been busy.

There were some polyplas crates of various sizes maglocked to the deck and the Storwo had worked around them. They had hung up rope, sheets suspended from it to form little living spaces. It was chaos but an organized chaos. People sat in small groups talking quietly, sitting near sleeping friends and family. They had even managed to form thin walking paths.

Impressive.

I looked across the faces, none standing out, wondering which was the stowaway.

I had decided that as long as he or she didn't cause trouble, I didn't really care.

The old Lancer luck helped that out.

CHAPTER SIX

The alarm sounded about two hours after I'd fallen asleep.

We had just completed the first hop when I had awaken Kaylia for her turn in the bridge and I had gone into the bunk to try to sleep. I doubted I would be able to. Too much to worry about, part of it about Kaylia being alone with all those refugees. Only a couple months into this guardianship and I was already the worried parent.

I'd laid down and surprisingly fell asleep.

Until the alarm.

Quiet, not the full on screaming claxon that signaled a massive failure. This one was calmer, just a beeping. I'd know that Kaylia would be getting it on the bridge, but I'd long since connected all the *Nomad Wind's* system readouts to my wristcomm. The ones that I could anyways. That included the ship's onboard alarms.

Glancing at the thin readout, I couldn't tell what the alarm was for.

Wristcomms are great devices but can be limited. They were created to link to a ship's control system or a space stations. You had all sorts of information available on the small device. Only about three inches long, it had a face barely over an inch wide that sat on the top of your arm with straps holding it in place. A couple of buttons that could scroll through the menus but only a very thin read out.

Some of the more expensive models had full holographic projectors.

Those were way out of my budget.

I silenced the alarm, which would cancel it on the bridge too. A sign to Kaylia that I was awake and aware. Grabbing my shirt I left the bunk, taking my boots in hand. As my bunk was the closest to the bridge, I stepped out the sliding door, took a quick left and stepped into the bridge.

From her co-pilot's station Kaylia looked up at me, a little panicked.

I don't know what it is.

Nodding I sat down at my station and looked the screen over.

"Someone was playing with the airlock door," I told her a minute later as I stood up. "Stay here."

I moved quickly, but quietly, down the stairs and into the galley. The readout said someone had tried to open the door but hadn't activated the lock. It wouldn't operate with the interior door open so there was no worry of someone making a breach. Part of me kind of wondered what would happen if someone opened the airlock. We were currently in wildspace again and that wasn't necessarily like the void of space. No one really knew what it was like. No one had been tempted to open an airlock and spacewalk in wildspace.

The galley was empty and clean. Everything had been put away. Any dishes used were cleaned up. The space was cleaner than I normally left it.

No one was in the lounge either. And it was picked up as well. There had been games, books and toys scattered around earlier. But now it was empty.

If it hadn't been for the noises, slight as they were, coming from the open door to the hold, I would have thought Kaylia and I were alone on the ship.

I walked to the door, glad that I had set all the doors down here to stay open, and looked into the space. With the sheets and crates, it was hard to see all the people. The ones closest to me were asleep, huddled together under blankets. Parents held kids closer, giving them most of the blankets. It wasn't cold in the ship but there was just something about sleeping wrapped in a blanket that provided comfort.

There were a couple of Storwo stirring, I could see a couple heads sitting up, but it seemed most were asleep. I knew that none of the five families in the bunks had gotten out, Kaylia would have known and mentioned it. So it had been someone down here.

I walked back into the lounge and to the airlock door. It was colored to match the wall, no view window into the space. Only the outline of where it opened marked it as a door. That and the control panel next to it.

Nothing looked tampered with. Someone, a kid maybe, had just played with the controls trying to open it. Curiosity most likely. Like the storage room doors, and engineering, it had been code locked.

That was normal for the *Wind,* all the doors being code locked. A bit weird for a ship with only one crewer, now two, but I'd had enough unwanted visitors and been boarded by pirates over the years that I had gotten a little paranoid. All doors were locked and there were cameras everywhere.

Almost everywhere.

The lounge's camera didn't cover the airlock door as it was mounted above it.

I could still look at the footage to try to see who had been playing with it.

Was it worth it? There had been no harm done but I was curious.

That it was done at night, when everyone else was asleep, was kind of suspicious.

Yawning, I made my way back up to the bridge.

*****

Kaylia stood behind me, looking over my shoulder, as I scrolled through the security cam footage. The monitor was on the console to my right and looked newer than the other readouts and controls next to it. Which it was. Most of the controls of the *Wind* were original but the security console was new. With all the modifications that I'd made and had done, the *Wind* itself wasn't close to original spec. I wonder what the Castellan designers would think? They'd probably have a fit. Shipbuilders were a bit touchy when it came to people messing with their designs.

I found the timestamp I wanted and slowed the video.

We watched a shadowed figure enter the lounge from the open door to the hold. They moved slowly, the head turning to indicate they were looking around as they walked. The way the shadows around the head moved, it looked like a being with long hair. A woman? The frame was a little more slight then the male Storwos. The figure disappeared from the camera's view, getting close to the airlock door.

The figure stepped back into view, just barely, before moving back to the door. Moving away to get a wider look or thinking of leaving and changing their mind?

Whoever it was had made a decision, as a couple seconds later we saw a small flash. Only visible because of the darkness in the lounge.

Another minute or so of thought and the figure stepped away from the door. As the figure started to move away I hoped they would turn their head just the right way. But they didn't and I was worried that we wouldn't get a look. But then they paused and turned towards the galley as if hearing something.

Still not the best picture but the person was recognizable. We both knew who it was.

Mostly because there were so few Storwo on board that we actually knew by name.

The late night creeper was Dresla.

*****

My instincts told me that I could trust Dresla.

They were rarely wrong.

But they were wrong sometimes.

Could she be the stowaway?

Out of all the refugees, she was the most forward, the only one interacting with Kaylia and myself. I thought it was because she had been appointed, or appointed herself, the leader of the group and the liason.

Normally, if you were keeping a low profile you'd do just that but maybe she thought by being more open and connecting that I'd think her less likely to be the stowaway?

Back in my Special Operations days, I hated the complicated missions. I wanted things to be straightforward. There's the enemy. Go shoot them. Nice and simple. But sadly too many of them involved politics and that always made things more complicated. I made a pretty decent intelligence operative when I needed to be but it was something I had thought I'd left behind. Too often though, things kept creeping up.

I had hoped this trip wouldn't be like that.

There wasn't enough information to really come to a decision, one way or the other.

Did I really need to?

Normally I would have said no. It was something that I could leave alone.

And I would have left alone but she had been doing something to the airlock. If she had just laid back and enjoyed the trip, could have left it alone. But the airlock thing showed there was more going on beyond just hitching a ride off a dying planet.

That could mean danger to me, Kaylia and my ship.

No way could I leave it alone now.

*****

Ship's morning and we had just hopped back into wildspace. Kaylia was asleep.

Now anyways.

It had been a struggle. She had wanted to be there when I talked with Dresla. She'd done her best to try to convince me but in the end I had ordered her to bed. For a teenager, or the Thesan equivalent of one, she listened to me pretty good.

The kid was smart. She knew when to listen and when she could push it.

I found Dresla in the galley, helping make breakfast for the refugees. It was mostly the same women as before and like before they pretty much ignored me. Except for Dresla. Again, she looked up and smiled.

"Can I talk to you a minute?" I asked her as I stood at the bottom of the stairs.

She nodded and leaned towards another woman that was at the counter behind her, saying something in Storwoi. The other replied and moved over to replace Dresla. She walked towards me, wiping her hands on her pants. I motioned towards the stairs and she followed me up.

"Need to show you something," I said as she stepped onto the upper corridor.

Very quickly I saw worry pass across her face. There and gone. She knew I was on to her but was still playing the part. Wonder what she was thinking?

In the bridge I motioned her towards my station and pointed at the security feed screen. It was paused, showing the empty lounge.

"Watch."

I hit a button and played the footage at normal speed. We watched the shadowy figure walk slowly through the lounge, disappear at the door, the flash, the figure reappear and turn to leave. I paused it at the image showing Dresla clearly.

She stepped back, only a couple steps, not enough to put real distance between us. Standing straight, she calmly looked up at me. No panic, no worry. Just acceptance.

I would have expected at least some panic from a stowaway. Maybe a quick explanation. Something. But instead she just looked at me, waiting on me to make the first move.

Studying her I sorted through all the information I had on her, the few and brief conversations. One thing stuck out to me. A comment from the first time she was on the bridge. She had pegged me as military or law enforcement. I thought she was the same. But now?

Now it was time to trust the instincts.

"You're a cop aren't you?" I asked.

It took a minute for her to respond, studying me the whole time. Finally she nodded.

"What gave it away?"

"Same reasons you had me pegged as a soldier," I replied. "So want to explain that?" I pointed at the paused screen.

She looked out the viewwindow at the cloudy white of wildspace, collecting her thoughts. I leaned against the bridge's rear wall, arms crossed, and waited.

"When the asteroid was first sighted, our scientists realized what it meant and informed the planet. There was rioting and looting as to be expected," she began and sat down in the co-pilot's chair, still looking out the window. "That died down as the evacuation plans were made public. That happened rapidly, surprisingly."

"I've never understood the idea of looting during an apocalypse event," I interjected. "You're not going to be able to take it with you and what is the point of having it for a few days or weeks?"

"Agreed. I had expected the looting to start with the announced evacuations, not before. Steal some items of value and sell them off planet. That did happen, but not to the extent we feared it might. Especially when it was announced that anyone that was caught would not be permitted off planet."

"That would put a stop to it."

"It did. For the small stuff. It allowed us to concentrate on the bigger stuff." She laughed. "That was hard. For years our job was to worry about a thief stealing credits from some rich *tiuk*. And now, in the end days of our world, we could care less about that."

I've always found it interesting that Tradelan does such a poor job translating curses.

"We started worrying about important cultural artifacts and documents."

That made sense. Destroyed planet relics go for big money on the black market. And those things would be important to the survivors. Some crooks would buy 'em from desperate survivors on the cheap and sell them at huge markups to the other survivors that wanted their relics back. Shady business. But profitable.

"Most were recovered before the moon cracked," Dresla continued. "I was assigned to track down one of the last. We tracked it to Touryon as that city was lower down the list of evacuations. It was the most likely place the thief would find a way off Storw."

"What's so important about whatever was taken?"

"It's called the *Daelot*," she explained, pulling her legs up and sitting cross-legged in the chair. 'It's...," she started and paused, shrugging. "It's hard to explain. Do you have anything on Terra that is considered vitally important but to an outsider would seem strange?"

I nodded. There was a lot of things that I could think of.

Really didn't matter what this D*aelot* thing was. Not to me. Just mattered that it was on the *Wind*.

"I assume that you suspect the person that stole Clerty's ID is the thief?"

It was her turn to nod.

"I've been searching for the *Daelot* since we left Storw. I thought that maybe the thief had hid it in the airlock, one of the few places that might be accessible and others would not go."

Made sense.

"The pad was alarmed?" she asked.

"Yeah, most of the doors are. Tied into cameras," I explained. "The *Wind* has had unwanted passengers too many times so I wanted to control access as much as possible."

Dresla looked up at me with an odd look. Surprised? Confused? Wondering what I meant about unwanted passengers.

I shrugged. It would take too long to explain.

Turning the pilot's chair, I sat down and leaned back. I tapped my fingers on the console randomly, thinking. Dresla sat quietly and watched me. I could hear noises coming up from the galley below. Sounds of people talking, chatting, trying to forget they were refugees from a dying planet.

I glanced at the door and the sounds.

"The *Wind* is a small ship. All is good now but that probably won't last. It's a long trip and tight quarters. I want you to find your *Daetot*," I said struggling with the word.

"*Daelot*," Dresla supplied, smiling.

"Thank you. I want you to find it but not at the expense of making life difficult on the ship." I sighed, answering my own internal question. Finding the stowaway wasn't worth disrupting the lives of the Storwo even more. "Does that make sense?"

"I won't stop looking," she said, a hint of steel to her voice. "But I understand and agree."

She stood up and headed for the door, pausing to look back at me.

"I will try to not set off anymore alarms," she said with a chuckle walking out the door. I heard her step back in and turned. "His name is not Clerty. Storwo do not have two names."

Dresla stepped back out into the hall and I heard her small footsteps descend the spiral stairs.

Learn something new everyday.

*****

The next day went smoothly. I was able to sleep. No alarms.

Things were proceeding smoothly.

Dresla had gotten to me and now I watched all the Storwo on the *Wind*, looking for suspicious behavior. Honestly, I really didn't have a problem with someone stealing credits or something to set themselves up when relocating from a dying planet. I really wasn't sure how I felt about stealing artifacts. That felt different. Wrong.

Weird. I know.

"Captain."

I paused as I was about to go up the stairs to the upper level. The galley was somewhat empty of people. They had just finished up the afternoon meal and there were five Storwo cleaning up the many dishes and putting food away. The stores were looking a little thin and I was starting to worry there wouldn't be enough to make it all the way to Hoin.

A Storwo woman was approaching. She was a little shorter than average with bright purple hair and eyes that matched. Short hair cut and kind of plain. I thought I recognized her. Maybe one of the ones that had spoken to me the first day? Aside from Dresla, Clerty and her husband and that Administrator guy that spent most of the time sulking in a corner of the hold, I didn't know any of the others on board.

As she got closer, I realized that it was her. The one that had come up and personally thanked me.

"Yes, what can I do for you?"

"I was wondering if you could give us access to the view screen in the lounge?" she asked pointing behind her into the other room. Through the door I could see some kids scattered around and playing or reading. The lounge had turned into the daycare. "It would be nice to show some videos for the children."

"Of course," I replied stepping back to the floor. Why hadn't I thought of that? "We're still in wildspace so you'll only have access to what is stored in the system."

"Why is that," she asked.

"Can't receive transmissions well in Wildspace. We'll be in the Yersk System in a couple hours and can get some new vids then. But we'll only be in Yersk for maybe thirty minutes, if that. Then it'll be about another eight hours until we're in the Tuint System and the next available time to download. You'll need to program the Feed to grab things for the kids at those points. We'll be in Tuint for longer as we'll need to stop at the station and refuel."

"That will be fine," she said. "Thank you Captain. I am Torsi," she said extending her hand.

"Arek is fine, Captain just sounds weird with only a crew of two," I told her shaking her much smaller hand.

Torsi followed me back into the lounge. I had to step around the kids and their toys as I walked to the viewscreen on the far wall. Mounted into the wall next to it was the control panel and I hit a couple buttons, unlocking the passcode.

"Do you need some instructions?"

"We should be able to figure it out," Torsi replied as the kids started to gather around. "We do not want to take you from your duties."

"There's not much for me to do," I replied stepping out of the way. Which was true, but the amount of kids and how close they were was starting to get a bit overwhelming.

I was not a kid person. Aside from Kaylia, I wanted nothing to do with them. Had a couple nieces and a nephew back on the Mars Colony, my sister's kids, but I had seen them only a couple of times. Talked to them sometimes via vid but it was mostly passing messages back and forth. They were growing quick, I knew that. Played some sports.

Really did need to visit my sister at some point soon, but whenever I thought about taking the trip back to Sol things always came up. I bet Kaylia would love them and my sister would love the kid.

I moved behind the couch and watched Torsi play with the controls. The screen came to life showing the standard Galactic Feed image, an artistic rendering of the galaxy, and then the menu options appeared. Hadn't taken long for her to figure it out. The kids starting talking, excited, and I smiled as I walked away.

That didn't last long.

*****

Yersk is a small system. Four planets, each with two to four moons. Only Yersk Prime is inhabited by the Yers, a race of mottled gray skinned amphibious humanoids with webbed feet and hands and four long tentacles growing out of their backs. Not the friendliest beings in the galaxy. They're grounders, planetlocked, meaning that they don't have the technology to starhop from system to system. Still see them out and about, not that common, but they hitch rides with ships coming out of the Yerbig colony on the planet as they end up working for the green skinned and big headed Yerbigs.

Yerbig's are somewhat amphibious so it's no surprise that they established a colony on Yersk. Their home system, Uin, is only a six hour hop away.

There's no reason for anyone else to care about Yersk Prime so the system is just a hop point. Lots of traffic at the edges as ship's hop in and out again.

My co-pilot and I were awake at the same time as we hopped in. One of her tasks was downloading the Feed for the latest updates. There was some automatic stuff, vidmail and the such, but the rest had to be grabbed manually.

I was checking the navorders, making sure all was in order when Kaylia tapped on the console. I turned to look and saw she was almost in tears.

"What?"

The planet.

She had to be talking about Storw and from her expression I knew it was going to be bad.

Hitting a couple buttons on one of my screens I brought up the latest news. It didn't matter the channel, this wouldn't be an unbiased report. The problem with such a large galaxy is that there is so much news out there and it's all biased in some way. It's hard to get an unfiltered view.

But for this it didn't matter. Everyone would be saying the same thing the same way.

"Tragic news for the last remaining people on the planet Storw in the Wils System," the newscaster was saying, a Kry. "The rogue asteroid's close proximity has cracked the planet's moon even more, sending larger shards to the planet's surface. Striking the surface has caused massive earthquakes over the entire planet, increased storm activity and other natural disasters. Because of this, no more ships can land and the evacuation has been called off. Nearly five million Storwi remain on the planet."

That was it then. The planet itself had days before the asteroid struck but for the people remaining, it was over. No ship would land in those conditions.

"Well damn," I said shutting off the video.

I turned to Kaylia, tears running down her cheeks, crying silently.

All those people.

"I know kiddo."

Walking over to her, I leaned down and pulled her tight. Her arms wrapped around me and she buried her head into my chest. I could feel her body shaking with silent sobs.

If we had never stopped to help, if she'd never met any of the Storwo, would she still have felt this bad about the planet's doom? Probably. I knew that Kaylia was a smart kid, but I was also finding out how empathic she was as well.

Wasn't getting it from me. Empathy was not one of my strong points.

*****

The news spread quickly. We didn't tell anyone but they got it through the Feed access that Torsi had set up. Didn't know if it was her or one of the others that had caught the news segment, but it spread throughout the *Wind*.

Somber atmosphere, lots of crying. No anger, just more of the resignation. I was afraid of someone taking that anger out on the ship or other Storwo. Didn't happen. It takes a long time for someone to stop looking at other races through the cultural filter of their race. All of us travelers through the galaxy based our reactions around our culture and judged others by those same guidelines. It wasn't fair, but it was what it was. That was the baseline and sometimes, more often than not, people were able to change and start being more understanding of the cultural differences. Not expecting other races to react the same as theirs.

I was looking at the Storwo through the lens of a Terran. I was expecting them to react as I knew my people would when faced with the same news.

Was one reaction better than the other? That kind of deep thinking is beyond me.

I was just glad no one was damaging my ship.

No way would I be able to get them to pay for the repairs and I didn't have the extra money. The *Wind* isn't the fanciest ship around and usually needs some kind of repair, but I try hard to not let her turn into a piece of junk. There are some that say it's only what's inside that counts, the engine and the strength of the ship, and well there is some truth to that the more important truth is that I have to live in the ship and take some pride in its appearance.

Everyone was silent, even the kids who picked up on their parents mood.

I had no idea what to say to them so I said nothing.

Torsi was in the lounge hugging another female Storwo as the vidscreen was on behind her. I recognized the same newscast as the one I had seen. It was now paused, the newsperson in mid-comment. I made my way through the crowded room and shut it off.

I saw Dresla walk in from the hold, wiping a hand across her face. She gave me a weak smile walking pass, stopping to talk quietly with a couple of the other Storwo. These ones followed her into the kitchen. I did as well and saw them start taking supplies out of the crates they had brought on board.

Smart woman. Get back into the routine. Give the people something else to think about.

I felt a vibration through the *Nomad's Wind* as we hopped into wildspace for the trip from Yersk to Tuint, a six hour hop. The course had been programmed in so all Kaylia had to do was watch the controls and make sure no warnings popped up. She knew which button was the hop override and since I had heard no alarms, figured it was a good hop. I'd go up and double check in a few. It was also time for her to get some sleep.

The vidscreen was turned back on and I heard the sound of some kids show. The language sounded Storwoi. Where had they managed to find that? Could hear the sounds of kids talking and starting to laugh, shuffling around to watch the show.

They'd have a proper mourning for their world when they arrived at the refugee camp on Hoin.

I stood at the bottom of the spiral stairs for a minute or two watching the meal prep. There wasn't any of the usually talking, sharing of stories. They were going through the motions, something that had to be done.

Everyone has experienced loss at one time or another. Death of a family member, a loved one or a friend. Hell, even a beloved family pet. But there is something different in experiencing the loss of a planet. There has to be.

There's another race, the Derty, that lost their world to pollution a couple of centuries ago. Way before humans were wandering the galaxy. Without the benefit of a home world, or a place to call home and set up most of the population, the race starts to die out. It's inevitable when there's no one location to find others of your own kind. Interbreeding with other races, if it's possible and it's normally not, doesn't help. No, for your race to survive, they needed to breed with others of their kind.

For most races, only a small percent of their population lives in space. The majority live on the homeworld, the colonies or the space stations. Some never even leave their place of birth.

I never heard why, but the Derty didn't have a planet to evacuate to. They scattered across the galaxy and over time just started to die out. That's why the Planetary Council tried so hard to find a place for the Storwo to go. There's a lot of life in the galaxy and all of it is precious.

Dresla directed the silent Storwo, keeping them on track.

I watched for a little longer and then went back upstairs to relieve Kaylia and send her to bed.

Sitting in the pilot's chair, watching the featureless and calming white of wildspace, I had time to think on fate and all that higher stuff but I try to leave that deeper thinking to others. I'm not a big picture kind of guy. Instead I thought about the galaxy and its people and how close we all were to disaster on a daily basis.

The Planetary Council, for the most part, is a waste of time and energy. They try to be big, come up with all these grand ideas and galactic law. The only true law is the basic law of society. You need people to live and help you survive so you don't try to piss them off because someday you'll probably need them.

A bit cynical, but true.

The Council is comprised of ambassadors from most of the major galactic races, at least those that have colonies outside their home system. Except the Tiat. They were invited and refused. No surprise. The group tries to have authority and some planets grant them more than others, but it's really just the different empires pushing their own agendas.

Every race that travels the stars is expansionist at heart. They want more, that's why they're out there. Sure, some went to other planets because their own couldn't support their growing populations anymore, but it's still expansion.

Most races learned a long time ago to give space to the others. It's a large galaxy, plenty of planets to go around. And that's why us earthlings are almost galactically hated. When we expanded, we basically started a galactic war.

Good times.

So I had to wonder what the Planetary Council had promised the Hoinites to allow the Storwo to settle on their planet. Had to be something major. Hoin was a large planet with a small population and there had to be some reason they had kept it small. It was a grounder planet, no spacefaring tech of their own.

Maybe that was what the Council was giving them? The ability to hop the stars.

And a population of people indebted to them.

Yeah, that made sense.

And it sucked.

The Council, or whatever planets pushed for this resettlement, would be reaping some kind of reward. This felt like a Coulson plan. General, retired, Frank Coulson was the Terran Ambassador to the Planetary Council. The head one anyway, there were a couple of them, each representing a planet or colony that Earth controlled. Coulson was just the big guy with the others essentially following his lead. I'd run into him a couple times during my soldiering days. He was behind a lot of black ops that unfortunately I was involved in. We didn't get along then and still didn't.

Luckily, we ran in different circles. His was the bright lights of the Inner Core worlds and the Planetary Council. Mine was the wilds of Deep Space.

I liked my circle better.

Guaranteed that Coulson had his hand in this resettlement. No clue why. It would mean the government of Earth would be getting something out of it but Coulson would be personally getting more.

Not my concern.

The Storwo, or at least some of them, had to know they were ultimately getting a raw deal. But if it was that or lose your entire species? Easy choice to make.

I had to remind myself to just think small picture. I was saving a shipful of people. A very small amount in the grand scheme of things but at least they would live. Doing my part. And not getting paid.

The kid and I would have to work twice as hard for a month or two after this.

But it was worth it.

I'd remind myself of that when struggling to buy fuel for the *Wind*.

CHAPTER SEVEN

The cloudy white of wildspace gave way to the black with millions of white dots of normal space. Same view as any other system. They all looked basically alike. Pilots had to rely on the navsystems to let them know what system they were in. Without it, they were blind.

Tuint was a large system. Twelve planets, making it one of the largest known, but only one inhabited or even livable. None of the other planets or even their moons could be lived on. Nothing even worth mining. Just the one lonely planet the furthest from its sun with the next nearest planet pretty far away. Tui, the only inhabited planet, was equidistant to its neighbor as it's neighbor was to the sun.

Basically Tui was pretty damn far from the sun and pretty far from any of the gas giants that made up the system. It had one moon that was just standard rock and iron. Nothing special, nothing making it worth mining.

That and the Tuis themselves were very territorial when it came to their moon. They didn't care to mine the sacred object and no way would they let anyone else. The surface was covered in the wrecks of those that had tried.

The strange part was that unlike most other systems, Tui wasn't a ball of ice. In every other known system, the further a planet was from the sun the colder it was. The closer and the hotter it was. The dream zone, for life, was the third or fourth planets usually. But not in Tuint. The sun was so bright that the last planet was a pretty moderate climate.

Lots of green, trees and water.

A decent place to live.

Not a decent place to fly into.

The Tuis Dock Control was notoriously difficult to work with. I'd spent hours waiting for their customs people to show up before I could even start to think about unloading cargo and it was hours after before I could unload. They went through everything. Multiple times.

And the bribes. I had always thought Dynuit was the worse, until my first trip to Tui.

At least the *Nomad's Wind* could enter the atmosphere and land on the planet. This was one planet where it paid to have a light freighter. There was no space station in the Tuint system, just the planet, so all large ships had to be unloaded in orbit. That added extra cost and time. Because of this, not many large trading guilds or companies wanted to travel to Tuint.

The bribes meant not many small freighters wanted to either.

There was talk of building a space station, but that had started a couple years ago with no momentum.

Tui didn't have much to offer and the Tuis themselves were notoriously cheap.

I had no desire to stop there but the *Wind's* fuel reserves said we were stopping.

Hearing some footsteps behind me, I turned and saw Torsi standing in the bridge's doorway. She was looking out the view window at the starfield beyond. It would be an hour or so before the planet itself was visible, so the view was just lots and lots of stars.

"I thought I felt the shift out of wildspace," she said motioning at the bridge.

I nodded, giving her permission to enter.

An old custom, not practiced by many. Besides no one being allowed to board a ship without the captain's permission, an old custom that had fallen out of use, was the one where no one could enter the bridge without the captain's permission. I'd heard it was still enforced on the passenger cruisers but everywhere else it had faded away.

Interesting that a Storwo would know of it.

"You've star hopped before?" I asked her turning my seat around again to check the controls.

"A couple times," she replied coming to stand next to me between the pilots and co-pilots stations. "Not extensively, only to the next system."

"How far out from the planet are we?" she asked after a bit of silence.

"Hour," I replied. "We'll be on planet for a while to refuel."

From the corner of my eye I saw her glance over at Kahlia's console and the chrono there. It was set to Terran time and had us midway through the *Wind's* night cycle. Everyone else on board was asleep. Not sure why she was up.

"So we'll be hopping out in a couple hours," she stated and turned to leave. "Goodnight Captain," Torsi said as she left the bridge.

When my instincts tell me to run, I run. And I've always been a decent judge of people. Something was making my instincts tell me that she was lying. Or at least not telling the full truth. I got enough of a read from her to know she was definitely hiding something.

Just like that I knew who the stowaway was.

There wasn't one thing that told me that Torsi was the thief. It was a lot of little things.

Her interest was the big thing. The only Storwo besides Dresla to show an interest in me, the *Wind*, or the travel times. Dresla's reasons were now known but the rest just tried to get through their days and it was understandable why they wouldn't want to know exact times. Even the husband that I had saved.

I was convinced that Torsi was the thief.

Now how to convince Dresla.

I remembered the time and realized it would have to wait. Dresla was asleep somewhere in the cargo hold.

It could wait.

Afterall, it wasn't like Torsi was going anywhere.

*****

I yawned. Tired.

Kaylia was at her station, adjusting the final navorders for bringing the *Wind* into the atmosphere of Tui as I watched the consoles and readouts. Everything was normal for planetary entry. No storms on our flight patch to Yorunital, the only major port on the planet. No other traffic, which was not a surprise.

Easy flight in and hopefully an easy flight out.

I should have been asleep in my bunk but the timing didn't work out. Kaylia had never done a planetary entry and this wasn't the time for her to do it solo. So here I was, awake after I don't know how many hours, piloting a ship full of refugees onto a planet to get more fuel.

Concentrating on the controls, I put thoughts of bed out of mind.

Tui was a lot of green, the sphere coming closer with the moon beyond the curving horizon. I adjusted the ship, feeling it shudder a little as the thrusters changed our angle. The view started as half green at the bottom of the view window, the moon beyond and the stars filling up the upper part of the view window, and it shifted to more and more green as the *Wind's* nose pointed down towards the planet.

Down was relative as from one viewpoint we could be flying up towards the planet, another could be flying sideways. But to us in the ship, we were going down.

There was a little shaking as we entered the atmosphere and entered the thin cloud cover. The view window filled with white, reminding me of wildspace, before we broke the barrier. Bright blue sky, green trees and blue of water filled our vision once past the clouds.

Like I had said, a good looking planet.

It looked pristine, almost untouched. The Tuis worked hard to keep it that way. They kept all off planet commerce in one location and maintained strict flight paths. There were around forty million beings on the planet, only a couple thousand not native and the amount of those that lived fulltime on the planet was even smaller.

I wasn't used to seeing this much untouched land. Even Storwo had more cities and tech spread across the planet. Here it was just green. We flew over a couple thousand miles of land and never saw a single city. Yorunital had maybe twenty million living there, so where did the other twenty live?

Ahead, by scanner only, I could see the city. It would be a couple more minutes before the skyscrapers would be visible to the eye.

We could see a series of mountains, dark gray against the green, appearing off to the side when the alarm sounded.

I glanced down at my readouts, looking to see what the noise meant.

The airlock.

Again.

Someone was tampering with the lock.

Torsi.

Had to be.

Cursing I adjusted the *Wind's* speed. I could have stopped the ship and put it in hover, but that would have made Tuis Ground Control contact us to see what was happening. A ship pausing in the flight path would delay their tightly controlled flight patterns. And Kaylia wouldn't have been able to communicate them.

And I was going to be busy.

Instead I slowed the ship. We might still get a ping from Dock Control, but at least we were moving.

"Keep us straight," I told Kaylia.

The poor kid looked panicked. The alarm, irregular sleeping, piloting the ship in atmo. It was a lot to put on her. I could see the questions, and the fear in her eyes. I tried to be as reassuring as I could be.

"You got this."

I didn't wait to see if she reacted and I bolted out of the bridge. I was down the corridor, down the stairs and in the galley in seconds. There was only a couple Storwo, all trying to push against the far wall, away from the door to the lounge.

The lounge wasn't as empty as the galley. Storwo hugging a few kids tight, crowding the edges. One woman was on her knees, hands outstretched and held back by two others. All were pushing and moving away from the airlock door. That space was clear except for three people.

Torsi, Dresla and a kid that Torsi was holding by the neck.

She had what looked like a knife, taken from my kitchen no doubt, held at the kids neck. I could see a thin line and a couple drops of blueish blood on the poor kid. He was terrified, eyes wide and crying. Looked to be only six or seven, maybe eight.

Dresla held both arms out, palms extended, so Torsi could see them at all times.

Both glanced at me as I walked into the room, Torsi's grip tightening and her eyes dropping to my waist to see if I was armed. I wish. She was lucky. If I was armed I would have shot her right then and there. I hated people using children as shields.

"Release the kid," I told Torsi.

I could see the faceplate for the airlock door controls had been ripped off the wall and some wires pulled, hastily spliced together. The door itself was open, she had one foot past the threshold and I could see a small wrapped object on the floor. The *Daelot* or whatever it was called.

"I didn't want it to be like this," Torsi said and I did believe her.

Her stance, her eyes, the hostage, all told me that this was something she had not anticipated. She had been hoping for a clean escape.

"Release the kid."

"She's the thief," Dresla said angrily.

"I know."

That earned a quick look from both. Each surprised.

I took a step closer. Torsi shifted back, pulling the kid who was too scared to struggle.

What was with beings and taking kids hostage lately? First Kaylia and now this?

More Storwo were appearing, crowding at the door to the hold. They were quiet, the whole place was quiet. It was surreal. I'd been in similar situations, sadly, and didn't remember them being this silent.

"Release the kid," I said again, putting more menace and threat into my voice. I really wanted to shoot her.

I could have too, without hitting the kid. She was taller than her hostage, all her head and most of her chest visible. Easy shot.

But the blaster was safely locked away up in my bunk. Out of reach. Too far away.

I've never been a good negotiator. I've always been a blunt force kind of guy. I prefered to shoot or punch my way out of problems. Not talk. It's always so much simpler.

Torsi was starting to look panicked. I could see it in her eyes as they darted around the room. The Storwo woman that was being held back was on her knees now, crying and reaching for the kid who was reaching for her. More blood was forming on the kids neck as he strained against the knife.

Dresla said something in Storwoi. She stared at Torsi calmly, arms at her side, body positioned to charge. Torsi's free hand chopped through the air and she spit something back at Dresla in their language. I had no idea what was said but it made Torsi angry and she took a large step back, dragging the kid.

"What did you say," I asked Dresla, voice loud enough for Torsi to hear.

"I told her that she was trapped and to give up," Dresla replied not taking her eyes off Torsi. "I also said that we would give her a lighter sentence if she gave up her contacts."

"That went over well," I muttered with a sigh.

What was Dresla thinking? She had no authority, not anymore. Not really. They both knew that. No one would care about Torsi's contacts, who she was going to sell to. Not yet and not for a long time. There would be no lighter sentence on Hoin. The refugee camp would administer frontier justice. If she gave herself in, Torsi knew she probably wouldn't survive long. All Dresla did was remind Torsi of what she was facing.

It was time to calm things down.

Just because I didn't like negotiation, talking, it didn't mean I had no idea how to do it.

Most of it was just to keep talking, engaging the person and basically stalling until you had an opening.

"What happened," I said getting both Dresla and Torsi's attention. "What caused this?" I waved my hand indicating the stand-off.

"I started to suspect that she was the thief yesterday," Dresla said, her attention returning to Torsi. She took a slow step forward, her motion barely noticeable. At least I hoped so. I glanced at Torsi who didn't seem to catch it. "So I kept an eye on her. Caught her trying to get into the airlock."

I filled in the rest. It was during the Storwo's sleep cycle, lights out. Torsi had tried to quietly get into the airlock, maybe to hide the *Daelot*. She had no idea about the alarm, like Dresla did, but it didn't matter as Dresla had caught her anyways. Torsi reacted quickly and grabbed the nearest hostage, a sleeping child.

Now what were we going to do about it? More accurately, what was I going to do about it?

Torsi looked from me to Dresla and shifted position so she could look behind her and still mostly see us. Her free hand reached out and touched the controls mounted on the inner wall of the airlock. The *Nomad's Wind* isn't a large ship. Most of the space is taken up by essential spaces: living spaces, engineering and the cargo hold. Because of this, the Castellan ship builders had built the escape pod off the airlock instead of a seperate room like in larger ships.

That meant that Torsi was steps away from the escape pod and was now trying to open the pod's access door.

And yes, the pod door was not code locked. Why would it be? The idea of an escape pod was to be able to get into it quickly. A code defeats that purpose.

The pod didn't have that much range. Limited fuel capacity, most of the space given over to life support. It had the capability of planetary landing, as well as launching in atmo. Torsi could get in the pod, launch it and land pretty much anywhere on the planet.

So why not let her?

I didn't care about whatever it was she had stolen. That was Dresla's concern. My concern was not getting my ship damaged.

Or letting that kid get hurt.

"Take the pod," I told Torsi. "Leave the kid."

Dresla turned to me quickly, angry. She started to say something but my look stopped her. It said 'my ship, my rules'. She backed down.

Torsi nodded as the pod door slid open. She gave Dresla one last look, waiting for the other to make a move. Nothing happened so Torsi pushed the kid forward and stepped into the pod, kicking the stolen artifact before her. The door slid shut behind her as Dresla caught the kid.

I ran forward to the airlock control panel. The wiring was a mess. The panel had not been opened with finesse, it had been forced open. The wires were ripped out, a couple quickly spliced together. No care, just speed.

And there was no way I could get it back together quickly. Not in time to stop the pod from launching.

I wasn't worried about the pod launching and opening the ship up to the atmosphere. The pod's access doors were a small airlock, two sets of doors. One on the pod and one on the ship. The seal on the ship side wasn't that great, I would need to get the airlock doors shut before the ship could go off planet but there was a bit of time.

The deckplates shuddered, a vibration building and sliding along their length. I heard the exterior pod doors opening, sliding back on their track. I half hoped they would jam open.

I had no intention of ever abandoning the *Wind*. She was my ship, I was the captain and I would go down with her. Fighting the whole way. I didn't keep up with maintenance of the pod, not like I should have. Pods were supposed to have regular operations. Getting them started, opening the doors. Basically everything short of launching it.

Which was supposed to be done every two or three years. I'd owned the *Wind* for five years and never done it. Not an expense I wanted to pay.

And now that I had Kaylia, maintaining the escape pod suddenly became very important. Just add it to the long list of things that I didn't have credits or time for.

There was a loud metallic snap, the maglocks holding the pod in place releasing. I could hear the engine and feel the *Wind* lurch as the escape pod shot out of the angled front end. Of course it would work perfectly.

I could picture it in my head. A ten foot long cylinder, barely the height of an average man, and maybe five feet wide, all a shiny gray color with no view window. It had two large thrusters mounted on either side of the cylinder at the back with wings that could be extended for atmospheric flight. Inside there were five padded seats along the sides and one seat directly forward, the pilot station. The thing was small and cramped but it did the job.

There was no noise that I could hear through the *Wind's* hull plates or over the sound of my ship's engines.

The pod would drop down, heading towards the ground, since that was where the *Wind's* front end was pointing. It's launch speed and trajectory would put it directly in front of our path. Torsi needed to be quick if she was going to avoid the ship crashing into her.

I felt the ship lurch to the side, the quick maneuver too much for the inertia compensators to deal with. I heard the sound of multiple things crashing to the floor, people and objects. There were cries of surprise and a couple of pain.

I ignored the movement of the ship, trusting that Kaylia knew what she was doing.

Honestly. I was impressed at the rapid movement. I hadn't expected her to be able to react that quickly.

"How could you let her go?" Dresla asked as the ship settled and smoothed out.

I spared a quick look over my shoulder. The kid was gone, probably in the arms of his mother where I couldn't see. Dresla was angry. I didn't care.

Finding the wires I wanted, I reconnected them to the control panel and hit the code. The airlock door slid shut.

Turning I started towards the galley and the stairs when Dresla stepped into my path.

"Why did you let her go?"

I fought down the urge to laugh. This tiny little thing looking up at me angrily.

Sighing I forced myself to calm down.

Dresla was only doing her job. Or what had been her job. Her dedication was commendable. There really was no point in apprehending Torsi and getting the artifact back. Who would she return it to? Who would judge Torsi?

As I looked at the anger in Dresla's eyes it hit me.

"She stole it on your watch didn't she?"

CHAPTER EIGHT

If stares could kill, I would have been dead.

Dresla was not happy, which told me that I had guessed right.

She stared up at me, angry and embarrassed. I ignored her, pushing past and into the galley. I was up the steps quickly, hearing her following behind me.

As soon as my head crested the floor I saw Kaylia standing in the opening to the bridge. She was frantic, hands moving too fast for me to keep up. I had no idea what she was saying. Normally she was good about doing her sign language slow for me to follow, but not when she was overly excited, nervous or scared. She was all three. A couple quick steps and I was standing before her. I took her hands in mine, lighting holding them.

"It's okay kiddo," I told her. "You did good."

And she had. That jerky maneuver had been just enough to get us clear of the escape pod. Torsi was stupid. We were in the process of landing, the pod shot out directly in our path. Of course Torsi had no way of knowing that but Kaylia had managed to get us just enough out of the way. The turbulence would have buffeted the escape pod heavily. No way was it a smooth ride.

The kid removed her hands and signed more slowly.

There's a transmission from Ground Control.

I nodded, and with hand on her shoulder, lightly directed her back into the bridge. She moved to her co-pilot's seat and pulled her legs up, arms around them, head resting on her knees. A clear sign she wasn't fully recovered.

Sitting at my station, I pulled the headset on and immediately heard the Tuis Ground Control.

"Unidentified ship, please acknowledge receipt of landing authorization."

I glanced at the comms and saw the incoming coordinates and clearance from the Tuis. As well as an indication that a message had been sent. Where had that come from? Kaylia or I hadn't sent a message recently.

"Ground Control this is *Nomad's Wind*, Terran registration SE6890. Landing authorization acknowledged."

It sounded innocent enough but I knew that if I hadn't acknowledged and given the ship's registry, we would have been shot out of the sky.

"Purpose of landing on Tui?"

"Refueling," I replied.

"Length of time on planet?"

I thought about how to answer that one. Buying and loading fuel would take an hour at the most, not even that. But Torsi had taken my escape pod. That would be expensive to replace. I knew Dresla would want to go after the thief. Could I make her stay on the ship somehow? I could leave her behind. Refuel and go. If she wasn't back, she'd be stuck here. That would be on her, her decision.

Dammit.

"A couple hours, maybe a day," I told Ground Control. "I have a shipload of refugees from Storw and they've been stuck in the ship for days. Could use some air and space."

I could feel Dresla's expression of surprise without even looking.

There was a long pause before Ground Control answered. Probably trying to decide how much they could overcharge me.

"There will be additional docking fees for an extended stay," the reply said finally.

Couldn't wait to see what this would cost me.

"Understood."

I removed the headset and programmed in the docking coordinates, setting the ship on auto pilot.

Now to see what that random message was.

"Captain," Dresla started to say but I held up a hand, stopping her.

Wasn't in the mood. Not yet.

The message was just an info burst, data sent out as a transmission. It had been hidden in the Feed drop when we had hopped into the Yersk system. When the ship's system had automatically downloaded the latest from the Galactic Feed, it had automatically sent out this preprogrammed message.

I almost laughed, a little upset with myself. It was a neat trick. Torsi had gotten me to give her access to the lounge's vidscreen which connected to the Feed, which allowed her to send the message. Smart.

The system quickly decoded it so I could read it. A simple encryption had been used, a basic one to protect the message well being transmitted across satellites and through wildspace. It also made sense that it didn't take long since the encryption had come from the *Wind's* own system. Tt would be easy for that same system to decode the message.

It was what I thought. A meeting time, here on Tui. Torsi's contacts.

The sale was happening on Tui.

"Did you do anything to tip Torsi off that you were on to her," I asked Dresla without turning around, pulling up the meeting coordinates.

"No," she said, a tad indignant. "Despite what you may think, I am good at my job." There was a pause and a sigh, the tone more humble. "It was only recently that I discovered that Torsi was the thief."

I wanted to make a sarcastic remark, something to make the guilt that Dresla must be feeling even stronger. She owed me an escape pod. But I couldn't. Even the most observant person needed to be forgiven if they were distracted by the destruction of their entire planet.

"Something tipped her off," I explained. "Otherwise she wouldn't have gone for the escape pod."

"I did think it odd that she tried to leave the ship now and not earlier," Dresla said stepping into the bridge and onto the top step that led down to navigation and weapons.

The *Wind's* bridge is two levels. Pilots on the upper left, co-pilots on the upper right. Down a couple steps is weapons and comms on the right and navigation on the left. Dresla stood on the first step down. She was short, by Terran standards and this made her even shorter.

"Her contact is here," I told her.

"How do you know that," she asked, surprised.

"She sent a message hidden in the Feed download," I replied. "Programmed to send when we were in Yersk and got connected to the Feed."

Dresla turned, stepping back up to the pilot's level, and strained to look out the view screen. With our angle it showed just the blue sky and white clouds of Tui, with the system's sun behind us. It was midday on the planet. A nice and sunny day.

"So you know where she is going," Dresla asked without looking away.

"I do."

I expected Dresla to make some kind of argument, something to persuade me to join her in going after Torsi. She didn't. At least not right now. I knew it was coming as soon as we landed.

That was fine.

But I was curious why Torsi had decided to go for the escape pod and not just wait for us to land.

*****

Yorunital was a tight city. Almost all skyscrapers, some reaching a hundred stories, all built close together. Overall the city took up a very small footprint on the planet. Maybe three-quarters or a half the size of other cities with the same populations. Very little in the way of parks on the ground level. What I could see was suspended at the higher levels, built on the tops and between skyscrapers. Trams connected the buildings at various levels. Not a single bit of ground space was wasted.

It grew in the middle of a large and flat plain. Green grass, the thick forests stopping miles from the first metal building.

Lots of space for the city to expand. None of it used.

Off to the side was the spaceport, nestled between the buildings and the forest. The only thing expanding out from the circle of skyscrapers. A matte black metal surface covered acres of ground, guide lights marking the various landing sites. A series of low hangers could be seen at the far edge. We were still too far away to see any ground control vehicles or shuttles and maintenance vehicles.

The buildings themselves were very utilitarian. No real design, just tall. An ugly and lifeless place. Why would anyone want to live there?

I adjusted the *Wind* and guided us towards our assigned docking pad. It was near the buildings, which was good as that would put us closer to ground transportation and other facilities. Hopefully near the refueling stations.

The ship flew slowly over the ground, the green of grass giving way to the black of the landing area. It wasn't that crowded, I could only see a handful of ships. All around the size of the *Wind*. One of them stood out, some kind of high-end yacht. Very shiny and fancy. Very expensive. Very out of place.

Using the thrusters I stopped our forward momentum, a small shudder moving through the ship. Another adjustment and we began to lower to the ground.

Because of the wedge shape of the ship I couldn't see anything below us so had to rely on the sensors and the external cameras. Through the monitor I watched the guide lights and the black surface coming closer. Glancing at the monitors I counted down the distance and signaled to Kaylia.

On her station she hit some controls and we could hear the Wind's landing gear lowering. A louder noise indicated they had locked into position. I could have done it from my station, all controls were routed to my console, but Kaylia liked being helpful.

And it was good practice for her. Someday she's do this by herself.

The sound of the *Wind* landing on the hard surface was loud. The ship shook, most of the shock being absorbed by the suspension units built into the landing gear.

I shut off the thrusters and leaned back in my chair. I could feel Kaylia's eyes darting from me to Dresla, who was still holding onto the edges of my station to keep herself steady. The kid probably guessed what was coming. I hadn't had a chance to explain it all, but she was very observant and a quick study. She'd picked up most of it already.

She shifted, taking the cue from my lack of movement, and began putting the *Wind's* systems into standby, prepping the ship for refueling.

I waited, knowing what was coming.

Dresla's hand released the console and she looked out the view window, the only things visible were the tall skyscrapers not that far away. A hundred stories of non-reflective windows and metal. Finally she turned to me.

Here it came.

*****

"Captain Lancer," Dresla began but I held up a hand to stop her.

I leaned forward and massaged my temples with my fingers. I knew Dresla was going to ask for my help, give me lots of reasons why I should. Recover a national treasure. Stop a thief. Blah and blah.

Looking to the side, past Dresla, I could see Kaylia. She watched me, expectant, and I wondered if she had an idea how close it was? The kid was a bad influence on me.

"I'll help," I told Dresla.

She looked shocked. Kaylia smiled.

"Torsi stole my escape pod, I want it back," I continued, not caring if either believed me. "Those things are expensive."

I really did want to get the pod back. They were expensive and I couldn't afford to replace it. Just me, I wouldn't have cared. But I had the kid to worry about. She'd been entrusted to my care and that meant I wouldn't let anything happen to her.

That was secondary though.

I can be pretty selfish sometimes but even I have some limits and some honor.

From the moment that I found Torsi holding that kid hostage and attempting to escape, I knew I'd help track her down and apprehend her. I'd done some work for the Territorial Protectorate through the years. The TeePees were the police force on Human controlled worlds and colonies. So I had no problem helping out the authorities.

I also had no problem helping out people on the other side of the law.

This whole situation with Storw was bad. These people were losing their planet and were becoming pawns of the Planetary Council. It was a crappy situation. They didn't deserve to have their cultural identity and history sold on the black market along with everything else.

Especially by one of their own.

Sometimes I wished I was more of an asshole.

"If we're going hunting you need to get someone to control your people," I told Dresla. Not the nicest way to put it, but I was aggravated. Mostly at myself for being a sap. "They need to stay on the ship and out of Kaylia's way."

"Understood," Dresla replied turning to leave the bridge. She paused, as if to say something else, but thought better of it.

Smart.

I glanced over at Kaylia. She was still studying me, smiling.

"Not a word."

She turned back to her station, still smiling. It was even bigger if that was possible.

I shook my head and keyed in the commands to track the escape pod.

CHAPTER NINE

My bunk was a mess.

A fifteen by ten space, it was never all that clean to begin with. But there were two of us crashing in it now. Crowded too. Or more crowded than normal. When just me, there was only the bunk with drawers underneath, a desk and a chair. Now there was a collapsible cot for Kaylia and bags of her stuff.

How had the kid gotten this much stuff in a couple of months? Lots of clothes. So much clothes. Where had she kept it all?

And when did she wear it? I prided myself on being pretty observant but I'd never noticed Kaylia wearing this many and this different of clothes. I figured she had two or three outfits like I did.

Shaking my head I made my way over to the bunk, stepping around the cot and piles of clothes. The cot really hadn't been slept in. The kid and I had been on somewhat off shifts so one of us was piloting and so been able to both use the bunk. I was just glad that Thesans didn't shed.

I pulled open the right drawer, which was empty and not that deep. Feeling around the underside of the bunk, I found the button and a panel slid open on the bottom of the drawer showing a keypad of six numbers. I input the code and the false bottom slid open to reveal the hidden compartment.

Inside was my Sig Sauer T1700 blaster and holster. Standing up, shutting the drawer, I belted the holster on. Low slung, there was a strap on the bottom that fit around my leg above the knee, the rest a belt.

The powerpack was full and I felt better having the weapon strapped on.

I could handle myself just fine in a physical fight but with the wide variety of beings in the galaxy, firepower was always nice to have. Especially with no idea of who or what we'd be running into.

And that was why I ran into the storage room between my bunk and the bridge. I thought about using the secret hatch off my refresher into the room, but that would be overly paranoid. So what if one of the Storwo saw me going into the room?

There are two storage rooms on either side of the bridge, but the one on the port side had been modified. So had most of the *Nomad's Wind*, but this one had a little more care involved.

I walked into the room and went to the far wall. There wasn't much in the room itself. I didn't have many possessions, just a couple of small trunks. If the Wind's systems didn't automatically keep the room dust free, I couldn't imagine how thick it would be. I didn't come in here or touch them that often.

Finding the latch and controls hidden on the wall, I opened a secret panel.

There was a thin compartment built between the wall of the room and the outer hull. There was a cavity running around the *Wind*, between the hull and the walls. Not enough space for someone to get into and there was a ton of wiring and piping but I'd managed to carve out some space and had the secret compartment installed.

This was where I kept the stuff I really didn't want people to know about.

Most of it was legal to own, in some systems, but not in others.

A couple different weapons, some blasters and rifles, and even some gear that I'd managed to take with me when I left the 2Es. That stuff was definitely illegal to own in any Planetary Council system. I grabbed one of the rifles, a Carlyle 600, checked the power pack and closed the hatch. Slinging it over my shoulder I reached down and grabbed a

Techon 750. A small blaster, it didn't pack a huge punch but it had range and was accurate.

Not knowing what Dresla usually packed this was my best guess on what would work for her. I pulled out the holster and belt for it, hoping it would pull tight enough for her to wear.

I looked the stash over, seeing if there was anything else that I would need. Really wished I'd managed to grab some body armor. The stuff the Earth Expeditionary Forces used was top notch. Even the slimmer stuff I had used in Special Operations. I missed the extra protection.

Also wondered what was wrong with my life that I had so many weapons and was concerned with not having armor.

Most freight haulers didn't worry about this kind of stuff.

It's not like I went looking for trouble. It just seemed to find me.

A lot.

I sure as hell didn't seek it out.

My sister called it the old Lancer luck. Trouble had plagued me my entire life. It's what basically forced me to join the Earth Expeditionary Forces.

Which didn't turn out that bad for me in the long run. Made me a better person. I'd always been scared of what my life would have been like if I hadn't joined up. Would never know but I knew what I was like before and the path I was heading down. I could just imagine how much worse it would have been.

Probably would have been dead by now.

Of course the time as a soldier could have led to my death as well but it would have been a better death.

Dead is dead, but how you die is pretty important.

I closed the hatch, sliding the panel into position where it looked just like another deck plate. The hidden compartment was well made, no visible lines to indicate the panel even existed. Well worth the credits I had spent.

Of course back then I was fresh out of the military, not a care in the world and had no idea how expensive it would be to maintain a ship. Even one the size of the *Wind*.

No regrets though. That hidden cache had come in handy far too many times.

Walking back out into the hall, locking the storage room behind me, I stepped into the bridge and went to my pilot's station. A couple clicks on the keyboard and I had the escape pods tracking data uploaded to my wristcomm.

*****

The ship was silent as I walked through the galley and lounge. The Storwo watched me, paying attention to the weapons I carried, but no one said anything. Did they know what Dresla and I were planning?

Did they care?

I was about to step into the hold when a Storwo woman stepped in front of me. Turquoise hair, violet eyes. Those eyes looked up at me, trying to convey something. It took me a couple seconds to place her, I'd only seen her in passing quickly and hadn't paid that much attention in the first place. She was the mother of the boy that Torsi had taken hostage.

She reached up and took my free hand, opened her mouth to say something and closed it. She didn't know the words. Neither of us spoke the others language. I just nodded, hoping it conveyed that thanks weren't necessary.

I hate bullies and I hate ones that target kids.

The woman nodded, tears in the corners of her eyes, and stepped out of my way.

I walked past her and into the hold. I threaded my way around the cargo containers, Strowo sleeping pallets, the blankets strung up for makeshift shelters and past the cargo I had been carrying when this all started. I still needed to deliver it. At some point.

Hopefully it wasn't that time sensitive. With my luck, it probably was, which would end up meaning I wouldn't get paid. And it probably wouldn't be something I could turn around and sell to get some of the credits back.

I didn't head for the loading ramp, which was still up, but instead went for the side door. Human sized, it was a foot or two above the ground. There was a set of retractable stairs that came out of the hull for when the landing gear was extended more, but here the ship rested a foot above the ground so no need for steps. The door was open and I could see a couple figures outside.

I could also see the form of a hovercar waiting just beyond the figures.

Kaylia and Dresla waited for me on the metal deck of the Yorunital docks. It was the matte black, painted dull to not reflect the sunlight. Painted stripes and landing lights dotted the surface, directing ships and people. The kid eyed the weapons as I walked out, she knew where I kept them even though she couldn't access them herself. Hadn't taught her the code yet.

There just hadn't been time yet to teach her gun safety. Hopefully she'd never need to use the weapons but I was going to make sure she knew how. We'd have to find a planet with a firing range. Just one of many things on my list. Never seemed to be enough time.

The look Dresla gave was one of surprise. She was wondering where I had gotten the weapons and probably wondering why I was carrying this much weaponry.

The blasters wouldn't be a surprise. Any ship carried blasters. There were pirates out there. Not that piracy happened often. There was a lot of coordination involved in piracy, and a hell of a lot of luck. It happened, just rarely. Both blasters were military spec, not civilian. But she knew my history so it shouldn't have been surprising.

On the other hand, the rifle would be. It was also military spec but not something that most ship captains would bother carrying. It was too strong to use on a ship. The rifle was an infantry weapon, built for the front lines and warfare, not on board ship combat.

I doubted that she knew the particular model but there was no mistaking the purpose.

"The belt should fit," I told her handing over the Techon.

Dresla took it and immediately drew the blaster. She checked the power pack and held it out at arm's length, sighting down the barrel. She examined the blaster, turning it around, maintaining good trigger discipline the whole time. She was professional about it.

You can tell someone that was professionally trained from someone that was just handed a blaster. They just carry the weapon differently. Hard to explain but if you know what to look for, it's there.

With a satisfied nod she replaced the blaster in the holster and started strapping the belt on. She had to pull the end pretty far to get it to fit around her tiny waist, having to wrap the excess around the belt itself so wouldn't be in the way. She adjusted the fit and nodded again.

"This will work," she said.

I looked past her at the hovercar. Getting it had been Dresla's job. I didn't care how she got it but we needed one that could go off roads. Most hovercars didn't have compensators for changing terrain, just made to hover the same distance above flat surfaces. The one she found would work nicely. It was short, a two seater with a low wall cargo storage behind the covered seats. No doors, but there was a windshield. It rested a foot or so off the ground on four thrusters.

"That will work" I said and pointed at the hovercar.

Dresla nodded and started walking towards the vehicle. I turned to Kaylia. The kid looked worried. She had seen me in action before, as I had her, but that was before she had been my kid to look after. I think she felt somewhat responsible for my safety as well.

"Don't worry kid," I told her putting a confident and carefree smile on my face. Never let them see that you're worried. That was one thing my old commander, Colonel Terrence Jessups, used to be fond of saying. Someone that commanded people should never show worry or fear, even if they are feeling it.

I was only worried because we were rushing into an unknown situation. I know my skills and what I'm capable of. There's not much that truly worries me in missions like this but the lack of intelligence is a big one.

Missions like this? I'd been out of the service for five years and some habits were hard to break.

"You know what to do and who to contact if we're not back in a day," I asked.

She nodded very reluctantly.

When I took her on, became her guardian, one of the first things I did was tell her who to contact and game plan what to do if I was killed or went missing. She's got a list of people memorized and who she calls is based on where she is and what the situation is. Getting her to memorize that list was not fun. It took awhile. I'm also pretty sure she has it written down and hidden somewhere.

I'm okay with that. As long as she knows who to call.

It was horrible that she couldn't go home to her own people. But some of those people wanted her dead, so yeah, not ever going back. The other reason she couldn't go home was the Tiat. I was pretty sure the Tiat had given up hunting for her, but better safe than sorry. They might remember what she was if she showed up back home. Could also prompt the Thesans to go down the genetic engineering rabbit hole again.

Like I've said, she was a smart kid. I had faith that she'd do the right thing. It just sucked that so far she hadn't met any of the people on the lists. She knew what to tell them to get them to trust her but beyond that, she would be entrusting herself to complete strangers.

That had to change. She had to meet some of these people.

But that kind of travel cost money and we never got that kind of extra money. We barely had enough to survive as it was.

"Don't let any of the Storwo off the ship," I repeated. She was probably getting tired of hearing it. "No matter how restless they get. We might need to take off in a hurry and having to chase down some tourists is not in the plans."

She nodded. Kaylia knew why this was important and had brought up some excellent points when I had told her to keep the refugees on the *Wind*. The main one being, why would they listen to her? That was where Dresla came in with whoever she had picked to kind of lead the refugees. Dresla wasn't the boss, but they all seemed to defer to her. I didn't know who she had picked but I was trusting she was also a good judge of character.

"Dresla," I called turning to her. She stopped midway in pulling herself into the passenger seat of the hovercar. "Your temporary group leader knows to listen to Kaylia?"

"Of course. I made sure of it."

"Good, I'd hate to have to kill any of your people if something happened to her."

Dresla studied me for a moment, no doubt wondering if I was serious.

I was.

Anyone that ever hurt Kaylia would not be long for this universe.

I returned my attention to the kid and Kaylia managed a smile. She threw her arms around me tight and I patted her back with my free hand, holding the rifle as far away as I could but I returned the hug just as tightly.

"Hey kiddo. It'll be okay."

She finally let me go, running a finger below her eyes which I pretended not to notice. She stood straighter. Trying to stand at attention, or mimicking the position she had seen. It wasn't close.

The Wind will be just as you left her Captain.

I chuckled.

"Back inside," I told her nodding towards the *Wind's* entrance. With a last wave to Dresla, Kaylia darted inside. "And lock the doors." The door slid shut, sliding out of the metal hull.

I heard the satisfying sound of exterior door locks being engaged.

Good.

I climbed into the driver's seat of the hovercar, handing the rifle over to Dresla to hold. It was pretty funny to look at. The rifle was almost as tall as Dresla was.

"How are we to find them," Dresla asked as I started up the thrusters.

The hovercar shook a little, wobbly, as the thrusters engaged and lifted it a couple more feet off the ground.

"Tracker in the escape pod," I told her looking down at the hovercar's navigation screen and trying to figure out how to operate it. Thankfully all the commands were in Tradelan and not the local language.

"You have a tracker in your escape pod," she asked surprised.

"Doesn't everyone?"

*****

I took a couple minutes to get used to the hovercars controls. Every planet and station had their own version of a hovercar. Mostly they were set up to be useable by the planet's dominate species with some variations. Busier ports have more generic vehicles. The Tuis one wasn't generic.

If we had just been going into the city, I wouldn't have bothered. They're easy enough to operate for quick trips like that. But going into the unknown? A potential firefight? Where we might have to make a quick get away?

Nope. I had learned the hard way to make sure I knew the equipment I was using. Sure there were times that I had to improvise but prior planning saved many a life and mission over the years.

I pulled the hovercar around in front of the *Wind* to see if there had been any damage from Torsi's escape.

The *Nomad's Wind* is a medium sized freight hauler, not designed for speed or agility. It's two levels, cargo and some living on the bottom and the rest of the living plus engineering on the top, the mid part of the ship on all sides but the back had a gray metal "wing" that came off the blue metallic sides and went around to the front. It extended beyond the front of the ship and angled in. The wing ran to the back of the ship but didn't extend beyond, also angling in towards the hull. Mounted on top of the wing at the back were two large engines. The rear of the ship was somewhat straight making the ship look boxy from that view, the cargo doors and ramp on the lower half. The front was different, the top and bottom halves were angled, sloping away from the wing.

It looked like a blue wedge with a gray triangle attached to it.

The top half of the wedge was the bridge and the viewing window, which was not visible from this angle. I liked the window but because of the steepness of the angled hull it was pretty useless for visibility well flying. Still had to rely on the sensors.

The bottom half of the angled front had two sliding doors. A larger one for the escape pod and a smaller one for the airlock. Both were closed, showing a tight seal from what I could see. There were some scorch marks along the edge of the pod door, where the thrusters would have hit the metal when the pod launched. Nothing that bad. Easy enough to repair. Just some cleaning and paint really.

Or not. There were already enough scratches, blaster marks and scorch marks on the hull. The little scars added character. Much like the ones I bore.

Looking at the tracking display on my wristcomm, I adjusted the hovercars trajectory and set off away from the city. We had flown in from the south, so that was the way I headed.

I took the car over the metal of the docking pad, not following any of the marked lanes. I swerved around the parked ships, most bigger than the *Wind* but a couple smaller. We moved quickly, almost but not quite hazardly.

The end of the pad came up and the hovercar's front end shifted as the thrusters went from the solid surface of the metal to the natural grass surface. The vehicle compensated once all the thrusters were over the grass. The plain stretched for miles in front of us, the trees distant. There was a flatness, almost unnatural, and I wondered if the land had been shaped to look like this. It was a decent defense, able to see anything coming along the ground before it even came close to the city.

But why would the Tuis need to have a kill zone around the city?

I had expected a bumpy ride but it was relatively smooth. The wind rushed by, blocked by the windshield and we left a trail of flattened grass behind us. The thrusters were quiet, no bounceback noise like you would get when over metal. The hovercar was almost gliding over the plain.

Now that we were in the open grasslands I increased the speed. No more having to worry about maglifters, other cars or people moving about.

Dresla gripped the side of the car, the only place she could grab, tighter. The small bounces were nothing to me, but they were bigger bounces to her.

"Shouldn't you slow down," she said as the windshield started to shake with the force of the wind and speed.

"We're on a time limit," I told her but didn't elaborate. She was a cop, she could figure it out.

Torsi already had an hour or so on us and she could have completed her deal and be on her way off planet by now. That's why I was going overland and hadn't taken the marked paths when we left. Speed was important now.

I also didn't want to get stopped by the Tuis Security. We'd deal with them when we got back.

And I'm sure there would be a lot to talk about. No doubt they were tracking us. An object, any object, speeding away from the docking pad was cause for concern. They probably thought we had stolen something.

They'd be on the right track, just not with who was the thief.

Security would be tightening around the dock and they'd be sending out some ships to investigate.

Which was part of my plan.

Instant back-up.

Briefly I wondered if they were tracking the escape pod. Had they even noticed it had launched? If they did, it would be a simple enough matter to track the ship it had come from. There could be Security Forces approaching the *Wind* and Kaylia right now.

Good thing I had briefed her on what to say if they did.

The truth.

Why lie? I had no problem lying to the authorities when I needed to but only when needed to. The truth would only help us in this case.

The trees grew taller as we got closer and I had to slow down. They were spaced pretty far apart, just enough for the hovercar to make it through. Dresla gripped the side even harder, if that was possible, as I sped and swerved through the trees. I really should have slowed down, I didn't know the forest, but I kept the speed constant.

Just shy of too fast.

It was like a slalom course. Swerve around one tree, then another, trying to maintain the same track. The branches were high, most above our heads but some low enough to break against the top of the hovercar. High and thick, casting most of the forest floor in shadow. The limbs started higher up the trunks, a bonus for us, as that was where they could get at least some sunlight.

I glanced down at my wristcomm and the tracker. It showed the pod at least twenty miles or more away. Too far.

CHAPTER TEN

Our progress slowed as the trees grew thicker and we entered a long valley. Trees along the top on all sides and down the slopes to the bottom where they were closely packed together and a river was barely visible.

The tracker put the pod down in the valley and using the rifle's scope I could see the burn marks on the trees where it had crashed through. Only two miles away. Or close to. I had parked the hovercar far enough back from the edge so the metal wouldn't catch the sun and along with Dresla we had walked to the edge.

On my wristcomm I could see the path the escape pod had taken. We hadn't been able to see it from the *Wind*, but Torsi had taken the pod in the same direction we had gone for awhile. That worked out for us as it shortened the distance.

I couldn't see any movement from up on the valley's edge.

Or any sign that someone was still there. Only the scorch marks told us that Torsi had been there. She wasn't a very good pilot. That clearing where she had landed was large, I could tell from up here, and any half decent pilot could have landed the escape pod there without damaging the trees.

I was afraid to see what damage she had done to the pod itself.

"Let's go," I told Dresla and started making my way down the slope.

It was steep but there were plenty of tree roots and small rocks to use as footholds.

I could feel the time ticking away. It would be just my luck that Torsi would leave just as we were almost there. I had to hold out hope that she had been early for her rendezvous and hadn't counted on me being able to track the pod.

Which was a logical assumption. Besides myself, I didn't know or hadn't heard of anyone putting trackers in their pods. I had been joking with Dresla earlier. No one did it.

Why would they? Pods were meant to be one way. Your ship was going to die somehow; run out of fuel, explode, lose life support, something. You used the pod to get away and survive. Why would you use the pod to go back? You got to where you needed to go, or drifted in space until somehow you were found, and that was it.

There was no need to track a pod.

Unless you were me and in your past life you had needed to.

Hitting the bottom of the slope, where the valley leveled out, I waited for Dresla. With a grunt she slid down next to me, breathing heavily. Her smaller legs were going to slow me down but there was no way I was going to let her lag that far behind with so many unknowns.

From this point forward, I was assuming we were in enemy territory.

I took off at a jog, adjusting my speed to make sure Dresla was able to keep up.

The trees were too close for the hovercar but far enough apart for us to run through comfortably. Plenty of space to adjust the course around ones that popped up in the way. Keeping the straight line was difficult so I relied more on the signal on my wristcomm. I kept glancing behind me, watching Dresla and making sure she was still there.

She was doing a good job of keeping up but my longer strides naturally pulled me ahead.

The spacing of the trees was nice in that it helped us run but it was going to be a drawback the closer we got. It wouldn't be good cover. We'd be too visible.

A problem for the near future. We had to get there first.

And hope our targets were still there.

*****

I slowed as the wristcomm told me the pod was just ahead, twenty feet or so. Ducking behind a tree I saw Dresla do the same another twenty feet behind me. I leaned around the trunk, hearing the faint sound of a hovercar some distance away. Torsi's contacts? Arriving or leaving? Were we in time?

Glancing back at Dresla, I sized her up and compared her to the rifle. She could hold it and shoot but not accurately. I looked up into the trees, finding one that would work. Waving my hand to call Dresla I moved to the new tree. She crouched down next to me as I looked at the branches, choosing my route.

Earth Expeditionary Forces Spec Ops had developed a series of hand signals, a code that conveyed a lot of information. Using that I could have told Dresla what I wanted her to do with three hand codes. Instead I'd have to speak the instructions. Quietly, of course, but if there was an Xhan or another of those species with crazy hearing that can hear a whisper a mile away, it would give our position away.

Of course if there was a species like that, they already knew we were coming. Another lesson from Jessups was to not overthink it.

"Circle around," I told her pointing towards one side of the clearing ahead. "Doesn't matter which side. Start firing when I give the signal."

"What's the signal?"

I half expected her to protest. She was the cop after all. Torsi was one of her people and had stolen from her. I was just a freight hauler. But instead Dresla just nodded.

"You'll know," I answered and adjusted the rifle slung over my shoulder.

I watched Dresla make her way through the trees and when she was far enough that any noise I might make would not draw whoever waited down on her, I started climbing.

I keep in decent shape. Do a lot of sitting around on the *Wind* so I force myself. I've seen too many fat and out of shape freight haulers. No way was that going to be me.

Also all the trouble that I somehow run into helps.

I climbed up the tree, jumping to catch the lowest branch, and made my way as high as I felt safe going. The tree was starting to thin out, the branches closer together but not thick enough to take my weight. I was high enough and with some shifting I got into a good position that gave me a decent sightline.

Carefully unslinging the rifle I rested the barrel on a branch and looked through the viewfinder. My vision narrowed to a small circle, lots of readouts around the edges showing me wind speed, temperature, elevation and anything else that could affect the shot. The rifle was a plasma blaster, like my pistol, so there were still outside and environmental effects that could alter a shot.

I located the hovercar first.

It was coming through the trees, moving slowly. The clearing had an opening at the far end and there were scorch marks along the ground. Looked like this spot got used pretty regularly. The hovercar was a basic four seater model with attached flat bed. Nothing special. Focusing in on the driver and passengers I was surprised.

I had expected Tuis.

Instead they were Herftos.

Each would stand about six and a half feet tall. Probably around two hundred pounds. Pale white skin. They had long arms that ended in three long and multi-jointed hands and fingers. Their heads were elongated. Thick at the top where they had two long eyes, thinner in the middle and thicker at the bottom with a wide mouth and whiskers.

What were Herftos doing here?

They weren't one of those races that typically got hired out as muscle. They weren't one of those races that were smarter than others. They didn't have a particular cultural dark bend, so they weren't seen as crimelords. I didn't think they were art fans either. I'm sure there were some among the millions of Herftos, but enough to deal in black market goods?

Question for another time.

I shifted my attention and found Torsi.

The clearing was long and skinny. The sloped grassy ramp at the far end, a stream that snaked in from the side and continued through the clearing, and bordered in trees. A peaceful enough spot.

Torsi was standing next to the escape pod, leaning against it. I couldn't see the *Daelot*, it had to be inside the pod. I could see some damage from where Torsi hit the trees.

I could also see the ground behind the pod was dug up, indicating that it had skidded to a landing. She hadn't even engaged the landing gear. That would make getting it up difficult.

The hovercar came to a stop and three of the Herftos got out. The driver stayed. There was nothing remarkable about any of them. Standard Herfto clothing and weaponry.

Who were these guys? Why were they here?

Slightly shifting my position I sighted on Torsi, the back of her head. I was a decent shot with the blaster and an even better one with a rifle but at this angle and distance I didn't need to be that good to make it. I laid my finger alongside the trigger and waited.

I wanted the deal to start going down, when they would be letting their guard down the most. Right now they were all amped up. Waiting for the other party to betray them, some kind of double cross, anything. Once the deal commenced, they would feel safer.

I'd participated in some black market dealings in the past. I knew how these guys would operate.

I just hoped that Dresla wouldn't get impatient.

The lead Herfto signaled to the other two to spread out, one walking around between the pod and the forest, the other moving closer to the stream and looking in that direction. I hoped that Dresla was well hidden. Also hoped they didn't have a bio scanner. Torsi watched them both, watched all three really. She twisted as one of the Herfto walked behind her. It was hard keeping eyes on all three, four if you included the driver, but she tried.

Torsi was lucky she was dealing with Herfto. They were generally honorable as long as you were honorable to them. She had no weapon, no backup, nothing to guarantee they'd hold up their end of whatever bargain they had agreed to. Lots of criminal groups would just kill her now. They'd get their prize and wouldn't have to pay for it.

The two guards spoke to the apparent leader. Probably in their language but I couldn't hear it. I hoped it was something like "all clear" instead of "there's a Terran in a tree and a Storwo in the bushes".

I didn't get shot at so figured it had been "all clear".

The leader stepped forward and started talking to Torsi, who evidently did understand the language. They went back and forth, gesturing, before finally both nodded. The Herfto touched a couple buttons on his wristcomm and Torsi glanced down at one she was wearing. Where had that come from? Must have snuck one onto the *Wind* in her bags. She glanced at hers and smiled, satisfied.

Money had been transferred. Deal was done.

Torsi stepped away from the pod but paused and asked a couple more questions. The Herfto leader tilted his long head and nodded after some thought. He pointed at the vehicle and Torsi started walking towards it. Looks like she'd asked for a ride back to the city. The leader then pointed at the two guards and gestured to the escape pod.

I think she sold my escape pod as payment for the ride.

Taking a deep breath I adjusted a little bit, holding the rifle steadier and put my finger over the trigger. I lined up my shot, watching a Herfto through the scope and waited.

One of the guards reached into the escape pod, bending down and lifting up a small object. I could barely make it out, but saw enough to know it was the *Daelot*. Confirmation that it was here, all that I had been waiting on. I hadn't shared that thought with Dresla, figured she had it as well. There was a chance that Torsi could have hidden it somewhere nearby to use as insurance to make sure the deal went through. But it was here. So it was time.

I waited for the Herfto's head to appear above the pod, the shiny metal catching the sun. The pale skinned being turned back towards the leader and the others. He grunted something in his language and I pulled the trigger.

The Carlyle jerked a little, a single plasma bolt streaking down to the ground incredibly fast. A bright blob of green, the bolt slammed into the Herfto's head and out the other side leaving a smoking hole.

It's body still moved for a moment as the limbs took a bit to stop receiving messages from the brain. The Herfto crumpled to the ground, the *Daelot* falling on top of it.

Silence fell across the clearing, everyone stunned.

Then the blaster shots came from the side, out of the trees.

CHAPTER ELEVEN

Dresla had gone to the right, choosing to take position on the opposite side of the stream. A good choice. It provided the most open attack vantage of the clearing. The pod was in the back, behind the targets. Lots of open ground, not much cover.

Her first shots went wide but caused the Herfto to duck. The leader lay on the ground, starting to crawl back towards the vehicle. I shot him in the leg.

The second guard crouched down and pulled up his weapon. Trained fighter, he started returning fire where he thought Dresla was. Or had been. Turns out she had moved after firing her first shots. Smart.

Torsi was close to the hovercar and ducked behind the front, just ahead of the door, while the driver took too long to come to a decision. I saw him reach behind the seat and pull out a weapon. He stepped out of the hovercar, eyes scanning everywhere, and took a shot from Dresla in the chest. Different angle, she had moved closer to where I was. Almost directly under me. If Torsi had been crouching higher, it would have hit her and I had to wonder if the shot had been aimed for Torsi and Dresla had missed.

The guard now tracked Dresla, whose position was exposed, firing rapidly in that direction, but leaving himself open for me. I caught him in the shoulder and he dropped, his weapon flying from his hands. The leader lay still, smoke coming from the wound on his leg. Couldn't tell if he was alive or dead, but either way the Herfto was effectively out of the fight for now.

That left just Torsi.

She was sliding along the hovercar, moving towards the driver's compartment. She crouched low. I couldn't get a good shot at her and doubted Dresla could either. Instead I took the shot I could make.

The plasma bolt slammed into the polycarbonite window of the hovercar. The material cracked and splintered, not breaking. The stuff is tough, but it did what I wanted.

Torsi stopped and stepped away from the hovercar, hands in the air.

I adjusted and leveled my weapon at her, head centered in my targeting sight. But I didn't pull.

Dresla walked out of the treeline, her borrowed weapon pointed at Torsi. She stepped around the fallen Herfto, giving the ones still alive a wide berth, glancing at them quickly.

"You're under arrest," Dresla said loudly, speaking Tradelan, probably for my benefit.

Torsi ignored Dresla and started scanning the trees, along with the tops of the trees.

"Captain Lancer," she said, her voice carrying. "Is that you out there with the rifle?"

I pulled the trigger.

Torsi jumped and yelled. The bolt had hit the ground a good two feet away, maybe a little closer. Purposefully missing. Dirt and grass shot up, falling all around, leaving a nice crater in the ground.

The shot had been to keep her honest and to give me enough time to scramble down the tree.

Which I did, quickly slinging the rifle and retracing my path back down.

Not my fastest or smoothest, but considering I hadn't done anything like this in awhile, I did good.

Landing on the ground I quickly made my way through the short distance of trees to the clearing, stepping out and walking casually towards the two Storwo women. I kept some distance between Dresla and me, stopping equal distance from Torsi. This made her have to turn slightly to keep an eye on both of us. She eyed the rifle hanging loosely from my shoulder, slung so the barrel was pointing down and an easy swing to being in hand. I left my blaster holstered, but my hand hovering over it.

"Sorry about the pod," Torsi said, smiling. "They were going to pay me extra for it," she continued indicating the Herftos. "A good chunk of credit. That's why it took so long for them to get here. Had to find a hovercar that could take it."

I ignored her.

She shrugged.

"What now?", she asked looking at Dresla.

"You're under arrest."

Torsi laughed.

To be honest, I almost did too. It was a stupid statement from Dresla.

Once a cop, always a cop.

"The Storwo government is reconvening on Hoin. I will turn you over to them for justice," Dresla said. It came out like she was reciting it. I wondered how long she had practiced the speech. "You will be tried for crimes against the people of Storw."

Torsi shook her head, disbelieving.

"What justice?"

"Storw is no more," she continued without a hint of remorse or sadness. "We're just a bunch of homeless beings spread out across the galaxy."

She paused and for the first time there was a hint of sadness in her voice.

"Those of us that got off anyways."

Was that also a trace of guilt? She had taken a pass meant for another and left the person behind. On purpose. She had no way of knowing that I was going to show up and save the guy.

Even if there was a trace of guilt, it was too little and too late.

"So I took an artifact. So what."

"The *Daelot* is a piece of our cultural history," Dresla replied, angry, no longer on script. "To sell it," she paused, unable to find the words. "*Yuintol, hui ta yuo*," she finally said.

Something in Storwoi. Whatever it meant, it made Torsi take a step back, shocked. Had to be a pretty bad insult.

"How dare you," Torsi said in Tradelan, clenching her fists and taking a step forward. She seemed to have forgotten that Dresla had a blaster pointed at her. She also didn't see me draw mine. "You judge me? You have no idea who I am or the life I've led. Storw is not the paradise you think it is. It's all lies."

She started to turn towards me as she talked. Was she trying to convince me? To sway me to her side?

I sighed and pulled the trigger.

*****

The pulse blast hit Torsi square in her chest. The green lines of energy wrapped around her, sparking and flaring. Her body jerked and spasmed before she fell to the ground in a heap.

Dresla looked over at me, shocked and surprised.

"Stun bolt," I said walking over to Torsi. "I was tired of her talking."

I knelt down and felt for a pulse, hoping it was in the same general spot on a Storw that it was on a human. It was. Faint but there. Torsi was still alive.

One of the benefits of the galaxy being made up of humanoids that are basically the same.

I'd hit Torsi with a full charged stun bolt. My weapon was calibrated for an average height and weight human. Stunning a different species can be interesting. Each species has lots of variables that makes calibrating the right amount of power for stunning a nightmare. A weapon can really only be set to work perfectly on one species. Or near perfectly. Any other species is a crapshoot. It can work. It can not work. It can work too good. Lots of different effects.

Sometimes it can cause permanent brain damage.

I doubted that would be the case here. It just probably meant Torsi would be out for an extra hour or two.

Standing up, confident that Torsi would live, I casually moved around the clearing and shot each of the Herftos. The ones that weren't dead anyways. I didn't want any of them waking up.

Holstering my blaster I grabbed the closest Herfto by the shoulders and started dragging him. He was heavy. A lot heavier than I thought he would be.

As I piled the sleeping Herfto in a heap, I watched Dresla walk over to the escape pod. She reached down onto the last Herfto and picked up the *Daelot*. She flipped it around, examining all the surfaces, looking for damage. I got my first good look at it.

About a foot high, three inches wide, it was a tube with carvings along its surface. There were pieces attached at the top, an inch thick, that came out to the sides and curled back in. These were also covered in carvings. It looked to be some kind of metal as it caught bits of the sun. Didn't look like it would be worth that much. Kind of ugly.

She was still standing there looking at it as I leaned down and grabbed the Herfto at her feet. I had to pull him to the side to get around her. So distracted she didn't even move. This one I had by the feet and smiled as his head bounced over the rocks in the clearing. I laid him alongside the others.

I was nice enough to keep the ones alive out of the pool of blood that still flowed from the head wound I had made.

"Torsi's right you know," I said breaking Dresla from the trance she was in. Her hands had been roaming the surface of the *Daelot*, tracing all the carvings. "About there being no more justice, not for Storw. No one will care about that," I finished pointing at the artifact.

Dresla sighed and lowered the *Daelot*.

"I know," she replied walking over to stand above Torsi. "On Hoin she would be tried and convicted and would be just another mouth to feed. One that couldn't help us rebuild or do anything useful. She'd use up valuable resources guarding her. Take people away from other tasks."

She looked up into the sky, staring off into space. The sky was blue, but I knew she was looking past and into the stars. Was she even looking in the right direction for Storw? Didn't matter.

"All in the name of justice."

"What she did wasn't right," I said coming to stand next to Dresla. I looked down at the unconscious Torsi. Looked peaceful.

"No it wasn't and getting the *Daelot* back will be a boost for my people. It had to be done. But it will also be a reminder of what we have lost."

She was silent for awhile, just staring down at her fellow Storwo.

"What do you want to do with her," I finally asked.

CHAPTER TWELVE

We left Torsi lying alongside the Herfto.

They could all help each other get back to the city, leave each other or kill each other. It wasn't our concern. Not anymore. She was resourceful, she'd find her way back. Or she wouldn't. The Herfto would probably abandon her but again, not our concern.

Sure the Herftos would probably be pretty damn mad that they paid some money and didn't get the item. Hopefully Torsi could reimburse them. If not, I didn't like her chances.

But she brought this on herself.

The people of Storwo might not be able to bring her to justice but there were other ways to get it.

*****

I maneuvered the flat bed hovercar around so the bed was facing the pod. It had a winch mounted to the back and I was able to connect the cable to the front of the pod. The bed also inclined, which was a bonus.

In the end it wasn't as hard as I thought it would be to get the escape pod onto the flat bed.

The pod needed a lot of repairs. The underside was damaged and got more so when we dragged it across the ground to get onto the flat bed. I had to use the thrusters which caused more damage.

Only about an hour and we were done.

Plenty of time before the Herfto and Torsi woke up.

Checking the straps I climbed into the hovercar driver's seat, Dresla already in the passenger side clutching the *Daelot*. She looked over at where Torsi was laying next to the Herfto. As I started the hovercar I wondered what she was thinking. As a cop, this wasn't normal. But she really wasn't a cop anymore. There was no Storw to police. Would she find a place in the refugee camp, doing the same thing? Was that why she was so focused on the artifact? It represented her old life, the one she was losing? Recovering it was doing the job she loved one last time?

But it didn't end like most of her assignments. Leaving the thief behind at the mercy of criminals. That wasn't what a cop did. I had no problem with it. I'd done worse in my time. How would she reconcile it? Would it change her? I knew how easy it was to step over the line again once you had done it the first time.

I turned the hovercar around, being careful not to get too close to the unconscious Torsi and Herftos. Their clothes and hair blew in the breeze generated by the hovercars thrusters against the ground, but that was it. Maybe they got pelted by some small rocks and sticks, got covered in leaves. Maybe I could have easily moved a couple of feet away so it wouldn't have been a problem at all.

Maybe.

The hovercar moved sluggishly up the small slope. The controls were sticky, not smooth at all. But I managed.

Taking it slow I got into the trees, following what looked like a logging trail. I could see from the marks on the ground that the Herftos had come this way. It circled around, looping back the way we had come from.

Made sense, there was just the one city around here.

"Our hovercar," Dresla asked.

She had been so quiet that I'd almost forgotten she was there. She was looking through the forest, towards the edge of the valley or where she thought it would be. Dresla wasn't any kind of a forest tracker or else she'd know we had passed it a couple minutes ago. For a guy that spent most of his time in space in a ship with a navcomputer, I had a very good sense of direction. I'd known when we had passed by our hovercar. It had been about a half mile into the forest, south of the logging trail we had been on.

I was a little annoyed. We had cut through the forest when this trail had been so close. It hadn't appeared on the map I'd downloaded onto my wristcomm so I wondered if it was more of a smuggler's trail. Either way, it would have been useful to know about earlier. Using the trail we could have gotten to Torsi before the Herftos.

Things could have been much different.

"Nothing we can do about it," I said. "We'll let the Tuis know where to find it."

Dresla looked like she wanted to say something but changed her mind. She settled back in the seat, staring out at the forest without really seeing it.

I concentrated on driving. The road was rough, the hovercar weighted down. It wanted to swerve and caught all the bumps. The thruster's compensators, designed to keep the hovercar level over any terrain, were having a hard time keeping up with the dips and rises. These things really weren't made for overland travel, especially when the land was not flat, and with the load it was carrying. A lot of places still used wheels and suspension systems when out of the cities. And a lot of places couldn't really afford the tech of hovercars.

The galaxy was not a fair place.

As Dresla was learning.

We passed the time in silence.

*****

The towers of Yorunital were visible long before we broke through the trees. The smuggler's road snaked through the thick trunks, the branches overhanging and growing close. Through the gaps we could see the gleaming metal of the city's skyscrapers. They dominated the sky.

It was an ugly sight.

We broke through the trees and the smuggler's trail disappeared, fading into the grass of the plains. The wind pushed aside the tall grasses as did the hovercars thrusters and we were able to pick up some speed on the relatively flat ground. I looked back and couldn't even see the trail. I'd have to remember that location, it could come in handy someday. Good smuggler's drops were hard to come by as the various planetary law enforcement groups got better and better tech.

I adjusted the path and aimed for the landing dock to the side of the city. I knew there was no way we'd approach undetected and we didn't have speed and surprise like we did when we left. There was going to be someone waiting for us.

The question was what story would we give them?

We sped across the plains, the sun setting behind the tall buildings casting shadows. We passed in and out of them, the temperature dropping each time with the strips of sun shrinking as the gaps between buildings shrunk. I couldn't imagine what it was like for the people that lived in the city itself. Did the sun ever actually hit the streets?

Probably not.

Because of the angle, the entire landing dock was covered in shadow. I could make out the shape of the Wind along with a couple new ships and a couple that had been there before. The yacht still stood out from the rest. Still shiny, still fancy, still expensive looking.

And there was the welcoming committee.

Two armored hovercars with official looking markings, some kind of symbol that I didn't recognize, patrolled the edge of the dock. There was a weapon mounted to the top with an armor wearing Tui manning it. Both vehicles turned towards me, heading at an intercept angle.

I slowed the hovercar and brought it to a stop. Dresla had been looking out to the side and now turned her attention to the two hovercars.

This was going to be fun.

The hovercars stopped about twenty feet away, placing themselves in a way to block me from moving forward and able to give chase quickly if I moved any other direction. Of course the weapons pointing my way were a pretty effective roadblock. The vehicles were armored but still looked faster than what I was driving. The Tuis that I could see, pointing the weapons at us, were fully armored as well. Head to toe. Tall and skinny, not much could be seen of them beyond the fact they were humanoid.

I lifted my hands from the wheel, holding them up so the Tuis could see. Dresla copied my actions.

Armored doors on each hovercar popped open and uniformed Tuis stepped out. Nearly identical. Dark gray uniforms, weapons holstered at their waists. The Tuis were tall, skinny and green skinned. Each a different shade with black eyes and no hair that was visible. They looked emancipated, their skin pulled tight against their bones and muscles.

Another reason that Tui is not a popular planet. The natives aren't that pleasant to look at.

The uniforms were trimmed in red and black, loose and not form fitting.

"Good thing the pod is registered," I said with a sigh.

Dresla didn't react.

The two Tuis walked closer, each coming to a different side of the hovercar. I noticed their hands resting on their blasters.

"Good evening," the one on my side said in accented Tradelan.

Not a good start.

I'd never had a good interaction with law enforcement on any planet that started with 'good evening'.

Both sets of eyes searched the inside of the hovercar. Noting both of our holstered blasters, the rifle on the seat behind us, the *Daelot* that Dresla was still holding and even giving the escape pod strapped to the back a glance.

I started to speak but Dresla was quicker.

"I am a duly appointed law officer of the planet Storw," she said turning to look at the Tui on my side, the one that had spoken and had to be the one in charge. "This man was assisting me in finding and securing stolen Storwo property," she held up the *Daelot* for emphasis.

The two Tuis stood up and exchanged glances, stepping back and coming together to confer. Not what they had expected. They talked quietly for a minute before returning and taking up the same positions except the leader was now on Dresla's side.

"Identification," he said holding out a hand, his other still resting on his blaster. "Slowly," he added unnecessarily.

The Tui on my side tensed up. I tried to project an aura of calm. Which I felt. Having some armed guard ready to draw standing so close to me wasn't that unusual. He was also standing in a way that I could easily and quickly disarm him if I had to.

Carefully Dresla placed the artifact on the floor and held her right arm up and away from the holster and blaster on that side of her body. With her left hand she reached into an inside pocket of her shirt and pulled out a thin card. I couldn't see what was written on it as she handed it over. The Tuis took the ID card and pulled a reader out of a pocket, inserting the card.

He spent a quick couple seconds looking the screen over before taking the ID card out and returning it to Dresla.

"Explain yourselves," the lead officer said.

And Dresla did. She started with the theft of the *Daelot* on Storw and ended at the roadblock. She was more truthful and gave more information than I would have. But she's the law officer and I'm the independent freight pilot that sometimes gets involved in shady stuff. It was probably better that she told the story.

Once she was done the two officers stepped back to the front of the hovercar and talked quietly again. I noticed the weapons on the officer's vehicles were still pointed at us.

"They are fellow officers of the law," Dresla said watching the two talk. "They will understand."

Was she trying to convince me or herself?

The two officers returned, the leader on Dresla's side again. They didn't speak, not at first, just gave us the glare and stare. Eyes roamed us and the hovercar, stopping on the weapons, studying us. A classic intimidation technique.

"Is there a problem?" I asked. I knew it was tempting fate but I was getting impatient. I wanted off this planet before the Herfto could come up with some kind of revenge plan or make another play for the *Daelot*.

"Are those weapons licensed," the officer on my side asked.

Yes and no. My blaster was. The other two, not really.

"Terran registry," I replied. "As well as Council."

Not that it would mean much. The problem with so many planets and their own governments was that each had their own laws and lists of banned weapons and objects. Some planets even banned beard shavers. The Planetary Council had a set of guidelines that was supposed to be galaxy wide and accepted but that didn't happen. Planets chose what to enforce and made changes how they wanted. Yet another example of what a colossal failure the Planetary Council really was.

Their registration was a joke but they still got to take our credits for it.

"The pod is yours?" the Tuis leader asked me, looking past Dresla.

"Yes. Registered to my ship, the *Nomad's Wind*." I looked past them to where I could see the wedge shape of my ship on the dock. They both looked that way and quickly looked back.

"Why did you not contact Yorunital Protectorate," the one in charge asked focusing on Dresla, cop to cop.

"Time," she replied, her tone gaining some authority and confidence. This was familiar territory for her. Different police organizations were always getting into pissing contests over territory and arrests. "By the time we would had gotten you involved, the deal would have been finished and the criminals escaped."

The Tuis officer thought it over for a minute before nodding.

It made sense. There really wasn't anything he could say to counter it. Bureaucracy was the same no matter what planet you were on.

"If you hurry you can catch the Storwo thief and the Herfto smugglers she was meeting," I said helpfully.

The lead officer stepped back and motioned to the other. They once again came together in front and got to talking. I could imagine what was being said. They had every right to hold us, question us further and generally make life miserable. But they had an opportunity now. Who was the bigger prize? Us or the smugglers.

Also how crooked were they?

We had the only evidence that Torsi and the Herfto had been up to anything illegal. If the Tuis went and arrested them, what would be the charge? Would it even matter? They could make something up or just arrest the Herftos and interrogate them until they had the information they wanted.

To some cultures, that was perfectly acceptable.

The conversation ended and only the lead officer returned to our car. To my side this time. The other officer went back to his hovercar and it immediately backed away. It moved past us and the other hovercar, heading the way we had come from. Towards the smuggler's road.

So far it was going good.

"How much longer do you intend to remain on Tui," the officer asked, his tone of voice telling me what the correct answer should be.

"I was landing to refuel before all this," I told him waving my hand back towards the pod. "And now I have to get that thing put back onto the ship. We're leaving as soon as both those things are done."

The Tuis stepped back, nodding. He looked towards the forest where the other hovercar was still visible and then towards the *Wind*.

"Both things need to happen quickly," he said and walked back towards the other vehicle.

I waited, not moving, until that hovercar was turned back towards the city and about a hundred feet away. Our hovercar lifted up and gained speed slowly. I didn't bother going too fast, we were close to the dock now and I didn't want to give the Tuis any reason to mess with us again.

CHAPTER THIRTEEN

Kaylia was waiting outside when we pulled up to the *Wind*.

The side door was open and she was standing there, pacing back and forth. She at least waited until I had shut off the hovercar and stepped out before running over and throwing her arms around me.

She hugged me tight and I returned it, finally pulling her arms off me.

"Hey kiddo."

What took you so long?

She looked past me at the hovercar, different from the one we had left in.

Where did you get this?

"Long story but the short answer is that we found Torsi and got the *Daelot* back," I replied and pointed at the artifact that Dresla still held.

Was there trouble?

I reached into the hovercar and grabbed the rifle, slinging it over my shoulder. I looked around the dock, out of habit, and saw no eyes on us. I didn't mind carrying around a blaster in public places, but having a rifle out in the open like this was a bit odd and I felt like it might draw more attention. Or the wrong attention.

"Nothing that we couldn't handle," I told her, putting my arm around Kaylia and pulling her in close as we followed Dresla into the ship.

*****

Besides the standard bribe, the cost of fuel was double what I had expected. Had to wonder if the Yorunital Protectorate officers had anything to do with it. I had no choice but to pay and it dipped significantly, and scarily, into my back-up credits. This trip was hurting.

It also cost a lot to get a lifter to help load the escape pod back into its berth on the *Wind*. Again, more than it should have. Larger ships had systems in place to help load the pods. Not mine. The Castellan designers never bothered with that kind of thing. It took up space that could go towards storage. Besides being able to reload an escape pod ran against the nature of it in the first place. It was an escape pod. When it was launched, it wasn't meant to go back because there would be nothing to go back to.

Sound reasoning. This was the exception and it was an expensive one.

I had to rent a magcrane with a Tui operator. He at least knew what he was doing. It didn't take long for the crane to lift the pod and maneuver it back into the bay. The thing that took the longest was me climbing up into the bay and adjusting the *Wind's* damaged clamps to hold onto the pod.

The whole thing was going to have to get repaired. The pod and the launching mechanism. More credits than I had or would have for awhile. Didn't look like it would be getting fixed anytime soon.

I climbed down out of the pod launch bay, squeezing between the pod and the hull. The magcrane had already left, taking most of my emergency credit fund with it. I hopped down, feet touching the metal decking and stretched. There hadn't been much space around the pod in which to work. As I worked out the kinks and knotted muscles in my back and shoulders I noticed a group of people exit the fancy yacht.

And of course they headed my way.

I'd been expecting this. I had a feeling the yacht belonged to whoever was controlling the Herftos. The style wasn't that of a business persons. This yacht was all about flash and being noticed. It belonged to someone with money to burn. Businesspeople wanted to look important but not flashy. It really only made sense for this yacht to be here if it belonged to whoever was meeting Torsi.

Turns out I was right.

I adjusted the holster on my hip, glad to still be wearing it. Working in the cramped spaces had been uncomfortable with the blaster on, but I wanted to be prepared.

This was also why I had ordered Kaylia and the Storwo to stay inside the ship.

There was no urgency to their walk, just calm and without a care. Like they were out for a casual stroll. I looked around the dock and didn't see anyone else around. Wonder how long they had been inside the yacht waiting?

They weren't in any hurry and neither was I so I leaned against the hull of the *Wind* and waited.

The front two were Herftos, both wearing a mix of clothing and holstered blasters. Their eyes moved around constantly, taking in everything, but always returning to focus on me. The two in the back were large Guykiks. Big, scaly and humanoid lizards. They made my 6'-0", 200 pounds, look tiny. Three clawed fingers on each hand, long and ridged tail with the ridges continuing up the back. Wide faces, short snouts and lots of razor sharp teeth. Bright yellow eyes with black slits stared at nothing but me.

Not good. Guykiks were tough bastards. Their scaly hides were pretty impervious to blaster fire. It took a lot to knock one of them down. That's why they were the favorite thug of a lot of criminals. The Guykiks were just muscle.

The being in the middle was the important one.

A Divut.

Humanoid, basically. Two legs, two arms, a head. Pale pinkish skin, backwards jointed knees that gave it an odd walk. Legs that ended in two large toes in front and one large in the back. Arms ended in wrists that attached to the hands perpendicularly so there were three fingers on one side and two on another, kind of like a pincer. The head was large, almost too large for the body. Wide at the top with a wedged shaped flat ridge of bone, small and dark eyes and a mouth hidden by tentacles that hung down onto it's chest.

This Divut wore pretty fancy and expensive clothes. Just like the yacht. Almost too flashy and both said how rich he was. But then when you had two Guykiks and a herd of Herfto on your payroll, broadcasting how rich you were wasn't a big deal.

Without showing it, I tensed up and got ready to move. I still leaned against the hull, but my hand lowered a little closer to the blaster where I could get it quicker and my boot slid a bit to the left to get a more solid connection for when I might need to push off.

The two Herftos moved to the side, the Guykiks staying behind their boss. The Divut stopped in front of me. The head moved up and down, examining me.

"You must be Captain Lancer," he said in Tradelan. The voice was bubbly, the tentacles quivering as he talked.

"And you are?"

I glanced at the two Herftos. They were a couple feet away, just barely in my line of sight. If they shifted a bit, I'd lose them both and really have to turn my head away from one or the other. But they didn't, they just stood there. Dumb or were they ordered to stand like that?

"You may call me Gur," he said with a slight bow.

Because of the small eyes and the tentacles, a Divut is hard to get a read on. You can learn a lot about a person by their eyes and how the face moves when they talk. Not so much with a Divut. Was this guy angry? Curious?

"Let me guess," I said, trying to sound casual. "Bet you're the guy that bought the Storwo artifact."

He started to say something but I purposefully interrupted him. He had come to me, trying to do this on his terms and under his control. It was time to show him that he wasn't in control.

"Did you get your money back or was it non-refundable?"

The tentacles twitched in a way that I took for annoyance.

"How much did you pay for that thing anyways?"

There was more twitching of the tentacles. Definitely agitated.

I smiled.

Gur took what I figured was the Divut version of a deep breath before starting to speak. He paused, waiting to see if I would interrupt. When I didn't, he continued.

"That was my transaction that you interfered with." He took a step forward, leaning in. Was he trying to be intimidating? "I was just curious why you did so?"

I shrugged.

"Something to do."

Gur made a strange sound. He stepped back, hands coming up and shaking, the fingers coming together. I think he was laughing. Whatever it was stopped and he got serious again. This time I knew he was trying to intimidate me.

"You are a funny man Captain Lancer but maybe not a smart one. You should not have interfered with my business dealing. I am not someone that you want to make an enemy of."

"Are you?"

That question caught him by surprise. The Herfto and Guykiks too. They weren't used to someone talking to their boss this way. They all had shocked expressions, or what passed for shocked on their various faces.

"I have no idea who you are so how am I to know if I should make an enemy of you or not?"

If something was going to happen, that remark would set it off.

I watched the Herftos as best I could. They were my first concern. Even though the Guykiks were the more dangerous, the Herftos were closer and to my flanks. I could easily take out Gur but I doubted that would stop his thugs. That made him last on the list. In a normal situation, but this wasn't normal.

Gur's tentacles twitched in that way that I thought of as irritation. I could see his fingers balling into fists, clenching tight. His eyes squinted. Whoever this guy was he was used to getting respect.

I probably should have been treading lighter. I really had no idea who he was but he had money and thugs, so he could in fact be someone I didn't want to mess with. I thought about backing off, trying to smooth things over, but that's not really my style.

"Who are you anyways?" I asked. I actually was curious. It's usually pretty smart to know who I'm dealing with.

"I am but a humble art dealer," Gur replied. He didn't sound it, but I could tell he was still annoyed.

"Humble? Don't think so," I said and nodded towards the gaudy yacht. "And I'm pretty sure you're more than an art dealer."

Gur's tentacles quivered a lot more. He stood up straighter, smoothing the front of his clothing and I could tell he was forcing himself to get calm.

"You have something that belongs to me," he finally said, trying to put threat into his voice. The Guykiks stood taller, seeming to increase their already intimidating bulk. Or trying to anyways. "I would like it back."

I fought the urge to laugh.

"Don't think so," I said instead.

He looked like he was going to speak so I continued talking.

"If you mean the Storwo artifact that you bought from Torsi, that was never hers to begin with and the transaction between you two would be considered illegal in pretty much every system in the galaxy." I paused long enough for Gur to start to talk and again I continued before he could. "If you want your money back, Torsi is off in the forest there. Maybe you'll get lucky and make it there before the authorities do."

Gur glanced that way before turning back to me, tentacles twitching.

"Maybe not," I finished and shrugged.

I stood straight, no longer leaning. If anything was going to happen, it would be now. Gur had to weigh his anger against starting a fight in the middle of the Tuis dock. I'd lose any fight. We both knew it. The numbers weren't on my side and we were in an open space. The question was how badly would I hurt him and his people? How hard would it be to put me down?

And would he then still be able to get the *Daelot*? Would he be able to escape clean or would Tuis Dock Control tag him?

He ran through all the scenarios and he had a lot. I was lucky. I had just one. How to do the most damage before I died. That was an easy one to work out. Kill Gur.

I smiled and stared at Gur. The smile was full of confidence, not a care in the world. The stare told him that he was going to be my target.

His tentacles quivered. A different movement this time. I took it to be the equivalent of a sigh. He raised his hand and made a quick motion. The Herftos stepped back to his side, never taking their eyes off me.

"Captain Arek Lancer of the *Nomad's Wind*," Gur said, voice filled with menace. "I think we will meet again."

He turned and walked away. The Herftos took the front and the two Guykiks stared at me for a bit before also turning and following their boss.

I waited until he was back on his ship, the boarding ramp retracted, before I fully relaxed.

Add one more to the list of the people that wanted to kill me.

It was a long list.

CHAPTER FOURTEEN

I couldn't find out much about a Divut named Gur. Not through the Feed or anything that was available at the time so when we left Tui I put some feelers out through some unofficial channels. It helps to know a lot of people scattered across the galaxy.

But because of the way the hops work, I had no idea when or if I'd get any replies or any useable intel.

So I basically put it out of mind. A worry for another day.

At that point in time Gur was the least of my worries. I had a ship that needed some repairs, some cargo that was very late in delivering, no other jobs lined up and a pretty close to desperate need for credits. What did it matter if some crime boss wanted me dead?

Tui to Hoin, with the hops in between, was uneventful. Dresla spent most of the time down in the lower level with her people so it was just me and Kaylia in the bridge. Neither of us went down that much, just when needed.

I was glad to hop into the Hoin System. I wasn't necessarily eager to see the Storwo gone but this trip had cost me a lot, in credits and time. As well as adding a new enemy to the list. I had to wonder when the good karma this should have earned me would arrive.

Hoin turned out to be a brown world. Not quite a desert planet, but close enough. Very different from Storw, which had been a water planet. That pretty much confirmed my suspicions that the Planetary Council had ulterior motives in relocating the Storwo here.

I could see some ships in orbit, larger passenger carriers and support ships. Shuttles moved between them and the surface. Lots of shuttles. The orbit was crowded. Beyond the passenger ships I could see heavy freighters and larger shuttles. Probably moving construction equipment and material. This many new residents needed places to live.

Wonder who was paying for that?

There was some blue on the planet and that was where I was being directed to.

In a way it proved lucky for my passengers that the *Wind* was the only ship around that could enter atmo. This meant they got on the surface faster and would be housed faster as well. I had no idea how many Storwo were still in orbit as facilities were being built for them, but it had to be thousands. My passengers would probably be in hastily built tents and shoddy buildings but at least they'd be on planet.

Which was a vastly different place from where they came from.

*****

The wind whipped across the plains, pushing the dust and dirt with it. Large and bare mountains, as brown as the ground, were visible in the distance.

Not a particularly welcoming place.

I walked back around the *Wind* to where the view was a little better.

There was a decent sized lake with large expanses of grass around it, a few trees. An oasis in the middle of the barren rocky land. The ship was parked on the edge of the grass, well away from where a collection of refugee housing was being built. The wind off the plains still cut through, pushing at the grass. A sharp wind, angry.

The buildings were all one story, square, plain and made of polyconc. It was a pretty common material. Pourable and hardened quickly. Common but cheap. The workers were all Storwo using borrowed machinery supplied by the Planetary Council. Beyond the homes I could see where some were starting to build a wall to help block the wind.

This was just one of a hundred or so similar new cities built around the oasises on Hoin. A lot of construction with cheap materials. Nothing like the new fancy port being built that we had passed over. A couple of gleaming new shipyards with the latest tech and what looked to be a landing deck twice the size of the one on Tui.

The Hoinite were making out pretty good on this deal.

Not like they needed the oasis. They all dwelled in the plains and liked it, tribes scattered across the planet. When we had first landed there had been a collection of them just on the edge, watching and waiting. They'd gotten bored and moved on.

Tall and gangly with long arms and legs. Thin looking arms and legs that were thicker at the joints: elbows, knees and shoulders. I couldn't get a good look at their heads as they were wrapped in some kind of cloth robes that left their arms and legs exposed. They had ridden some kind of reddish beasts that looked like giant lizards.

This was the best planet the Council could find for the Storwo?

And what were the Hoinites really getting out of this? Did all of them even want it? How angry would they be with their new neighbors? Would they get along over time?

I watched a stream of Storwo walking down the *Wind's* ramp. Kaylia was at the bottom, hugging some and laughing and poking the kids. Other, more official Storwo, were directing them on where to go. They were heading towards a large building closer to the lake's shore. Some kind of community building.

It had been funny to see the self-important Cortl run immediately to the officials only to get brushed aside.

Dresla walked down the ramp still holding the *Daelot*. We hadn't spoken since returning to the *Wind* on Tui. She paused on the ramp so our heads were level and looked out towards the lake.

"You were correct," she finally said and paused, shaking her head before continuing. "I have always upheld Storwo law, followed it exactly. As I thought it should be. Torsi stole the *Daelot* because I followed the law exactly."

No wonder she had taken it personally. She felt it was a failure. Not just her own but of the system she had upheld for so long. I knew what that was like, finding out the thing you held as sacred really wasn't what you thought. I glanced at the *Wind*, the thing that had replaced my sacred following of being a soldier in the Earth Expeditionary Forces and wondered what Dresla would find.

Maybe she'd stay a cop. The settlements would need good ones.

"Leaving Torsi behind like that was not the letter of the law," Dresla said and turned towards me. It was not exactly a question or statement, she was looking for validation.

"No, but it was justice," I replied.

I looked out towards the new homes, watching the Storwo walk through the grass towards the larger building. There was no excitement about their new home. They were tired, disappointed and sad. A raw deal but at least they were alive and could rebuild.

"Sometimes the law and justice are not the same."

ASTEROID RETURN

Originally Published:
January 26, 2019; eBook on Amazon

CHAPTER ONE

"They did what?" I asked, surprised, shocked and angry.

"They released Commander Arskli."

I looked at the vidscreen, at the image of the Turesan Planetary Governor Yoterra, a Thesan. She was upset, almost as much as I was, that was obvious. We both had reason to be.

"A prisoner exchange," she went on to say but it really didn't matter.

The reason why it had happened didn't matter. That it happened at all, that mattered.

Not like I wasn't paranoid enough already.

"Thanks for the heads up," I said and switched off the vidscreen, leaning back in my seat.

I stared out the *Nomad's Wind* view window, watching the stars drift by. We'd stopped in this system long enough to get the download from the Feed. That was the plan until I had gotten Yoterra's message to contact her.

Had to get going. We were heading to the Tuyo system for a job. It was the first job we'd had in a week and one we needed badly.

We being me and my crew.

The *Nomad's Wind* could carry a crew of six but I had retrofitted it to be operated by a crew of one. Currently there was only two. Me, the captain, and a thirteen year old Thesan girl named Kaylia. For a long time there had been only one, me. But I'd picked up Kaylia a couple of months ago.

She was the reason that the release of Arskli was a problem. A Tiat, high ranking in their military, Arskli was responsible for me meeting Kaylia in the first place. She, Arskli, had kidnapped Kaylia and the kid had escaped, literally running into me on a mining asteroid in Deep Space.

I'd been responsible for the Commander's capture on the Thesan controlled planet of Turesa.

Tiat were not a forgiving people and they never could be relentless and brutal. As far as Yoterra, Kaylia's legal guardian, and I knew the Tiat's bounty on the kid had been removed. The Tiat seemed to no longer be interested in her. But I knew it was just a matter of time before Arksli came looking for revenge on me, and the kid as a bonus, for the loss of reputation she had suffered. Tiat were big on their version of honor and there was no way Arskli would let it go.

Something to look forward to. One more name on the long list of people out to get me. A list which, despite my best efforts, seemed to be growing. Lately it seemed I couldn't go anywhere without picking up a new enemy. The latest was a Divutan black market art dealer by the name of Gur. I'd gotten on his bad side by helping some refugees from a dying planet.

Would have thought doing a good deed would have helped my karma. Nope.

In the meantime, we'd stay as far away from the Tiat as we could. Which shouldn't be a problem, I tried to avoid them anyways.

Tiat and Terrans weren't allies, never would be. We'd fought against each other in the Third Galactic War and were engaged in a kind of cold war over new territories to this day. That was old news for me though. I hadn't worried about the status of the war in five years, ever since I had left the Earth Expeditionary Forces Special Operations and became an independent freight hauler. I'd gotten my ship, the *Nomad's Wind*, and set off into space.

Should I tell Kaylia about Arskli? Naw. No need to worry the kid. She had enough to deal with. The main reason the Tiat wanted her was that she was the last of a group of genetically modified Thesans. A kind of super trooper of the species. More feral, claws, speed. The works. Kaylia's parents had been the ones whose DNA had been messed with. They'd passed it onto the kid.

An example of the Tiat not forgetting or forgiving. The Thesa Wilders had done some pretty nasty damage to the Tiat and it had taken years, but the Tiat had gotten their revenge. Or most of it. There was still Kaylia, alive and well and a reminder that they hadn't killed all the Wilders. And that would never happen. Not on my watch.

So no telling her. Not now anyways.

"Kid," I said turning on the ship's intercom system. "Come on up. It's hop time."

I leaned back in my chair and looked out the viewwindow at the stars. Lots of small white dots, pinpricks in the blackness of space. In the distance was a small planet, the only one close enough to be visible by the eye. This system had no sentient species, or habitable planets, and was used mostly for mining. The Kry controlled it.

We were just stopping by, had only been here for thirty minutes or so. Long enough to get the updates from the Galactic Feed. That's how I had known that Yoterra was looking for me. We would have been out of the system a while ago but I needed to get ahold of Yoterra.

Traveling from solar system to solar system is done in a series of hops. You hop into the space between systems, some kind of strange realm that is nicknamed Wildspace, and then hop out again somewhere else. Going from A to C means hopping to B and sometimes E. It takes time. Well in that in-between space, you can't receive transmissions of any kind. Well you can, but they're so garbled that there's no understanding them or cleaning them up. So when a ship enters a system, there's a rapid influx of downloads from the Feed, the galaxy wide information system. News, letters, videos, books. Takes awhile to go through it all, but what else are you going to do well hopping through wildspace?

It also means that by the time you get anything, it could be days old.

I turned as the door to the bridge slid open and Kaylia walked in. About five feet tall, slender, she looked like a humanoid cat. Gray and black striped fur, tufts at her wrists and ankles and long black hair that ran halfway down her back. Short and pointed ears, bright yellow eyes with green slit irises.

And a long tail that was always moving, swishing back and forth.

Only thirteen years old, or the equivalent of that anyways, she'd seen a lot in that life. I didn't know why she had chosen me, but she had and I would do whatever I could to protect the kid.

She'd grown on me fast.

When I started out in space as a freight hauler, I never wanted a crew. It was always going to be just me. Going where I wanted, when I wanted. Then I met Kaylia and well it took some getting used to, I was now okay with a crew.

Just her though. No need for anyone else.

Smiling, she was always smiling, she sat down at the navigators station in front and down from me. The *Wind's* bridge had four stations. The pilot's on the right, co-pilots on the left and down a couple steps were the navigators and weapons/communications. Lots of screens, buttons, dials and controls. She busied herself with some of the buttons for a minute.

"Navorders all set," I asked her, looking at the back of her head.

She flashed me a thumbs up over her shoulder, one of the first earth expressions I had taught her.

The kid was mute and primarily communicated through sign language.

I glanced at my station. Since I had everything rigged for a single crewer, my station had controls and readouts for all the ship's systems and I looked quick to double check. She'd set up the hop perfectly.

Normally I'd set all the hops from the system where we left to the destination system and let the navcom make the adjustments as we traveled. No route was ever perfectly set in stone. The galaxy was in constant motion and things changed rapidly, so whenever a hop brought you to a new solar system there was some downtime as the navcomp made adjustments before hopping out. I'd been training Kaylia on how to do that manually, so now whenever we hopped in she would plot the course out.

She tapped on the console to get my attention.

Six hours.

Space travel was not quick.

I leaned back, put my feet up on the edge of the console and my hands behind my head.

"Whenever you're ready."

With a nod, smile and eyes bright with excitement Kaylia stood up and sat down in the co-pilots station next to mine, the small aisle between us. She adjusted a couple of dials, tapped some buttons and hit the controls. The *Wind* started moving forward, the distant planet growing a little bit in size. We couldn't feel the motion inside the bridge, the inertia compensators working, but the stars started to elongate as we gained speed. I could feel the familiar vibrations through the metal decking of my ship. The white pinpricks became lines, more and more of them closer to together until the black was all gone and replaced with a landscape that was best described as fuzzy clouds of white.

The space between space. Wildspace.

Not all ships had view windows but I made sure mine did. I found the view of both, space and this wildspace, to be peaceful. It was where I belonged. The view here was unchanging, just the weird cloudy white, so it did get old after awhile but I tried to spend the first couple minutes of most hops just enjoying the view.

Out of the corner of my eyes I could see Kaylia shift to mimic my position. Feet up, hands behind her head, leaning back. I smiled and watched wildspace drift by.

*****

Tuyo System contained six planets, three of them were gas, another a ball of fire and two that were inhabited. None of the planets were capable of sustaining life but they had three colonies on the two planets. Since there was no life native to the system, the first settlers got to pick the planets names. Tuyo Major and Tuyo Minor.

Very imaginative.

Major had two mining operations from the Pierd, one in each hemisphere. Minor, our destination, had an operation run by the Huyit Trading Consortium. We'd left a system with mining operations by the Kry to come to one with operations by the Pierd and one of the galaxies many trade consortiums. There was a lot of mining done in the galaxy.

The *Wind* wasn't capable of transporting ore. Too heavy for light freighters like my ship, an Earth made Castellan Model F497. The heavier transports did the bulk of the ore, those also usually belonged to whatever Trading Consortium or planetary government owned the mine. That left guys like me to deliver the cargo needed for the people working and running the mines.

It wasn't big money but it kept me and my ship flying. That was all I wanted.

A little extra would be nice but can't have everything.

We'd been traveling in-system for three hours when the first of the planets became visible to the eye. Star hopping brings you in at the far edge of a system and you have to use thrusters to get the rest of the way. They're slow. At least it appears to be, but when talking the distances between planets, three hours really isn't that bad.

Tuyo Major was coming up off to the port side. Our port anyways. With ships in space, directions like up and down or left and right were kind of meaningless.

It was an ugly planet. Gray, cratered. No lights could be seen from this distance but there were plenty of ships in orbit. Large freighters and even a small space station, a long cylinder with a ring around the middle. It served as a terminal for ships as well as defense. I could see the weapons mounted on the ring.

My console lit up, telling me that we were being scanned. I hit a button and transmitted the ship's ID and our purpose for being in Pierd controlled space. It was just a routine check. We continued past Major with no problems. Hadn't expected any, but can never tell. Last I had heard, things were fine between the Pierd and the Huyit Consortium. That wasn't always the case, but for now it was. Which was good. I hated flying into warzones, I'd been in too many of them back in the soldiering days. The *Wind* had shields and some weapons but it was still a freighter, not good in a fight.

I could see some of the ships docked at the space station. Some light freighters like the *Wind*, lots of different makes and models, lots of different species. There were a couple heavy freighters drifting in orbit with the station. I could see smaller shuttles moving between them and the planet. Major couldn't handle ships landing in atmo and most heavy freighters weren't designed for landing and flying through atmosphere. Another benefit that my ship had.

Shuttles brought cargo and personnel up from the surface to the freighters or the station. The surface was nothing but gray rock, lots of cliffs and mountains. Barren and stormy. Not a fun place.

And Minor was worse.

It would be another six hours before we came upon Minor along its orbit on the far side of the system's sun. We could have hopped in on that side, closer to the planet itself, but that would have required hopping to another two systems.

More time and more fuel. In-system travel wasn't that fast, but sometimes it was needed as it didn't use up fuel as much as hopping. As we passed the sun, I tilted the ship so the viewwindow was away from the light. We were still light years away, a lot of them, but it was bright.

Gravity on a spaceship is weird. It's centered on the ship itself, whatever the manufacturers consider the deck. What is down for one ship would be up for another or sideways for a third. It makes things interesting when approaching space stations and planets.

As we flew through space I leaned back in my chair, feet up on the console, and drank an ale. What I called an ale anyways. Tradelan works pretty good most of the time. It takes the word in the other language and substitutes the closest word in yours. So what I was drinking was an ale, it also wasn't. That was just the only word that came close to the translation.

Because of the translation issue, while Tradelan allowed the varied beings of the galaxy to communicate, it still led to a lot of miscommunication. Which more often than not was answered with blaster fire.

This particular ale came from a planet called Ture and was pretty good. The closest to true Earth ale that I had found. And this far out in Deep Space it was easier to find.

My console started beeping and I sat up. The lights on the comms were flashing, indicating there was an incoming message. Not live, a recording. Someone had sent a message out into the Galactic Feed to my address. It was just luck that the Wind was in-system currently, otherwise I might not have gotten it until after the next hop, wherever and whenever that would be.

The Feed was the galaxy wide, at least the known galaxy, system of connected satellites and relays. It bounced data across the stars. Anything from messages to entertainment, news and pictures. Each system paid a tax to have the Feed satellite's there, but they were all willing to pay it. No inhabited system went without, even the Tiats. While they had their own system they still used the Feed.

Glancing at the delivery mark I was surprised. One of the last people I would have expected a random message from. Well we were still on good terms, and did communicate, it wasn't just for social calls.

I wondered what my former commander, Colonel Terrence Jessups, wanted.

CHAPTER TWO

I was in the Earth Expeditionary Forces for ten years and most of those were spent in Special Operations. All of that time was spent under the command of Colonel Jessups. He was pretty much responsible for me being who I am. When I had joined, at eighteen and just out of high school, I was the stereotypical troubled kid. It had been my mother, my sister and me. We had it rough and I'd fallen in with a bad crowd.

A bad decision led me to the best one I had ever made.

I'd been given a choice; jail or the military. I chose the military and everyone, including me, was surprised to find I had a knack for soldiering.

Except the following orders part. That I had never really learned. But my skills made up for that and led me into Special Operations. Jessups took that wild kid and turned him into a soldier. I'd risen quickly up the ranks and had left as a Captain.

Without Jessups, I wondered where I would have ended up. Nowhere good that was for sure. I glanced around at the *Wind*. Some would have said that I hadn't upgraded when I left the 2Es, might have taken a step back, but I was happy and free. On my own.

Putting on the headset I keyed the transmission and watched Jessups appear on the screen. Gray haired in a close cut military style, brown eyed, more crows' feet and wrinkles around the face than the last time I had seen him. Jessups was looking weary. He'd been looking that way the last few times but now it was really noticeable. He was run down. Tired. Should have been long retired but the man knew too much and was too good. The 2Es wouldn't let him leave. Not that he really wanted to. The Forces were his only family.

"Captain," the message started and just hearing his voice almost made me jump out of the chair and stand at attention.

"I am messaging for two reasons. I cannot go into many details over the Feed as encrypted as it is." Here he paused. To send me a message meant he couldn't use the standard military codes. The *Wind* didn't have the software to decrypt them. Jessups was trying to figure out what he could tell me. "The first reason is to inform you of the deaths of three members of your old unit."

That caught me by surprise. The deaths must have been recent as I did check in with some old war buddies now and then. For three of them to die around the same time and recently, as they must have been or I would have known, was pretty suspicious and I could see why Jessups would want to inform me. I wondered how many others of the old units were getting similar messages.

I saw that there were data packets attached to the message. Those would be the news items on the deaths.

"The other reason is we believe connected to the first." Again Jessups paused, staring at the screen. It caused me to look at him instead of at anything else. "The rock is active."

Jessups leaned away from the screen, giving it a nod. That was the message. Nothing else. I could tell by his posture that it was all delivered.

It took me a couple seconds to figure it out, which was all the time Jessups gave me in the message. He started speaking again.

"I am stationed at the new colony if you would like to get together to raise a drink to old friends. I will be there for a month."

The message ended and I opened the data packets.

Anyone that intercepted the message would know that Jessups had given me some coded phrases. There was no way to hide that. They'd comb through the packets, dissect them, looking for whatever information Jessups would have passed on to me. They wouldn't find anything. There was no information.

Everything Jessups had to pass on, he had in the message.

Just four simple words.

The rock is active.

But there was so much more in the message. Jessups was always a fan of hiding messages in plain sight. The intelligence division wanted to be tricky, always coming up with new and complicated ways of passing information from one source to another. Jessups, and myself, we preferred the simple ways.

He used the plural 'we' when saying that the first reason, the deaths of my old unit mates, and the second were connected. This meant that it was the 2Es that thought it. The intelligence division more than likely.

'New colony' meant that he was on Rewe, a frontier world and Earth's newest colony. There was a sizable Expeditionary Forces base there. The 'raise a drink' meant that he wanted to meet with me, face to face.

I skimmed the packets. Each was an obituary and news article on the death of three men. Jon Herrin, Harald Devry and Stuart Thoms. Three good soldiers. Three good men. Each had died from various accidents. Also in each packet was a file, more details on their deaths. Police reports. Skimming those I quickly realized that none of the deaths was an accident.

Made to look like accidents, but they weren't. They were assassinations.

I knew what those looked like. I'd done my fair share during the Spec Ops days.

It really didn't shock me. Aside from Devry, the other two had still been active duty. There was a cold war going on with the Tiat. After the truce and the end of the Third Galactic War, we had settled into an uneasy peace with them. That didn't stop either side from still trying to wipe the other from the galaxy. Some of my missions had been against Tiat operations. The Tiat were bastards. We were as well, but nowhere near as bad as the Tiat. Reprisals, from both sides, were common.

What was surprising was the frequency of the deaths.

I had been right. They were all recent and pretty close together. Not a coincidence. They had been targeted. Which was odd, as one was retired and the other two weren't that high up the food chain with the 2Es. Not high value targets.

Not worth the effort.

There was also the fact that all their names, including mine, would have been redacted and not on file. Not supposed to be anyways. It was information that no one should have had access to. But if it existed in some computer, someone could always get at it.

That was one of the reasons I tended to keep to the area of the galaxy known as Deep Space. Out on the fringes and away from all the activity. Keeping a low profile. Trying to anyways. Because of Kaylia I knew I was probably on the Tiat's radar but did they connect the freight hauler with the 2Es soldier?

Jessups had said that it was assumed the deaths were connected to the other part of his message and I knew he was right.

The rock was active.

There was only one rock he could be talking about. One place that the three dead men, Jessups and me would have been connected.

An asteroid located just a few systems, and hops, from Tiat controlled space. It had been used by them as a development factory. Lots of nasty stuff created there. Thankfully none of it had been used.

Thanks to Jessups, Devry, Thoms, Herrin and myself.

*****

I thought about ignoring the message. Going deeper into the fringes and staying there.

I wasn't a soldier anymore. Not my fight. I could defend myself if the Tiat came hunting. Getting involved would just put me fully back on their radar and in their sights.

Low profile.

Tuyo Minor came into view. Half the size of Major but with twice as much nastiness. More valleys, more inhospitable. But the mining was better.

We had a job lined up. Quick delivery to a system a few four to five hour hops away, the Youtin system. Not much in the way of credits, but it was money.

Youtin would also put us that much closer to a hop to Rewe. It would still be a couple days and more time without a job or income.

Just more reasons to not go.

As I followed the coordinates from Minor's Dock Control to the landing pad I was already doing the calculations that would take us from Youtin to Rewe and already angry at myself.

CHAPTER THREE

The white of wildspace became the black void of space with nothing visible ahead of us. We'd hopped into the fringes of the Rewe system. It shared the same name as the only inhabited planet. A colony world with a small population of natives.

It had been discovered about ten years ago by an Expeditionary Forces vessel and us earthlings, Terrans, had laid claim to it. It had taken about four years of skirmishes and battles before the claim had been solidified. Three gas giants, one desert and one earth like planet with one lifeform that was near civilized. At least as judged by the standards of the galaxy. The native Rewens had never really advanced far or grown in population. Which was odd. No one had yet been able to find out why.

Really, no one cared. It was essentially vacant and the system was the edge of known space so a perfect jumping off point for exploring further into the galaxy. The planet didn't boast many natural resources so unlike the other colony worlds, or moons, Rewe's real purpose was as a staging ground. Sure there were colonists, people setting up settlements across the planet but Earth's government tried to ignore them. They only cared about the 2Es base.

I'd been to the system a couple of times. First was before it was a true colony world, during the height of the claim fighting. Some deliveries but the funnest had been about two years ago when I helped out a friend in the Territorial Protectorate with a pirate problem.

Well not really fun. The pirate part wasn't the fun but the couple days after were. I hoped that Kristin was still stationed on Rewe.

Kaylia stepped onto the bridge and my thoughts drifted away from TP agent Kristin Higareda and to what I was doing. This was a mistake, I knew it. And the kid's presence, taking her seat in the co-pilot's station, reminded me of it. My main goal in life now was to protect her and coming to Rewe was not going to do that.

But I had to do something.

Those men that had been killed, they were brothers. And I needed to know why they had been killed and what that could mean for me.

And Kaylia.

*****

A nice and green world, lots of bodies of water, Rewe was very flat. No hills or mountains, which made for a constant wind across the plains. Pretty in its way. Very small, fourth from the sun, the climate was pretty moderate. Lots of rain though.

Last time I had been here, there had been no cities of any size to be called cities. Just collections of buildings scattered across the plains. But in just a year or so a real city had grown up. Population of a hundred thousand or so. Made up of two and three story buildings, utilitarian, not much to look at. It was a true frontier world. Lots of different species came here to mingle with the human colonists. Most came to get away.

The largest structure was no longer the spaceport. It was the 2E base.

But I wasn't getting a look at either. Or the planet.

This trip I was stopping at the space station in orbit.

The larger ships don't have the ability to enter a planet's atmosphere so they can't land on that planet. To allow for these ships, the systems that could afford to ended up building giant space stations at the edges of the systems. A side benefit was it kept the in-system traffic down. The stations all basically followed the same designs to make them easier to use. All to make commerce better. Credits made the galaxy run, in space and on planet. Everything was done to make the transfer of credits easier, not the lives of the billions of people.

The Rewe station was different. Not a place for merchants, it didn't follow the standard design. This was a military station and that was how it looked. Unlike the merchant stations, which were long cylinders, this station was squat. Kind of globe with the top and bottom flattened. There was a docking ring around the middle but it wasn't as big as the merchant stations. Two large gun platforms were mounted on the flat parts of the globe with smaller emplacements along the docking ring.

It hadn't been built the last time I was here and wasn't as big as I thought it would be. The crew wasn't large so there wouldn't be a need for much in the way of creature comforts. The planet and all it had to offer was close enough for that.

The ring was empty, as I figured it would be, except for one large ship. A Kry made vessel, heavy freighter that looked pretty beat up.

I transmitted the *Wind's* ID codes. Didn't bother with calling the station's dockmaster, I knew I was expected. Sure enough, without any questioning I got landing authorization. A couple bays down from the Kry freighter. If this had been a merchant station, I might have let Kaylia do the manual dock but not here.

We got closer and I turned the ship so our aft end was facing the docking ring. The *Wind* was a giant wedge in shape with the aft end having slight angles on the two decks. The lower one had the ramp with a smaller door in it. Multiple cameras gave me a good view of the airlock now extending out from the docking ring. Using the thrusters I slowed the *Wind* and adjusted it so the airlock fit around the ramp.

There was a bump, the ship moving slightly, as we connected with the airlock. The maglocks engaged, the black gasketing resting tight against the ship's hull, and we were secured.

hit a couple buttons and put the *Wind* into standby.

"Let's do this," I said to Kaylia and got up from my seat.
I just knew I was going to regret this.

*****

Didn't take long to regret it.

I opened the *Wind's* hatch and came face to face with blaster rifles. All pointed at me by six armored 2E infantry soldiers.

Somebody must have forgotten to tell them I was invited.

I felt Kaylia grab my shirt and shift so she was fully behind me. I kept my arms out to my side, palms turned towards the grunts. Good thing I'd left my weapon in the bunk.

Not much had changed in the standard 2E uniform in the last five years. Dark green with black lines down the sleeves. Black blaster resistant armor pads at the knees, upper and lower legs along with the lower arms and elbows. The same chest covering tactical armor with various pieces of equipment attached to it. Pretty empty right now as these were on-station soldiers. I knew there would be clips on the back straps for other equipment to be connected. Things like environmental tanks. They all wore the green helmets with dark visors. Couldn't see in but they could see out along with lots of other useful information on the helmet's heads-up displays.

"Hello," I said with a smile.

None of them moved but I did watch someone walk out from behind the soldiers. He was in a base uniform, clean and crisp and also unchanged over the years. About six foot, brown hair, clean shaven. Dark green pants, matching dark green jacket that was closed. Black trim down the long sleeves and down the front along the zipper. Patches depicting rank and unit were on the arm. Belted to his waist was a standard issue blaster.

An officer.

Even worse, a non-combat officer.

He stood there, just off to the side, hands clasped behind his back.

"Captain Lancer," he said in greeting.

"Hi," I replied and nodded at the weapons. "Can you?"

"No," the officer replied. "You are authorized but she is not," he said and pointed at Kaylia who still hid behind me.

I rolled my eyes. Ridiculous.

Kaylia was just a kid, what were they expecting? This was the response I would expect from a visiting Tiat. I mean, Kaylia could be dangerous, but this was an overreaction.

"Okay," I told the officer and turned back towards the ship, taking the kid by the shoulders and steering her into the hold. "We'll just leave then."

I heard the airlock door open behind the soldiers and didn't bother turning. I had a feeling I knew who it was.

"Lieutenant," a voice said. One I recognized. Full of command and annoyance. "What are you doing?"

I turned around, trying not to smile. I still held Kaylia behind me hough.

Colonel Jessups looked the same as the last time I saw him in person, over five years ago. Just older. Lots older. He looked worse then he did in the video. Very worn out, tired and old.

"Sir," the officer said snapping to attention. "Just following protocols. Captain Lancer brought an unannounced being on board the station."

Jessups sighed.

He stood straight, arms clasped behind his back.

"I will personally vouch for Captain Lancer's associate," he said in a tone that dared the officer to argue.

The officer had the right to argue and by all the rules of the 2Es, he really should have. Kaylia was an unvetted non-human that was not part of the 2E. But he was young and Jessups was old, a colonel and a living legend. Sometimes the most important lesson a person could learn was when to back down.

"Sir, yes sir," the lieutenant said.

"Back to your stations," Jessups said.

The officer turned on his heel and walked out the airlock. The soldiers all stood, adjusted their weapons to at-ease, and followed. In seconds it was just me, Jessups and Kaylia.

"Not much has changed I see," I said.

"Davin is a good officer," Jessups replied. "A little too by the book but the 2Es need those just as much as they need the ones that don't follow the book," he finished and smiled towards me.

That was a reference to my time in the 2Es.

I extended my hand and shook his.

There probably wasn't anyone in the galaxy that I respected as much as this man. More than anyone, he was responsible for who I was today.

"Hello Kaylia," Jessups said turning to look behind me at her, extending his hand.

She tentatively reached out and shook it.

He stepped back and moved his fingers in sign language. I could feel Kaylia's laughter as she was still leaning against me.

I shouldn't have been surprised that Jessups knew she communicated through sign language. The colonel seemed to know everything.

*****

Jessups led us through the corridors of the station. I hadn't asked him what it's official name was. The 2Es liked to name their capital ships after former world leaders and the stations after major battles. There was a lot of those to choose from.

They may not have even had a name. Lots of secret 2E installations around the galaxy, in Terran controlled space and some in territory controlled by others.

It was too big to be a secret station. Rewe too well known and occupied. This was an official installation.

This station was pretty empty and had the new station smell. I could see some areas still under construction. Besides the uniformed soldiers there were workers, including some Europans.

That was different. First time I'd ever seen non-humans working on a 2E station. Visitors, sure. But working there? And Europans? They were from the largest moon of Jupiter in the Sol System. The same system that us Terrans were from. It was very rare to find a Europan anywhere outside of Sol. The furthest most of them ever got was the Sol Station at the edge of the system. But there were a half dozen or so working, moving some beams.

Kaylia stopped in an open doorway to watch them.

Seven or eight feet tall, one long furry body. Short legs, wide and flat tail. Long arms. Their heads were part of the body, just bent forward. No neck, just a flat head. Small eyes, large mouth. Different shades of tan and grays.

"Europans?" I asked Jessups. "That's new."

"They were bound to start leaving Sol," the Colonel said with a shrug. "They started joining the 2Es about two years ago."

"Hadn't heard about that." I was no longer part of the Expeditionary Forces but I did get some news now and then. Europans joining the 2Es should have been galactic news.

"It's been kept fairly quiet," Jessups said as he motioned for us to continue.

Interesting.

We continued down the corridor and after about fifteen minutes or so stopped in front of a sliding door. It was unmarked and a small waiting area was set up in the wide hallway. A couple chairs and couches, table and vidscreen. It looked pretty hastily put together.

"Kaylia will have to wait out here," Jessups said.

I was going to argue but she tugged at my sleeve.

It'll be okay.

"You sure?"

She nodded.

I still hesitated, thinking back to the soldiers in the air lock, but she was essentially under Jessup's protection and I would be right inside the room. She was safe enough.

Nodding I gave her a quick one armed hug.

Jessups inputted a code into the keypad. The door slid open and I could see a long conference table, vidscreen on the far wall and a couple people sitting. Not good enough to see who they were yet.

"I should warn you," Jessups started as I got a better view of one of the men in the room.

Sitting on this side of the table, standing up and smiling, was Planetary Council Ambassador Frank Coulson.

CHAPTER FOUR

I should have turned around and left.

Nothing good ever came out of anything Coulson was involved in.

Former General in the 2Es and now currently the Terran Ambassador to the Planetary Council. One of the most powerful people in the galaxy. And as crooked as they came. He had his hand in everything. Always Pro-Earth, but he didn't do anything that didn't benefit him in the end.

We'd had a couple interactions during my time in the Expeditionary Forces. None of them went well. We didn't like each other.

He still looked the same, hadn't aged in the years since I had seen him. Hair perfectly cut to military standards, all gray. Clean shaven, square jaw. Blue eyes in his pale skin. Wore his old dress uniform with lots of shiny medals at all times. Bragging by showing.

Our last official interaction had really been our last. A couple months before I left the 2Es, so about five years or so ago. That had been a big reason that I had left really. I got tired of the politics and Coulson was always political, doing what would gain him positioning at the cost of the men.

It worked, which made it worse.

What Coulson didn't know was that I had run across him on a planet called Buhin on the edge between the Inner Worlds and Deep Space. A trade hub. He had walked past and I had avoided him. Not that he would have done anything or even pretended to notice me. But he would have noticed me and that could have been trouble later on.

Really, I've always thought he was connected to the business that happened on Buhin. I'd run into another old 2E associate, Thomlin Romer, or more accurately he had forced me into a meeting. Romer was an old 2E Intelligence officer and just as crooked as Coulson. Equally good at his job.

When he had left the 2Es it had been under a dark cloud and he was considered persona non grata. Had started up an illegal information brokering business which meant that all of Earth government ignored his do-not-touch status.

Made him a rich man.

Romer had tried to force me to a do a job for him. Didn't work out in his favor. Barely did in mine. I had always wondered if Coulson had been involved in that. Not Romer forcing me, but in the job itself. Coulson would have loved the results of it. Could only have aided him.

So yeah, being on Buhin at the same time, he was probably involved.

Just had no proof of it. Not that it would do any good anyways.

Coulson was standing up, moving from his seat to the right of the head, and coming my way. He was smiling. A big and obviously fake one.

His hand reached out for mine.

I felt like ignoring it but ended up clasping his and shaking.

A strong grip. He had always been strong and age hadn't weakened him any. I always forgot that Coulson had got his start in the same units that I had, Expeditionary Forces Special Ops. He knew how to fight.

"Captain Lancer," he said moving back towards his seat. "Glad you could join us."

There were three other people at the table but I hadn't taken the time to see who they were yet. Coulson had all my attention. Jessups motioned to a chair towards the end of the table, one person between me and Coulson, and started for the head of the table.

Sometimes I don't know when to be quiet. I let my mouth just go when I would be better off just staying silent. I really didn't need to provoke Coulson but this was one of the times I couldn't shut up.

"How's Romer," I asked Coulson as I sat down.

Coulson paused before finishing to sit.

It was a quick reaction, brief and gone, but I caught it. A tightening of the eyes, flash of surprise. Coulson had not expected me to say that name.

"I do not know Captain," Coulson replied. I wasn't sure if he was acknowledging me as captain of my ship or referencing my old rank. Probably the rank. He was trying to put me back into the chain of command which had him on top. "I have not spoken to Thomlin Romer in years." Which was true, in a way, as far as anyone officially knew. "Over five or more if I remember."

"Whatever Coulson," I said, purposefully not using any of his many titles, current or former. Petty of me, sure. "Next time you're on Buhin, I'm sure you'll try extra hard to avoid him."

I turned away and focused on Jessups, but not before I saw the reaction I was hoping for. There was no way for Coulson to hide that one.

Coulson's expression proved it. He had been involved in that Buhin job Romer had forced on me. Now he was worried about what else I knew or more importantly, had proof of.

Sadly there was nothing.

Not that it mattered, but I took my victories where I could find them.

Just making him squirm a bit was enough.

Jessups was looking from me to Coulson. He gave me a curious expression. One that also said "you're going to tell me later". I shrugged. If he wanted to know, I'd tell him.

I finally looked at the other three in the room. Two men and a woman. None I recognized at first glance.

One of the men reminded me of Davin, the Lieutenant that had met me when I first got here. Uniform perfectly pressed. Trying to look all official and important. A desk jockey. A little older than Davin had been, handsome enough, blond. Probably some rich guy's kid.

The other guy looked like a pilot. He was leaning back in his chair, looking relaxed. Hair was cut in regulation style, but he had a cocky air to him. Fighter pilot.

I studied the woman. She was attractive. Black hair, sharp nose, brown eyes, short shoulder length hair. But that wasn't why I studied her so intently. Not fully anyways. I was trying to figure out if I knew her. She was Special Operations. My old unit. Don't ask me how we can tell, but Spec Ops can always spot Spec Ops.

Only the desk jockey looked at me as I walked in.

Felt out of place. Here I was in my standard outfit: pants and shirt. If I had been wearing my weapon it would have been in a low slung holster, definitely not military issue. At least I had my old military jacket on. All of the others were in current uniforms, clean and up to date. The Spec Ops lady's jacket looked a little worn. Coulson's uniform wasn't current, but it was cleaner than any of the others. More medals too.

Jessups took his seat at the head of the table.

"For the record, Captain Lancer's security clearance Delta has been reinstated for the duration of this meeting."

That did send some glances my way. Delta was pretty high, there was only one level higher. One of the more interesting aspects of getting clearance that high is that you're bound to it for life. Even when you leave the 2Es, you're still under oath. So my clearance wasn't really reinstated, I had never truly lost it. More accurately I had just lost access to the information that clearance gave me but I was still bound to not reveal anything I knew.

Another side effect was that my rank of Captain was also temporarily reinstated. It had to be to reactivate the security clearance.

What Jessups meant was that for this meeting, it really was like I had never left the Expeditionary Forces.

The Spec Ops soldier now studied me. I smiled at her. She rolled her eyes.

"As long as Captain Lancer understands that the Delta oath binds him to silence over anything heard here," Coulson added.

"I haven't revealed anyone's dirty laundry so far," I replied leaning forward so Coulson could see me. "Why would I start now?"

It was Jessup's turn to roll his eyes. I knew I had to rein it in. This little back and forth with Coulson wasn't gaining anything. Just me being petty. Jessups wouldn't say anything because I doubted the others in the room knew anything of my history in the 2E, let alone how it connected with Coulson. To say something more would be to invite questions.

And the only part of my history that I really cared to deal with right now was how the murders affected my future.

Jessups settled back in his chair, glancing around the room. This brought the others to attention and concentrating on the Colonel, except the desk jockey who was fiddling with the tablet in front of him. That guy was obviously in charge of the presentation aspect of whatever this was.

"First introductions," he said. "Lieutenant Gott," he pointed at the desk jockey. "Intelligence Division. Captain Devin Yearly," he continued and pointed at the pilot. "Lieutenant Lysa Harrow, Spec Ops. Ambassador Coulson," Jessups finished.

No one bothered to get up so neither did I. They didn't bother to look at me, so I didn't either.

Quite a mixed group.

"Captain Arek Lancer, former Spec Ops," Jessups said for benefit of the others in the room but I had a feeling they already knew who I was.

I really wanted to ask why I was here but held back. The more I let Jessups talk, the more I was going to end up being involved.

This was starting to feel familiar, like any of the dozens of mission briefings I had attended. I could feel myself slipping back into old routines. It's true what they say, you never really leave the military.

"Most of this will be old news for the rest of you but we'll bring Captain Lancer up to date on where things stand with the conflict."

Ask the soldiers, we were still at war with the Tiat. Ask the government, and it was just a conflict.

One of the longest continuous wars in Earth history.

Twenty years and counting. Officially the Third Galactic War had only lasted seven years but the sides were still fighting even after the treaty had been signed, a cold war. My time in the Earth Expeditionary Forces had been in fighting that cold war. I had joined up two years before the war ended.

Jessups signaled to Gott and the screen mounted to the wall went from black to showing a star map. Four systems were visible. Just from the map with no labels, I couldn't recognize any of them. Maps like this one had no scale. The left system could have been twice the size of the others, or half the size. No way to know. Also no way to know the distance from one system to another.

Navcomputers were needed to calculate the actual distances. Maps were just used to get an idea of how many hops would be needed to get from one system to another. Good reference to know where you'd be traveling through and what to expect.

Gott made some quick movements on the tablet and labels started to appear.

I wanted to curse.

The far left was one of the Tiat's major systems. The next one over was a colony system of theirs. The one where the rock was located. The third system was one I didn't know the name of. The fourth, on the right, was Rewe.

I had never realized how close Rewe was to the rock and Tiat space. Only three hops and judging by the numbers I now saw on the screen, it was three very short hops.

No wonder the Tiat had fought so hard to take the system from us when we tried to secure it.

Rewe was practically in their backyard.

CHAPTER FIVE

"On the left is the Towrandru System," Jessups said. Definitely a Tiat name.

"Three habitable planets, controlled by the Tiat," he continued. "There's a major shipyard mid-system, two military stations at either edge and a civilian trade station orbiting one of the planets."

Civilian trade for the Tiat meant more of their people, which meant somewhat less military. The Tiat were a matriarchal military society. Everything was run through the military. The civilian station just meant that there was no overt presence of soldiers. It was also where their allied species would do their trading.

There were a lot of species governed by a militaristic society. The Dyer was another. Allies of us humans. But the Tiat took it to a whole other level.

"The right system is where we are now, Rewe," Jessups said as if we didn't know.

I didn't miss that about briefings. Going over things that everyone in the room already knew. Gott was hanging off of Jessups every word. Yearly was pulling the typical flyboy, listening to every word but pretending he wasn't. Coulson was the politician. Perfect mix of attentive interest and studious remembering. Harrow was like me. Ignoring the parts she already knew.

The reasoning for it made sense. I got it. I just didn't like it and my attention would start to wander. I'd gotten reprimanded enough back in the day but I'd always retained what I needed for the missions.

"To Rewe's left is an unclaimed system called Jeffern."

"Who named it," Harrow asked.

Which is a question I would have asked back in the day.

There is really no such thing as an unclaimed system. Someone found it, planted the navsats and named it. If it had a name, that meant it had something within the system that was worth having. Ores, gases, water. Whatever. No one would bother naming a system that had no purpose.

And because it had a name, it meant someone was there. Unclaimed was just saying that none of the galaxies many empires or expansionist species had bothered to claim it yet. Some trading consortium was there, mining or harvesting, and bribing the right people.

"The Saxit," Jessups answered.

A trading consortium. Engyn if I remembered right. Wonder how secure they felt knowing they were between the Tiat and Terrans. I wouldn't feel secure about my hold on anything in that situation.

"The last is the important one." Jessups returned to his presentation. "The Tiat have designated it as Unitouro and there has been nothing there. No habitable planets. No asteroids of size worth mining. No reason to go there except as a hop point."

"And the rock," I muttered.

Jessups nodded.

He motioned to Gott and the image on the screen changed. Now we were looking at an asteroid belt, a very large belt of small rocks. Lots of them. Like Jessups had said, there was no asteroids of size to make mining worthwhile. Ores, all of the various kinds, were somewhat plentiful in a galaxy full of planets made of rocks. Unless an asteroid had a rare ore, and lots of it, the expense to mine it wasn't worth it.

But other uses for asteroids could be found.

"The rock is what we called a very specific asteroid," Jessups said finally getting to the good part. "Six years ago, 2E Intel got wind of the Tiat building a weapons development lab in the Unitouro system." He paused and looked down the table at me.

I wasn't looking at him or the screen. I knew what the rock looked like. Knew where it was located in the asteroid belt. I could feel his eyes on me. The others all glanced at me, now starting to understand why I was here if they hadn't known already. Didn't take a genius to figure it out.

"Turns out they had already built it," Jessups said.

My mind flashed back those years to that mission. Not one I wanted to remember.

It was supposed to have been an insertion to destroy a facility that was in mid-construction. It wasn't. It was fully built and occupied. Heavily occupied.

Somehow we succeeded in destroying it. Once we found what they were building there, we had to. There was no choice.

"When did we start picking up chatter that it was up and running again," I asked, still looking down at the table.

"Started about three months ago," Jessups said. "Rumors, nothing substantial. Until recently. But nothing indicating that it's an R&D facility again. We think it's a staging ground. There has been an increase in terrorist activity on Rewe as well."

Part of me wondered if that was why Rewe had been so contested by us. It was on the edge of the frontier, a good staging ground for exploration into the unknown regions but also a good staging ground for operations into Tiat controlled space.

"When do we go in," Harrow asked.

Right to the point. I liked her.

"The problem is that we don't know the exact location of the asteroid," Coulson said speaking for the first time. "Six years ago we were never able to pinpoint the exact location. We sent in scouts and lost every one."

"How did we finally find it?" Yearly asked.

"Ask him," Coulson said and pointed at me.

I sighed. This was why I was brought here.

The level of tech in the galaxy is pretty high. We can travel from solar system to solar system in a matter of hours. We can live on planets that are poisonous. There is so much we can do. But there is also a lot we can't. Asteroid belts are perfect hiding spots. If the right kind of ore is in the rocks, no sensors can penetrate the belts. With the asteroids constantly moving, maps aren't that accurate either. They're hard to fly around in, so any mining is usually the edges. Going inside a belt can be extremely dangerous if you don't know the path.

"We got lucky," I said, leaning back in my chair and now staring up at the ceiling. "We hid out in a drop ship for days on another rock just waiting for a Tiat supply ship that we could follow in."

I paused, remembering. Drop ships are never comfortable. Ugly, bare bones. They're not meant for long term use but we did it. Somehow. Twelve of us plus the pilot. Four of us made it back.

"Lucky," I laughed, a bitter one. "Not sure how lucky it really was."

"You're here so you must have destroyed the place," Harrow said. "How are the Tiat able to use it again?"

I liked Harrow even though she was questioning my ability to do my job. It was the right question to ask and she didn't mean anything personally, just doing her job. She was the one that was going to lead the mission, that much was now obvious, so she had to know everything.

"Remember it was supposed to be under construction," I said leaning forward. "Just one of many times that Intel let us down." I stared at Coulson. Everyone knew he was ex-intel and now started to wonder at his involvement. "There were twelve of us. Four times that many Tiat. We blew the place up, destroyed their equipment and whatever they were developing. Barely made it out alive."

"During the war we kept an eye on the place," Jessups said. "The Tiat never went back. Over time the intelligence resources were deemed better used elsewhere and we abandoned our watching of the rock." He looked at Coulson.

A pretty big indication of who had deemed the resources wasted.

"Again I ask, when do we go in," Harrow said it as a statement, not a question.

"As soon as Captain Lancer agrees to lead us in," Jessups said and all eyes fell on me.

*****

I wanted to say yes, to agree to the mission. Part of me really wanted to get back into action again. But a bigger part of me was saying no. I thought of Kaylia, sitting alone in the other room wondering what was going on. I couldn't leave her. She was my responsibility. My job was now taking care of her.

With the other survivors of that mission now dead, I was the only one that had been on that rock. I was the only one that knew the way. Our ship had been destroyed on the rock and with it the navrecords. The belts ore had prevented us from sending a signal out or being tracked. No one had expected to need those records years later.

That mission was the first time I had flown outside of simulators. And it had been a Tiat ship. I had been, and still was, surprised that I had gotten us off the rock and out of the belt.

I could feel every eye in the room on me, waiting for my answer. The tension was thick, dragging. I returned to looking at the table, leaning forward and resting my head on my hands, elbows on the table.

"I'm sorry Colonel," I said finally after a couple minutes and meant it. "I can't. I'll help any other way that I can but I can't go with the strike team."

Jessups nodded and in that instant I knew that I was going. He had anticipated me.

"I thought you might say that," he told me with regret, true regret. He was sorry to play the next card but he did it anyways. "I'm sorry Captain but we really need you for this mission and I knew that you would not leave young Kaylia to be watched by just anyone." He leaned forward and hit a button on the desk in front of him. "You can come in now."

There was a very short list of people that I would trust to watch the kid. I ran through it in my head and it didn't take long. There was only one person in the immediate area that qualified.

I thought of the planet Rewe orbiting below us.

Dammit.

The door slid open and I turned to look, knowing who would be there.

Kristin Higareda stood in the doorway.

CHAPTER SIX

Short, eyes even with my shoulder, long black hair pulled back in a ponytail that she always seemed to have. A couple strands of hair fell down on either side of her face, which always seemed to happen. Very striking, beautiful, she had dark eyes and tannish skin. A long time officer in the Territorial Protectorate, even with her size she carried herself in a way that warned people not to mess with her. I knew just how tough she really was.

And loyal.

The badge hung on it's chain around her neck, the only indication of who she worked for. Low heel boots, up to the calves, black pants, white shirt and the same black jacket that she'd had the last time I saw her. A little more worn, little more faded.

Just like I was.

Kristin had spent some time in the 2Es. That was where we had first met and gotten together. Which had happened a couple times over the years. We liked each other. Really liked each other. But time and distance and life seemed to keep getting in the way.

We exchanged a look and a lot was communicated in that look. There was some pity in that look, a little guilt as well.

She may not have known exactly what the mission was but she knew enough. It was important otherwise she wouldn't be here. The pity was because she knew her presence was the tipping point, what would get me on the mission. The guilt was because she felt sorry for having to do it.

"When do we leave," I finally said.

*****

"I'm sorry Arek," Kristin said once we were alone.

Jessups had called a break, the others leaving the conference room. When the door had slid open I could see Kaylia sprawled out in one of the chairs watching the vidscreen. Kristin had followed my sight line. When the door slid closed, she'd turned back with a smile.

It hadn't lasted long.

"Not your fault," I said standing up and walking over to her.

I folded her into a hug, holding tight. She felt good in my arms, felt right.

"Are the attacks on Rewe that bad," I asked as we stepped apart.

She looked good.

"Yeah," Kristin answered. "Just took down a cell the other day, right before Jessups contacted me." She sat down in one of the chairs and I took a seat in the one next to her, swiveling it to look at her. "There's always been terrorists on Rewe ever since we claimed it. You know how much fighting there was over it. That never really stopped."

It probably hadn't taken much convincing on Jessups part. Kristin had been born to be a cop. She was a good soldier, excellent one, but it had never suited her like being a cop did. Looking out for the people, protecting them, that was where she was at her best. If Rewe really was under attack that much, and it could be traced back to the Tiat, she would have signed up for anything that ended those attacks.

Kristin had probably volunteered for the mission.

For her to accept being a babysitter then this mission was that important.

"She's a good kid," Kristin said motioning to the door. "Got to spend some time with her well you were in here."

I nodded, smiling.

"Great kid."

"Look at you," Kristin said with a chuckle. "Arek Lancer as a dad. Never imagined it."

"Me either," I replied with a shrug.

"Why," she asked, head tilted as she looked at me.

I thought about it, leaning back in the chair, arms crossed.

"Don't really know," I finally answered with a shrug. "She needed my help." I could still remember, probably always would, the look on Kaylia's face when she ran into me on that asteroid a couple months back. Scared and hopeful at the same time. Scared of who chased her. Hopeful that I would help her.

How do you explain why you did something that you had no choice in? There was never a question. I was going to help Kaylia and continue helping her as long as that needed to be. First as her rescuer and now as her guardian.

What kind of guardian was I though? Roaming the galaxy, barely making enough credits to keep flying, and now leaving her on a military station so I could play soldier again?

Kristin must have caught something in my expression.

"You're doing good," she said. "Sure it may not be the most stable life but Kaylia is safe, fed and happy."

I nodded. She was right. And leaving Kaylia here, under Kristin's protection, was keeping her safe. Short term and long term.

"How's Abboud," I asked changing the subject.

Waleed Abboud was Kristin's long time partner. An older officer, he was more mentor and father figure than just partner. A good man. He really didn't like me.

Which just made me respect him more.

"Doing good, had his fifth grandkid last month."

"Back on Earth?"

"Nope," she answered. "His family's over on Zahn."

That was interesting, not that many people left Earth for Zahn. I really didn't care about Abboud's family. It was just a way of steering the topic away from areas neither of us really wanted to get into. Zahn was an Earth colony world. Terran as the wider galaxy called us. All planets are 'earth' in their native tongue. To the rest of the galaxy, my Earth was Terra. Kind of confusing but Tradelan, the galaxy wide near-common language, could only do so much. I hadn't been to

Zahn in a long time and what I remembered wasn't a big draw.

"Is he ever going to retire?"

"Not until his family is off Zahn."

Damn, that took a turn I hadn't been expecting.

"Come on," I said to move around that topic. "Need to talk to the kid."

I stood up and headed for the door, Kristin behind me.

*****

Kaylia took it pretty well.

I had been expecting a fight, some guilt trip from her. Something. But instead she had surprised me. Yet again. She was good at that.

I understand. They need you.

"Yeah, but you're more important," I told her. And that was the truth. If she wanted me to not go then I wasn't going.

We were sitting together on the couch. She had shut off the vidscreen, turning to face me so we could talk. I glanced at the screen, not sure what show she was watching. It looked like a documentary. There was a space battle happening. Lots of ships, capitol and fighter. Some explosions. The ships were all Terran models. Couldn't see who they were fighting.

Kristin was leaning against the wall, watching us. She concentrated on Kaylia's hands, trying to decipher the sign language the kid spoke in. It was a mix of Tradelan, Thesan and some other languages thrown in. Took me a while to understand it, Kristin would have a hard time with just a couple days.

And there was no way it was going to take longer. I would make sure of that.

"I'm going to grab some coffee," Kristin said pushing away from the wall. "Need anything?"

We both said no.

I watched her walk down the hall and turn out of sight.

Turning back I saw Kaylia studying me and smiling.

"Not like that."

The look she gave me said she didn't believe me.

"It's complicated," I said with a sigh.

Kaylia's face scrunched up in a soundless laugh.

I like her.

"So do I."

She's on the list.

I nodded. The list was a small group of people I had told Kaylia to contact if something ever happened to me. People I trusted and people that would take care of her.

The kids mood shifted. Acknowledging the list was also acknowledging that I might not return. I wanted to tell her that I would. Promise that I would. But I wasn't going to do that to her. There was no way that I could truly promise it. She knew that I would do my best, everything I could to make it back to her. But some things were beyond my control.

"What are you watching," I asked, changing the subject.

I was doing a lot of that.

Battle of Irisk.

I studied the vidscreen, noting the placement of the ships. One of the last major battles in the Third Galactic War. Many said it was the the one that finally got the three sides to sit down and work out the treaty that really didn't stop anything. A lot of lives were lost in the fighting. Tiat, Thesan and Terran.

Not too much available in the library.

Figured. Good old Earth Expeditionary Forces. Guaranteed the documentary was completely bias and heavily edited.

"The *Wind* will still be docked here," I said and felt a momentary twinge. I really did not like the idea of leaving my ship behind. Not as bad a feeling of guilt as I got for leaving

Kaylia behind, but damn close. "You'll have access to your own vids."

Can I go down to the planet?

I shrugged.

"Up to Kristin but don't see why not. Rewe is a nice enough place."

Except for the terrorists.

Some guardian I was.

*****

Once I made my decision, things moved quickly.

The plan was to launch and head for the Unitouro system in the local system's morning. One of the most annoying things about travel between solar systems is that time is relative to that system. Each ship kept their own measurement. The *Wind* operated off Terran Standard, which Rewe as a colony world did too. That made it easier for me. No disruption to my sleeping pattern.

But then I didn't really have one.

And there was no way I was sleeping that night anyways.

We reconvened the briefing and immediately I had noticed that Coulson was missing. Wonder if he was now avoiding me?

"Unlike last time," Jessups had said continuing the briefing. "We're not sending in a team to destroy the facility. Lieutenant Harrow will lead her team into the station and plant the beacon. Once planted and out of the facility, Captain Yearly's squad will begin their bombing run."

A beacon? I liked that idea better than another full frontal assault. Let the flyboys do the heavy lifting. 2E tech had advanced since my time if they had a beacon that could penetrate through an asteroid field.

"What's my part in all this," I asked but I knew, I just wanted confirmation.

"You're to guide Harrow's assault team to the asteroid," Jessups confirmed for me.

"What will I be flying?"

I had flown the previous mission but I had been in the ship's cockpit when we had made our way through the asteroid field. I could do it again and would feel safer flying my way in.

"An Assault Dropship," Yearly answered for Jessups. "But you're not flying, one of my guys will be"

"We'll see about that," I said and could tell that Yearly was ready to start a pissing contest. "Your guy will be better than me," I told him wanting to stop the contest before it started. That wasn't why I wanted to fly the Dropship. I really didn't want to fly the Dropship, those things were boxy and unwieldy. I honestly didn't want to fly any ship into the asteroid belt. "I'm just a freight pilot but once there I might need to fly instead of navigate."

I could tell that Yearly wasn't happy about it but he understood. He was probably still going to tell his pilot to not give up the seat no matter what. I'd deal with that if and when it needed to be dealt with.

"How long, once the beacon is activated, will we have to get out of the target zone," Harrow asked.

Jessups looked over at Yearly. The pilot shrugged.

"No clue," he replied. "We'll be going in blind until the beacon is activated. No way of knowing how deep in the belt the rock will be."

"Twenty minutes," I said and again all eyes were on me. "I assume you're flying X-6932s as escort for a BT6894?"

Both ships were built by the Castellans, the same as my own *Nomad's Wind*. The BTs were bombers. Slow, heavily armored. The Xs were the standard starfighter used by the Expeditionary Forces.

"Yes," Yearly replied. "But the BTs are faster than you remember."

By his tone of voice, I knew he felt like he needed to defend his pilots and their ships. I was sure there had been some improvements in the five years since I had left the 2Es but there wouldn't have been that much to shave time off. There was only so fast that a ship the size of a BT6894 Hammer could fly. Especially when it was loaded with bombs.

"Eighteen minutes," I said without a trace of sarcasm.

"So fifteen," Harrow said not having time for the Alpha Male pissing contest I had found myself in. "Size of the target zone?"

"We'll be carrying a load of plasma bombs," Yearly answered. "2 tonners."

"Pretty much the whole rock is the target zone," I said after running the numbers in my head. A full load in the Hammer's bay for 2 ton plasma bombs. That was a lot of explosion.

There would be nothing left of that rock.

"Any further questions?," Jessups asked the room.

I managed to keep my mouth shut. I had always been sarcastic but it had only gotten worse in the last five years.

Always had liked Jessups briefings. Short and to the point. There was only so much to go over. Plans were only good until the first plasma bolt was fired and after that they were useless. Jessups trusted his people to be able to improvise so his briefings gave just the right amount of information. The who, why, what, when, where and how.

"The mission is straight forward," Jessups said signaling to Gott to turn off the vidscreen. "Find the target, paint the target and destroy the target."

Simple but something would go wrong. It always did.

CHAPTER SEVEN

When we had first flown in I had wondered what the Kry heavy freighter was doing at the station. The only ship there. I found out pretty quickly when the mission launched.

It was our transport.

I didn't get to see much of it. We entered through the airlock and inside the cargo hold was a 2E Assault Drop Ship. Harrow hustled us into the Drop Ship's hold. There were a pilot and co-pilot for the Kry ship and a set for the Drop Ship. The only other people on board were Harrow, myself and her five Spec Ops commandos.

One of which was a Europan.

He had to duck to make it through the bulkheads. The Drop Ship was tight for normal sized humans. Not designed for taller and bulkier Europans. Made to sit twelve people and gear in the back, the GH-5971 was bulky. Another ship made by the Castellans, it was a box with jets and stubby wings. Two forward thrusters mounted on either side of the slightly sloping front. A thin view window at the top. The rest of the ship was the hold with two larger rotating thrusters mounted at the top. Small wings swept off from the front with small stabilizers in the back.

Not fast, it was a tough ship. Heavily armored, lightly armed. The ship, nicknamed the Meteor, was designed to be carried close to a planet where it would live up to its name and drop to the surface to unload its cargo of soldiers. The nickname came from the speed and force which the ship would drop.

No one would ever call riding in one comfortable. It was to get the soldiers to the surface safely, not in comfort. Besides angry and uncomfortable soldiers made better fighters.

At least that's what one of my old drill sergeants used to say.

The Meteor, no specific name for this one and only a unit number that was not painted on the dull gray hull, took up most of the space in the decoy ship's hold. Just enough space to squeeze by between both hulls. The freighter's cargo doors weren't big enough to get the drop ship out so I was curious how we'd get out into space.

That part hadn't been included in the mission briefing.

Not my concern.

I settled into my seat. Straight backed, barely any cushion, the bottom low to the ground so my knees were elevated. Pulling the crash webbing across my body, the whole thing started to feel familiar. Too familiar.

The ship's inside was just how I remembered. Six seats mounted to the hull along each side. Clear space down the middle. Handles hanging from the low ceiling. To my left was the hatch that went to the small cockpit and to the right was the hatch that opened to the outside.

All of it in black.

Lights blinked on some readouts across the exposed piping and conduit. The metal hull that I could feel against my back was cold. Just like I remembered.

It actually wasn't that bad. Of course we hadn't left the space station yet. Had two couple hour hops to look forward to. It was going to be long and boring.

I may not have been that uncomfortable but the Europan was.

His seven foot long frame and width were too much for the small seats. He stretched out across the ship, parts on seats on either side of the hull. One of the other commandos helped him with the crash webbing. Once secure he shifted a bit and promptly fell asleep.

The commando next to me caught me staring.

"Ever seen one up close," he asked me. His name was Derek Fortin.

Bald, black eyes. About my height and size, a couple years younger.

"Yeah," I replied thinking of the time on Corric Station when my ship was almost stolen by a Europan and his human sister partners.

"Took some getting used to," Fortin said glancing over at the Europan. "When Treuto first started coming with us on missions but when we're in a tight spot, glad to have him along."

I nodded remembering how strong and tough the race was. And those climbing claws they could unsteath were sharp. Europa, the largest moon of Jupiter in Earth's Sol System, was a giant ball of ice. Hollow inside, the Europans lived in caves within the ice, using their claws to climb and tunnel.

They cut through ice pretty easy. A human was a whole lot easier.

The other three commandos were named Ryan Sweet, Mark Gilbert and Joe Carleton. None of them really talked or acknowledged me. Couldn't blame them. I was the outsider and these Spec Ops squads were a pretty tight knit bunch.

At least mine had been.

I'd also been on a couple missions with tag-a-long consultants. They were never fun.

"Feels like coming home," I said trying to remind the soldiers that I used to be one of them.

Nobody made a comment.

At least I had tried.

Harrow came into the hold from the cockpit where she had been talking with the pilots. She said down in the empty seat across from me, staring right at me. I smiled at her.

"The Colonel said your rank was reinstated for the duration of this mission," she said, loudly, so the others could hear. I saw one of the Europans eyes open and fixate on me. "So that means you outrank me but this is my mission."

I nodded.

"It is," I said getting that out of the way. I didn't need Harrow worrying that I'd take over her mission. I had absolutely no desire for that. "I'm just along for the ride."

She looked at me for a minute before nodding.

"We launch in five," she told her squad.

The Europan grunted and closed his eyes.

*****

I started out somewhat comfortable.

That lasted about two minutes after we launched from the station.

I could feel the vibrations of the freighter through the metal hull and up into my legs. Was this how new people felt on the *Nomad's Wind*? Did they feel the vibrations and I was just used to it? I hoped not. My ship was a little beat-up, in need of constant repairs, but it was built better than that.

Settling as best I could in the webbing, I closed my eyes. Besides Treuto, Fortin and Carleton had already fallen asleep. I used to be able to do that, but no longer. I'd gotten used to the limited comforts of the *Wind*. It felt like the height of luxury compared to this.

I couldn't see the stars, which was the thing that felt the most off to me. I always looked out the *Wind's* view window everytime I left a station or exited atmosphere of a planet. I wanted that view. I craved it.

Undoing the crash webbing I stood up. Harrow barely spared me a glance, the others watching with curiosity. I didn't care. I moved over to the hatch that led to the cockpit, hit the open button and slid into the cramped space.

Two stations were at the front, open space between them, about a foot or two of clear space to stand behind. Pilot on the left and co-pilot on the right. Both of them looked back at me, surprised and questioning.

"Need to see that," I said and pointed at the thin strip of view window that was at their sitting eye level so I had to crouch a little.

The drop ship was inside the hold of the larger freighter so most of the view was blocked but the maintenance techs had put some windows into the cargo hold to allow the drop ship pilots to get a view of space, so they would have some idea of what they were flying into.

Through the drop ship window and the other window I could see the black of space with the millions of tiny white dots that were the stars. Just like when in the *Wind*, I felt a sense of calm come over me. The pilots must have recognized one of their own because neither said anything, just turned back to their controls.

I stayed like that for a couple more minutes before returning to the hold.

*****

Usually the soldiers didn't spend this much time in the cramped confines of a Rock drop ship. The carrier would fly into the system, get close to the planet, and then soldiers would get into the drop ships. At the most they spent half an hour or so in the small holds.

Before this trip the longest I'd been in one had been an hour.

Interestingly enough, it had been the last time I'd gone to the same asteroid. That mission we had taken the drop ship to the asteroid, following the Tiat supply ship. Well waiting we had stayed in the carrier ship hidden at the edges of the system.

Periodically each of us would unhook from the webbing, which we really didn't need to wear for now, just to stretch and get some circulation back in cramped muscles. Treuto also moved a couple of times. When that happened, the rest of us had to crowd near the front so the Europan could rotate his body as he couldn't stand up fully.

He hooted and grunted each time.

I had never learned the Europan language. The species couldn't speak Tradelan and most other species couldn't speak Europan but could learn to understand it.

Communication was key during missions. I wondered how it was handled between Harrow and the Europan.

It was a couple hours later, I'd lost track, when the hatch slid open and the co-pilot stuck his head into the hold.

"Just hit system," he said and the hatch slid closed again.

Harrow readjusted her crash webbing, tightening it. The others followed her lead, LaPlante helping Treuto. I did the same.

Once settled we waited. For what I didn't know.

It was about an hour when the ship started to shake.

The hatch slid open again.

"Contact," the co-pilot said.

He kept the hatch open so we could hear what was coming through the comm connection with the freighter carrying us. It was one way. We could hear the freighter, they couldn't hear or connect with us. A hard wire line, not broadcast. No signal to intercept.

"Approaching ships identified as Tiat patrol ships. Three XTs."

The Expeditionary Forces knew what the Tiat called their various ships, what the names and classifications were, but it was of course in the Tiat's own language. Our guys had just started giving them nicknames. XTs were the common fighters, called that because of the distinctive shape. The ship had a long and thin body, just wide enough for the pilot, that ended in a point at the front. In the rear it widened out with two engines mounted on either side of the body. That created the 'T' shape. The 'X' came from the four wings. Two coming off at angles from the top and another two at similar angles from the bottom. When one of them was coming towards you it looked like the letter X. From above it looked like a T.

Never said the nicknames were clever.

"Hailing."

We waited in silence. Couldn't hear anything as the freighter's co-pilot has disconnected the link to communicate with the Tiat patrol ships. He was probably being asked why a Kry freighter was so far out in the middle of nowhere. The Kry ship was a good choice.

There were not many planets in the galaxy that considered themselves allies of the Tiat. And the Tiat were fine with that. They had their Empire, the largest in the known galaxy. The strongest too if being honest. It had taken the combined might of the Thesans and Terrans to hold off the Tiat in the Third Galactic War and then it was just barely. The list of planets that did not deal directly with the Tiat was pretty long. Much shorter were the ones that would deal with the Tiat. The Kry was one of those.

Kry were business people first before anything else. They did not care about the war or which side was "right" since really no side was. They just wanted to turn a profit. So they did business with the Tiat.

Seeing a Kry ship in Tiat space wasn't unusual. Seeing one coming in from this direction was.

"Let's hope they buy the cover story," Harrow said quietly.

I wanted to make a sarcastic comment but it really wasn't the time. My old unit, it would have been a race to see which one of us made a comment first. But this wasn't my unit and I didn't know the dynamics of the squad.

"Hope you're all strapped in," the co-pilots voice came back. "Going to get bumpy."

Guess that meant the Tiat hadn't bought the story.

Probably thought the Kry were smugglers.

Or just didn't want intruders in this system.

Either way this mission had just hit its first snag.

CHAPTER EIGHT

Part of me was worried that this was the end, for the mission and myself.

But I'd been in enough of these tight spots to know that there was always a way out. Any mission, pretty much every second was walking along that thin line between failure and success. This was no different.

The mission planners back on Rewe Station would have thought about this scenario and come up with a way to make it work.

We just had to survive long enough for it to work.

It was a bumpy ride.

The freighter lurched back and forth, up and down, as the pilot kept the ship moving erratically. The only way to avoid laser lock. I don't know much about ship to ship combat in the void of space. I was a ground pounder even though I was a decent enough pilot now. I'd never flown a combat ship but I knew the basics.

The vidshows liked to show space combat as ships swooping and diving, barrel rolling around the enemy. It really wasn't like that. Mostly it was boring.

But from inside the hold of the drop ship, I had no idea what was happening and it was frustrating.

The movements of the freighter were not that violent considering how much the ship was moving. The inertial compensators were working overtime. We were still being thrown around but not as bad as it could have been. I felt bad for Treuto and the way he was forced to sit. The lurching would be worse on him. He'd feel every movement. Glancing at the Europan, he didn't appear bothered.

When we arrived in the system, the goal was to get as close to the asteroid belt as the pilot could and then launch the drop ship. We had to hope that the pilot was still heading in that direction. To the pursuing Tiat, it would make sense.

Under constant barrage, there wouldn't be an opportunity for the ship to hop into wild space. The navcom wouldn't be able to make the calculations. The only option would be to head in-system and find a way to hold off the Tiat long enough for the navcom to compensate for the erratic movements and plot a hop.

That would bring us closer to the asteroid belt.

The race was on and we would probably lose.

Starfighters have the advantage of freighters in speed and maneuverability. They may not move like in the vids, but they can still move better than bulky freighters. Three of the Tiat XTs and sooner, rather than later, one of them was bound to make a direct hit.

"Get ready," the freighter's co-pilots voice said over the link.

Ready for what? I hadn't been briefed on the insertion scenario, how we would get from the freighter to the asteroid belt, but I had an idea. I'd run quite a few missions like this back in the day.

The trick was older than I was. Probably older than Colonel Jessups.

"Do we really think the Tiat will fall for this," I asked no one, just said it outloud.

Next to me Fortin laughed.

"I said the same thing," he remarked.

"Stow it," Harrow said.

I would have shrugged if I could have in the crash webbing.

We all felt the sharp turn the freighter took, pushing us against the webbing that fought to hold us still. The pilot had shifted to take a parallel course to the belt. The ship bucked even more now. Besides the side to side movement, there was a pushing as the gravity of the asteroids themselves acted against the ship. Singularly there wasn't that much gravity to an asteroid, nowhere near enough to push a ship.

But a belt was different. So many together generated quite a lot of gravity. Especially around the edges of the belt.

"Good luck," the co-pilots voice said.

"You too," our co-pilot replied and the door between us slid shut.

I grabbed the webbing with both hands, crossing over my body, and braced myself.

There was an audible sound, a whooshing as the air was sucked out of the ship and into the void. A cracking of metal with multiple small explosions. We only heard it because of the atmosphere that remained in the freighter, just enough to bounce sound.

I felt the drop ship falling backwards any noise lost to the void.

Picturing what was happening in my mind, I saw the front half of the freighter falling away as the rear half with us in it continued. The engines were on our end, so the thrusters would push as forward until they ran out of fuel or fell apart. The cockpit in the front half would spin and spin, unable to stop.

Had the pilots just commited suicide?

The drop ship shook and the vibrations changed. I could feel the ship's metal floor almost throbbing in time with the engines as they powered up. We were pushed back in our seats, pushed to the side away from the front, as the drop ship burst out of the shell of the freighter.

With the hatch closed we couldn't see anything but had to hope the pilots were quickly getting us into the asteroid belt.

The freighter had been detonated, probably exploding in time with a blast from an XT laser. Make the Tiat think the ship had been destroyed. Explosions, set by the techs back on station, would have ripped the ship in half. They would have been placed where they would have done the least damage to the cargo hold, with the drop ship, or the cockpit but also where they would split the ship and expose the hold to space so we could escape.

I knew we had entered the asteroid belt when the shaking of the drop ship increased. The entire structure vibrated as well as the ship itself being pushed and pulled by the asteroids. Well they weren't comfortable, drop ship had very strong thrusters. They needed them in order to power through storms, thick air and other obstacles on the various planets.

An asteroid belt's messed up gravity shouldn't have been a problem.

Had the previous trip been this bad? I couldn't remember. Or had I purposely blocked it from memory?

*****

Twenty minutes later we got through the belt and to the other side into relatively clear space.

We had to hope that the Tiat had bought the ruse, thinking the freighter had been destroyed. An old trick but as Jessups was fond of saying, the reason they were classics was because they worked so often. The XTs couldn't fly through the belt, not as easily as we had. There had been some close ones. We could feel the many times smaller asteroids had hit the hull of the ship. The sound had been a deep boom with each one, the hull echoing with the impacts. Thankfully the ship's armor was thick and held up.

The star fighters would have been destroyed by any of those smaller impacts.

Belts had earned the name because of their shape. They resembled a belt wrapped around nothing but more space or a planet or moon. There was a width to them, they didn't go over the top or bottom.

The Tiat ships could have flown over the belt and into the clear space we now occupied.

So we had to move fast. The rocks themselves would protect us from scanners. But only until a Tiat ship was in a position where it's scanners went over or under the asteroids at just the right angle. And there probably would be Tiat patrols in this area as well.

Or maybe not.

The mission planners, who I had always thought needed to actual go on missions sometimes, had figured the Tiat wouldn't patrol inside the belt as no one was expected in system and no one should know they were operating out of the belt.

I wondered if anyone had tried to point out that the entrance we made would put the Tiat on alert and probably have them run patrols to be safe. I mean that's what I would have done if I was them.

The tough part was going to be finding the rock before the Tiat inevitably found us.

Again.

The hatch to the cockpit slid open and the co-pilot looked my way.

"Captain Lancer," he said. "You're up."

With a sign I unhooked my crash webbing. I stood up a little shakily, getting the feeling back in my legs. Using the handles mounted to the top of the hold I walked the short distance into the cockpit. No handles inside, I had to hold onto the back of the co-pilot's seat to stay steady. We were still being thrown around a bit by the asteroids gravity and the pilot was continuing the erratic movements to confuse any possible sensors even though the mission planners said there wouldn't be any.

"You got the coordinates," I asked and the co-pilot nodded.

He pointed at a screen and I leaned over his shoulder to look. Only a couple thousand kilometers away. We'd lucked out and gotten pretty close even accounting for the movement of that point over the years.

Jessups had wanted me along on the mission because I was the only person alive that knew how to get to the rock. That was true. But they would have still been able to do the mission without me. Just more difficult.

When we had escaped the last time in the borrowed Tiat ship, there were no navrecords we could use that showed the path well within the belt but we did have a record of the point I had exited the belt from. That gave us our starting point.

The real reason Jessups needed me was because I knew the layout of the facility on the rock. Or most of it. The Tiat had probably changed it and rebuilt the parts we had destroyed. But some knowledge was better than no knowledge.

"Let's get this over with," I said.

The pilot and co-pilot laughed. No one behind us did.

The thrusters kicked on and the drop shop made for the coordinates in the navcom.

I looked out the viewwindow, the ship orientated so the belt was above us. Or above to our relative location. In space direction was fairly meaningless. Up was someone else's down and so on. But we still needed a fixed point of reference in order to function. Our minds couldn't handle the concept of no direction. So we acted as if the directions were just like on the ground, using ourselves as the fixed point.

For us the asteroid belt was above us.

Jagged, uneven rocks of different shapes spun and moved. The rotation was opposite our travel so they appeared to be moving faster than they really were. For the most part they kept a constant distance. When one would break apart, as they were all bound to do eventually, the smaller pieces would go flying everywhere. Their own gravity so small compared to the larger masses that they would be sucked into those asteroid's wells.

We could see some of the impacts, lots of smaller rocks and dust erupting into space, when those smaller ones slammed into the larger ones.

The asteroids gravity would push against the gravity of the ones around it, keeping the asteroids pretty much locked into place.

Which would help us to pilot our way through them.

"What happens to the freighter pilots," I asked as we made our way to the entry point, my former exit point.

"The freighter was modified so the bridge was the escape pod," the co-pilot, I hadn't gotten his name yet, said. He didn't look at me, just focused on his read-outs. As he should have. "It had a small one-hop engine. They were going to hop back into the Jeffern system where some Expeditionary Forces ships will meet them."

I was glad to hear the pilots had a plan for getting out of Unitouro.

One-Hop engines were a relatively new technology. About ten years ago the Xertin had taken the standard hop engines, their design of course, and stripped it down. Only enough fuel and power to make a short hop, no more than six hours. Once used it was done. There was a lot of work involved in getting it operational again. Let alone the cost of the fuel. One-Hops burned a lot more of it.

At first no one could understand why there would be a need for such an engine but then someone in the military got ahold of the idea and adapted it.

History, not just Terran, is filled with such examples. Pretty much all species' first thought, when seeing new technology, is how to convert it to military use. How to weaponize it.

It happened with the One-Hops. Each species sought to duplicate the Xertin tech, reverse engineer it and make it their own.

Terrans were the first to succeed.

The Xertin's had intended it to be used for escape pods. Normally a pod would launch and you were at the mercy of the system. Your beacon would go out but if there was no one in ear shot, no one within the solar system, then you weren't getting saved. The idea with the One-Hops was to give the people in the escape pods more of a chance. If you struck out in that system, hop to the next one over and try again.

Of course your life support would be halved, if not more, but the intent was at least noble.

The Earth Expeditionary Forces took the tech and used it for the purpose the Xertin intended. No escape pod that the 2Es commissioned was without a One-Hop drive. I wanted one on the *Wind's* escape pod, which we still hadn't gotten repaired, but the cost was so damn high. The 2Es could pay for it, but no one else could swing it.

They took it one step further and started wondering what would happen if you sent a One-Hop equipped ship in the other direction. Instead of being used for defense, saving a life or lives, why not use it for offense.

Send a bomb from a neighboring system to your target system.

No actual ships or personnel would be directly in harm's way and it could inflict a lot of damage.

Take an idea meant to save lives and instead use it to take lives.

Typical 2Es.

*****

"You're up," the pilot said.

I hadn't moved from the cockpit, standing there behind the pilot and co-pilot as they made their way to the entry point. I was watching the stars and the asteroids above us, thoughts turning to the last time I was here.

Focusing on the present I checked the readouts. We were there. The pilot shifted the ship so we were looking straight into the asteroid belt. It looked familiar and at the same time it didn't. The rocks here were large, ship sized gaps between them.

The pilot undid his harness, standing up and sliding out of the way. He pointed at the seat.

"Figure I would get an argument over this," I said strapping myself in. I held off from adjusting the seat. That would be going too far.

"Captain Yearly did tell us not to give you the stick," the pilot said with a shrug. "But he's not here so…"

Yearly should have known better. The mission always came first. Things like ego had to be put aside to succeed. All he had accomplished was lowering his standing to his men.

I put my hands on the controls, studying them, getting familiar with them. I'd never flown a drop ship before but it really wasn't that different from a freighter.

Adjusting the thrusters we moved into the belt. The ship rocked, pushed by the gravity of the asteroids. I held the controls tight, keeping it from moving as much as possible. Once inside, rocks all around, what had appeared to be large gaps between them got much tighter.

The Tiat facility was not that deep inside the belt. It had to be close to the edge, or in this case the inner edge of the ring. Too deep in and it ran the risk of being too buried, too hard to get to.

Looking out the viewwindow, which I had used to navigate by the last time as well, I tried to find a landmark. I had to quickly determine if relative up was the same this trip as the last. If we came in with the wrong orientation we could end up going left when we had meant to go right.

Very easy to do.

Landmarks were hard to establish when all the possible choices were in constant rotation. There was no fixed point. With nothing to find, I just decided to wing it.

I remembered how deep in the facility was, how long it took to reach it. I knew the exit point I had taken. Most importantly, I knew how I flew.

Trying to escape a destroyed Tiat facility, I would have flown in as straight a line as possible.

With that in mind and my memories, I retraced the path I had flown over six years ago. Around asteroids, threading the needle between others, avoiding and swirling debris.

And found the facility in ten minutes.

The asteroid that we had nicknamed The Rock did not look different from all the others. Dark colored stone, rough and jagged, canyons and mountains off the surface. Nothing special.

Until it's rotation revealed the facility.

It looked nothing like I remembered.

*****

The first time I had seen the building it had been two stories sticking above the surface of the rock. A wide space, no valleys or canyons, not mountains or hills. Just flat surfaces of stone with this gray building looking like the asteroid was trying to get rid of it but the building refused to go. It looked quickly built, barely attached to the asteroid.

When we had left, the facility had a large hole in the wall. Both floors were exposed to the atmosphere. We could see gases and liquids escaping and falling out of now exposed piping and ducts. Flames could be seen in the windows of some spaces. It had been damaged enough to no longer be able to be used.

We knew the secret location, the Tiat abandoned the facility. Until recently.

Now the building was vastly different. One much larger story. The buildings footprint had changed in size and scope. The walls were taller, lights only visible in one row of windows. There was a second story, much smaller, that rose out of the middle of the first. Walls were the same height and there were windows on all four sides, continuous glazing and frames.

Both stories, the walls were completely intact. Not a hint of damage was visible.

It had been rebuilt. Everything about it was new.

I turned the drop ship and brought it up close to the rocks, keeping as far from the facility as possible. No telling what kind of sensors it had.

This new facility seemed to be more important to the Tiat then the previous.

Getting up I gave the seat back to the pilot. My first part of this mission was done.

"Nice bit of flying," he said strapping back in.

"Thanks," I replied and made my way back to my original seat to strap back in.

"How's it look," Harrow asked.

"Like a Tiat facility," I replied. Fortin laughed. Harrow just rolled her eyes.

I felt the ship pick up speed and pictured the flight in my mind. The pilot was bringing us around the asteroid, looking for the perfect insertion point.

Assault insertions were always tricky things. There were so many variables in play. An insertion on an asteroid was one of the hardest. A blind insertion was equally as hard, if not harder. Put the two together and it was near impossible to do successfully.

But we were going to try.

CHAPTER NINE

The pilot set the drop ship down on the blind side of the asteroid where it was protected from any Tiat scanners. There had only been a minimal amount of turbulence in the landing. The pilot, I later learned his name was Jack Warren, was good. Warren had put us as close to the facility as Harrow would allow him to risk it. Risk of detection versus length the team had to run. There was a sweet spot to find.

Once settled the team unstrapped ourselves and started suiting up. I'd been given a standard 2E assault suit which doubled as an enviro suit. The typical dark green, black trim and armor plating. Attached to our chest armor were oxygen tanks that plugged into small ports in the back of the armor. The Tiat breathed oxygen just like seventy-five percent of the galaxy. Some species had different mixes to their air, just slightly different enough to be unbreathable, but not the Tiat. It would be a little harder for us to breath, like we were at the top of a mountain, but nothing too difficult.

The tanks were for the run across the asteroid's surface.

It had been a long time since I'd worn a full suit of armor and tanks. Had to shift it a bit to get the fit right. I hoped that it would start to feel familiar again. Fighting would be difficult enough if I wasn't forced to compensate for the armor and suit.

At a command from Harrow, the co-pilot slid the door shut between hold and cockpit. I could hear the slight hiss as they environmentally sealed the door. Fortin and Gilbert were helping Treuto into his specialized suit. I'd seen an environmental suit on a Europan before. Tubes along the arms, body and legs connected to a tank that filtered a cold agent. Europans came from an ice moon, they needed cold. This suit had the tubes but also plates of armor for limited protection. The tactical vest he wore was larger, the tanks larger. No helmet, just a pair of goggles and special mask that went over the somewhat pointed face.

Watching them help with the suit made me realize that Treuto had not been wearing one before. None of the Europans on the station had been and the temperature there and the drop ship had been Terran standard.

"Why didn't he have an enviro suit before," I asked Harrow.

"I thought Jessups had said you were pretty observant," she replied sarcastically. I let it go. She did have a point. "Training and a new pill from some Earth corporation."

That sounded interesting and potentially dangerous.

"It lowers their relative body temperature so it seems they are in an environment more friendly to their needs," Harrow finished turning back to her preparation.

Whatever this pill was, it appeared to work pretty good. I just had to wonder at the future issues. Europans had never been a starfaring race. No great desire to get out and see the stars. A limiting factor had been their body's need to be cold all the time. The young had gotten restless and started venturing out but it was very rare to see one beyond the Sol Station at the edge of the solar system.

"Helmet's on," Harrow said.

I had no more time for thinking about the Europans. The helmet was already connected to the tanks and I pulled it on, activating the seals. A slight hiss and pressure around my neck and I was breathing recirculated air filtered through the tanks. Lose the tanks or the tubes connecting the helmet, and I had maybe about a minute before I was dead.

Why did I sign up for this?

The helmets heads-up-display turned on and I got a lot of information at once. A lot to process. Had a graph showing how much oxygen I was using and how much was left. A read out with the rest of the team located and their levels. Lots of other information. I'd forgotten how much there was.

It took a lot of training to filter it out and concentrate on what you saw through the helmet's visor. It was overwhelming at first.

Harrow had us line up and check the connections of the person in front of us. I noticed that I was put in front of the line and had no one to check, Harrow pulled double duty. I wasn't bothered by that. They knew my history but also knew I would be rusty.

Keying in a code, Harrow opened the weapons locker and passed out our armament. We each got a standard Expeditionary Forces blaster rifle, a Carlysle T200, and a blaster pistol, a Carlysle P320. I already missed my trusted Sig.

Once we were checked out, armed and good to go, Harrow rearranged the line. Gilbert and Treuto were in the front. Harrow and Sweet, then myself, then Fortin and Carleton in the back.

"Ready," Harrow's voice asked through the helmet comms.

She got a chorus of affirmatives, one "let's get this over with" from me and a hoot from Treuto. Satisfied she signaled the cockpit.

I felt the air pulled out of the hold as the door slid open. The vacuum around the asteroid claimed it and anything not strapped down. The ship shook as the pressure also pulled at it. I knew the pilot was adjusting the thrusters to help keep the ship level on the surface of the rock.

Without a word, Gilbert and Treuto jumped out the back and onto the asteroid.

Neither of them floated off into space so I knew they had activated their boots weights. No gravity and since none of us were given flight packs, we had to do something to increase our weight to keep us firmly on the rock. 2E infantry were given special boots that could be adjusted as needed to provide that extra weight and still allow us to move.

Our normal gait and run were affected of course, but a small price to pay to not float off into space.

The activation timing was always tricky. It got better with practice. Too soon and you could trip as you left the drop ship. Too late and you'd be a couple feet higher off the ground before activating.

I paused when it was my turn, took a deep breath, and jumped out the door.

Landed just fine.

I caught Harrow watching me. She had been wondering how rusty I was going to be. This showed her that there wasn't much rust on me at all.

Or I had just gotten lucky.

She turned away and I started to follow.

I looked out across the surface of the rock. Nightmarish was an accurate descriptor.

Jagged spikes of rock grew everywhere at odd angles. Large cracks covered the surface. The land rose in hills, fell into valleys. All lined in sharp and serrated rock.

This was going to be fun.

*****

An hour of running and we were there.

I knew I was out of shape but I was proud of myself. I managed to keep up.

Harrow kept a steady but slow pace. She wanted the team to be combat ready when we got to the facility. Or maybe she was compensating for me. I liked to think it was to keep us combat ready.

Gilbert and Treuto were on point, ranging further ahead. It was comms silent for the run. We avoided most of the valleys and hills, as well as the major rock outcroppings. Gilbert was transmitting a map back to Harrow on the best path to follow.

I got some quick glances at the rocks as we ran past. The edges were razor sharp, serrated. Just brushing one would be enough to cut through the suits we wore. One small tear and it was game over.

Working in open space like this, planets with no atmosphere or deadly environments, was always dangerous. One false step and you'd be done. I'd seen that happen too many times. You had to be extra careful, senses heightened to the dangers, but at the same time cognitive of everything else around you. Especially if you were in a combat situation.

It wasn't just running from cover to cover. It was running to cover, keeping low enough to protect your tanks and suit but at the same time not scrapping either, getting to the cover and hoping it was big enough to cover your entire body including the tanks. Also hoping not to get the lines from tank to helmet snagged on anything. And finally hoping not to slam the tanks too hard against the cover when you ran behind it.

And the boots. Couldn't forget the boots. Always had to make sure you didn't damage them somehow.

We made it across the asteroid to where Gilbert and Treuto crouched behind some cover. It was essentially just another outcropping of the jagged spikes of stone, but thick enough to hide behind. They kept far enough back from the sharp edges to not cut their suits or their tubes.

The team gathered around and Gilbert pointed past the outcropping.

"Just over there,' he said.

Both Harrow and I moved to look over the rocks. Her helmet turned towards me quickly and if I had been able to see past her visor I was sure she was giving me a very dirty look.

Ignoring her I concentrated on the facility that was about three hundred feet away. The walls were tall, about twice the height of a terran building. The Tiat were taller than us, a couple feet on average, and for some reason they liked very high ceilings. This resulted in the floor to floor of their buildings being almost double that of a Terran building.

Harrow had a pair of imagers and spent a couple minutes studying the building. From here I couldn't see much without some form of magnification, but there didn't appear to be any patrols or guards or surveillance equipment.

There had to be something. The Tiat were many things but stupid was not one of them. The remoteness of this place was very good security itself but they wouldn't rely on just that.

"Launch the eyes," Harrow said.

Sweet crouched down, reaching behind him. Under his tanks was a square container. He pulled it off and opened it up. The insides were padded, most of the space padding. A wristcomm came out and he pulled it on, hitting the buttons to activate it. Next he carefully pulled out a small tube. It was only about three inches long and an inch in diameter. There were small jets attached to front and back ends, at least that's what I thought they were.

He set the tube on the ground and hit a button on the wristcom. The jets kicked up a small amount of dust from the asteroids surface and the tube rose into the air. It settled at a height of twenty feet or so and sped off towards the facility.

"Next gen drone," Sweet said as I watched the small tube disappear to the eyes. "Full range scanning, all spectrums."

A small screen appeared in my heads up display and I realized I was seeing what the drone was seeing. Neat little device. I wondered how much one cost and how I could get my hands on one. Could come in handy. I'm sure it would be illegal to own one but that never stopped me. I had a good collection of Expeditionary Forces gear that was illegal for civilians to own.

The drone moved fast, the image changing rapidly. I was surprised how wide the camera on the thing was. I'd expected a small picture but what I saw was big. Could see the edge of the building come into view. The wall we saw had no doors, no openings of any kind. The roof of the one story structure had running lights and painted markings. A door was off the second story building. No windows.

The roof was a landing pad.

Good security. No openings except on the top and so far only that one. A ship would need to land on the roof to access the entrance

The drone did a quick run around the entire building and the full roof.

Just the one opening.

"That makes it easy," I said and got a couple chuckles.

Harrow glared at me.

One way in didn't mean one way out. That's what explosives were for. Just had to hope that what we had for explosives was enough to get through whatever the walls were made of.

Worry for once we were inside.

*****

We ran across the open space one at a time.

Cover was provided from behind the outcroppings, all weapons pointed towards the Tiat facility. Gilbert went first, followed by Treuto. Fortin was next and then they sent me.

I felt exposed and I was. Any Tiat on top of the building would see me. The distance wasn't that great but it wasn't close either. About a five minute run from start to when I slammed tight against the wall. No shots had been fired at me and none had been fired back.

The ground was rocky, the footing unsteady. The trek to the facility had been done carefully, making sure of each footstep. Not this time. This was a quick and wild run. Just get to the wall as fast as you can.

I waved my arm indicating that I was there safely.

Sweet followed. He ran quickly. I saw his foot land awkwardly and he fell. He rolled along the ground, scrambling to get up and protect his suit and tanks. Sweet lay there for a minute or two, unmoving. I looked at Gilbert and Fortin, unsure what to do. Should we run out and get him?

But he finally sat up. Slowly, carefully.

With greater care he finished his run, coming to a panting stop next to Fortin who quickly looked Sweet over looking for rips or tears. Finding none, Fortin flashed the thumbs up.

Sweet waved his hands to signal the next runner.

"You run like you dance," Fortin said with a laugh.

We all chuckled. Treuto grunted and hooted ending with a repeating squeak that I assumed was laughter.

"Not you too," Sweet said to Treuto, causing the Europan to squeak with laughter even more.

Some private in-joke that they didn't bother to share. I didn't ask.

Carleton came next and made it without incident. Sweet muttered something that no one caught.

That left just Harrow. She had volunteered for the hardest run. She would have no cover. From our angle we couldn't provide any covering fire without stepping away from the building's wall. We couldn't even see if any Tiat appeared on the roof until they started firing on Harrow.

We saw her stand up, step away from the cover, and start her run. She ran smoothly, a straight line. A steady pace. She got to the wall. No one had fired on her.

She took a couple steps away and looked up towards the roof of the building.

"Let's do this," she said.

CHAPTER TEN

Climbing in zero G is as easy as it sounds.

Turn off the boots and pull yourself up the rope. Easy.

Just don't let go or you'd float away.

Climbing in an environment with low gravity isn't as easy as it sounds.

The low gravity worked against you. Instead of climbing carefully, you could go too fast and end up overshooting. Your own momentum would keep you moving up. Too slow and you'd go nowhere.

*****

Sweet seemed to be the bag of tricks guy for this op. Every operation I'd ever been on had one. It was the guy that carried all the extra miscellaneous equipment. Stuff that you knew you'd need and stuff that you didn't think you'd need but ended up needing it. And you never could figure out how the guy stored all that gear.

He pulled out a grapple line from somewhere and stepped back from the wall. Estimating the distance, made some adjustments to the grapple, and fired. The hook shot out at a little bit of an angle, trailing the rope behind it. We couldn't see it from where we hid tight against the wall and couldn't hear it land or catch either. Only knew it had caught when Sweet pulled on it and the hook didn't fall.

Giving a thumbs up to Harrow he let the rope fall against the smooth side of the Tiat facility.

Harrow pointed at Sweet, Treuto and then myself. The three biggest people.

Six foot, two hundred pounds, I was a big guy. But the other two were much bigger. Treuto was average for a Europan, which put him at close to seven feet. Sweet was about six or so inches taller than me, wider and heavier.

Sweet and I looked at each other, wondering who would be the first up.

That was not a fun job. You were basically a sitting duck to anything that was at the top of your climb, with no way to defend yourself. Second person up had at least the first to provide cover if needed.

"Rock, paper, scissors," I asked.

Sweet laughed.

Treuto grunted and held out his hands. With a flick, three long climbing claws extended out of his wrist. About six inches long with a slight curve at the front and serrated edges, they looked and were sharp. The Europans lived in icy caves, the claws on their hands and feet helped them move through those caves.

"Put those away," Harrow ordered.

With another grunt and what looked to be a shrug, Treuto resheathed the claws.

"Sweet, you first," Harrow added.

"I would have thrown rock," Sweet said passing me with a smile.

Grabbing the line with two hands, he set his left foot against the wall.

"Scissors," I said and Sweet gave a soft curse.

Hand over hand, setting each foot solidly against the smooth wall, Sweet made his slow way up the wall. His blaster rifle hung by it's sling and he kept his body angled so the weapon would not bang against the wall.

Finally making it to the top, he paused before reaching a hand over the wall. There was no weapons discharges that we could see, no noise from Sweet through the comms, so we assumed it was safe enough. One hand on the wall, the other still gripping the rope, Sweet swung a leg onto the top of the wall. Pulling himself the rest of the way over, Sweet disappeared.

"Clear," his voice said through the comms.

My turn.

I grabbed the rope in both hands, pulling at it. Adjusting the weight of the boots, I pulled myself up by my hands. One over the other, a bit at a time, feet flat against the wall for stability. At the top I reached over the wall, my fingertips gripping. The wall was only about eight inches thick, if that. I looked over the top. No body laying down, no weapons. Sweet hadn't been ambushed and killed. I could see him crouching about five feet ahead, weapon to his shoulder and pointed at the one door.

Hoisting myself up, I swung a leg over the wall, and let myself slide down to the roof. The parapet was only about a foot high. Not that far. Pushing myself up, I pulled my weapon around and pointed it at the door.

"Clear," I said through the comms as I stepped away from the wall.

The walls were a dull gray, flat. The roof, some kind of membrane, was the same color. Dull and lifeless. Also empty. Which was good.

Crouching down next to Sweet, both weapons trained on the door, we waited for the rest of the team to climb up.

*****

Once up we quickly ran to the door. Harrow had us spread out, a V formation with the point facing the door. Each of us had a clean line of fire and enough space between us to make it hard to target more than one at a time.

We made it without incident, again holding tight to the wall. Harrow and Gilbert were at the door, both crouched down and examining a keypad mounted next to it. We waited for what seem an eternity but was only a few minutes.

Gilbert was the first in, followed by Treuto. Harrow held the rest of us back for a minute as we all slid down the wall to the open door. I could see inside the opening. There was nothing visible, just darkness. Treuto poked his big head out and waved a hand up and down. His version of the all-clear thumbs up.

Harrow pointed, motioning at me to come closer.

"You're second behind Gilbert," she said. "Since you know the way."

"This place is nothing like it was the first time," I pointed out but knew it didn't matter.

"As the only one here that has ever been in a Tiat facility, let alone multiple like your record says, you're second behind Gilbert."

I walked over to the door, Treuto stepping aside so I could enter. It was dark just past the door. The ceiling was probably three times my height, double a Tiats, and dark tiles. The walls were the same drab metal panels as the exterior walls. There was another door directly across from the one I had entered by. An airlock.

Gilbert leaned against the wall, the keypad faceplate removed. He was fiddling with the wiring. The entire team crowded into the small space, feeling very vulnerable. When the exterior door closed, Gilbert opened the inner door.

It slid open soundlessly into the wall revealing a well lit corridor that ran left and right with another door directly across. Gilbert stepped out and looked right, Fortin followed and looked left. Harrow and I walked across the hall.

Touching the door with my hand I could feel vibrations.

Carleton tapped Gilbert on the shoulder, switching positions.

He was getting better at opening these doors. Gilbert had this one open almost instantly.

Harrow and I followed Gilbert into a large room. Judging by the size, it took up pretty much the entire upper level. And it was filled with machinery. Ducts penetrated the floor in multiple locations, connected to large units the hummed and vibrated.

"Ventilation," I said and the other two nodded.

"Fortin, get in here," Harrow ordered.

A couple seconds later Fortin entered, looking around. The visor on his helmet was blackened so couldn't see any expression. Aside from Sweet's size, the others were hard to tell apart. In a squad where everyone wore the same armor, you started identifying people by the way they walked or held themselves. I hadn't been, and wouldn't be, with this group long enough to get to know them that way.

I wondered if Harrow was using their names more often for my benefit.

"Set one up."

With a nod, Fortin walked deeper into the room. He wandered around for a bit, looking at all the machinery, examining the duct work, before finally settling on a spot. I couldn't see what he was doing, just that he took something off his vests harness. A couple seconds he returned, flashing a thumbs up.

Probably set a homing beacon.

Which meant the countdown had started.

CHAPTER ELEVEN

We moved quickly after that.

I understood what Harrow was thinking. The engine room, as that was what it seemed, was a good place to set the bombs. If we couldn't penetrate deeper, bombing that would pretty much destroy the facility. Place the bomb, start the timer, and see if could complete the rest of the mission.

Same move I would have made if I had been in charge. Just didn't like it now as I wasn't a soldier anymore and I was heading down to the floor below the bomb.

At the end of the hall was the stairs down. The door's security was easy for Gilbert to bypass and we made our way down. Quickly and silently. The stairs themselves were a little awkward. Tiat were taller than us humans, the shortest would be a very tall human. The treads and risers were only an inch or two different but it was noticeable. Was that what it was like for the Storwoi that had recently been on the *Nomad's Wind*?

Probably worse. Instead of inches, they were feet shorter than humans.

Fortin, at point, paused at the lower level door. He looked up for the okay from Harrow. Given, Fortin moved to the right of the door where the pad was located. Carleton took his spot to the left of the door, where it would slide into the wall. Tapping the pad, we all waited for the door to open.

It opened at normal speed but felt very slow.

The door slid into the wall and Fortin locked that way. Carleton pivoted around the jamb and into the opening. He was crouched low, weapon to his shoulder, eyes scanning what he could see. We saw lights coming in through the opening and that was it. Carleton took a step forward.

He flew backwards, slamming against the far wall. Smoke rose from the blaster mark on his chest armor. More shots hit the door jamb, head and the floor around the opening. They were pinning us inside.

I glanced at Carleton's status in my heads up display. Still alive. Just unconscious.

Not for long if we couldn't move him.

One of those blasts would hit in and the way he was crumpled up, chances were good it would be where he wasn't armored up.

"Four of them," Harrow said. She was staring at the wall from her position on the stairs just behind me. Must have been scrolling through Carleton's helmet cam images.

Random patrol that got lucky? I doubted it. There had been no surprise from Carleton, no body language to suggest the Tiat attackers had appeared from around a corner or anything. He was just shot. That meant they were already in position and waiting.

"Ambush," I said. "We must have tripped an alarm."

Harrow looked like she wanted to argue but backed down.

"Agreed," she said. "We need to get out of this stairwell. Time's wasting."

She didn't need to remind anyone of that. We all had a ticking clock in our heads.

The problem was that there was only one way to go and no good way of getting through it.

Or was there?

I looked up the stairwell at where the floor and ceiling would be in the hall beyond. Last time in this facility, or the first one here, there was some duct work that ran in a cavity space between the ceiling and floor. In Terran facilities there wasn't enough space to crawl, but in the Tiat one there had been.

Our ceilings were fairly weak, the Tiat's had been strong made of the same metal as the walls. I'd seen the ceilings above and they were like I remembered.

Would there still be a cavity?

It was worth a try.

Harrow agreed.

*****

Fortin and Gilbert, now on the side of the door where Carleton had been, provided cover fire out the door when they could. Alternating, waiting for pauses between the continuous fire of the Tiat. We'd managed to drag Carleton out of the way during Fortin and Gilberts fire.

Treuto and Sweet stood against the wall facing me, Sweet with his hands cupped. I placed a foot in the cup and he lifted. I used my hand on his head to help balance until I was level with Treuto and stepped on the Europans shoulder. One was a little taller than the other, but it worked good enough to support me.

Holding the torch that Sweet had brought, I started cutting a large hole in the wall, hoping I was above the ceiling. The walls were a hard metal, the torch having a hard time.

I was regretting my plan.

But it was my plan so I was the one that would do it.

A minute or two later, after what felt like an hour, I had the four sides cut. The wall finish material proved to be pretty thick. A sheet of metal attached to some kind of structure. Enough space for me to work my way through. The hole I made opened into the cavity space, just like I remembered. I could see the floor above, the structure it rested on and about two feet of space before the ceiling. There were numerous ducts, tubes and squares, along with wires, running everywhere.

Just like I remembered.

Leaning into the hole as far as I could, I pushed against the ceiling. Awkward angle, I couldn't put my full strength into it, but it felt strong enough. Would have to hope it held.

With a final boost, I crawled into the space. Spreading out as much as I could, distributing the weight as evenly as possible, I started working my way through the cavity.

I'd reviewed Carleton's helmet cam video and had a rough idea of where the Tiat soldiers were positioned.

We knew there were four. Had more shown up? That was the risk.

I had to remember to keep my mouth shut next time I had a brilliant plan.

A slow foot by a slow foot I made my way down. The cavity was dark and I had to switch on my helmet's light. The ducts ran straight, avoiding the corridor, which made some sense. I could hear the noise of blasters, both sides, coming from below.

Ten feet, twenty feet. Twenty five and I was where I needed to be.

I hoped.

I didn't need to be right on top of the Tiat but I needed to be behind them.

It was awkward holding the torch with one hand but I needed to be quick. When the piece of the hard ceiling dropped, the Tiat would react. I needed to be quicker. Hitting the activation switch with my left thumb, I held my hand over where the hole was cutting.

I moved the torch slow, not wanting to make noise or much light. I figured the Tiat weren't hearing it or they'd be firing into the ceiling. No shots, I had to be safe enough for now.

Watching the cut line carefully, I followed the bright light as it sliced through the metal of the ceiling. The front got closer to the end and I held my left hand up, just above the soon-to-be-hole. I could feel the heat, even through my gloves.

There was a snap and the small slightly oblong circle of metal ceiling dropped to the ground. I couldn't hear the noise it made over the sound of blaster fire and I didn't hesitate. My left hand lowered, I released the button my thumb was holding down, and the plasma grenade fell through the hole.

I rolled away from the hole as far as I could.

The blast was loud, the ceiling beneath me buckling. A great concussive noise and impact. The hole I'd cut enlarged, pieces of ceiling splitting. Cracks formed around me and I could have sworn there was a leaning to the ceiling now. The firing below stopped, that of the Tiat, but the return fire from the 2Es Spec Ops continued. It came closer, the two blasters joined by a third and a fourth.

Twisting myself around I started working my way back to the hole into the stairwell.

*****

The plasma grenade had made a mess of the corridor, all three legs. We'd come onto a straight run out of the stairwell door that ended in a longer 'T' intersection. Doors were off all three corridors. The walls had buckled, dented and cracked. There were black burn marks across the smooth and polished metal.

Four Tiat lay on the ground. Two bore burn marks from the grenade, the other two dead from blaster shots. I recognized the burn mark and hole that 2E rifles made in Tiat bodies.

Not one of my more marketable skills, recognizing the burn marks left by different weapons.

Fortin was down one hallway, tight against the wall. Gilbert was down the other.

Carleton was hobbling in the rear. Treuto and Sweet were clearing rooms with Harrow reviewing the contents behind them.

None had waited for me to exit the ceiling cavity or offer to help me down.

I was starting to wonder where the rest of the Tiat were. There had to be more.

There had to be more soldiers and where were the scientists? Tiat eggheads were almost as dangerous as the soldiers so we had to worry about them as well.

Were they all holed up somewhere? Had someone called in reinforcements?

Hopefully the Tiat didn't keep a capital ship in the system.

Our scans hadn't shown anything but there were a lot of places to hide in a solar system, especially a large one, and scanners weren't all that reliable.

"Look like offices," Harrow said. She had a collection of small devices in her hand. They looked like parts to a computer. Data drives? "I can't read Tiat, can you?" That was directed at me.

I shook my head. Not a language I had ever bothered to learn.

No guards had come to bother us yet so Harrow directed Sweet and Treuto to start with the rooms across the hall. That should be the first of the labs, I thought, working the layout in my head. It would make sense that the stairs would lead to the offices first before the labs. One of the halls would lead to facilities like a break room and locker room, maybe a barracks, and the other would lead to the labs.

50/50 odds either direction.

Sweet worked the door and it slid open. He entered, followed by Treuto. Looking straight in, we could see they were in a large airlock. The walls were some kind of see-through material. Not glass but the Tiat equivalent. The inner door opened and a cloud of gas or something billowed out the door.

Everyone held still.

"Safe," Sweet called out as his helmet's system ran a quick biohazard check.

He stepped into the room along with Treuto. Lights automatically came on. I couldn't see much but the room looked large.

"Clear," Sweet said a couple minutes later. He was still inside the room, Treuto near the door. "Better get in here boss."

Harrow walked forward, motioning at me to follow.

I felt the temperature drop even through my biosuit as we walked through the airlock. That's what the cloud was, frost as the warmer air met the colder coming from the room. It was freezing in the space.

It was an operating theater. Examination tables lined the walls, each with a collection of different equipment next to them. There were saws of various sizes and shapes. One had weird tubes connected to a pump. Another group looked like scanners. The sizes and shapes were varied, which made me think they weren't meant for Tiats.

Against the back wall were five cubes. Made of that clear material, each was about fifteen feet by fifteen feet. There was a single door leading into each. Harrow was standing in front of the middle one, Sweet walking around and recording everything with his helmet cam. I walked over next to Harrow. I couldn't see what her expression was but I could imagine because chances are that it matched mine.

Inside the glass cube was another examination table, this one at an angle. Strapped to the table was a body. Not human but that sized. Green skinned. Male. Naked.

Dead.

A Dyer.

Tubes ran from the Dyer's arms to machines mounted to the floor.

"What the hell," I said.

Harrow moved left, I moved right.

The other two glass boxes held a female Thesan and a male Engyn.

Both were naked with tubes attached to them.

Both were dead.

Harrow and Sweet were both at the far end. I headed that way, avoiding looking at the Dyer. I was starting to have an idea of just what was happening in this facility. The next two boxes held a dead and naked Serit and a dead and naked Human.

"Please tell me this isn't what I think it is," Sweet said. He sounded scared, or at least worried. Which coming from such a big guy was a little disconcerting.

I shared his worry.

Harrow looked at me, wanting confirmation but not wanting to say it aloud.

So I did.

"They're developing bioweapons."

CHAPTER TWELVE

A Human, Dyer, Thesan, Engyn and a Serit.
I really wanted it to be the start to a bad joke but it wasn't.
My race and the closest allies to our people.
Basically the Tiat's biggest enemies.

*****

Each of the clear cubes was a lab. Each had their own air supply, I could see the ducts above leading from the ceiling to the cubes. The tables were the same, sized for each race. The banks of monitors and tubes, all the same.

The occupants were interesting. I mean it made sense that the Tiat would develop a weapon that would only work on their enemies and not their allies. The Tiat really didn't have allies, just acquaintances, but you still wouldn't want to kill every race in the galaxy. Just the ones that gave you the hardest time and were the biggest threats to expanding the empire.

I couldn't imagine how difficult making such a weapon would be.

This was the testing chamber. This was where whatever bioweapon they were cooking up was tested.

Which meant the actual production lab was elsewhere.

"Look for anything of value," Harrow said to Sweet and me. "Computer drives, files, anything."

There was a note of anxiety to her voice. She was worried. She had every right to be. We had thought the Tiat were developing some new tech or weapon. It was a weapon, but not the kind we thought. This was epic level scary.

Disease was the scariest thing in the galaxy. The hardest thing to control as well. There were so many varied beings in the galaxy, with so many different immune systems, that it was very easy to bring a benign virus from one planet to one where it was lethal. Contamination was a real concern at ports.

Would think that with everyone knowing what a danger it was, there would be more safety measures in place and people would pay attention more. No. That didn't happen.

But bioweapons were things that the various species did not mess with. It was hard to believe the Tiat would open that box. Too much risk, everyone knew. No matter how well designed your virus, they were still living things and could adapt and evolve.

The three of us tore that place apart.

And found nothing.

"Time?" I asked.

"Not enough," Harrow replied and motioned for us to go.

Back out in the hall, we regathered and followed Fortin down the left hall. Going for the break room and barracks wouldn't help us but it was a 50/50 chance either way.

And we still hadn't come across more guards. Or the lab techs. Where were they holed up?

Probably where the good stuff we wanted was.

*****

"We need to get going," Fortin said. He was standing at the corner, leaning against the wall and ready to swing around.

There was no noise or anything coming from down the new corridor. At least not yet.

"Not yet," Harrow said.

I agreed with Fortin. Time was not on our side and we needed to move. But I agreed with Harrow as well.

"The boss is right," I said. "We need to try to find out what they've developed."

"We need to do it quickly," he said. "Clock is ticking."

I did the quick calculations in my head. Assuming the timer started when Fortin placed the transmitters in the machine room, we had twenty minutes before the bombers got here. Twenty minutes to get through the asteroids.

"Where were the bombers launching from," I asked Harrow.

"Next system over but only a thirty minute hop."

I did the math in my head, knowing the others were as well. Thirty minutes from reception of the signal to get from the Jeffern system to Unitouro, twenty minutes to get through the asteroids. I assumed the bombers would have hop coordinates that put them pretty close to the belt. Probably another beacon on the ship we had come in on, acting as a hop satellite.

So on the low end, fifty minutes. On the high no more than sixty.

We'd already used up twenty five of those minutes. Halfway to out of time.

"Right," Fortin said coming to the same conclusion. "Time to move."

He nodded to Gilbert who was in position behind him. Gilbert grabbed a strap on the back of Fortin's tact vest.

Leading with his weapon, Fortin turned and leaned out into the corridor. He looked down the hallway, scanning.

"Pull," he yelled, depressing the trigger on his blaster.

Gilbert yanked hard, pulling Fortin away from the corner just as blaster bolts slammed into floor and corner of the wall. Both soldiers slid back and away from the corner. The metal wall panel was heating up from the repeated blaster bolts, burn marks radiating through the material.

"Four, maybe more beyond the next intersection," Fortin said. "Doors down the right side, the outside wall. Couple more on the left but further down."

I'd always been good at mapping, able to think in 3D and 2D geometry. Lefts, rights, sizes of the rooms. Somehow I could put them together to create a rough layout of a space. The doors on the left would put those rooms past the large examination room. A shared wall.

Most likely.

More shots slammed into the corner, the far wall, some getting a better angle and forcing us back from the corner. If I was the Tiat in charge I'd be advancing down the hall under the covering fire. Concentrate the fire along one side of the corridor, advance up the other.

That's what I'd do and I really didn't have the urge to look to see if I was right.

Looked like Harrow was agreeing with me.

"Back the other way," she said with a curse.

Sweet in the rear became point. With Treuto, they advanced back the way we had come. Fortin and Gilbert stayed behind, covering our backs. Sweet passed the exam room door, where Harrow and I stopped to wait. Carleton was between our position and Sweet, looking back and forth, ready to cover which side would be needed.

"Contact," Sweet yelled through the comms and we heard the sound of blasters against metal wall.

"Dammit," Harrow said, her eyes on the stairwell that would lead back upstairs and the roof.

Where we could escape to.

With mission not fully accomplished.

And if we left now, before the bombers were close, the Tiat could find the beacons and simply turn them off. We couldn't retreat. I knew it and Harrow knew it.

"Inside," I told her, pointing at the exam room.

"We'll be trapped," she said, looking back into the room.

"I think we can get out," I said.

"You think?"

"Yeah," I answered watching as blaster bolts slammed into the walls at either end.

If we stayed here, we'd be dead. The Tiat would take the corners and then just keep firing down the corridor until we were no more.

Harrow didn't want to follow my plan but couldn't think of anything else. It wasn't her ego making her hesitate. She would never let her ego get in the way of keeping her men alive or completing the mission. I knew this because I never did. She hesitated because she didn't like the idea of the unknown.

"Inside," she said into the comms.

I led the way inside, moving quickly towards the back wall in the right corner. I ran my hands over the smooth metal where wall met wall. I tapped on it, hearing the noise. It sounded solid.

The others followed me in and I could hear our side returning fire. Now that we were inside, we only had to defend the one opening. Glancing back I saw Fortin and Sweet in the airlock, one on each side, firing down the corridors.

"Well," Harrow asked eyeing the wall.

"Need a torch," I said tracing an outline of a door on the wall.

"Look around," Harrow ordered, thinking there had to be something in the room we could use. She had pretty quickly figured out my plan.

"Doesn't Sweet have a breacher in his bag of tricks?"

Harrow cursed, annoyed at not thinking of it herself.

"Sweet!," she yelled.

Gilbert switched positions. The big man ran over to us, saw the wall and reached behind his back. He pulled out a small device that I recognized. It was a newer model of the one I had on board the *Nomad's Wind*. Of course it was legal for Sweet to have it. Not legal for me to have it. Which is why I never told anyone I was in possession of a breacher. Or any of the other equipment I had borrowed when I left the 2Es.

Harrow and I moved aside. He placed the device against the wall. I heard the hum as Sweet traced a large square. He placed the device in the middle of the square and hit a button. It stayed in place. Taking a small controller in hand, we all stepped back. He hit the button, lines of energy coming out of the bottom of the device, sliding along the surface of the wall and outlining the square that Sweet had traced. The lines of energy sparked and snapped, crackling against the wall. Hitting another button, smoke started rising up from the metal as the lines of energy started cutting through the wall. The energy lines were bright, the smoke thick. Within seconds the section of wall fell to the ground.

It landed with a loud crash.

We were immediately through the wall. Harrow led. I followed.

The new room was an office. A Tiat equivalent of one. There was a piece of furniture that looked like a desk, another that was probably a chair, and some weird abstract sculpture that I think was supposed to be shelves. There was also a door to the hallway.

This was good news for us. We had chosen the right corridor to go down. The other must have led to the barracks which was not what we wanted.

And the most important part was that it wasn't flying open with Tiat swarming into the room. They hadn't heard the giant section of wall falling.

Good for us, bad for them.

With Gilbert and Fortin back in the lab providing covering and distracting fire, the rest of us gathered at the office door. Harrow started ransacking the desk thing and the shelf art. Carleton leaned against the door with Sweet and Treuto ready to burst out. I was to follow them. They would go right, I'd go left. Not what Harrow had told me to do but technically I wasn't part of her team.

Carleton hit the pad and the door slid open. Sweet stepped out into the hallway, body looking right towards the corner. He went flying, a body coming in from the left quickly and suddenly. We all heard the impact against the wall.

The Tiat are tall, the shortest is seven feet, and skinny but they are super dense and strong. Hitting one is like hitting a wall. Being hit by one hurts a lot. I've done both and regretted it everytime. Sweet had just been body tackled by a Tiat and slammed into the wall. Even a big guy like him was going to be hurting from that.

I stepped out to help but immediately had to start firing down the corridor. The Tiat had turned at the noise. They were now trapped between me, and Carleton who swung out into the corridor, and Fortin on the other end. We couldn't help Sweet who was under the Tiat and unable to move.

Luckily Treuto was there.

The Europan stepped into the hall, covering the distance in just a couple steps, and reached down. He grabbed the Tiat by the collar, lifting the heavy alien as if he weighed nothing. I knew Europans were strong, but not this strong. The Tiat reached behind and punched at Treuto, the Europan staggering under the blows, but holding up as there was no real strength behind them because of the angle. A human would have gotten broken bones but Europans seemed to be as tough as Tiat. I heard the sound of Treuto's climbing claws unsteathing followed by them slamming into the Tiat's back. There was a scream that turned to a gurgle. The Tiat spit blue blood and sagged, Treuto letting him drop to the ground.

Humans were no match physically for Tiat. If we got into hand to hand with them, we'd lose, every time. Even if we somehow managed to kill them, we'd be a battered and bloody mess. It appeared that Europans were a match.

Between Carleton and myself, along with Fortin now backed up by I presumed Harrow on the other side, we made short work of the Tiat caught between us. Once they fell, I expected to see the others come barreling down the corridor with Tiat in pursuit. Instead they came through the office space.

With a loud explosion behind them.

The building shook and could hear pieces of it falling. A dust cloud came down the corridor.

"That'll hold them for a bit," Fortin said with a chuckle.

"Unless that corridor loops," Gilbert mentioned. "Then we'll be seeing them again."

"Let's go," Harrow said stuffing some items she'd taken from the office into the pack attached to her vest. "You good," she asked Sweet who was being helped up by Treuto.

He gave a thumbs up. His helmet wasn't cracked, which was good, but it looked like a rib or two might have been. At least he was walking. He was a big boy, only Treuto would have been able to carry him.

We started down the corridor, Gilbert on rear guard just in case the Tiat had breachers of their own. None of us mentioned that we'd just blown up our way out of here.

CHAPTER THIRTEEN

The other rooms were more of the same. Offices. Small labs. Not what we wanted. Or at least not that we could find wanted.

Or read what we wanted.

It was all in Tiat and none of us could read it. Fortin could read some but nothing related to what we were seeing. I had a few words but mostly they were curses. The Tiat equivalent of 'Your Mother'. I also knew some Tiat ship commands and notations from the time I had to fly a Tiat ship out of this asteroid belt. Nothing that helped us now.

We had no idea what we were looking for either so we just grabbed all that we could, hoping that 2E Intel could make something out of it. There was plenty of signage, but again all in Tiat.

They speak a very short language. Sharp consonants, very little in the way of vowels. It's very direct. Short and to the point. The Tiat had no time to waste on unnecessary words. They had no time to waste on entertainment either. Not a fun people.

The corridor continued and turned just like it did on the other side. This confirmed what we had been worried about, that it was a continuous loop around the building with rooms on the inside and outside. A pretty basic layout but one that worked against us as it allowed the Tiat to come at us again from the other side.

This time when they started shooting at us, just as we had gotten down the new corridor about twenty feet and found cover in doors on either side of the corridor, we only had to worry about them shooting at us from one direction.

For now anyways. No doubt they were working their way through the debris barrier or using their own breachers to pass through the walls. Sooner or later they would flank us again.

There was also the part about the 2E bombers that were incoming.

I didn't bother to ask Harrow for an update on the countdown. I really didn't want to know.

Fortin and Carleton were just ahead, the furthest out, in a doorway on the right side. Myself and Gilbert were on the left side, the first of just three doors on that side. Harrow, Sweet and Treuto were in a right side door, closest to the corner.

Letting Gilbert provide the fire I looked around the room.

It wasn't an office.

Not as big as the lab with the five bodies, which was an examination and testing room, this one was still a decent size. Judging by the equipment, this had to be a research or development room. If there were viruses being generated in this facility, this room was where they were created. I had no names for the equipment or any idea what exactly they did. It was more what they looked like.

I'd seen enough vids to know what an evil scientist's machines looked like.

Working my way around the room I searched everywhere, or as much as I could when doing it quickly. I pulled open drawers and cabinets, tossed stuff off counters. I had no real idea what I was looking for but hoped I would know it when I found it.

I wasn't really worried about accidentally exposing myself to anything. I was wearing a pretty high end environmental suit. I should be safe as long as nothing tore the suit or smashed the helmet. Should being the word. I didn't want to take the risk but I was here and we needed to know what the Tiat had developed.

That examination room scared me.

Disease was the scariest thing in the galaxy. It could wipe out entire civilizations and then spread to others. With so many varied beings in the galaxy, what was specific for one species inevitably would affect many others. Maybe not in the same way, but there would be consequences.

Quarantines were strictly enforced and one of those rare things that seemed to bring everyone together.

The last time a planet had come under a world and species wide plague, that system had been blockaded by pretty much everyone. There had been Tiat ships next to Terran vessels. No one was allowed in or out. The planet died, the entire population destroyed.

It had then been bombed with geothermal explosives. Everything had been burned which hopefully included the virus.

There were survivors of the species, those that had been off planet, but they were few and far between. The Bintu were a fairly peaceful race, had to be when there was no homeplanet and just a collection of ships orbiting a dead planet. They were in the process of building a giant space station to house what remained of their population with the hope that someday their planet would be livable again. They'd been building the station for a decade.

No way in hell would I allow that to happen to Earth and our people.

And not just Terrans. Apparently the Dyer, Thesans, Engyn and Serit were also at risk.

The Tiat scientists could be super geniuses but there was no way that a virus or viruses designed to attack five different and such varied species wouldn't adapt and kill or harm others.

Or maybe that was what they wanted?

Wipe out their five greatest enemies and decimate the rest of the galaxy while they remained safe and secure in their isolated little empire? The Tiat had stopped expanding into the known galaxy over fifty or more years ago. They solidified their hold on what they already had and just sat back, enjoying life as the largest empire in the galaxy. When we started exploring the unknown systems, they started doing so as well.

A whole new direction for them to expand into.

Was that the plan? Take out their biggest threats, weaken the rest of the galaxy and look towards the unknown and eventually come back and take over what was left of the known systems? Rule it all someday?

Biochemical weapons were the worst. I mean war sucks and physical weapons do their fair share of destruction but nothing on par with biochemical attacks.

We needed to know how far along the Tiat were. For all we knew they had started this program during the Third Galactic War and they were nearing completion of the virus. Or it was only a year or so old and they weren't far along. Or there were another twenty facilities like this scattered around.

I doubted that part. This was probably the only one.

Developing viruses was dangerous work. Asteroids were really the only truly safe space to do it. If there was an accident it would be isolated on the rock and not contaminate anywhere else. The asteroid could be destroyed and the virus could be attempted again.

I came up empty. The room was clean. Nothing that looked to be research notes, materials or even a computer. There were plenty of places that looked like input for a wired computer, but those did me no good without the system itself.

Walking back to the door, I stood in a way so I could look down the corridor at the door behind me without exposing myself to the Tiat. I could see Sweet at the door firing down the corridor with Treuto and Harrow just inside the doorway. I held up my hands, showing them empty. She did the same.

"Carleton," Harrow's voice came over the comms. "Anything?"

"Nada boss," he replied.

There were only a couple more rooms down this corridor and sooner or later we'd start hitting the barracks and break room, along with whatever other creature comfort rooms there were here. I doubted there would be a game room or entertainment center like there would be in a Terran facility but never know.

What it meant was that we had to get to the other rooms and check them out.

That meant advancing down the corridor with the Tiat firing on us.

There was really only one way to do it in this situation.

"Lancer, take over for Gilbert," Harrow ordered.

Gilbert was crouching down, weapons held against the door jamb to keep it steady, and continuously firing down the corridor. Hearing Harrow, he started standing up well firing. I crouched down and maneuvered myself in line with him, holding my rifle. Looking down the blaster's barrel, I was the room and then the door jamb and finally the corridor.

Long and straight, made of the gray metal, with a couple doors on it. Nothing remarkable except for the four lines of fire coming our way. It was all I could do to not fall backwards, every instinct telling me to take cover. But I had to stay here and return fire.

Once I was firing, Gilbert stepped back and out of the way. I slid forward and hugged the jamb. I could see Fortin ahead and on the right.

"Gilbert and Carleton," Harrow said, everyone knowing what she wanted. "Sweet and myself. Treuto is pick-up. On my go."

I continued firing down the corridor. I did controlled bursts. Three at the bottom where wall met corridor, three in the middle and three at the top where I thought a Tiat's head would be. I didn't hit anything but hoped my fire would keep them buttoned up. Just ahead and across Fortin was doing the same. We waited for Harrow's command.

"Go," she ordered.

We increased our fire, no longer aimed or controlled bursts, but a steady stream up and down the wall and the corridor. Gilbert stepped out into the corridor, standing up, and starting firing down the corridor. Up ahead, Carleton did the same. We waited for return fire from the Tiat but none came, Fortin and I had done a good job of keeping them hiding.

Gilbert started walking and as soon as he was past me, I stopped firing. I stood up and waited. He was a couple feet ahead when Sweet passed me, weapon raised and ready to fire. Coming even with Fortin, Gilbert adjusted his walk as Carleton stepped out next to him. Fortin stopped firing and stood up, waiting.

With Sweet and Harrow passed, I stepped out into the hall and raised my weapon. Sweet was directly ahead of me and I could feel Treuto behind. If any of us fell, the others would continue and Treuto would grab the fallen.

They passed Fortin and he stepped out, waiting until I was even with him to start walking.

"Drop," Harrow ordered.

Carleton and Gilbert continued firing and then abruptly stopped. They dropped to the ground in a crouched position weapons still raised. As soon as they were below the weapons barrels, Sweet and Harrow opened fire. They kept advancing as Gilbert and Carleton moved to the side. They stayed crouched, firing until Sweet and Harrow were past. They waited until Fortin and I passed by then stood up and starting following us. I could feel Gilbert's weapon pointed at the back of my head.

"Drop," Harrow ordered after walking ten or so feet down the corridor and she and Sweet did so.

My firing was a second or two behind Fortin as I had to wait longer for Sweet to get out of the way. He was a tall guy, much taller than Harrow.

I kept the barrage up as I walked. Not the easiest thing to do.

"Drop."

Stopping firing, at the same time lowering my body, I could hear and feel the plasma blasts from Gilbert only inches from my head. Crouching down, weapon raised, I shifted to the side as Gilbert and Carleton walked by.

This was a risky maneuver. It required precision and timing, all members to be synced up. If one faltered, it gave the other side an opening. The idea was to keep a continuous barrage of fire down the corridor, keep the Tiat pinned down. The reason for the switching was to keep everyone fresh, give the lead a quick break.

It may have seemed like the hardest part, when the first team stepped out into the corridor and started walking but it really wasn't. It was the riskiest, that was for sure. If the timing wasn't right or the enemy was daring, they could take out one of the first pair and the whole thing would be over. That was the riskiest. The hardest was keeping up the constant fire well walking and ducking. Dropping and maintaining your balance, then sliding to the side, well keeping synced with the guy next to you. Yeah, that's the hardest.

Harrow was showing a ton of faith in me. Only teams that had been together a while would attempt it. I was an unknown quantity. No way was I going to let her or the team down.

Sweet and Harrow walked by us, weapons raised and ready. I stood up, Fortin next to me, raised my weapon and followed. Treuto was behind us. The Europan had his large blaster hanging over his shoulder on a sling. Wouldn't take much to flip it around into ready position.

Continuing past the next door on the right, Gilbert and Carleton stopped. Harrow was on the right side and when she came level with the door, she dropped her weapon on its sling and started working on the keypad. Fortin walked around her as we both passed the door. I moved to the side closer to the wall so I could fire around Gilbert and Fortin did the same.

I hoped that Treuto was keeping an eye behind us.

Harrow cursed, the door not opened. She took out her pistol, stepped back and fired at the lock. The door slid open, smoke rising from the ruined keypad. She rushed into the room. I couldn't spare a glance inside. I was busy firing down the corridor trying to keep Tiat from peeking around.

They were going to try something soon. They had to.

And we didn't want to be in the corridor when it happened.

A minute later, while Harrow still searched, the Tiat made their move.

CHAPTER FOURTEEN

The Tiat, as a society, are fanatical. They are single minded, following the will of their Empress without question. When first encountered, we thought they might have some kind of hive mind, they were that singular in focus. Win at all costs. They had no problem with sacrificing themselves if ordered. It was expected of them.

So it shouldn't have been a surprise when two Tiat stepped into the corridor.

Instinctively we targeted them. They went down, dead, smoke drifting up from the many wounds. Well we were taking out the two sacrifices, a third Tiat leaned around the corner and threw something.

It was small. We didn't see it so much as we heard it. It landed on the floor with a metallic clink, then bounced towards us a couple of times, clinking with each bounce.

"Dammit," Gilbert said.

The object came to a stop about thirty feet away. The moment it stopped, bright light exploded outward. We all turned to shield our eyes, the envirosuit helmets visors tinting to help but not quick enough.

My eyes burned, blinking to push away the flash spots. Thankfully it had been far away so the damage wasn't as bad as it could have been. But it was bad enough.

Gilbert grunted as a Tiat's plasma blast caught him in the stomach. He fell just as I turned back towards the corridor, spots still in my eyes. Leaning tighter against the wall I fired rapidly at the Tiat, moving my fire top to bottom.

Another grunt of pain and Fortin stopped firing. Sweet stepped up into his position but it was too late. We'd lost the advantage. Behind us Treuto hooted. I had no idea what he was saying and the others were too busy, or hurt, to translate.

"Inside," Harrow said through the comms. "Now. Treuto covering fire."

We all increased our fire, trying to pin the Tiat back behind the corner again. I saw a long and furry arm in my peripheral. It reached down and grabbed Gilbert, who was still firing from a sitting position, by the handle on the back of his tact vest. Treuto yanked Gilbert, who slid backwards across the metal floor quickly. He stopped firing, almost losing his weapon the pull was that strong.

I heard Gilbert curse as Treuto pretty much threw him into the room. Fortin managed to get himself inside. Instead of an arm, I saw the Europan's whole body step into view. He filled up the corridor, a large presence, with a giant cannon of a blaster pointed down the corridor.

Pulling the trigger, the blaster was loud. Thick beams of energy shot out and down the corridor. Treuto moved the weapon, covering the corner, the far wall, top, bottom and middle. But he was one weapon, no matter how big and powerful it was, so there were gaps.

"Lancer, move," Carleton said and so I did.

I slid along the wall so I was past Treuto. Carleton shifted along the floor, keeping lower than my line of fire. I stopped firing and moved behind Treuto, using the Europan as cover. Quickly I stepped into the office, Carleton standing and following. Glancing back I saw Sweet pull back so he was in the door, using it as cover.

"Now," he said.

Treuto stopped firing and quickly took the two steps he needed to get into the room. Immediately Tiat blaster trails filled the space the Europan had occupied.

Essentially we were all trapped inside the room now.

It wasn't a large room. Twenty by twenty. Another research and development space.

Harrow had already torn it apart and didn't look happy.

I assumed that meant she hadn't found anything good.

The others were spread out, Carleton standing behind Sweet ready to relieve him. Right now Sweet was the only one able to fire at the Tiat. One weapon but it was better than nothing. Gilbert and Fortin were leaning against a set of cabinets, comparing blaster wounds. Harrow had a bunch of stuff spread out before her, pawing through it.

"Anything good," I asked coming alongside.

"Not that I know," she replied indicating the pile of what I assumed was data chips and readers. "And we're out of time."

All heads, except Sweets, turned towards her at that. None of us had forgotten the impending arrival of the bombers but we had been a bit preoccupied.

"How the hell we getting out of here," Carleton asked. "The Tiat have us pinned down pretty damn good."

"Through the wall," Harrow replied calmly, like it was her plan all along. Probably was.

She had done the same mental mapping that I was doing currently. The wall opposite the door should have been an exterior wall.

"The breacher strong enough to make a hole through that," Gilbert asked running his gloved hand over the metal surface of the wall, reaching over the cabinets that were mounted against it.

"Sure," I replied. "That wall is probably pretty thin and cheaply made."

"You remember that from last time you were here?," Gilbert asked.

"No," I answered with a shrug. "This is a military installation. Sure, might be Tiat, but the military mindset is always the same. Big budgets but spend it all on weapons and ships and none on buildings." I tapped the wall, it made a nice metallic echo. "This'll come down easy."

I hoped and they all hoped.

They all knew I was making it up. I had no clue how thick the exterior wall would be. No military installation was the same across the planets and asteroids. Each place was different. Different gravity, different radiation, different weather and so on. Each facility was designed for that specific planet.

We all knew we were in it deep.

Also knew we could have been out of here, on the drop ship, and heading back to Rewe. We'd set the beacon, our job was essentially done. But we had gone for more. The discovery of the bodies had pushed us for more still.

None of us would ever second guess that decision. The risk was worth it.

Or would be if we could escape.

"Get Sweet's breacher," Harrow ordered. " Move those cabinets."

Gilbert and I studied the cabinets. Metal, about fifty inches high. Higher than Terran cabinets, accounting for the Tiat's greater height. There was a counter, made of some weird plastic material and the metal cabinets themselves. The counter was attached to the cabinets, the cabinets to the wall. Opening the doors we tried to find the attachment points.

Couldn't.

Gilbert was banging against the back wall of the cabinets, trying to find some way of pulling it off to get at the attachment points. I looked around the room for anything useful and found it. I kicked apart a piece of lab equipment. It hurt, that stuff was solid, but I got a strip of thick metal about an inch wide and two feet long.

Back at the cabinets I motioned for Gilbert to move and set my new pry bar in the seam between counter and wall. Jamming it in, I pulled and pushed. Quickly, but it felt so slow, I managed to pull the counter and cabinet away from the wall. Another metal pry bar joined mine and a couple minutes later we were pulling a set of cabinets away from the wall.

By the time we were done the makeshift pry bars were bent and twisted but the cabinet was moved and the wall was clear.

"Get the breacher," Harrow ordered.

Gilbert ran over to Sweet, who adjusted his positioning so Gilbert could grab the breacher from Sweet's vest. Running back, Gilbert squeezed around the cabinet, Treuto grabbing and pulling it further away. The metal of the cabinet screeched across the metal floor.

Tracing a large rectangle on the wall with the breacher, Gilbert stuck the unit in the middle.

"Everyone check your suits," Harrow said.

I looked the read-outs over in my heads up display. Everything still looked good. Plenty of air, no leakages. Good to go. The guys that had taken hits had others look over the exterior of their suits, checking for any damage that the built-in sensors couldn't pick up. Everyone checked out.

Harrow gave Gilbert the thumbs up and he hit the button, stepping back.

"Everyone grab on," Gilbert said.

Even though there was some gravity on the asteroid, there wasn't enough to match the artificial inside the station. There was going to be a big change in pressure when the room was exposed to the atmosphere.

We, except for Sweet who continued to fire down the corridor, all watched the breacher go to work. The lines of energy snaked out from the device and followed the path Gilbert had traced out. Connecting, the lines flared and started burning.

They burned for awhile.

The wall was thick.

Still burned and finally the glow faded, the lights dying out.

We waited for the section to fall.

It didn't.

CHAPTER FIFTEEN

We all stared at the wall. The breacher had burned through it or through most of it.

"Well damn," Fortin said.

The same thing we were all thinking.

I glanced at Harrow. Couldn't see much of her face through the helmet's darkened visor but could tell she was fuming. Mad at herself. That was the one shot we had at escape. Now we just had to wait for the bombers.

Not the way I thought I'd go.

I thought about Kaylia. She'd be okay with Kristin. Maybe it would be for the best. Flying round the galaxy hauling freight, barely scraping by, that was no way for a kid to grow up. She needed stability and that was not something I could provide. Not that Kristin would be any safer. She was a cop, Territorial Protectorate, on a new colony world.

My biggest regret was not seeing the kid one last time. She had grown on me. I knew there were better places for her but I wanted her with me.

I stared at the burn mark in the wall, the breacher out of power.

"What's the max thickness a breacher can go through," I asked, suddenly not wanting to just sit down and give up. I had told Kaylia I was coming back and I was going to fight to my last to make that happen.

"Depends on the material, usage and lots of other conditions," Fortin answered.

"Rough idea," I prompted.

I knew the variables probably better than he did. I had one of my own that I'd needed to use now and then. I wasn't going to mention that since I wasn't supposed to have it.

"Two feet," Harrow answered starting to catch on to what I was thinking.

What were the chances the wall was over two feet thick? We'd already used the breacher once. They cut through the material using the power stored in the device. The thicker and harder the material, the more power was used. So when Gilbert used it, the breacher was not at full strength.

How much wall remained? That was the question. There could be air leakage now and we wouldn't know it because of our suits. Or there may not have been and there was still feet of wall to go.

Only one way to find out.

"Treuto," Harrow pointed at the wall. "You're up."

We all backed away, Fortin and Gilbert pushing the cabinet further out of the way to give the Europan completely clear access. Bending over, unsheathing his climbing claws. Treuto stuck one into the gap burned by the breacher. It disappeared but that really didn't tell us anything. The claw was only nine inches long or so.

Pulling the claw out, the Europan leaned against the section of wall. He pushed at it, testing the strength. Stepping back, he leaned into it with force. We could all see the section shake a little.

He slammed into it harder, the wall seemed to slide forward a bit. Treuto slammed his shoulder into it again, the wall did move this time. It started to shake, vibrating, as the pressure difference started to move it.

We could see the wall shift with each hit from the big Europan. Again and again he slammed it, the sound of him striking the metal mixing with the continuing blaster fire from Sweet and the Tiat.

Taking a step back, Treuto ran at the wall, slamming into it full force.

The section of metal didn't fall, it was ripped from the wall. The pressure change pulled it out, sending it flying across the asteroid propelled by the Europans hit. Treuto stumbled and fell, half in and half out. We could see the surface of the asteroid through the opening, feel the pull against us. Small objects started flying through the air and out the opening.

"GO!," Harrow yelled.

We were already moving. Treuto lifted himself up and stepped outside, feeling and looking over his biosuit for damage. I watched Gilbert step over the thick threshold, awkwardly bending his body. As he stepped onto the asteroid he was pushed up into the air and slammed down as he adjusted his boots.

My turn came. The wall was a little under two feet thick, the opening only six foot or so tall. Too wide to step over in one move so had to step halfway through, which meant bending the body and sliding all the way through. Not quick, but I stepped out onto the rock of the asteroid. I adjusted my boots and ran a couple steps away.

Treuto and Gilbert were facing away from the opening but at the building, watching the corners. I raised my rifle to my shoulder and took aim at the roof. The others joined us. Sweet was last and he had the hardest part.

Tall, big, he'd have the hardest time getting through the opening. But he was also going to have the Tiat on his back. The second he stopped firing and ran for the opening, the Tiat were going to rush down the hall.

We waited.

A shadow filled the opening, Sweet stepping through. He was pretty much diving through, landing outside and slamming against the ground. Reaching down, Fortin and Harrow pulled him through and helped him up. We all moved away from the opening as blaster fire quickly followed.

"Run," Harrow ordered and we did.

*****

We spread out to make it harder for any pursuit to take shots at us. No evasive maneuvers though, just straight running towards the spiked rock hills ahead. The Tiat in the corridor wouldn't be able to chase us, not with their atmosphere leaking out. The facility might have had automatic airlocks as well. Just meant pursuit would be delayed but it was coming. We needed to get into the cover of the hills before it happened.

Also wanted some distance between us and the facility before the bombers got here.

Halfway across the expansive open space between the wall and the rocky hills, blaster bolts started hitting the ground. I looked back over my shoulder, turning and firing back. A couple Tiat had gotten on the roof. They had enviro suits and long range blasters.

That had been quicker than I thought.

The range wasn't good, we were moving quickly and spread out. The Tiat had to choose their shots. Bolts came close, throwing up bits of sharp rock, but none hit. Not yet. It was only a matter of time.

They didn't even need to hit us directly to take us out. If any of those rock shards punctured one of our enviro suits, we'd be dead pretty quick.

I hated fighting out in the open on non-earth-like planets. Blaster fights were dangerous enough without the element of having to protect your suit.

We were too far away for my blaster to do any damage. I was just firing wildly, trying to keep them pinned down. So were the others. Run, stop, shoot, run. Rinse and repeat.

The low gravity helped us, pushed us along faster.

But the further away we got, the less impact our return fire was doing. Our blasters weren't long range. The Tiat's were.

It didn't end up mattering.

I fired off two quick shots, turned and started running, seeing four dark specks coming in low over the asteroid. Just high enough to avoid the rock outcroppings. Coming in fast. They got closer and I recognized the shapes.

The two Raptors led. Starfighters, they were fast and deadly. Two engine pods sat out on long wings, the cockpit in the middle. It was sleek, mostly canopy, just big enough for a pilot and gunner. Two lasers were mounted on either side, two more cannons extended out from the front. The ships were kind of blocky and bulky, but I knew how fast and deadly they could be. They were easily a match for the Tiat XTs.

Opening fire with the large forward plasma cannons, the Raptors strafed the top of the building. The Tiat that were attacking us either got killed or ducked out of the way. Either way they were out of the fight and we were able to find cover behind the jagged outcroppings of rock. The Raptors banked and turned around, strafing the building again. The plasma bursts tore up the roof, sending large chunks of the metal material flying into space.

They peeled away, turning in opposite directions, and clearing a path for the bombers.

Hammers were small ships, long and skinny. All black, the canopy was up front with two small cannons that were pretty ineffective. The ship was all body, small wings for in-atmo travel, mounted on either side of the canopy and two more small multi-directional ones mounted on either side of the rear engine pod. The entire middle was taken up with the bomb bays. A slow ship, not very maneuverable, it was very ungainly in space and in-atmo. But it wasn't there to be quick or look flashy. A Hammer's only job was to destroy whatever it flew over.

And they were good at their job.

The two ships flew in low and slow, one after the other. The Raptors had returned, taking up position on either side of the Hammers, between the two, to provide cover fire if needed.

We watched the bombers level off and the first fly over the building. The bay doors in the middle of the ship opened and we saw a half dozen small canisters fall out. The doors closed and the ship quickly, for a Hammer, headed sharply away from the asteroid. The other ship was above the building, higher than the leader, before the first canisters struck. It opened it's bomb bay doors and dropped it's half dozen canisters, before angling up and away.

The plasma bombs fell in a line across the top of the building. We saw the explosion as the first hit. No sound but we could feel the pressure. A large funnel of red flames shot up from the gray metal building, followed by six more. The structure shook, the concussive blast from each bomb sending shockwaves throughout the building.

Then the second wave hit, falling through the gaps in the roof made by the first salvo. These hit the second floor, some falling to the first. We saw smaller fountains of fire as those struck. But the sides of the building flexed out, bursting at the seams.

And then it did.

The entire building shook and the walls exploded outward. Great balls of flame erupted into the air, metal sections sent flying. We ducked behind the rocks as smaller pieces were flung even this far.

A minute later it was over. The Raptors flew over the debris to make sure the building was completely destroyed. It was. Just a large pile of rubble. Even the flames had died out in the thin atmosphere of the asteroid.

Mission accomplished.

CHAPTER SIXTEEN

A bit anticlimactic.
But that's a good thing.

*****

That was it. Mission over.

The dropship came about ten minutes later, flying in from where it had been waiting outside the asteroid ring. It landed in the open space between the debris and us, we wearily boarded and within five minutes were were spaceborne and heading back to Rewe.

There were congratulations passed around inside the hold and I was included. Fortin pulled a bottle of whiskey from somewhere and we all shared a shot, even Treuto.

I'd forgotten what that felt like. Enjoying a successful mission. No wounded or dead. We'd accomplished our goal. I remembered plenty of missions that had failed, or someone had died. There wasn't any celebration then so the rare ones that were no dead and a success, those got celebrated.

None of us mentioned what we had found and what we hadn't found.

That would be for the debrief back on the still nameless station.

Now was just for being thankful we were all still alive.

"We're making the hop," the pilots voice came across the loud speaker about forty five or so minutes later.

The small ship shook and made its first hop.

*****

We felt the small ship shift as it turned to back into a docking slot. We heard the clang of the dock maglocks clamp onto the hull and the swish of air being blown into the airlock.

"Welcome back to Rewe."

The rear door slid open and we all groaned. Inside the airlock were a half dozen 2E techs dressed in white hazmat suits and carrying assorted equipment that they were setting up in the corner of the airlock.

Portable decontamination showers.

I'd forgotten how much fun those could be.

Treuto moaned. It was going to be even worse for him.

CHAPTER SEVENTEEN

After decontamination was debrief time. I spent an hour, if not more, in a small room with three uniformed 2E officers. They asked me question after question, trying to trip me up and get me to tell the sequence of events differently.

I was an expert at these. They hadn't changed techniques in five years.

Bored after the first five minutes I started playing with them, purposefully changing things in noticeable ways. They got on another five minutes later and we were able to get down to business.

The real debrief.

*****

I walked out of the small conference room and saw Colonel Jessups in the hallway waiting for me.

"Thank you," Jessups said.

Nodding I shook his hand. He turned and kept pace with me as we walked.

"You'll find some credits added to your account."

I glanced sharply at him, biting back an angry jab. I hadn't done this for money.

"We reinstated you in the Expeditionary Forces for the mission duration," he said raising his hand to calm me down. "Also some back pay and Contractor payout."

"Seriously?" I asked, part annoyed and part incredulous. What kind of strings did Jessups pull to manage to get all that from the notoriously money tight 2Es. Also, what kind of future favor would be owed?

"We owed you," Jessups said and I understood that he meant for more than just this mission.

Curious I linked my wristcomm to the stations system and pulled up my account. It took a bit but once I got connected I was a little shocked. That was a lot of money. Well, not really in the grand scheme of things, but for me it was a good chunk of credits. More than I'd had in the account for awhile.

The amount of money that definitely owed a future favor.

I'd be hearing from Jessups in the near future.

The question was now how to spend the money. Could get some needed repairs done on the *Nomad's Wind*? Or save it for future rainy days which tended to be almost all of them? Some of both?

We kept walking towards the docking ring and I could tell that Jessups had more to say. I knew him well enough to know that what he wanted to say, he probably shouldn't.

A couple Europans walked by, providing their version of a salute to Jessups who returned it. I looked over my shoulder at them. One almost all gray, the other black with some gray spots.

Humans were no match physically for the Tiat and that had always been a big advantage the Tiat held over us. Thesans had their natural agility but us Terrans had nothing to counter that advantage. But the Europans were the Tiat's physical equals. It looked like the 2E leadership had finally come up with a way to offset that disadvantage.

"So did the Europans volunteer to join the Expeditionary Forces or were they convinced?"

Jessups gave me a sad smile. He suddenly looked older, more weary. The load on his shoulders was heavier than I had thought. I suddenly had the realization that he wasn't being allowed to retire and fade away into the sunset. The 2Es needed him.

And he now had his opening to speak.

"Things aren't as peaceful as they seem," he said glancing around. We were alone. "We think there will be another Galactic War in the next ten years, maybe less."

Things were never truly peaceful as I well knew. I'd just helped blow up a Tiat facility afterall. But what Jessups was saying, that was shocking. Not good at all. The truce and cold war was fine, the rest of the galaxy didn't care if we sniped at each other in the background. But things were moving towards a full on war?

I lived the last war. Parts of the galaxy were still recovering.

A new one would be worse.

"And we may not have the allies we thought we would," he added.

I looked at him. That was surprising. The Tiat were hated. To a lesser extent so were we but no one sided with the Tiat ever, not even their supposed allies.

"The greater galaxy has always been angry with us," Jessups began. "Our early expansions sparked the Third Galactic War and we didn't learn our lessons. Even now with the threat of war and the trouble on Rewe, we're planning an Expeditionary Flight. Probes went out over a year ago and next month the scouts are scheduled to leave. The rest of the Flight will be a couple months after that, long enough to make sure the beacons stabilize. The Planetary Council has been trying to talk us out of it for months."

We had expanded quickly to the two other planets we controlled, the ones outside our home solar system of Sol. But those had been planets we knew about, colonization aided by the Thesans.

There had been only one Expeditionary Flight in my lifetime. The one to Rewe. Standard procedure was to send out drone probes into wildspace with programming to hop out randomly. They'd do a rudimentary analysis of the system, if they managed to arrive safely in a system, and then hop to the next charted system. Eventually, after a set time, they'd follow the hop path back. Lots of smart folks back on Earth would analyze the data and determine the next system to expand into. Scout ships would go out, set up beacons and colonists would arrive soon after.

Honestly, I didn't blame the galaxy for being angry with us. Humans and our need to expand had caused millions of deaths in the galaxy already. And it seemed like we were going to cause more. There was a lot of risk in our style of expansion. Who knows what we'd run into out there. What other civilizations or beings. We could end up poking the bear and not liking the response.

We walked a while in silence. I could tell the future was weighing heavily on Jessups.

"You said we may not have the allies, but once they're told about the virus the Dyer, Engyn and Serit will stand with us?," I asked.

Jessups long pause really told me what I needed to know.

"The speculation of a virus you mean," he started with a sign. "Until we can decode what the team brought back, we have no proof. We'll inform the planetary governments of the experiments and they'll do what they want with the information. Can't inform the Planetary Council without true proof. We may not even tell the Engyn."

Which might be a good idea. The species was blunt to a fault. They had no filter. They did what they said, didn't hide what they felt. They were not good at keeping secrets. Telling them that the Tiat were experimenting on captured Engyn would probably be enough for the Engyn to start the next war themselves.

"The Serit have been moving towards isolation for years and this could just push them further. The Dyer, we'll tell them, and they'll start their own clandestine investigation and operations."

We stopped outside an unmarked door and Jessups looked up and down the corridor before speaking again.

"Destroying the facility was a mistake in hindsight," he said. "Now the Tiat know we are aware of the experiments. If there are other facilities, they'll tighten security or move them. They could cease operations altogether and all this concern will be for nothing. It'll be us and our allies chasing our tails and wasting resources. That's what I'd do." He shook his head. The situation was not good and was only going to get worse. "Or they double their resources into the project and finish it that much quicker. There are too many variables and I'm afraid we may never catch this one."

I didn't envy Jessups or anyone in the 2E right now. Not even Coulson who was also going to be neck deep in this mess and of course doing what he needed to come out smelling good.

But that wasn't my concern. Not today.

The door opened and Kristin stood there, smiling at me. She was pushed aside and Kaylia ran out of the room, jumping into my arms.

I hugged her tight and for that moment there was no impending war, no potential species killing virus, nothing but her. And all was right in the galaxy.

Author's Notes

Welcome to the first collected edition of Arek Lancer's adventures. All these stories have appeared before except for Europan Switch, which was written for publication but never submitted.

I envisioned Arek as a mix of Jack Reacher, Malcolm Reynolds and a little Han Solo. The introduction of Kaylia kind of changed that. Which was a surprise for me but Kaylia just kind of took over and said she wanted to be in the books, so she is. Which allows that side of Lancer to appear in the prequel stories.

Delivery To Orso was written to serve as the "magnet", or giveaway, that entices readers to sign up for my mailing list. I don't remember where the name 'Yortusk' came from and the Dyer meaning is never revealed in this story. That happens in Volume 4 of Lancer, when the Yortusk reappear. Coulson and Romer were created initially for this story but each will appear in other novels. They're too fun, and their history with Lancer too rich, not to use again.

Kinn's Pirates is another story written to serve as a "magnet". This one was put into an anthology available from the New England Speculative Writers mailing list. There are a lot of homages in this story to one of my favorite cartoons from the 80s, and one of the favorite of all time. The Adventures of the Galaxy Rangers. Captain Kinn is based on Captain Kidd from that cartoon and the aliens that make up his crew were also patterned after Kidd's pirates from that show. I like doing little homages like that. This story has a couple others that appear at the back of the story. Kristin Higareda is based on the character of Kristin Ortega from Netflix's first season of Altered Carbon, as played by Martha Higareda.

Her partner, Waleed Abboud, is based on her partner in Altered Carbon, Samir Abboud as played by Waleed Zuaiter. Kristin pops up throughout the stories.

Europan Switch was written to submit to a anthology put out by a small press publisher. I missed the deadline, which was my fault, so the story sat around until this collected edition. It was meant to serve the same purposes as the other two, a magnet to draw readers to the rest of the stories. I don't remember where the story came from, but I wanted to do something with the moon Europa and my wife loves otters so the race was created. I liked the idea of giant space otters so much after this story that I put one into Asteroid Return and came up with a reason for them to appear in more stories.

One of the themes I want to hit with Lancer is that there is no good or evil, just people living and doing the best they can. In the books, Terrans aren't good. To a lot of the galaxy, earthlings are expansionists that started a galactic war. That plays out with how the Terrans treat the Europans.

Lancer himself isn't a good or bad guy. He's just a guy trying to make a living and protect the ones he loves. He tries to do the right thing and sometimes he fails.

The Last Child didn't go how I thought it would. The idea of Lancer came first and then the first story just kind of happened. I didn't really intend for Kaylia to stick around, that would put a crimp in Lancer's wandering lifestyle and romantic interactions. I had three different women thought up for him to interact with. Then Kaylia showed up and changed things. Somewhat. Changed for the better I think. I threaded things throughout to set up future storylines and worked up a rough timeline of what the next stories would be. That timeline didn't last long.

Armageddon Theft came out of nowhere. I was watching or reading something about a world ending and the idea just built from there. Can't remember exactly what caused this one to happen but it kind of messed up my roughly laid out plans for the series. This was never meant to be book two. But it works. It pushed the other stories down. As did the next book.

Asteroid Return wasn't meant to be book three, it just kind of happened. I also had meant this story to be told in the past, a story from Lancer's soldiering days, and in the present. Two parts telling the same story. The original mission to the asteriod and the present day mission to the same asteroid. But it didn't end up that way. Before I started writing the first past chapter I decided not to tell stories about Lancer's days as a soldier. The period between when he left the Expeditionary Forces and The Last Child are open to any story but I think I'll leave his days in the 2Es alone. Like other stories, there are a couple of homages here as well.

The Castellan Ship Builders tend to take their ship design ideas from the same inspiration. LEGO. *Nomad's Wind* is based on an old LEGO set, 497-1 from 1979, the F in the ship's designation comes from Serenity from the TV show Firefly. The *Hammers* BT6894 are based on the LEGO Blacktron 6894-1 from 1987 and the *Raptors* X6932 are based on the LEGO Stardefender 6932-1 from 1987. Expect to see more such homages in more Castellan ships.

That's it for this edition. Thank you for reading and I hope you look forward to the rest of Arek Lancer's stories. Check out my website below for a full listing of my published works as well as other writings.

Thanks for reading,
Troy

Ossy Writes website: https://www.ossywrites.com

Patreon: https://www.patreon.com/troynos

Facebook: https://www.facebook/com/ossywrites

Newsletter: http://eepurl.com/dilUn9

About The Author

Born and raised in the granite state of New Hampshire, Troy is a lifelong and avid reader of comic books and novels (mostly in the fantasy, sci-fi and adventure/thriller genres). The ongoing serial storytelling methods of comic books and television has always fascinated him and provided inspiration for his writing. He's always had a love of creating and world building and dreams of someday seeing his creations expressed across all media: books, comic books, movies, TV and even toys.

When not writing, Troy can be found outside hiking, kayaking or out back at the bonfire with beer in hand. Don't expect to bother him during football season, especially when the Patriots are playing.

First Edition 2019
Copyright 2019 by Troy Osgood

ISBN: 978-1-7338562-1-8

Published in the United States by Barking Fire Publishing, Northwood New Hampshire

Barking Fire Publishing and its logo are registered trademarks of Barking Fire Publishing, LLC

Cover art by GermanCreative
Barking Fire logo by Kat Howell

BARKING FIRE
PUBLISHING

http://www.barkingfirepublishing.com

www.ingramcontent.com/pod-product-compliance
Lightning Source LLC
Chambersburg PA
CBHW030543020726
47494CB00005B/1467